A Shift in Ashes

Lost Legacies Book 4

Maddox Grey

GREYMALKIN
PRESS

Published by Greymalkin Press
www.greymalkinpress.com

This is a work of fiction. Names, places, characters, and events, and incidents are the product or depiction of the author's imagination and are completely fictitious. Any resemblance to actual persons, living or dead, events or establishments is purely coincidental.

Copy-editing and Proofreading by Ashley Olivier

Cover Design by Seventhstar Art

eBook ISBN: 979-8-9881893-0-5
Paperback ISBN: 979-8-9881893-1-2

The Lost Legacies Series

A Shift in Darkness*

A Shift in Shadows

A Shift in Fate

A Shift in Fortune

A Shift in Ashes

A Shift in Wings

A Shift in Death

A Shift in Tides

*A Shift in Darkness is available for free download at maddoxgreyauthor.com.

Quick Note From The Author

Hey there! I just wanted to chat real quick about what you can expect in this book. This is a fantasy novel that contains adult content and situations. If it was a movie, it would probably be rated "R" for violence, language, and sexual content. If you want to go into this book completely blind and prefer not to read content warnings, you can skip on ahead, my friend.

If there are certain topics that you need to avoid for the sake of your own mental health, or that you simply don't like, please take a look at the list below for some things you will find in this book.

- Consensual explicit sex scenes (there is no dub-con or non-con)
- Similar to previous books, this one has lots of fantasy violence and gore, and one scene of someone being tortured by being burned

Also... quick little note on language. I am a strange, strange person, and I've lived a bit of an odd life. I was born and raised in California, but was mostly raised by my Canadian grandmother and was then unofficially adopted by an Irish family in my late teens. You might be wondering why I'm mentioning this, and the reason is that I have a bit of a magpie approach when it comes to the English language.

Sometimes I like the American English spelling… sometimes I'm really attached to that extra "u" and go for the non-American version. Variety is the spice of life y'all.

Bless the soul of my copy-editor because she just sighs heavily at the start of each manuscript and deals with my eccentricities. So if you're an American and looking at a word and thinking it's not spelt right… it is most likely the non-American version of the word.

To Puff, my cranky yet adored bearded dragon. I promised you more dragons. I fucking delivered.

Chapter One

"I'm not lost!" I snapped at the vampire to my right. The one on my left wisely said nothing.

We'd finally reached the top of the hill we'd been trudging up, and I gazed across the desolate landscape that stretched before us. No plants or any hint of life anywhere. Even the dirt was an odd grey color, as if life had been leeched from the earth itself.

As a realmwalker, I'd been to a lot of different realms, so many I'd lost track over the centuries, but this was a new one for me.

One I had no interest in ever returning to again.

Something horrific had happened here, and I could still feel the echoes of it across my skin. Even my magic was uncharacteristically quiet and had retreated deep within me, as if it wanted nothing to do with this realm. I didn't blame it.

"There." I pointed to a pile of debris not far from us. "Told you I wasn't lost."

Mikhail shrugged. "If you knew where it was, then why

didn't you open a gateway closer to it instead of making us trek across this godsforsaken land?"

"Oh, I'm sorry. Did you have something better to do with your day?" I stepped towards him and poked him hard in the chest. "I don't even remember inviting you on this gig in the first place! And I'm not sharing any of the cut with you, so don't even ask."

Mikhail narrowed his eyes at me, but before he could speak, Magos cut in, ever the peacekeeper.

"Let's go take a look, shall we? The sooner we find it, the sooner we can get out of here." Without waiting for our agreement, he headed down the gentle slope, choosing his footing carefully amongst the loose rocks and rubble. I curled my lip up at Mikhail, displaying a fang, and followed after Magos.

"How did Chamosh even know this thing was here in the first place?" Mikhail asked.

"He has a piece of it that he acquired a long time ago. He doesn't know where it came from, which is why he's never been able to gain more of it. But when he learned of my ability to access any realm, he wanted to know if I could find one based on something that came from it. I agreed, and here we are."

I slipped on a piece of loose shale, and Mikhail's hand shot out to steady me. I grumbled a thanks, and he let go after a long moment, letting his fingers trail across my skin. My magic that had been content to lie sleeping within me started to stir, but I slapped it back down. Mikhail had been doing that more and more. Finding reasons to touch me and gauge my reaction. I was only partially successful at hiding my responses, and my fae magic was all too eager to come and out and play with Mikhail.

There had always been this pull between us. It scared the shit out of me, so I shoved it down into the darkest pit of my soul and kept it there. For a while, Mikhail had seemed content to ignore it as well. Until Andrei and I ended things for good. Now Mikhail seemed determined to pursue this connection we felt towards each other, and I was struggling to maintain the distance between us. Every time he touched me or I caught him giving me a heated look, the wall I'd built up crumbled a little bit.

My emotional wall was looking pretty patchy and pathetic these days. But it was still standing, damn it.

"How widely is it known that you can travel through the realms?" Magos asked.

"At this point, I'm pretty sure every single daemon and fae are aware," I said tiredly. "Pele is still managing my gig requests, but there are too many coming in at this point. A lot of it is from people who don't even need anything; they just want to meet me. Some of them are finding ways to get around Pele, but I've been ignoring any direct contact requests."

Chamosh was the only one I'd agreed to take a gig for lately. He was a grumpy old bastard, but the daemon was an excellent spellcaster and the reason Magos and the vampire brats could freely move around in the sun. Plus, Chamosh was paying well, and he'd owed me a favor.

I'd told the rest of those who'd come asking about my abilities to take a hike. I wasn't enjoying my newfound fame. Most of my life, I'd hidden my magic from everyone else because it would have gotten me killed or enslaved. But recent events had forced me to come out of the shadows and make my abilities known. I was part fae, courtesy of my father, and both he and my mother belonged to the Unseelie Court. Now I did, too.

I hated it.

It'd only been a few months, and really nothing in my life had changed that drastically aside from my newfound popularity. But I still chafed at the idea of *belonging* to a court. Previously, I was just a feline shifter who had a solid reputation for finding lost things, nothing more. Now I walked into a room and everyone stared at me and whispered in the ears of their companions.

That's her, the daughter of that insane murdering bastard, The Erlking.

Her mother is a real piece of work, too. She'd have to be, to be with that thing for centuries.

The Unseelie Queen's new pet.

Devourer freak.

Magos reached our destination first and looked over his shoulder at me. His bright copper eyes seemed so out of place in this realm devoid of life and color.

"This was a ship." He knelt down and picked up a broken piece of what indeed looked like a mast. I crouched next to him and picked up a few more pieces, looking them over. "Which means there was once water here," he said, dropping the broken mast piece he'd been studying and gazing out over the wreckage. "What happened to this realm?"

I rose and brushed my hands against my pants. "I have no idea. Chamosh doesn't know anything about this realm. He acquired the chunk of meteorite in a daemon realm a long time ago. Might have fallen to the devourers during the first Cataclysm. It doesn't really feel like devourers, though." I frowned and looked around the remains of the ship. "I think something else happened to these people, and honestly, I don't want to know. I already have enough crap haunting my dreams, I don't need more."

"Fair enough," Magos replied. "Still, I wonder what these people were like. If any of them made it to another realm or if their entire existence ended here."

I stared at the broken ship, left behind in a forgotten realm. The shifter realm my parents had come from had fallen to devourers. So had Magos and Mikhail's home realm. Countless realms had been lost. So many beings forgotten. Some had vanished without the rest of us even knowing about their existence.

"Let's find this expensive hunk of rock and go home," I said, dragging myself out of my melancholy thoughts as I stepped over more debris. "I felt the tug of its magic as soon as we arrived in this realm, and it's even stronger now. It's definitely here."

We carefully sorted through the wreckage. I kept expecting to find some bones, but there was nothing. No trace of whoever had manned this ship. I hoped some of them had made it out of this realm alive, even though I knew that was unlikely.

"Found it," Mikhail said, pulling something from underneath several broken boards.

He held up the chunk of meteorite, and it glinted in the fading sunlight. Despite being buried in debris and left to the elements all this time, the black rock sparkled in the light, bits of purple glowing brightly against the black.

Mikhail's dark purplish-blue eyes, which always reminded me of twilight, found mine, and I saw the amusement glittering in them. "Seeing how I found it, I do believe I earned my take."

I snorted. "You only found it because I led us here." I held my hand out, and he tossed the chunk to me. The rock was cool against my skin, and something about it felt strange. I shoved it into a pouch attached to my belt. "Besides, you don't even pay rent."

"I'm not paying rent to sleep on your couch."

"It's a nice couch!" I countered.

Magos cleared his throat politely. Right. We had gotten what we came here for. It was time to get out of this damn realm. I carefully picked my way out of the wreckage and stretched out my hand. Magic flowed from me, and a ripple formed in the air. A few seconds later, it widened, revealing a modern-looking apartment with floor-to-ceiling windows. I stepped through and waited for the two vampires to follow before closing the gateway.

"I'm going to shower, and then we can head to The Inferno." I walked down the hallway towards the bathroom. "We'll drop this off with Pele. One of her minions can bring it to Chamosh. Eddie is going to meet us there. He wants to talk to us about something."

Ten minutes later, I walked into my bedroom with a towel wrapped around myself. I was pretty sure sand was still ingrained in my skin. I loved our apartment but would honestly kill someone for access to a nice soaking tub right then. The memory of the beautiful wading pool from the fae queen's palace floated to the surface. I grimaced. That pool *had* been really nice, right until a monster had appeared from under the surface and dragged me through a gateway. I'd probably chance going in it again, though. I'd just bring my swords with me.

Movement from the corner of my bedroom caught my attention, but I refused to look.

"No. You just got fed yesterday." I strode over to my dresser and pulled out some clothes. "We've talked about this. You're not getting fed every day. You're already too big for this room, and I don't know where I'm going to move you to yet."

I closed the dresser drawer a little too hard and tossed the clothes on the bed, along with my towel. I reached for my underwear but snatched my hand back as a green vine snapped at where my fingers had just been. The vine wrapped around my underwear and pulled it away.

I glared at the plant that now took up an entire corner of my bedroom. When Kaysea had given it to me as a house-warming present a year ago, it had been barely a foot tall and contained in a pot on my dresser. Now it was easily four feet tall and was in a massive stone pot in the room's corner in front of the window, where it could soak up all the sunshine.

The dark green stem that rose out of the dirt was nearly as thick as my waist. Narrow vines with small leaves wound up the stem; amongst them were several thicker vines, like the one currently waving my underwear around. The large electric-blue flower at the top of the stem was shaking its petals in frustration, and its bright orange center was opening slightly.

"If you eat my underwear, I'm not feeding you for a week," I hissed. "And I'll make sure the kids don't sneak in here to feed you either!"

The orange center of the flower split open, revealing rows and rows of impossibly sharp teeth that curved backwards at abrupt angles. The vine shoved my underwear in and swallowed it down while I stared at it in disbelief.

Fuming, I grabbed another pair and yanked the rest of my clothes on before stalking out of the room. Mikhail was grinning widely, and Magos was clearly trying to keep from doing the same.

"It's easy for both of you to find this funny!" I snapped. "You don't have a giant plant in your room with a bottomless fucking appetite!"

"I don't have a room," Mikhail replied.

I growled in frustration and headed towards the apartment door. "Get cleaned up and meet me downstairs. I'm going to have a chat with the vampire brats. This plant is their damn fault from overfeeding it all the time, and they're going to help me move it!" I slammed the door and stomped down the stairs, passing the apartment on the second floor where Bryn and Finn lived.

Luna usually stayed on that floor as well, which meant Jinx was there most of the time. I was happy for my friend. He deserved to find love and happiness. But even though he was only one floor below me, I still missed him. He'd been my one constant companion my entire life. I knew I wasn't being rational about it. He still lived in the same building, and he breezed in and out of our apartment all the time. But I felt like my life was radically changing, and I didn't know how to deal with it. I just wanted at least one thing to remain the same.

Laughter erupted from the first-floor apartment, and it checked some of my annoyance. I didn't bother knocking but froze after taking only a few steps inside the apartment. Two vampires, barely past their teenage years, stared back at me. Between their pale skin, dark hair, and striking features, they could easily pass for brother and sister. Given that we didn't know who their parents were, it was a distinct possibility.

The slightly younger vampire they had pinned to the floor between them looked at me desperately. Something red was smeared on his face, but it appeared too thick to be blood, and small yellow chunks lay on the floor around him.

A giggle tore out of the curly-haired girl standing behind the three others with her hands tucked suspiciously behind her back.

"Elisa, dare I ask what you and Misha are doing to Damon?" I opened my mouth slightly and inhaled, parsing the scents. "And why Isabeau is hiding a piece of pizza behind her back?"

Cheese and toppings slid to the floor with a plop as all four vampire kids gazed at me guiltily. "Damon says pineapple has no place on a pizza?" Elisa replied, somehow turning her answer into a question.

"He won't even try it!" Isabeau tossed the slice, now without cheese or toppings, onto Damon's shirt and leapt the five feet to the couch like it was nothing. "It's the best, and he would know that if he would just take a bite!"

"I genuinely don't know how to respond to this other than

I'm not cleaning up this mess, and I better not be smelling cheap cheese and pineapple for the next month."

"Yes, Nemain," Misha and Damon intoned.

"Also, I have to head to The Inferno for a bit. But when I get back"—I pointed a clawed finger at them—"all of you are helping me move that damn plant out of my room. We'll put it in the living room, somewhere it can't reach anything sharp or important."

"Let's move it down here!" Isabeau yelled. We were trying and failing to explain the concept of "inside voice" to her.

"No!" everyone said at once, and she slumped against the couch cushions, a sulky expression spreading across her face.

"Is it okay if I get a ride with you?" Elisa asked.

Suspicion crept over me, and I narrowed my eyes at her. "Why?"

"Pele offered me a part-time job as her assistant." Elisa paused. "On a trial basis. Just to see if I can do it."

"Of course you can do it," Bryn said from where she'd been sitting across the living room, well away from the pineapple pizza assault, and gave Elisa a knowing smile. Elisa smiled back at her, while Misha and Damon rolled their eyes.

"I strongly suspect that allowing you to train under Pele is a bad idea, but I'm not going to stop you. Just be prepared to take a lot of shit for being a vampire." I had no doubt Pele had already discussed this with her. Vampires weren't well-liked or respected in most of the magical community. Pele in particular didn't like them, but she'd grown to accept, if not respect, most of the vampires who lived with me. Elisa had been locked away for most of her life, but anyone who spoke to her for more than a minute could see the cunning mind and political savviness she wielded like weapons. Gods knew what she would be capable of underneath Pele's tutelage.

"I'm prepared, and I'll deal with it," Elisa said smoothly.

From her position, she couldn't see Bryn's face as it tightened slightly, and red flashed briefly across her eyes. Elisa could stand on her own two feet, but if anyone seriously came after her, they'd quickly find themselves at the mercy of a pissed off valkyrie.

"All right," I said. "Get cleaned up. We're leaving as soon as Magos and Mikhail are ready."

Elisa nodded and scooted off to her room. I walked over to the kitchen, where Finn was perched on one of the stools. He was settling in but was still very quiet. At least he no longer looked alarmed or worried at the constant outbursts from the vampire brats.

"Hey, kid," I said and grabbed one of the last cookies from a plate in the center of the counter, no doubt dropped off by Zareen earlier because nobody in this building could bake. "Luna upstairs, I'm guessing?" I knew she was because that's where Jinx was. I had felt his presence when I walked past the apartment on the second floor. But asking Finn how he was feeling would result in only a one-word answer. I'd learned other tactics to get the kid talking over the past few months.

"Yes. She's taking a nap."

Finn studied the plate of cookies as if he couldn't figure out if they were a trap or not. I rummaged around in the kitchen and poured him a glass of milk. Setting the glass in front of him, I nudged the cookies a little closer.

Finn's eyes flicked to mine, and I kept my expression calm as those strangely colored eyes looked at me. The inner part of Finn's eyes was golden yellow, like the color of leaves in the fall. The color shifted to a bright green around the outer layer, the color of spring. Eyes of change.

According to a fae prophecy, Finn, the son of the exiled fae king, would bring about the end of the realms. Unless I changed his fate. Unfortunately, the prophecy hadn't come with a helpful guide on exactly how I was supposed to do that, so I just pushed the plate of cookies a little closer. When in doubt, eat more sweets.

I was *so* not cut out for this.

"Luna doesn't mind the noise down here," Finn said quietly as he reached for a cookie and carefully took a bite. His eyes lit up as he chewed. "I don't think Jinx likes it, though."

I snorted and got myself a glass of milk and dunked my cookie in it. Finn watched with wide eyes and then, with slow, deliberate movements, repeated the process with his cookie and took a nibble. He pulled the milk a little closer and did it again.

A smile tugged at my lips as I took another bite. "Jinx is grumpy. He always has been. Luna is good for him. She helps balance him out."

"Balance is good," Finn said with a thoughtful expression. "Like Bryn and Elisa."

"Exactly like that," I agreed. Elisa joined us again, running a hand down the well-tailored suit she was wearing. "I see Pele already has you dressing like her." I shook my head in mock disgust.

Elisa blushed slightly. "She said a certain level of dress was expected given the work she does. Looking professional is important. I didn't really have anything, so she, uh, sent some stuff over."

"You look good, kid." I wasn't lying. Elisa was stunning with her dark hair and creamy white skin. She had a willowy frame, but the suit complemented her build without swallowing her. The way Bryn was staring at her, the valkyrie was very much a fan of this look.

"You look old and stuffy," Isabeau chirped from the couch.

Elisa huffed a laugh. "Thanks, Bo. Stay out of trouble while I'm gone, okay?" The young vampire girl gave her an innocent smile, and Elisa peered at Bryn in concern.

"It'll be fine," Bryn said, rising and giving Elisa a quick kiss. "Have fun on your first day of work. We'll have to do something to celebrate tonight." She toyed with the edges of Elisa's jacket.

"Can you not do that?" Damon said. "She's like our sister, and it's gross."

Misha and Isabeau voiced their agreement, and I laughed. Elisa and I headed to the front door, and just before we left, I saw Finn reach out for another cookie.

Chapter Two

Vampires have excellent reflexes. Feline shapeshifters have better reflexes. That's why when we walked through the doors of The Inferno, I was able to dodge the shot glass headed straight for my face, but Elisa wasn't fast enough to dodge it completely. Still, it only hit her shoulder instead of her nose.

"Sorry!" a gruff voice called from the bar.

I glanced over my shoulder at Elisa, who was wiping the whiskey off her jacket with a frown. Mikhail and Magos had moved to either side of her and were surveying the room for more threats. Or flying shot glasses. An enormous being ambled over from the bar; he would almost pass for human if not for his ridiculous height. And then there was the issue of all that hair.

"Your aim is still terrible, Kuya," I said, tilting my head back so I could look up at him.

"Sorry," he said in a low, rumbly voice and sheepishly handed Elisa some napkins. "I wasn't aiming for ya, girlie. Those damn lokis were annoying me, and my aim was off."

Elisa took the napkins from him and pressed them against the wet spot on her jacket. "It's all right. The lokis annoy everyone." She smiled brightly at him, and Kuya blushed all the way to the tips of his ears.

I reached up and clapped him on the shoulder. "It's fine. Elisa's right, the lokis do annoy the shit out of everyone. I'm pretty sure they believe it's their sole purpose in life."

He chuckled and thumped me on the back, not noticing when I stumbled forward a couple of steps. "I was just about to head out, but it was good seeing you, Nemain."

We stepped aside to allow Kuya's colossal form by.

"What was he?" Elisa asked quietly.

"A kapre," I answered and headed towards Pele's office. Elisa followed me while Mikhail and Magos split off to grab a table towards the back of the tavern. "It's unclear what realm they originally came from. Most of their population lived in the Philippines when they first came to the human realm, but they've spread out over the past few centuries. They're one of a few species largely responsible for the Bigfoot myths."

"I'm not surprised," she said with a laugh. "He had to be at least eight feet tall and that was . . . that was a lot of hair."

"Yeah, they're a hairy lot," I agreed. "Harmless, though. Kuya is a great cook and throws barbecues during the summer. We'll go to the next one."

"I'd like that," Elisa said as I moved the thick purple curtain aside and waved her through.

Pele glanced up from behind her desk as we entered her office. "Give me a moment," she said, returning her attention to the book in front of her.

Elisa and I obediently sat in the chars in front of the desk while Pele finished up whatever she was working on. Interrupting her usually resulted in a fireball being thrown at your head. I was used to it. If Elisa wanted to work for Pele in the long run, she'd have to get used to it, too.

"The suit looks good on you, Elisa." The young vampire preened at the compliment, as Pele closed the book and stacked it neatly with a few others. She turned her piercing turquoise eyes on me. "Do you have it?"

"Of course I have it," I scoffed and pulled the chunk of meteorite from my pocket and tossed it to her.

Pele snatched it out of the air and studied it. She wasn't skilled in making amulets and magical artifacts the way Chamosh was, but she had enough knowledge to evaluate those objects, as well as the materials used to make them.

To me, the meteorite felt cold and a little off, but I couldn't tell anything about it beyond that. "I still don't see what's so special about it."

Pele shrugged and set the meteorite piece down on her desk. "Any material from another planet is useful in crafting amulets and artifacts. Their properties make them difficult to create counter spells against because of how different they are from any material collected from here. That amulet of yours to prevent tracking spells being used on you relied on meteorite fragments."

"That explains why it was so expensive." I hadn't bothered wearing the amulet in months. Sebastian was the one who'd had my blood, and he was dead now.

"That, and Kali charges a premium price."

I snorted. "I trust you're good to deliver it to Chamosh?"

"Yes," Pele said. "He has some plans in motion that will require some careful arranging, and I'll be working with him." She turned her attention to Elisa. "You'll be assisting me with those plans. Chamosh likes you, and he doesn't like most beings."

Elisa smiled, keeping her expression calm and professional. "Wonderful. He was pleasant to work with in our previous engagements and provides exceptional services."

I glared at Pele. "You are the worst sort of influence on her."

Pele smirked and dismissed me with a wave.

I shook my head and rose from the chair. "See you later, kid."

I left Elisa and Pele to their scheming and weaved through the bar patrons until I spotted Eddie's dirty blond hair towards the back. Mikhail and Magos were already seated with him, but my pace slowed when I saw the other two people at the table.

Badb and Kalen, known as The Morrigan and The Erlking to most, and more recently, as Mother and Father to me.

Although I never actually called them that. I still thought of Macha and Nevin as my parents and always would, despite them technically being my aunt and uncle. Both Badb and Kalen accepted that, and I was getting used to them being in my life. But I still felt a pang in my heart every time I saw Badb. Her and Macha had been identical twins, and the seeing the familiar features hurt even though Macha had died centuries ago.

"What are they doing here?" I muttered as I continued walking over to the table.

Eddie kicked out a chair, and I slid into it. He set a shot glass in front of me and filled it with whiskey. I immediately slammed it back and enjoyed the burning feeling down my throat. Eddie smirked as he slyly looked at Badb and Kalen, then poured more whiskey into my glass.

"Just leave the bottle in front of me," I grumbled.

Eddie's smirk grew into a full-fledged grin.

I gave Kalen and Badb my best hard stare. "Why are the two of you here?"

Kalen's features showed polite interest. "Perhaps we wanted to check on you after the way you left our last training session?"

My left eye twitched, and I counted to ten in my head. My parents were the only ones in existence who could help me master my magic. In the few months we'd been practicing,

I'd already improved drastically. I would have made even more progress if half of our lessons didn't end with me and Badb going for each other's throats and Kalen pulling us apart.

"Oh, come now, love," Badb said. "We had plenty of time to see she was fine since it took her so long to open the gateway to get back home."

I gritted my teeth as I wondered exactly how upset Pele would be if I broke her rule about no magic being used in her bar. "I repeat, what are you doing here?"

"My apologies. We're intruding." Kalen held a hand apologetically to his chest. "Your friend here has something important he wants to share with you."

Even though I hadn't known him for long, I knew there was no rushing Kalen to do anything. It wasn't a coincidence he and Badb were here at the precise moment Eddie had something important to tell me. Which meant whatever they were plotting was related to Eddie's news.

"Fine," I ground out, turning away from my parents before I lost the small amount of patience I still had. "What's going on, Eddie?"

The playful smile that had been plastered on his face while he watched the exchange between me and my parents slid away as his true self peeked out. Eddie was all fun and games most of the time, but at his core, he was a predator. A dragon to be exact, and even though I'd seen him in his true form only once, it had left a lasting impression.

"I found something," he said. "An artifact from my home realm."

"Do you have it?" I sat up a little straighter.

Eddie and I had gotten off to a bit of a rough start that had resulted in him swearing a blood oath to never reveal the magic I'd been hiding from everyone in exchange for me taking him to his home realm. Now I considered him a friend and would have taken him to his home realm even without the blood oath between us.

Unfortunately, Eddie had been exiled quite thoroughly, and I couldn't use him to find a path back to his realm, so we'd been searching for something or someone from his realm. The search had proven to be far more difficult than either of us anticipated.

"No." He shook his head. "But I know where it is. We just have to go and get it."

"All right." I swallowed another shot of whiskey. "Where is it?"

"The seraphim realm." Eddie couldn't hide his wince.

I stared at him. "Tell me you're joking."

"Sorry, can't do that, I'm afraid," Eddie replied and grabbed the bottle of whiskey. He didn't bother pouring it into a glass but drank a third of it straight from the bottle. I had a high tolerance for alcohol, but apparently dragons were on another level.

Badb and Kalen maintained neutral expressions, but Mikhail and Magos looked at me with confusion. "What is the problem with going to the seraphim realm?" Magos asked.

"What do you know of the seraphim?" I gestured at Eddie to give me back the bottle. The greedy bastard clutched it tightly to his chest.

Magos glanced at Mikhail. They were both too young to remember the seraphim, and unlike me, they hadn't spent most of their life traveling through the realms. But Mikhail had served the Vampire Council for centuries, and they had collected vast amounts of knowledge in their quest to gain power in this realm.

"The seraphim inspired most of the angel mythology in the human realm," Mikhail said. "They vanished from this realm roughly two thousand years ago. Rumor is, they were asked to leave by the fae. I've never met one, so I know little about them other than they have wings and fire magic. They were apparently quite formidable in battle."

"Bits of that are true," I said. "The seraphim *do* have wings and strong fire magic. Their culture is barbaric and militaristic. When they lived in this realm, they found humans to be quite tasty. They had a bit of fun hunting them down and fire-bombing cities. It was the daemons, not the fae, that made them leave this realm. After the fae and daemons perfected the magic of creating wards to protect realms from the devourers, they suddenly cared quite a bit about the human population. The spells to protect the daemon, fae, and other realms from the devourers required a constant source of magic, and humans provided that."

"They are excellent magical batteries," Eddie agreed, tipping the whiskey bottle in my direction. "They generate all that lovely magic, and the vast majority of them never use a drop of it. Must be delicious to snack on." Everyone at the table stared at Eddie, and he shrugged. "I said what I said."

"I was really hoping you would find what we needed in a nice realm. Maybe one full of sushi and sunny spots to nap in."

"Sorry. I checked those realms first, but they were fresh out of dragon bones."

"They have a dragon bone?" I raised my eyebrows.

Dragon bones were highly sought after because of the amount of magic they contained. Since the dragons had been locked away in their realm, finding bones was nearly impossible.

I'd assumed Eddie had been searching for a relic or trinket from his home realm. We didn't need anything with significant magic; I just needed something from the realm to lock in on. A plain old rock would have worked just fine. But the daemons were overachievers, and when they banished the dragons to their home realm, they threw away the key . . . and every trace of the realm they could find.

"How the hell did you learn this?" I asked.

"Not bone, dragon fangs. One of my regulars came by yesterday. Pele's cousin actually, Azrael."

Alarm bells went off in my head. Pele had barely batted an eye when I told her that Eddie was a dragon, and she had been surprisingly hands off about our plan to break into the dragon realm. Which meant she was plotting something, and every time Pele plotted something I ended up being almost swallowed by underground devourers or rescuing lost fae princes.

Argh.

Seeing the alarm on my face, Eddie finally relinquished the whiskey bottle to me, and I slammed down another shot. "What did Azrael have to say?"

"He was picking up some rare books I'd acquired for him, druidic shit, and he stayed to chat a bit. Told me he'd just gotten back from the seraphim realm where he'd been conducting some business, under the table of course, and the seraphim he was dealing with was some big-shot general."

"What a *coincidence*." I gripped the whiskey bottle and poured myself and Eddie another shot. Mikhail pushed his shot glass towards me, but I ignored it. He could pour his own damn whiskey.

"The general's name is Zephon." Eddie swiped his glass and downed the whiskey in one gulp. "He was bragging about his various conquests and showed the fangs to Azrael. Apparently, he has a room somewhere in his house full of trophies."

"Azrael is sure they're the real deal?"

Eddie's burnt amber eyes met mine. "We both know he only went to that realm to confirm they were real. This is Pele's doing."

"Which means they are very likely the real thing." My head fell back, and I stared at the ceiling. "Fuck. We have to go to the seraphim realm."

"Why the concern about going to this realm?" Magos cut in. "Is it forbidden?"

I looked at Kalen and Badb, who'd remained suspiciously quiet during this entire conversation. Between that and Pele playing cat's-paw with us, my irritation was reaching all new levels.

"It's not forbidden exactly, but it is . . . highly discouraged," I explained. "The seraphim are one of the few species that rival the daemons and fae in terms of raw magic power. They've been slowly and quietly expanding beyond the realm given to them, but they've made no move on the human realm or any realms belonging to the fae and daemons, so it's been ignored. I have no doubt it's being closely monitored, but the daemons and fae have more pressing concerns at the moment."

"Doesn't seem wise to annoy such a threat and let it grow stronger," Mikhail pointed out. Magos and Eddie nodded.

"Not my call, not my mess." I shrugged. "I've run into the seraphim in other realms, and it has always been a less than pleasant experience. I was lucky to limp away the last time. We'll have to plan this as a smash and run job."

"My favorite kind," Eddie said.

Magos and Mikhail didn't look happy about this plan, but they didn't disagree. If I had it my way, they wouldn't be coming on this trip, but I doubted I'd get my way. Still, I'd fight with them about it later.

"Technically, no one is forbidden from going to the seraphim realm, but for those who belong to a fae court, it's understood that they'll ask permission first," Kalen said smoothly.

"Ask permission?" I bristled. So this was why they were here. Somehow, they knew what Eddie had found and that we'd be going to the seraphim realm. I was getting really tired of my friends and family plotting behind my back.

"You're part of the Unseelie Court," Badb cut in, her emerald-green eyes practically glowing. "I understand the leash chafes. But you entered the court willingly, and there is no going back now. The Unseelie Queen won't stop you from going. She'll just ask for something small in return."

I glanced back and forth between my parents, suspicion taking root. "You've already spoken to her about this."

Kalen's dark eyes sparked with amusement. A small grin played across my mother's lips.

I let out a long breath and rubbed my temples. "Just tell me."

"The Spring Equinox is in one week. Your attendance is requested," Kalen replied.

I looked at them in confusion. "The price for me going to a forbidden realm . . . is going to a party?"

"You will be there as a member of the Unseelie Court," Kalen explained. "Your mother and I keep a presence in the court—" Badb snorted, and Kalen let out a low chuckle. "Let me rephrase. I keep somewhat of a presence in the court, and your mother is occasionally dragged kicking and screaming to court events. But the Unseelie Queen wishes for you to have more of a presence. The Spring Equinox will serve as your coming out."

Eddie made a strangled noise, and I glared at him. At my expression, he lost it, and the laughter he'd been holding back came pouring out of him. A positively wicked smile spread across Mikhail's face, and even Magos started chuckling.

"I hate all of you," I spat. Thank the fucking gods Jinx wasn't here for this. Although I had no doubt one of the laughing idiots at the table would be filling him in later.

Kalen and Badb glanced around the table, taking in the reaction of my friends and what was no doubt a murderous expression on my face.

"Was it something I said?" Kalen asked.

"I haven't known our wonderfully cheerful Nemain for that long, but even I know there are two things she absolutely hates. Well, three things." Eddie held up a finger and counted off. "One, fae politics. Two, fancy parties. And three, being the center of attention." Eddie shook his head in amusement. "I know both of you are quite proud of yourselves for working out this small bargain on behalf of Nemain and your fae queen, but it just demonstrates how little you know about your daughter."

Kalen and Badb both stiffened at the insult.

My father recovered first, slipping into that calm and bemused expression he wore as a mask most of the time. I got the distinct impression that if Badb were in her feline form, she'd be snarling right then. I watched as she reeled her emotions back in until they were hiding behind a bland expression, but her eyes still betrayed a hint of wildness.

Her vertical slit pupils slid to mine, and she matched my stare. I looked away first.

"I'll do it," I said. "You're right. I willingly joined the Unseelie Court so Finn could remain free of bullshit like this for the next few decades, and I'll hold up my end by going to this party and letting everyone gawk at me. I'll ask Pele or Kaysea to come along. That will make it slightly less miserable, and they can keep me from saying the wrong thing." I sighed.

The party would be terrible. To say I was awful at fae politics was an understatement. I'd have to watch every word I spoke, and everyone at the party would be looking for a weakness, something they could use to their advantage later on. We might all belong to the same court, but that didn't make us friends or allies.

"That won't be possible, I'm afraid," Kalen said. "The court of the sea fae is in transition since Kaysea's father only recently stepped down. It's tradition for those of the former ruling family to avoid political events for the first few years while the new king or queen steps into their power."

"Fine," I conceded. "Why not Pele, though?"

"Daemons aren't invited to these types of events," Badb said. "Furthermore, Pele isn't just any daemon. She's the daughter of the leader of the Assembly. Everyone knows she'll be taking his place one day. Likely one day soon."

"Well, on the plus side, if I go by myself, I can avoid dancing for most of the night," I muttered. "I'll just have to glower threateningly at any sidhe who attempts to ask me."

"You can't dance?" Mikhail arched an eyebrow at me.

"Not well," I said. "Definitely not at the level expected at a fae court event."

"You're over four centuries old. How can you not dance?"

"Because learning how to kill all sorts of beings in all sorts of ways was more important than figuring out how to twirl around on my toes!" I snapped.

Mikhail grinned at me, flashing his fangs. I was calculating how far I'd have to push back in my chair to be able to leap across the table at Mikhail to wipe that grin off his face when Kalen cleared his throat politely. "You will be expected to dance. It's the Spring Equinox, and you're new to the court."

"Fuck," I groaned.

"I'll go with you," Mikhail offered. "I'm a good enough dancer for the both of us."

I narrowed my eyes at him. "Why do you know how to dance?"

"Apparently, the vampires have something in common with the fae. They both like their fancy parties." The words were casual, but Mikhail's expression tightened slightly. "First impressions matter, Nemain. Kaysea can show us some dances to practice, or one of them can." Mikhail gestured at my parents. "Your ability to stab things indeterminately will only get you so far in the fae courts."

"I'll stab you indeterminately," I grumbled.

Mikhail ignored me and turned to my parents. "Will there be any problems with me going?"

Kalen studied Mikhail, and I had to give the vampire credit. He didn't look the least bit unnerved by Kalen's gaze. Several types of daemon had solid black eyes, like Zareen. Mikhail had been around her often enough that he was used to it. But Zareen's black eyes still shone with joy and happiness. Kalen's bottomless obsidian eyes were cold and touched with cruelty. Even I found them unsettling at times.

After a moment, Kalen looked at Badb and something passed between them. Some silent conversation only people who'd been together for centuries were capable of having.

"It will be fine," Badb finally said. "It's well-known that you've left the Vampire Council. Some members of the court might be intrigued by your presence and will likely try to test you, but given your experience with vampire politics, I suspect you'll be able to weather fae politics just fine."

"This is going to suck so much," I said in defeat. Eddie laughed, and I kicked him under the table. A thought occurred to me, and I glanced at Kalen. "Is the Seelie Queen going to be there?"

"Queen Áine will not be in attendance." His lips quirked up in an amused grin. "By tradition, each queen celebrates the Spring Equinox separately, in their own court. The Unseelie celebration is being held in Mag Cíuin, which is the realm Queen Elvinia spends the most time in."

"Good," I said in relief.

The last time I'd seen Áine, I'd broken into her private chambers and threatened to kill her if I found out she had anything to do with the death of Macha and Nevin. They may not have been my parents by blood, but they had raised and loved me all the same, and they would always be my mother and father.

The warlocks had played a direct role in their deaths, but I strongly suspected Áine had been the reason Badb and Kalen hadn't learned about the danger they were in until it was too late.

"I'll work on getting you something to wear. Your"—Badb stumbled at the words—"Kalen . . . he can show you some of the basic dances." Uncertainty flashed across Badb's pretty features, and Kalen reached out and laid a gentle hand on her arm.

"Right." I stood up, looking away from their small intimate gesture. "There should be a room upstairs where we can begin this torture. Magos, you can head back to the apartment or hang out here. Eddie, let's chat tomorrow about the seraphim realm. It'll be difficult to find updated maps, but if you can, that would be really useful. Maybe Pele can pull some out of her ass since she's decided to involve herself in this."

"But I want to stay for these dancing lessons." The corners of Eddie's lips turned down in a pout.

"I will stab you. Repeatedly."

"Fine, fine. We'll talk tomorrow." Eddie rose and swiped the bottle of whiskey on his way out.

Mikhail walked over to me and held a hand out, a look of challenge on his face. "Shall we?"

I ignored him as I stalked up the stairs. Kalen's voice carried after me, "You sure you don't have a death wish, vampire?"

"The threat of death is what makes life interesting."

Chapter Three

Sidhe fashion was not meant for someone built like me. In general, the sidhe were tall and slender. I had the tall part but not the slender part. My build was far more muscular than most sidhe, not to mention my hips were wider and my breasts fuller. All of which meant any fae clothes brought to me had to be adjusted.

Badb wasn't as tall as me, but she had a similar build, so she knew we'd be spending some time making a sidhe outfit work. She brought along a tailor who adjusted her clothing and was used to these sorts of adjustments. It was a wise move because if she'd brought someone who made judgmental comments about my body, I likely would have thrown them out the window. Even with Badb's experience and the tailor's skill, it still took us hours to find something and tweak it so it worked for all parties involved. Then the discussion about what type of makeup and hairstyle I would wear that night started.

At that point, I considered throwing *myself* out the window.

And all this was just to get ready for the party that was still almost a week away. Badb had ambushed me in my own damn apartment that morning, and Magos had done nothing to save me, the treacherous bastard. All he'd done was make us some coffee and then politely excuse himself.

I didn't know if Mikhail was going through something similar. Kalen had shown up shortly after we'd started with another sidhe tailor in tow, and they'd whisked Mikhail off to the second floor. I hoped he was suffering every bit as much as me, but I suspected Mikhail would enjoy all this primping.

"Quit messing with the dress," Badb said without looking at me.

I scowled at her. She was wearing loose-fitting black pants and a black top with open-flowing sleeves. I'd dubbed it her casual, menacing look. No weapons were visible, but I had no doubt she had some tucked away somewhere. "Shouldn't you also be getting fitted for something just as ridiculous?"

Badb glanced over her shoulder at me and grinned. It felt like being sucker-punched. Most of Badb's mannerisms were different than Macha's. My mom always had this quiet determination around her whereas Badb had more of an intensity. Like she was always one breadth away from going on a murder spree.

But that damn grin. It was the same one Macha would give me and Cian when we'd steal our father's favorite book and hide under the bed waiting for him to find us. It was the grin she'd wear when we'd convince her to stop working for a few hours and play tag with us in the meadows instead. That grin was tied to almost every good memory I had of her.

Every time I saw it on Badb's face, something inside me broke. Not just because it brought back a flood of memories, but because I was terrified that those memories would start to slip away, and I'd associate that grin with Badb instead. I hated her for it.

It wasn't fair. I knew that. Macha had been her sister. The only family she'd had left since their older sister had already died. She had known and loved Macha for far longer than I had. They'd had centuries together whereas I'd had barely twenty years. I hated her a little for that too.

The grin slid off Badb's face, and her eyes darkened as she stared at me like she could see into my soul. Which to some extent she could; I'd inherited my abilities to sense and read souls from her. It wasn't a particularly strong gift, only allowing us to get a basic read on someone's nature. But I hadn't been bothering to keep the pain off my face, so she likely knew what I was thinking even if she hadn't been able to sense it in my soul.

"You're not the only one who misses her." There was an edge of pain to her voice I'd never heard from her before. "This is hard for me, too."

The muscles of my jaws tightened as I looked away from the emerald-green eyes that were a match to my own. That had been a match to Macha's, too.

Fuck. I needed a drink. Or to stab something.

Badb let out a low, raspy laugh. "That look is exactly the one Macha would have when our older sister critiqued her stance while sparring. Nemain taught us both how to fight and she could be overly critical at times."

"Maybe you can tell me about her more sometime." I swallowed, and some of the pain in my chest eased. "It'd be nice to know more about the person I was named after."

It was her turn to look away. After a moment, she nodded and said softly, "She would have liked that. She would have liked *you*."

We sat there quietly for a few minutes before I cleared my throat. "So explain to me why you don't have to get fitted for a stupid dress but I do?"

"I've already paid my dues," Badb replied gruffly. "I've earned the right to dress however the hell I want, and everyone in the court knows better than to challenge me on it."

"Must be nice," I muttered as I let the remnants of grief fade away.

Echoes sounded from outside the apartment as two people came up the stairs. A few seconds later Kalen entered, followed by Mikhail. Kalen greeted us and asked something, but every part of me was focused on Mikhail.

He was wearing a daemon garment commonly referred to as a khikri that fell somewhere between a robe and a dress. The top was sleeveless with a high collar and was practically molded to his upper body before it loosened enough to flow over his hips and fall to the floor in a dark curtain. The deep indigo color matched his eyes, and vibrant purple vines were stitched elegantly throughout it in a simple pattern.

Lately Mikhail had taken to braiding his hair back, but now it fell in loose waves around his face. Mikhail was a vampire, but at the moment, he looked like a daemon prince, whereas I felt completely out of place.

"Nemain?" Kalen's voice finally cut through my short-circuiting brain.

I blinked and looked at him. Based on his expression, I got the impression he'd said my name a few times already. "Yes?"

"Is something wrong?"

"Why a khikri?" I asked, instead of answering his question, my gaze already back on Mikhail.

"Dressing him in fae fashion would have given the impression we were trying to hide that he's a vampire. There is no hiding that. Everyone not only knows what he is, but they know *who* he is." Kalen gave a small smile. "I find the best way to keep the fae on their toes is to lay all your cards on the table sometimes. You will be escorted by the former assassin of the Vampire Council who is wearing a daemon garment made infamous by the current head of the Daemon Assembly, whose daughter is your oldest friend and occasional lover."

My attention snapped back to Kalen, who merely

shrugged. "Despite your attempts to hide in the shadows and avoid the politics you constantly remind everyone you hate, you've managed to collect some powerful friends in your life, my daughter. That is not something you should hide."

I held Kalen's stare for a moment longer before turning to Mikhail, who was giving me an odd expression. Looking down at myself, I ran a hand across the light crystal-blue fabric. I usually wore black and other dark colors, but when I saw this dress, I couldn't resist.

"I know I'm not as pretty as you, Mikhail, but I don't think I look that bad," I said wryly.

My words seemed to snap him out of it, and Mikhail blinked slowly. "You're stunning."

"Oh," I said awkwardly, trying to fight back the blush. *Gods, what the hell is wrong with me?*

"I. . ." Mikhail's gaze slowly looked me up and down. "I wasn't expecting the dress."

"My options were limited," I said, biting my bottom lip. "The sidhe tend to use a fabric that doesn't have much give to it, and fighting in the fancy tunic I tried on would have been difficult. Not that we're going to be fighting at the party, but just in case." I realized I was babbling and took a breath. "It would have irritated me all night. The dress is less restrictive."

"I can see that," he murmured.

The intensity in his dark eyes was usually only visible when he faced off against an opponent. The damn pull I felt towards him rose, just as it had the first time we'd met before I'd even known who he was. I'd tried ignoring it, smothering it, and would have tried setting it on fire if such a thing were possible.

Everything about Mikhail was complicated, and my life was already complicated enough. He was Magos's nephew and came with a whole lot of baggage thanks to centuries of serving the Vampire Council.

What really worried me was that Mikhail knew a lot about

me. He knew some of the terrible things I'd done in my life while I'd been hellbent on revenge. And he didn't care. It didn't bother him in the slightest. I didn't know what to do with that. In the short amount of time I'd been with Andrei, I'd worked hard to keep my dark side under control just as I had when I'd been with Myrna.

The only person I'd been with who had known about and embraced my darker side was Sebastian. And that relationship hadn't exactly gone well. Mikhail and I were too much alike. I couldn't let myself go down this path no matter how much part of me wanted it.

The longer we stood there in awkward silence, the more it felt like my skin was on fire. Unable to stand it any longer, I turned towards Kalen to ask him a question but stopped at the look of concern in his features. I glanced at Badb and found her staring at Mikhail with outright suspicion.

I was way too old to be feeling this awkward. "So do we just show up at the party or do we have to do some type of dramatic entrance?"

"It's a fae party, daughter, and you are the special guest of the evening." Kalen smiled. "Do you even need to ask that question?"

"No," I sighed. "I guess not."

"This is where we need to go," Eddie pointed to a city sketched out on some parchment that one might call a map. If you squinted and tilted your head to the side. A few sections had squiggly lines that we weren't sure represented mountains or water. General outlines of buildings and streets were laid out in the city. Eddie's finger rested on a square building towards the city center.

"That's the general's house?" Magos leaned in closer and

scrutinized the map. "Given what both of you have told me of the seraphim, their city will be well-guarded. If Nemain opens a gateway within the city, we risk immediately being seen. But if we start outside the city, we'll have to sneak past whatever guards they have and whoever is still awake."

Eddie stared at the map, but I could tell he wasn't really looking at it. He'd been uncharacteristically solemn since arriving at our place in the early afternoon. I thought he would have been more excited about being one step closer to returning to the dragon realm, but instead, he seemed troubled, as if convinced something was going to go wrong.

"This is Zephon's house. We have to figure out how to get there," he finally said. "Azrael never saw the trophy room itself. Zephon sent a servant to retrieve the fangs, so it might take us time to locate them within the house."

"I still can't believe he has a pair of dragon fangs," I said, still not over my disbelief that a pair of dragon fangs had been found in the seraphim realm of all places. "Did he tell Azrael where he got them from?"

"He did," Eddie said absently, still staring blankly at the map. "Azrael was concentrating on sending out his magical subtly to confirm they were, in fact, dragon teeth, so he missed most of the story. But every part of a dragon is soaked with magic. There will be enough in the teeth for me to summon a vision of whom they belonged to when I touch them."

I nodded. Eddie wasn't a seer like Kaysea, but all dragons had the ability to draw memories from magical artifacts. That ability was what had allowed him to track me down in the first place.

"If I recognize the dragon the fangs belong to and they still have someone left when we get to the dragon realm, we can return them." His fingers clenched into fists. "At least then they'll know what happened to their loved one."

I thought about what it must feel like to lose a loved one

like that. To know that they had likely met a terrible end but never knowing for sure. On the one hand, we would be ending whatever hope someone might have that their loved one was still alive out there somewhere. But we'd also be giving them closure so that they could hopefully move on with their lives.

"All right, moving back to our original problem, I think our best bet is to start outside the city." I placed two polished stones on the coffee table, one a deep blood red and the other a pearl white. "These were delivered this morning. Apparently, Azrael swiped them while he was there. One is from just outside Zephon's house, and one is from outside the city walls."

The vampires stared at the stones suspiciously. "Have you talked to Pele yet?" Mikhail asked.

"No." I tapped my fingers aggressively on the table. "I looked for her yesterday after Kalen was done torturing us with those dance lessons, but surprise-surprise, she was nowhere to be found. Elisa hasn't seen her in days either, she's been helping Zareen behind the bar while she works through some reading that Pele assigned to her before pulling her vanishing act."

"I don't like this," Eddie said. Mikhail and Magos nodded.

I tossed my hands up helplessly. "I don't either, but Pele will tell us what she's up to when she wants to and not a moment before. Trust me, I've known her for almost my entire life. The only reason we know about these dragon teeth is because of her, because she wanted us to know."

"You're *certain* she won't betray us?" Eddie asked.

"Yes," I said with no hesitation. "Regardless of the history between daemons and dragons, Pele would never betray me. However, having been on the other side of her scheming before, I can promise we won't like whatever she's planning."

"Then we proceed without her," Magos said. "Based on the little intel we have, this is a fairly large sprawling city. Even under the cover of night, some seraphim are bound to still be awake. Plus, we can't search the house while Zephon is inside, and trying to take him out quietly is risky. If something goes wrong and others are alerted to our presence, we'll have to flee, and the house will be highly guarded after that."

"We need a distraction," I said, gears already turning about what we could do to distract an entire city of seraphim. "If someone stays outside the city and causes a distraction, I have no way to quickly get to them when it's time for us to leave. Once we find the fangs, I can open a gateway and get us the hell out of there. But it's still hard for me to open a gateway within the same realm. I've been practicing, but it's not something we can rely on, and I'm not leaving whoever is causing the distraction behind."

"Could just go back and get them after we leave?" Eddie suggested.

I shook my head. "What if something goes wrong for them and they need a quick retreat? The seraphim don't fuck around, and their favorite thing to do after a battle is *eat* whoever or whatever they killed."

"Lovely." Magos grimaced.

"We'll do it," Badb chimed in.

The four of us flinched and turned around to find Badb and Kalen in what had been the empty kitchen mere seconds before. I had watched both of them leave shortly before Eddie arrived and hadn't felt her open a gateway to return here.

"How?" I glared at her.

Badb smirked. "One's never too old to pick up new tricks."

"We'll bring the valkyrie with us," Kalen said, smoothly stepping between me and Badb. "The three of us can cause a distraction. You four and Jinx can search the city for the fangs. Stay together as a group and get out once you have them."

"I'll be able to feel you opening a gateway," Badb said. "I'll do the same to get us out once you're gone."

"There's no reason to drag Bryn into this," I said. "Why can't you two serve as the distraction?"

"The seraphim have a bit of a vendetta against the valkyries," Kalen answered. "The entire city will empty just so they can take a shot at her."

I stared at him in disbelief. "I'm not throwing Bryn into that!"

Badb snorted. "She's not a child, and she's been training with Sigrun. This will give her a chance to cut loose." Badb glanced at Kalen with a purely feline expression. "This will give us a chance to cut loose, too."

Kalen grinned. "It's been a while. It'll be fun."

Mikhail looked at me. "I'm starting to understand why you're such a violent person."

I ignored him. "Fine, we'll ask Bryn, but I'm not making her do this." She'd say yes. I knew she would. I didn't like it, but Badb was right. Bryn was twenty-one years old, and for a valkyrie that counted as an adult no matter how much I still viewed her as a kid. She was old enough to make her own choices.

Jinx? I pushed the thought out.

A few seconds later, an annoyed voice rumbled through my mind. *What?*

Don't take that tone with me. Silence. I rolled my eyes. *You should be up here planning with us.*

Why? I'm not going to listen to what any of you tell me to do, anyway.

Get your ass up here and bring Bryn with you. I need to ask her something.

Fine, he grumbled.

I smiled and stood up from the couch to move one of the chairs over for Bryn, feeling a pulse of magic. I recognized it instantly, but before I could do anything about it, I stumbled over the rug and slammed my foot into the leg of the coffee table. Pain exploded in my foot, and I jumped back and promptly tripped over Magus's extended leg, falling on my ass and slamming my head into the hardwood floor a moment later.

Godsdamn grimalkin.

"Nemain? Are you okay?" Magos asked as he crouched beside me.

I lay there panting, the pain in my foot and my head battling for supremacy. I was pretty sure I had broken a toe and given myself a concussion. I would be fine in a few minutes, thanks to my shifter healing, and hopefully during that time the bad luck Jinx had sent my way would pass.

Speak of the devil. The door opened a second later, and he trotted in, Bryn closing the door behind them.

Shoving the pain aside, I arched my back and pushed up with my hands, flipping myself to my feet. "You." I pointed at him. "I'm going to make a fucking scarf out of your hide."

Jinx leapt onto the kitchen counter, completely unconcerned by my threats, and pawed around the leftover pieces of chicken until he found one he deemed acceptable. *Maybe next time you'll watch the tone you take with me and not interrupt my nap.*

"You're always napping!" I snapped and took a step towards him.

Echoing Kalen's movement from before, Magos smoothly stepped in front of me, amusement dancing in his copper eyes. "Why don't you take a seat, Nemain, so we can discuss things with Bryn?"

Jinx snickered. I glared at him and pantomimed punching him in the face before I stalked over to the couch, reclaiming my seat.

"He gets that from his mother," Badb observed. "She has quite the vindictive streak. She once gave me bad luck for a month because I barely stepped on her tail."

Kalen glanced sideways at Badb. "As I recall, you slammed

your foot down on her tail and then dumped a pint of ale over her head."

"Whatever." Badb waved her hand at him.

Jinx and I just stared at her wide-eyed and then looked at each other. It was weird to think of Badb having a similar relationship with Jinx's mother like he and I had. Especially after meeting his mother. She seemed so refined and above such pettiness. Then again . . . stomping on the tail was a bit much.

Magos grabbed a chair over by the sparring mat and brought it closer. The back of the chair had a cutout that allowed Bryn to sit comfortably in it. She nodded in thanks and plopped down in the chair, her golden wings tucked in behind her.

"What's up?" She glanced around us and then focused on the map on the table, leaning in for a better look.

"We're planning to enter the seraphim realm to retrieve a dragon artifact for Eddie," I explained. "We've decided to split into two teams. Badb and Kalen are going to cause a distraction outside the city while the rest of us search for the item. Badb thinks it would be a good idea for you to join them. Apparently, the mere sight of a valkyrie will stir up the seraphim."

"Why?" Bryn looked up from the map at Badb and Kalen with her serious grey eyes.

"The seraphim caused all kinds of trouble when they were in the human realm. But one inciting incident set things in motion for their eventual expulsion." Badb's mouth tightened slightly. "I'm assuming none of you are aware of the rituals the seraphim take part in when a new generation is coming of age?"

We all shook our heads. Dread formed in the pit of my stomach. The seraphim were violent and psychotic. Any ritual they took part in wouldn't be good.

"They believe that by sacrificing beings that possess magic, their own magic becomes stronger when they're going through their settling, which, for them, is usually between fifteen to eighteen years old. They come into their magic much younger than most species," Badb explained. "The stronger the sacrificed being, the more magic the seraphim will absorb. Or so they believe; it's never been proven. Usually, the seraphim used humans for this. They'd find some that had more magic than others and be satisfied with that. No one particularly cared about the humans, so no one fought them about it."

"I bet the humans cared," Bryn muttered.

"None of them were strong enough to do anything about it. Not to mention a significant portion of the humans worshipped the seraphim and were more than willing to be sacrificed." Badb shrugged. "But some of the highest-ranking seraphim had children scheduled to go through the ritual together, and they wanted something stronger than humans for their children."

"Tell me they didn't." I looked sharply at Badb. How the hell had I never heard about this?

"They did," she said flatly. "Odin and those who followed him were in the human realm. Quite a few young valkyries were in their group. They hadn't gone through the awakening yet, but they still possessed vast amounts of power. The seraphim stole six of them and sacrificed them that very night."

Bryn sat unmoving in her chair, barely breathing. Her magic flooded the living room, making it feel like a static charge.

"How did they even get the children?" I asked, as the horror of what they'd done still settled within me.

"The children were playing in a field. While things were tense between Odin's group and the rest of the Yggdrasil realms, it was understood the children on either side would never be targeted. And no one in the human realm, or any realm for that matter, had any interest in messing with the valkyries."

"Still"—I shook my head—"given how precious children are to the valkyrie, I'm amazed they didn't have better protections around them." Everyone in the room except Badb and Kalen gave me a questioning look. "Valkyries are one of the few species that are truly immortal. Well, technically they can die, but only by violent means," I explained. "Once they awaken, they continue to age for a few years, but then their aging stops completely. They never get sick or contract any diseases. They're even immune to most poisons. Their magic is formidable in combat, and their melee fighting abilities are well-known. But all this power comes at a cost. They can only reproduce once in their lives."

"So, the mothers of those six children. . ." Bryn shuddered.

I nodded grimly. "They lost the only children they would ever have, and they would carry that knowledge for the rest of their lives."

"I'm surprised they didn't tear apart this realm," Eddie said.

"When that happened, things were tense in the Yggdrasil realms, particularly among the Aesir," Badb said. "Even so, the valkyries on both sides set aside their differences and joined together. They slaughtered all the seraphim responsible and proceeded to tear apart a good chunk of Mesopotamia. Eventually, the daemons stepped in and negotiated with the valkyries, promising they would deal with the remaining seraphim. The valkyries returned to their homes. And the seraphim found themselves with a third less of their population," Badb finished, a savage grin spreading across her lips.

"And that is why," Kalen said softly, "the sight of a valkyrie outside their city gates will draw out the seraphim."

"You don't have to do this." My gaze met Bryn's. She'd managed to pull her magic back, but her eyes had a red sheen to them. "We can find another way to draw them out. The seraphim will try to tear you apart, and you'll only have Kalen and Badb with you."

Badb snorted. "I'm a bit insulted by that. We've earned our titles through blood and battle. Don't forget that, *daughter*."

"I've seen you fight. Wasn't all that impressed, *Mother*," I retorted.

Magic sparked in the room, and Eddie and Mikhail leaned back slightly in their chairs. Magos looked like he was ready to leap between me and Badb, but Kalen spoke first.

"You've never seen your mother or me truly fight before. All those previous incidents were"—he paused—"scraps. Barely above barroom brawls. We'll get to truly unleash ourselves in the seraphim realm." Kalen's endless black eyes seemed to glow slightly, as if the magic he contained sensed this upcoming battle.

"I'll do it," Bryn said before I could argue further. "It'll give me the opportunity to practice some of the moves Sigrun has been teaching me. I've been limited in how much I could practice because I didn't want to hurt anyone." Her jaw tightened. "I won't have that problem against the seraphim."

"Fine," I said. "But talk to Sigrun about it. There's a pretty good chance she'll want to join this seraphim slaughter party, and I'd feel better if she was with you."

Eddie chuckled, and the tension eased in the room.

"I realize that this is probably a foolish question to ask this group," Magos started. "But are we sure that using a"—he closed his eyes as if uttering the words pained him—"*slaughter party* as a distraction is the best course of action? Perhaps we could simply lead them away from the city instead of killing them."

"The seraphim have been pushing their boundaries for centuries. All they understand is war and violence," Kalen said. "Neither the Daemon Assembly nor the fae queens have done anything about it because the realms they've attacked have all been minor ones with beings who have no power and no ability to pay for protection."

My eyebrows raised; this was the first time I'd ever heard anything like reproach in Kalen's voice when it came to the fae queens. He didn't always agree with them, but this was more than that. The neutral mask was still firmly in place, and his tone was even, but I saw the slight tightening around his eyes and the way his fingers twitched like he was forcing them to remain open instead of clenched. Kalen was pissed off about no one doing anything about the seraphim.

"I've seen a realm after it's been attacked by the seraphim." The smell of burnt decaying flesh and mournful wails flickered through my mind. "The seraphim aren't picky eaters, but children are their favorite."

Magos's eyes darkened. "Slaughter party it is then."

Bryn rose from her chair. "I'll reach out to Sigrun now. I'll also need to let Elisa and Finn know where I'll be. What time do we leave?"

"We'll wait until nightfall."

Bryn nodded and left. After we hammered out further details of our plan, we had nothing more to do but wait.

Chapter Four

"I'M JUST SAYING it'll be easier for Eddie, Jinx, and me to sneak in," I repeated for what was probably the dozenth time.

"Eddie is blind as a bat at night," Mikhail countered. "He'll need light to see by, which will increase the chances of you being seen snooping around. Therefore, it's worth the risk of having a bigger group if you have to fight your way out."

"I'm pretty sure bats aren't actually blind," I said.

"It's just an expression, Nemain."

"A stupid one." I shrugged.

Mikhail narrowed his eyes at me, and I smiled at him.

"One of us will stand guard outside the house," Magos said firmly. "In our mist form, we'll be undetectable and therefore well-suited to keeping an eye on things outside while the rest of you search for the fangs."

"Then you can come, and Mikhail will stay here," I countered.

"Nemain," Magos said in the patient tone he so often used with me. "We're both coming. If I truly thought it would put the mission at risk, you know I wouldn't push this."

"Fine," I said reluctantly. "Mikhail will be on watch outside the house."

As Mikhail opened his mouth to no doubt argue being regulated to guard duty, the purple triangular crystal that rested above the mirror in our living room started to glow. After I'd come clean to Pele about all my abilities last year, she'd been annoyed at me for a few weeks but still couldn't resist putting some structure into my life. She'd given me a few matching pairs of crystals with instructions on how to link them to specific people so they couldn't be activated by just anyone.

I used the silver crystal set for my brother Cian and his partner, Dante. The purple set had gone to Sigrun after she'd agreed to train Bryn. The crystals themselves couldn't open gateways, but they let me know whenever the folks who had a crystal wanted a gateway opened from their home to mine, and it made it easier to open a gateway in their house because it gave me something to pinpoint.

I raised my hand to open a gateway but heard Badb's chiding voice in the back of my mind. "Is there a reason why you want to broadcast to everyone what you're about to do? Is this some new fighting tactic kids are using these days?"

Grinding my teeth, I lowered my hand and focused. Crystal-blue flames briefly flickered across my arms and disappeared.

My devourer magic came from Kalen and was essentially bastardized fae magic. It wasn't truly sentient but something close, and it often reacted to emotions. I'd been making further strides with learning how to wield it because it felt more natural, and Kalen didn't aggravate me as much during our training sessions as Badb.

The magic I used to open gateways came from my shifter side and was completely different to control. It required precision and was more like muscle memory. Unfortunately, the way

I'd been opening gateways my entire life was wrong, and I was having to unlearn everything.

It sucked. Massively.

Finally, my magic snapped out of me, and a gateway rippled open, revealing Bryn and Sigrun. Without wasting a moment, the two valkyries stepped through the gateway into our living room. I held the portal open as two more creatures came through, a white wolf and a cat with a shaggy brown coat and tufted ears. Gunnar and Viggo.

"Brought the entire crew, I see." I released my magic and let the gateway shut.

Jinx and Viggo pointedly didn't look at each other. Gunnar peered at me with his solemn, light blue eyes. If the wolf had been capable of rolling them, I had no doubt he would have.

"Of course." Sigrun extended her hand, and I gripped her forearm in greeting.

The dark-skinned valkyrie was one of the few beings who made me feel small. Magos had a much larger build than me, but he dressed in a way to tone it down. Sigrun always dressed like a warrior. I wasn't entirely sure she had a casual look. Tonight, she came dressed for battle in leather and chainmail, her favorite axe strapped to her back and several long daggers at her waist.

Sigrun went on, "Bryn told me what you were up to, and I thought me and mine would come along to see how well our young valkyrie puts to use what we've been teaching her."

"And swing your axe a bit? Perhaps separating some heads from shoulders?"

"Exercise is important at my age," she said solemnly.

We grinned at each other and headed into the kitchen where I'd already left out some shot glasses and poured some whiskey into them. "Elisa is with Finn and the others downstairs. Zareen and Kaysea are there, as well."

Bryn nodded at me in thanks. If she was worried about the

both of us going on this mission and leaving Finn behind, she didn't show it. Given we were about to visit a realm full of psychotic killers and pick a fight, I wouldn't have blamed her for being worried. Hell, *I* should be worried. It probably didn't say anything good about me that I was kind of excited.

"Everyone ready to do this?" I asked as the others joined me around the kitchen counter, each picking up a shot glass.

"We're ready," Kalen said, Badb at his side.

I picked up my glass and looked around the group. Sigrun and Bryn both gave me steady nods. Mikhail merely arched an eyebrow, while Magos looked at the shot of cheap whiskey in front of him with obvious distaste. "Let's do this then." We all threw the whiskey back and slammed our glasses down on the counter.

"Time to kill some angels and steal their shit." I grinned wickedly. Sometimes, I really loved my life.

I CROUCHED behind the crumbled remains of an old wall a short distance outside the city. Magos, Mikhail, and Eddie were next to me, and Jinx was sulking a little further back on timeout.

We'd made it to the realm without attracting any attention, but then Jinx and Viggo had almost blown our cover. Jinx claimed Viggo swiped at him, and Viggo made the same claim against Jinx. Sigrun and I separated them quickly, but I was surprised their snarling and hissing hadn't attracted unwanted attention. Once we had them under control, we'd decided our group should move closer to the city, so we'd be in a better position to make our move.

Viggo came with us because not only could the skogkatt fly, but he could also turn himself invisible, which made him an incredibly useful scout—a fact that annoyed Jinx to no end.

Grimalkins might have more powerful magic, but even with all his abilities, Jinx could neither fly nor make himself truly unseen.

We waited quietly for Viggo to return. Best-case scenario, he would be able to locate the general's house. But even if he couldn't find the exact house, he should be able to determine the area of the city where he would most likely live. Generals were revered in seraphim society and often held high positions within the government. He would have a large house, likely decorated with symbols of his victories in battle.

The minutes ticked by, and I could feel Jinx's anger through our bond. *You okay?* I asked. Viggo had definitely scored some good hits before we'd separated them.

Fine.

His tone made it clear he didn't want to discuss the matter any further, so I dropped it. Mikhail and Magos remained perfectly still, their eyes tracking the occasional seraph that flew over the city. The crescent moon provided some light, but even if it'd been pitch black, the vampires would have no problem seeing. Out of all of us, they had the best night vision.

The city was larger than I thought it would be. It sprawled outward instead of up, which I was a little surprised by given that they were a winged species. A thick stone wall encased all of it, and surrounding that was a moat. A few times I was pretty sure I saw something dark and serpentine rise silently from the water before sinking back down.

I wasn't exactly sure who they were defending against, as this entire realm belonged to them, and while the seraphim clans warred with each other, the defensive measures in place wouldn't keep out anything that could fly.

Either the seraphim were just obsessed with turning their cities into fortresses, or they thought there was a distinct possibility of their cities being under siege at some point. Elvinia's suspicions about them having an alliance with Balor were definitely looking more possible now that I was here. The only ones who would launch a ground invasion against the seraphim were the daemons or fae—and they would need one hell of a reason to do it.

Eddie shifted again, and it drew me from my thoughts. I was worried about him. It was unnerving how quiet and tense he'd been all day. I understood it. He'd been looking for a piece of his home realm for years, and this might finally be it. I didn't know of anything I could say that would make him feel better, so I waited with the others in silence, willing Viggo to return soon with good news.

Got it. Viggo appeared directly behind us.

Every single one of us jumped except Eddie. I glared at Viggo. *Not cool.*

His tufted ears twitched, and he spat out a piece of flat stone that looked like it might belong to a roof. *I'm sorry, were you expecting someone else capable of turning invisible?* Light green eyes taunted me before he turned invisible again. *The roof of the house is empty, so you should be good to open a gateway there once we start our distraction.*

"We'll wait until the general enters the field," I said quietly.

Very well.

Viggo didn't say anything else, so I assumed he left. I glanced at Eddie. "Could you see him?" I asked, and Eddie nodded. "You could have warned us!" I hissed.

"I know." A spark of mischief lit up his eyes, and I was so relieved to see it that I forgot my annoyance.

"Here we go," Mikhail said.

I turned on my heels and looked behind us at where the others waited. Fire lit up the night sky as two giant bonfires burned, setting the golden wings of the valkyries aglow.

"IS THIS WHERE YOU'RE COWERING THESE DAYS, VERMIN?" Sigrun's voice boomed across the field.

Within seconds, shouts came from within the city.

"VALKYRIE!" Seraphim shot up into the air, their white wings beating hard. We crouched down as best we could, and I pulled my hood up to hide my ash-blonde hair. We were counting on our hiding spot being off to the side and the seraphim being in enough of a frenzy that they wouldn't notice us.

My heart beat wildly as what had to be over a hundred seraphim poured out of the city, flying straight towards our friends. I can't believe I dragged Bryn into this insane plan of ours.

Badb had been right about the seraphim hating the valkyries enough to fly out to meet them without thinking it through. Screams of rage tore out of them as they flew across the field, but one voice raised itself above the others. "Kill them all!"

The seraph general had arrived. That was my queue to open a gateway and get us inside the city. I raised my hand and started to release my magic when I saw Bryn and Sigrun drop from the sky like stones and crouch on the ground. My breath caught as Kalen stepped forth. Even from here I could feel the devourer magic practically dripping off him. The civilized mask he always wore was gone—only The Erlking remained.

The seraph general shot up into the sky. Half of the seraphim surged up with him, but the remaining half dove towards Kalen. Their feathered white wings tucked in tight as they picked up speed. A few pulled out curved daggers, but most didn't bother with weapons, choosing instead to rely on their talons and teeth to tear my friends apart.

Kalen raised his hand in the air and closed it into a fist. Blue flames so similar to mine shot out from his fist in multiple tendrils, slamming into the first wave of seraphim and punching through their bodies and into the ones behind them.

The seraphim, speared by the flames, pulsed in the air, screaming as Kalen drank down their magic. The ones who hadn't been struck by his flames scattered at seeing half their battalion wiped out in a blink.

I stared at the battlefield, my hand still stretched out in front of me, but I was too shocked to even try and open a gateway.

The general barked orders, and the seraphim reformed far above their dying comrades and used their fire magic to create giant burning spears. They flung them at Kalen, but the blue flames of his devourer magic spread out from the seraphim they'd been attacking and formed a web. The fire spears slammed into the web and snuffed out of existence.

Kalen opened his fist and flicked his fingers. What remained of the seraphim who had been ensnared by his magic fell to the ground in chunks of frozen ashes. The web of blue flames remained spread across the sky, preventing the seraphim from firebombing Kalen and the others.

"Holy shit," we all breathed out at the same time.

I was proud of myself for making a shield out of my devourer flames last week and holding it for a few minutes. The web Kalen had created had to be close to half a mile wide in each direction, and he was holding it like it was nothing.

"I knew your father was powerful . . . but holy shit, Nemain," Eddie said, staring wide-eyed at Kalen. I nodded, too stunned to respond or make my normal retort that he wasn't my father.

The general managed to rally the remaining seraphim, and they split into smaller groups, flying out to the edges of the devourer web and ducking underneath. Kalen pulled a sword free, blue flames dancing along the black metal. I didn't know how he was still standing after absorbing all that magic. I'd never consumed that much in one go, and the few times I'd consumed a fraction of the power Kalen had just taken in had left me feeling giddy and in desperate need of a nap.

The first group of seraphim were about to reach Bryn, who

had once again flown up and hovered over the others. With the close quarters, the seraphim couldn't fling their firebombs, but they still had fire magic to wield. Flames erupted along their swords, and as two of them closed the distance between them and Bryn, a gateway snapped open above them. Badb dropped out of it and neatly sliced off both seraphim's heads, dropping into another gateway and reappearing on the ground beside Kalen.

Gunnar surged up from the ground, great white wings unfurling as the wolf grabbed one of the falling heads and flung it at the approaching seraphim. It struck one in the chest, and he pulled up his flight, only to have his throat torn out by an invisible Viggo. The skogkatt briefly became visible as he ran across the sky as if leaping from one invisible branch to another before flickering out of sight again. The seraphim hovered in the air, almost like it was unsure who to attack.

The general barked another order, and they once again dove towards those gathered on the ground.

Panic seized me when two seraphs broke through Bryn's guard, and I heard her scream as they tore into her wings. Before I could take a step forward and say to hell with opening a gateway, Sigrun was there hacking the seraphs apart.

Despite the damage to her wings, Bryn was still in the air and Sigrun was now guarding her back. Kalen's devourer flames shot out and caused the seraphim who had been ganging up on the valkyries to scatter. More seraphim poured out of the city.

"This really is a seraphim slaughter party," Mikhail commented. Badb made a gesture and everyone started moving back, away from the city.

"We need to search the general's house fast." I returned my concentration on opening a gateway and pushed the battle raging behind us out of my mind, focusing on the problem in front of me. "I doubt Kalen can do what he did again, and they can't hold off those numbers forever."

Mikhail and the others gathered around me as I gripped the smooth piece of tile Viggo had given me earlier.

My magic surged forward, and I pulled it back, gritting my teeth. Not too much. I let a little more out, but once again too much spilled forth and I had to rein it back. My magic faltered.

Nemain. . . Jinx growled impatiently.

I'm trying, I ground out.

Fuck. Why was this so hard? My magic kept trying to punch through this realm entirely and take us somewhere else. I yanked it back and squeezed my eyes shut, focusing on the cool tile. Slowly, I let a little of my magic out at a time until it was just enough to create a gateway.

Once I felt the gateway snap open, I opened my eyes and saw a roof deck beckoning us forth. "Let's go."

We all quickly passed through the gateway and onto the roof. I didn't want to risk struggling to open the gateway again, so I left it open for now in case we needed to get back outside the city.

"I'll keep watch. Don't try and ditch me here, shifter," Mikhail said, and vanished in a swirl of mist.

We didn't waste any time and quickly made our way downstairs into the home. The four of us searched floor by floor. The top floor went quickly because it was a large kitchen and general sitting area that didn't seem to get much use. The next floor had several large bedrooms and a bathing area, but no signs of any dragon teeth. Eddie's tension grew as we went down to the ground level floor.

"I smell humans," Magos said quietly as he surveyed the room.

"Are you sure?" I frowned.

There was no reason for humans to be here. Unless... warlocks maybe? Even if the warlocks were Balor's allies, I still couldn't see the seraphim working with them. As far as they were concerned, all humans were cattle.

I inhaled and caught the faint scent that Magos had picked up on. Sloppy of me to miss that, my sense of smell was just as good as Magos, I just hadn't been paying attention to it. The scent was recent.

"They're still here," I said softly.

We all looked around the scattered furniture in the room. Movement caught my attention, and I turned just in time to see a few fingers wrap around a doorframe and a head poke out.

A young girl who looked around the same age as Finn stared at us. Her honey-brown eyes were wide with fear as her heartrate sped up.

"We're not going to harm you," Magos said, keeping his voice calm and even as he slowly moved towards the girl. She froze like a rabbit caught in a snare as he knelt in front of her, palms raised. "No harm," he promised.

Words poured out of the girl as tears tracked down her face. My brows furrowed together, and I looked at Eddie. "You get any of that?"

He shook his head as he rubbed the translation mark behind his ear. "Never encountered anyone who spoke a language that couldn't be translated before. Have you?"

"Yes, a couple times, but. . ." I stared at the girl.

Magos rose and extended a hand towards her, which she latched onto, cowering beside him. The clothes she had on were nothing more than torn rags. Based on how skinny her arms were and the hollow look of her face, she was severely malnourished.

I sighed, "We don't have time to deal with this now. We'll take her with us and figure out how a human girl came to be here." And why the seraphim didn't just eat her like they normally do with humans. "There's one more room to search."

"Come with me," Magos told the girl.

Even though she didn't understand him, she didn't argue as he gently led her into the next room. I didn't know if that was because she recognized Magos as someone who wouldn't harm her or if she was simply used to following orders without question.

Two steps into the room, Eddie stopped and sucked in a breath. "They're here. I can feel them."

"Then let's find them and get out of here," I said.

This room clearly served as a mix between a weapons room and trophy display. Various axes, swords, and spears lined the wall. I recognized the designs from a few different realms. These were the weapons of fallen warriors the general seraphim had bested in battle. Stone tables sat against the wall with silver boxes ranging in size. I flipped some of them open as Jinx padded around the room, stopping here and there to study boxes for a few seconds before moving on.

Eddie tore through boxes on the other side but stopped abruptly, opening a long silver box with trembling fingers. He pulled out a curved fang that had to be almost a foot long.

"Is that it?" I asked, peering into the box and seeing a second identical fang laid carefully inside. When I looked back up at Eddie, his eyes were squeezed shut but moving rapidly back and forth beneath his eyelids. Seconds later, they snapped open, burning brightly.

"I know who these belonged to. He has . . . *had* a younger brother." Eddie carefully laid the fang back in the box. "He'll want to know what became of his brother."

I laid a hand on Eddie's shoulder. "And he will. We'll find him when we get to the realm." Eddie nodded once and clutched the box to his chest while I went to retrieve Mikhail.

Less than a minute after we arrived back in the apartment, Badb opened a gateway, and the rest of the group joined us.

Everyone appeared to be in one piece, but that didn't stop

me from moving towards Bryn and looking her over. The young valkyrie was streaked with blood, and a few seraphim had clearly gotten close enough to dig into her with their fangs and talons. Sigrun had gotten armor made specifically for Bryn that covered all her vitals. Based on the fresh nicks in the dark metal, it had done its job.

"Go get cleaned up." I jerked my head towards the door, and Bryn left for the second-floor apartment. I walked over to the kitchen where everyone had gathered around the counter and stopped mid-step. "Where is Sigrun?"

Badb, standing in front of the coffeemaker, shrugged, a frown on her face. "She had other business to attend to in the seraphim realm."

"You left her there?!" I hissed.

Badb tore her gaze away from the coffeemaker, bright green eyes identical to mine glaring at me. "She had. Other business. To attend to. What part of that was not clear? How does this coffeemaker work?"

I would murder her.

As I took a step, Kalen wrapped an arm around her shoulders. I glowered at him, trying to tell him to keep Badb under control, but he quirked a dark eyebrow up in amusement. He hadn't fully put away the Erlking persona yet. His bottomless black eyes swirled as if they contained smoke, and blue flames periodically danced across his skin. I could feel the cold power radiating off him still.

"You should ask Pele about whatever Sigrun is up to. I suspect she had a hand in it," Kalen said.

"Of course she did," I snapped. "I'll reach out to her, but I wouldn't be surprised if she's still avoiding me."

Kalen tugged Badb out of the kitchen towards the open space of the living room. "We'll return to collect you tomorrow. Rest up, daughter."

"You're going to need it." Badb smirked and opened a

gateway. With all the planning we'd been doing for the seraphim realm, I had completely forgotten about the Spring Equinox.

I stared at the spot where Badb's gateway closed behind them. "Any chance we can just go to the dragon realm now?"

"And miss your misery at the fae party?" Mikhail gave me a sinful smile. "Not a chance."

Chapter Five

"How WILL we know when to enter?" I tugged at the fabric of my dress again and continued pacing across the room. Badb had picked us up from the apartment a couple of hours ago, and we'd been waiting in this room for the past thirty minutes after getting dressed and dolled up.

Mikhail waited with a quiet focus, his gaze tracking every step of my movement. It both unnerved and thrilled me at the same time to be the center of his focus like this.

While I was still annoyed at being forced to go through that gods awful dress fitting and attend this party, that was likely going to be incredibly boring . . . I loved this dress.

Instead of a tight-fitting bodice, two strips of fabric flowed down from my shoulders and over my chest where another band of fabric wrapped around my waist, holding them in place. The bottom half of the gown fell to my feet, but two high slits on both sides kept my movement free. The silky fabric was light and airy, and I secretly adored that the light crystal blue color matched my devourer flames.

Honestly, the most annoying part of the look was what they'd done to my hair. My long ash-blonde hair was swept away from my face and pinned in place with what felt like a thousand pins digging into my scalp.

But I wasn't too vain to admit the effect was stunning as the waves of slightly curled hair cascaded down my back. I'd stared at my reflection earlier when I'd had a few minutes alone, twisting enough so that I could see the blue flower tattoo between my shoulder blades. Myrna's final birthday gift to me.

So far, no one had brought up that my birthday was in a few days. Even though Sebastian was dead, and I no longer had to worry about what fucked-up gift he was going to give me, I still wasn't looking forward to it. My birthday would forever be intertwined with Myrna's death. I would be happy to let my birthday pass without commentary this year and every year after.

My fingers itched to pull the pins out of my hair or rub off the bronze paint that had been applied to my eyelids and lips.

I'd tried asking Kalen earlier about what I should expect tonight, but the only bit of advice he'd been able to give was, "Always expect the unexpected when it comes to the fae queens."

Which was exactly what I was afraid of. The Unseelie Queen had barely asked anything of me since I'd officially joined her court, and it made me anxious.

I went to run my fingers across my silver bracers and felt skin instead. My lip curled as I stared at my bare forearms. Since they were fae-made, I assumed my bracers would be acceptable to wear. Their design was exquisite, and they looked more like jewelry than armor, but more importantly they provided a way for me to hide two throwing daggers. But Badb and the sidhe who had helped get me ready vehemently disagreed. After arguing about it over ten minutes, Badb had finally threatened to tie me down and tear them off me. I'd relented after that.

"Someone will come and get you," Kalen said. "The guests

started arriving an hour ago. You're the main event and the official kickoff of the party."

"Wonderful." My shoulders slumped forward. "You both will be with us, right?"

Kalen shook his head. "This night is about introducing you to the court. Our presence would overshadow that. You will be announced as our daughter"—he paused at the word and swallowed—"but we will not be by your side. We'll make our way through some back hallways and join Elvinia by her throne. It's important you stand on your own when you make your entrance."

"As a sign of strength?" Mikhail asked, one dark eyebrow arched in that annoying manner of his. "Or an attempt to make sure your enemies don't immediately transfer to her?"

Kalen laughed softly, which made the hairs on the back of my neck stand on end. "You are a clever one. As long as you use that political savviness to protect and help my daughter, I won't kill you for the way you look at her."

I bristled at his words, but Mikhail responded before I could. "If *Nemain*"—I smiled at the way Mikhail pointedly said my name instead of referring to me as Kalen's daughter. The mark clearly struck home as Kalen stiffened—"has a problem with how I look at her, I have little doubt she'll let me know. Either with her sharp blades or even sharper tongue. But don't fool yourself into thinking you could take me out. I've survived far worse things than you."

"So arrogant," Badb scoffed. "Vampires always are. Perhaps if you still had your mist sword like your uncle, you'd be more of a threat. But as it is, you're only a fraction of the warrior you once were."

It was Mikhail's turn to stiffen as Badb's words sliced into him. I'd only asked Mikhail about his sword once before. I knew the reason he could no longer call it. He felt he was no longer worthy after the things he'd done in the war against the werewolves. I moved without thinking and looped my arm through his, leaning against him slightly.

I met my mother's eyes. "Careful, Morrigan."

Her nostrils flared slightly at the use of her title and my mocking tone.

A loud knock on the door ended our standoff, and a moment later, a sidhe dressed in a brilliant blue tunic opened the door and announced it was time. Without another word, I turned and pulled Mikhail with me. We were halfway down the hallway when Mikhail stopped. I halted with him and once again was distracted at how he looked tonight.

On its own, the dark indigo khikri was striking. But delicate silver vines had been painted up his arms and part of his neck in a beautifully intricate pattern.

I'd been so stunned when he'd entered the waiting room that I'd run my fingers across the paint and traced the pattern. Luckily, it'd been applied via magical means and hadn't smeared. Mikhail hadn't moved the entire time I'd been touching him, as if he'd been worried about breaking a spell.

Now as he leaned towards me, it was my turn to freeze when he whispered in my ear, "Thank you."

"Don't thank me yet," I said, my voice trembling slightly. I took a breath and continued more steadily, "We still have the actual party to get through. Something tells me the last hour was the simple part of the night."

Mikhail let out a soft laugh. "The no shoes thing weirds me out," he admitted. I glanced at his bare feet, which had the same silver pattern painted on them as his arms.

"It's a fae thing," I said. "Parts of the ballroom have bare earth exposed. The rest is stone that holds small amounts of earth magic. The fae don't like to be cut off from nature, even when they're in buildings."

"Just don't step on my toes when we're dancing."

"No promises." I smirked. "Even with the dance lessons, I'm not exactly a skilled dancer."

The fae who had collected us cleared her throat from where she waited in front of tall silver doors. Mikhail held his arm out for me, and I looped mine through his. At our approach, the fae stepped aside, and the silver doors slowly swung open. My stomach fluttered, and I was glad I hadn't eaten anything while waiting because I was pretty sure I would have hurled if anything had been in my stomach.

I took a deep breath and let it out, along with my magic. Unless someone attacked me, or the Unseelie Queen directed me to, I wasn't allowed to use my magic against anyone tonight. But Kalen had specifically told me that I was allowed to *display* my magic if I chose to.

My first inclination had been to keep my magic contained because that was what I'd done for most of my life. But everyone here would know exactly who and what I was, so there was no point in hiding it. I wouldn't be walking out of this ballroom tonight without having some enemies, but I could at least make sure they understood what I was capable of so they would think twice about making a move against me.

A warmth spread over my skin as my magic settled around me. I heard the quick intake of breath from the sidhe who had led us here. The fae were capable of seeing magic. I was a little jealous I hadn't inherited that ability since I was only half fae. I could only feel it. The music and talking within the ballroom died as Mikhail and I walked out onto the top of the stairs, and all attention fell on us.

"I present the newest member of the Unseelie Court," Queen Elvinia called out from where she stood on a raised platform, Kalen and Badb at her side. "Nemain, daughter of The Morrigan and The Erlking. Guardian of my own flesh and blood." She paused, her lips parting in a wide smile. "And my new knight."

It felt like everything around me stopped as those words clanged around in my mind.

And my new knight.

Her reference to me being the guardian of her nephew was bad enough, since most beings didn't know about him. But no one had told me about this knight business. I didn't even know what that meant. The shock faded slightly as my blood simmered in rage at the queen. And Badb and Kalen. They had to have known this was coming and hadn't thought to warn me.

I stood at the top of the stairs, frozen as rage and shock battled against each other, and would have remained there if Mikhail hadn't pulled me forward slightly. I looked away from where the queen sat with my parents and found the waiting crowd wasn't much better. Most of the gathered sidhe looked at me like I was a feast they couldn't wait to sink their teeth into.

It was too late for me to hide my emotions behind a neutral mask. Every emotion I'd been feeling since I entered the ballroom had been displayed for all to see. They knew just how far I was out of my depth and were excited at exploiting my weaknesses. But I wasn't prey, and I certainly couldn't be viewed as such by those here tonight.

A fierce grin spread across my face, putting my fangs on display. I pushed my magic slightly, and it responded with glee. Crystal-blue flames erupted across my shoulders and trailed behind me like a cape, leaving frozen ash in my wake.

That was all I intended my magic to do, but between one blink and the next, it spread to Mikhail. It mirrored what it had done for me and raced across his shoulders, giving him a cape of matching flames. Mikhail kept his steady pace down the stairs, as if the display were completely expected. Only the tightening of his grip on my arm told me he was unnerved. The sidhe that had been looking at me with interest and hunger mere moments before now looked at me, at us, with wariness. When we reached the bottom of the stairs my flames smashed outwards and they took several steps back, clearing a path for us.

"Thank you for joining us on this night of celebration," Queen Elvinia said smoothly when we reached her throne. She glanced behind me at the frozen ash I'd left behind. "And for providing the festive decorations."

"It is my pleasure to attend, and to serve as your *knight*," I said, adding a little bite to my words.

The queen merely smirked at me. "Of course. Please enjoy the party." She raised her eyes from me and addressed the rest of the court, "Let us all enjoy this first day of spring and welcome Nemain to the court."

The sidhe of the Unseelie Court immediately split off into groups at her words. Some headed to the dance floor, others to where drinks were being served. I had no doubt all of them were discussing what had just taken place and how they could use it to their advantage. But for now, I had a moment with Elvinia, Badb, and Kalen all to myself.

The Unseelie Queen snapped her fingers, and a faint green circle glowed on the floor around us. A privacy spell. Perfect.

"Any particular reason you didn't warn me ahead of time of this knight business?" I practically snarled at Badb and Kalen.

"Because they didn't know," the queen interjected. She rose from her throne with a casual grace and joined us.

She was dressed almost the same as every other time I'd seen her, in a black tunic with dark green pants. These ones were actually clean and had a stylized pattern of a tree embedded in the fabric. Her short black hair hung loose, barely brushing against the top of her shoulders. Apparently, like Badb, she wasn't required to dress up for these events either.

Must be the perks of being the queen.

"If I'd told them, they would have argued with me about it. Just as you would have argued with me about it." She waved a flippant hand at all of us. "I didn't want to deal with it. Being my knight will offer you an additional layer of protection from those in my court who might wish to strike out at you in an attempt to hurt your parents. This adds another angle for those who would have taken such measures to consider."

"It also ingrains her that much more in the court," Badb growled. "You haven't had a knight in centuries. I thought Kalen and I were covering those duties just fine. There was no reason to do this to her."

Kalen's expression tightened in agreement. Some of the tension loosened within me. At least my parents hadn't been lying to me the past couple of days. About this, anyway.

"What exactly does it mean to be your knight?"

"For now . . . not much," Elvinia said. "Badb is correct in that she and your father have been covering most of the duties my knight would usually do. I would have declared them my knights long ago, but their history with the Seelie Court complicated things, so instead they've served as my unofficial knights. Essentially, they are the enforcers of my court."

"So they're your assassins," I said flatly.

"If only," Badb muttered.

The queen chuckled. "It would make their lives a lot easier if that were the case. But sadly, most of the time, they have to solve problems that arise in the court without killing." Kalen snorted, and the queen amended her words, "Without *just* killing."

"Why me? I'm not qualified for this." I gestured towards the ash trail behind me. "I was about ten seconds away from unleashing my magic on everyone in this room when you announced to everyone I was your knight and they all started staring."

"But you didn't, and you handled it all quite well. I was curious how you would respond, and you exceeded my expectations." The queen studied her nails, which had been sharpened into points with silver tips. "As to why I chose you, Fionn will one day rule the fae realms over both the Unseelie and Seelie Courts. Many will work against him to keep him from ruling, and once he sits on the throne, they will continue to undermine him. He will need a knight. You *will* be that knight." Her eyes bore into mine. "Consider the next fifty years training."

I tried to calm the pounding in my ears. With one declaration, the Unseelie Queen had just radically altered my life. It was bad enough belonging to a fae court, but this . . . did this mean I had to relocate here? Was I expected to always be at her beck and call? Just how much of my life had just been given up?

Kalen's worried gaze fell on me before turning to the queen again. "Elvinia—"

"For crying out loud," she cut him off. "You act like I have sentenced her to death when I have done no such thing. We don't have time to coddle her."

"Come." Badb tugged on Kalen's arm. "Let's go get something to drink." She half-lead, half-pulled him away, and I started to follow after them, still in a pissed-off haze about what had just happened.

"Stay," Elvinia commanded, and I felt a slight tug in my chest.

I froze before whirling to face her. "What the fuck was that?"

Out of the corner of my eye, I saw both of my parents halt and spin back towards us. Mikhail stood in a loose stance with a calm expression on his face, which meant he was a hair's breadth from trying to murder the queen and everyone around us.

Elvinia rolled her eyes, which I absently noted was very unqueenlike. "All of you are truly ridiculous." Her eyes flicked to Mikhail. "Vampire, go with her parents to get something to drink. Wine or blood. I don't care, just don't kill anyone. Nemain and I are going to have a little chat and everyone is going to calm the fuck down and stop acting like I just declared her to be executed at dawn."

"It's fine," I said tightly, meeting everyone's eyes. "Just a knight having a chat with her queen."

Badb and Kalen looked at me for a moment before offering a stiff nod and walking away. Mikhail's jaw hardened, and he made no move to follow them. I placed a hand on his arm, and he blinked at it before turning those intense twilight eyes on me.

"Go, it's okay really," I said quietly.

With one last dark look at the queen, he left to join my parents across the ballroom.

"Until tonight if you'd told me that a vampire could kill me, I would have laughed in your face," Elvinia drawled. "It's still highly unlikely, but I'm pretty sure that one would at the very least test my skills."

"What did you do earlier?" I asked coldly. "What the fuck was that pull I felt?"

"Oh that." She glanced sideways at me, a quick grin darting across her lips. "That was just a nudge. Trust me, I can do far worse now that you're not only a member of my court but also my knight."

"How?" The word came out as more of a growl than anything.

Power rippled off her as she let her magic flow. The fae gathered around the ballroom continued their conversations, but they all glanced towards us nervously while creating more distance between them and the queen.

"How?" More magic poured off Elvinia, and my own rose

up to push back against the tsunami of power that was washing over us. I gritted my teeth against the onslaught while she leaned forward, crowding my space. "Because I'm the fucking Unseelie Queen."

Just as suddenly as she unleashed it, the magic pulled back into her, and the entire ballroom seemed to let out a collective sigh of relief. My magic settled down but didn't retreat completely, ghostly blue flames flickered down my dress.

"So, are you going to tell me what you want me to do as your knight? Or do I have more surprises to look forward to as you unveil the plans you have in store for me?"

"You're already doing it," she said and gave me a satisfied look. "Balor has allies outside of the realm he's trapped in. Some of them are fae who have made the unfortunate choice to support him, your parents can handle hunting those ones down."

A muscle in my face ticked at Badb and Kalen casually being referred to as my parents, but I let it go. I'd have to get over that at some point because that's how everyone viewed them even if I didn't.

"The warlocks and vampires are allied with him as well," I pointed out.

"They barely count; their magic is nothing."

"Someday the fae are going to pay for their arrogance." The warlocks and vampires might be weaker in magic than the fae and daemons, but I'd learned my lesson in underestimating them. They were crafty bastards. Plus, they'd already grown in power since allying with Balor. He was sharing all kinds of tricks with them.

"Perhaps," she acknowledged. "But I'm more concerned about the other allies he's gathering."

I titled my head as I thought about her words, and suddenly it all clicked together. "You think the dragons have formed an alliance with Balor. That's why you've been leaving me alone these past few months. You want me to go to the dragon realm."

"I thought about *ordering* you to do it." A self-satisfied grin curved across her lips when I immediately bristled at the idea of being ordered to do anything. "But I figured it would be less of a headache this way. Plus, it was fun starting the rumor and make sure your little daemon friend heard about it."

"You're responsible for that rumor?" Gods, Pele was not going to be happy to know that the fae queen had manipulated events like this.

"Don't look so surprised," she said dryly. "I have been at this whole queen thing for a while now."

"Anything else you want to drop on me?" I scowled. "Might as well do it now."

"The seraphim are also working with Balor. There are other pieces of dragons lying around that you could have used, but I specifically started the rumor using the seraph general because I was curious if the daemon would figure it out." She tapped a sharp nail against her dark red lips. "She is quite clever. I've been watching her these past few years; she knew something wasn't right, but she was missing a big piece of the puzzle."

"If you're expecting me to apologize for telling her about your asshole big brother, you'll be waiting a long time." I gave her a pointed look. "And just to avoid any confusion in the future, I tell Kaysea and Pele everything. They have my loyalty. Just because you ensnared me in your court doesn't mean I owe you shit."

"You're so much like your mother." She let out a low laugh. "I'm not going to lie and say I'm happy with the secret of Balor's existence being known to others. Although Pele appears to have mostly kept that information to herself,"—the queen cut a sideways glance at me—"methinks that she doesn't quite trust everyone on the Daemon Assembly the same way I do not trust everyone in my court."

Shit. Pele was so not going to like Elvinia knowing that she suspected there were Balor supporters amongst the daemons, specifically in the Assembly.

A suspicion came to me, and I narrowed my eyes at the queen. "If you know all this, why haven't you done more to stop it? Why put on ridiculous parties like this one when your time could be spent stomping out your brother's allies?"

She pursed her lips together, and I realized for the first time just how tired she looked. There were faint dark circles beneath her eyes. She hid it well, but now that I knew where to look, it was all I could see.

"The ward my sister and I placed around the realm we trapped Balor in is weakening," she admitted. "He still can't get out, but he's able to send more of his army out. My sister and I patch up the holes as fast as we can find them, but they're growing in number. Balor is getting stronger, and we are getting weaker. We cannot allow him to gain powerful allies like the dragons and seraphim, but just as importantly, we need to know what he's planning to do with them."

I started to raise my hand to rub my face but dropped it when I got halfway. *Fucking makeup.* "Have I ever told you how much I hate the fae? And all your bullshit?" I felt so goddamn tired, and we were only in the opening hour of the party.

"You do realize that you're part-fae, right?" She arched an eyebrow at me.

"It's called being in denial," I growled. "Look it up!"

She shook her head ruefully. "I'd say I was sorry for laying all this on you, but I'm not. Your fate is tied to that of my nephew. You were always meant to be involved in this. So quit whining, and get to work."

With those parting words of encouragement, the queen glided away to join Badb and Kalen.

Mikhail drifted back over to stand beside me. I instantly felt better at having him by my side and then immediately felt pissed off for feeling that way.

"You okay?" Mikhail asked, not taking his eyes off the sidhe gathered near the dance floor.

"I'm annoyed I didn't see this coming," I admitted. "I should have known it wouldn't have been as simple as me coming to this party, that the queen was plotting something else. The sidhe are always plotting at least a dozen different things."

"True enough." He slid an appraising glance at me.

"What?" I snapped.

"Just wondering if now is a bad time to tell you that the band will start playing in ten minutes."

"Great." I grimaced. That meant we'd have to twirl around on the dance floor soon while all the fae gawked at us.

"Is it weird having the Morrigan and Erlking as your parents?" Mikhail asked as he continued to study me curiously. "I always knew who they were obviously, but seeing them here and how the other fae treat them . . ."

Confused, I searched the room until I found them, walking slowly around the room a short distance from Elvinia. All the other fae gave them a wide berth, a few practically tripped over themselves to get out of their way. Badb's posture held a slight stiffness, and she was tapping her fingers against her thigh rapidly. I grinned to myself. She clearly didn't enjoy these types of events any more than I did. Kalen wrapped an arm around her waist and pulled her in close. Whatever he said made her throw her head back and let out a throaty laugh.

"I'm getting used to them, but when I think of my parents . . . I think of Macha and Nevin. They raised me, and they loved me like a daughter. I was their daughter." My throat tightened, and I paused, allowing my emotions to settle. "I don't think I'll ever think of Badb and Kalen as my mother and father. That feels weird. Also, I'm over four centuries old. I don't need a new mother or father at this point."

"They don't seem like the type to ask that of you."

"No, I don't think they ever will. I think we're all a bit confused about what to do with our relationship. But everyone views me as their daughter, so I'll have to get used to being referred to as that even if it doesn't seem right." I chewed on the inside of my cheek. "Maybe it'll be less weird with time."

"Perhaps." A sidhe couple made their way over to the queen, and she greeted them with what seemed like genuine fondness. Mikhail's gaze stayed on them. "Do you know anything about any of the sidhe gathered here tonight?"

"Not much about them personally. Most of those here are the Tuatha Dé Danann, which are the oldest and most powerful sidhe families. I've probably done jobs for some of them indirectly through Pele in the past. The Tuatha are always jockeying for more power within their court, and those who aren't Tuatha are always trying to knock them down a peg. But other than that basic generalization, I couldn't tell you much about court politics."

"Sounds like you've got the next fifty years to figure that out," Mikhail said, his lips twitching in amusement.

"You're hilarious," I said dryly. "I'm going to stomp on your feet when we dance."

"Please, we both know I'm faster than you." I punched at his shoulder, but Mikhail moved out of the way in time. "I noticed the dancefloor was dirt when we walked by it earlier. You weren't kidding about the fae preferring to be close to the earth. I'm surprised everyone here isn't more dusty."

"You can thank earth magic for that. The dance floor and other areas might be dirt, but none of it will rub off on you. Usually, the fae also use their magic to create patterns with various minerals on the floor. It can get pretty elaborate." I frowned as I looked at the dance floor. "This all seems a bit plain, to be honest."

I looked more closely at the ballroom, taking notice of little details I'd missed before. Really, the only stunning part of the room was the ceiling, which was mostly open to the night sky. Before we could continue critiquing the fae ballroom, the band started taking their place. Dread coiled in the center of my chest. The dance had been what I was most worried about tonight until the queen had sidetracked me with that knight announcement. Now all that anxiety was rushing back in full force.

Mikhail twisted towards me and bowed slightly, holding out his hand. "Dance with me, shifter."

I slipped my hand into his. "Only because you asked so nicely, vampire." I looked him over and added, "And because you're so pretty."

"I *am* pretty," he agreed without a trace of humility.

I huffed a laugh and let him lead us to the dance floor where all the sidhe had gathered on the sides. Magic pulsed slightly with every step that brought us closer. That was weird. I subtly glanced around, but no one seemed alarmed by this, and nothing about the magic seemed hostile. When we reached the dirt square of the dance floor, Mikhail looked at me with an eyebrow raised. Tension roiled through me, but there was no going back now. I gave him the barest hint of a nod to let him know I was ready.

In one smooth motion, which I had to admit he was really good at, Mikhail spun me away from him. The band was ready and instantly started playing. I closed my eyes and let my feet carry me across the dance floor, my dress swirling around me and the magic that had been building exploding across my skin. After a few more spins, I paused with my hands held up, palms to the ceiling, and opened my eyes.

A small gasp escaped me as I saw what the magic had

done. The dance floor had bright traces of a gold mineral running through it in some sort of pattern.

Mikhail slipped an arm around my waist, and I followed his lead around the dance floor. The beat of the music picked up, and we moved faster in our elaborate dance. Every time Mikhail spun me, the earth magic increased and more of the pattern within the dirt became visible, until it seemed like most of the floor was glittering gold. After a particularly long spin that allowed me to see glimpses beyond the dance floor, I saw the entire room had been transformed. A light silvery blue mineral ran up the columns and resembled flames stretching towards the inky blackness of night sky above us.

Mikhail pulled me close, one hand gliding up my back, leaving behind a trail of heat. His twilight eyes were fixated on me, and I couldn't look away as we moved around the dance floor. I forgot about the sidhe surrounding us and the magic pulsing beneath our feet and racing up the columns. There was only him and the feeling of his hands on me as we moved with the beat of the music. The band played faster, building to the end. Mikhail spun me one last time and pulled my back against his chest, one of his arms wrapping around my waist while the other rested on my hip.

Both of us were breathing hard, and the crowd was silent as they took in the magic that had poured from the floor and outward, transforming the plain ballroom into something so much more.

Our dance had ended on one side of the dance floor, where I could see the golden pattern that had come alive as we danced. It was stylized, but there was no mistaking the golden feline shape snarling on the floor. Silvery blue lines glowed across the columns, creating elaborate patterns of flames.

I looked straight across the dance floor and met the Unseelie Queen's gaze. This wasn't just a beautiful display; it was a message. No more hiding who and what I was. I nodded once, letting her know I had received her message loud and clear. She gave me a short nod in return, and the band picked up on some unspoken signal to start playing again. Mikhail and I moved off the dance floor. I'd had enough dancing for one evening.

Kalen and Badb took turns leading me around the room and introducing me to other members of the court. Mikhail remained by my side the entire time. My head was swimming from all the introductions.

Hours later, I was grateful the apartment was quiet when Mikhail and I returned, and surprised to see that the monstrous plant had been moved to the living room. I pulled the pins out of my hair and shook it loose as I looked around. Magos must have helped the vamp brats move it because no obvious path of destruction was visible, and I doubted it had been cooperative about the whole thing.

I heard Mikhail move behind me, and I remembered what it had been like to dance with him. The way his skin had felt on mine. My mouth went dry, and I was acutely aware of how fast my heart was beating.

"Nemain?" His voice was soft, with so much more conveyed in that question.

I never backed down from a fight. For better or worse, I liked to face my enemies head on. But this wasn't a fight. And Mikhail wasn't my enemy anymore. So I did the only thing I could do.

I fled.

Tossing a quick good night over my shoulder, I didn't stop moving until I was in my bedroom with a solid door between me and Mikhail.

Chapter Six

I MANAGED to avoid being alone with Mikhail for the next couple of days while Eddie and I plotted our return to the dragon realm.

Unfortunately, during that time, Pele also continued to avoid me. I'd even gone to her home in the daemon realm but found it empty. For the third time today, I tapped on Pele's glyph on the mirror, the one connected to her mirror at The Inferno.

Maybe if I just continued to harass her constantly, she would answer me.

The large piece of glass at the center rippled, revealing Asmodeus seated at Pele's desk. They regarded me with unreadable turquoise eyes. "You've called this mirror fourteen times in the last two days. Did you really think that would accomplish anything other than annoying me?"

"To be fair, I was trying to annoy Pele into answering me, not you," I said. "You could have just answered and told me Pele wasn't there."

"But then I would have had to listen to you complain about Pele ignoring you. Possibly followed by you trying to bribe me to tell you her whereabouts. I had neither the time nor the patience for such a thing."

"Zareen at least offered me pie as an apology for not being able to tell me anything," I grumbled.

"Pele is on her way to you now," Asmodeus said, and turned their attention back to whatever they were working on, scribbling away on a long scroll. The dismissal was clear, but instead I peered at them through the mirror.

"Do you know what she's plotting with Sigrun?"

The writing paused. "Yes."

"Care to fill me in?"

"No."

Mikhail laughed softly beside me, and a small smile played across Magos's lips as he slid me a cup of coffee.

"Fine," I huffed. "We'll wait for Pele to get here. Good chatting with you, as always, Asmodeus."

I raised my hand to tap the glyph and end the call, but stopped when Asmodeus leaned forward slightly. Something flashed across their face, gone before I could settle on what it was. I got the sense they were fighting some type of internal battle, so I waited. Asmodeus had worked for Pele for over a century and was one of her closest confidants. I also knew Asmodeus was totally and completely in love with my fire-hearted friend.

"Watch her back, Nemain," they said slowly. "Pele is pulling on some strings to see where they go. And if she's right, this will have far-reaching consequences. Things are changing rapidly in the Assembly, and some would gain a lot from Pele *not* unraveling this plot. And *not* picking up her father's mantle."

What are you up to, Pele? I'd been annoyed at her for avoiding me because it was a clear sign that whatever she was plotting was going to directly involve me and that I wouldn't like it. But Asmodeus was almost certainly aware of all of Pele's scheming, past and present. And if they were this worried that they felt the need to warn me . . .

I met Asmodeus's eyes. "I will always have her back. If someone makes a move against her, they make a move against me." They nodded once slowly, acknowledging my words, and I ended the call.

My stomach growled, letting me know that despite everything going on, I still needed to eat. When Pele arrived a short time later, we were all sitting around the living room, snacking on meat and cheese. Elisa was perched on the armchair over Bryn, playing with the valkyrie's long auburn hair. She dropped the braid she was twirling around her finger as soon as Pele walked in, sitting up a bit straighter.

My eyes narrowed on Pele when she casually walked across the apartment and took a seat in the remaining empty chair as if I hadn't been hounding her for a week.

In a rare moment of familial resemblance, Mikhail and Magos both wore identical wary expressions. Eddie was seated in the chair directly across from Pele. My easygoing friend was nowhere to be seen. It was only the predator with us now, and he was tightly wound, as if he would spring at Pele at the first hint of danger.

It felt wrong for them to be pitted against each other. Eddie was a frequent patron of The Inferno and had known Pele for longer than he'd known me. But that was before we all knew he was a dragon, and I suspected Pele's avoidance this week bothered him even more than it had me.

"What would you like me to answer first?" Pele asked.

In the bright light of the living room, her pupils were thin vertical slits standing out in stark contrast to the bright turquoise of her eyes. My feline shifter eyes were similar, but daemon eyes had no sclera, which always made them a tad unsettling.

"What did you ask Sigrun to do?" Bryn cut in before I could ask Pele what the hell she was plotting.

"I have reason to believe the seraphim are working with Balor, much the way the warlocks are." Pele glanced at the little girl we'd taken from the seraphim realm, who was currently curled up on some pillows in the corner and fast asleep.

She'd wolfed down an entire block of cheese and several helpings of meat before setting her head on the pillows and passing out. We'd set up a spot for her to sleep in the living room because we wanted to keep an eye on her until we figured out what her deal was. She remained wary of us but seemed to understand we only wanted to help.

"I take it you found that girl in the seraphim realm and she speaks a language your translation mark doesn't recognize?"

"Yes," I said slowly, narrowing my eyes at Pele in suspicion. "She can speak a few words of seraphim, but it's still hard to understand. She doesn't have a translation mark of her own, so she can't understand us. You've come across others like her?"

"A few weeks ago, five children appeared outside The Inferno. It was a couple of hours after sunrise, so no one was around except me and Asmodeus. The kids were clearly human but spoke an unrecognizable language and were half-starved. They came with a note written in an old fae dialect."

That would have been nice information to have earlier, I thought but held back my snarky commentary, mostly because I was curious about the note. "What did it say?"

"The seraphim are assholes."

I blinked. That was a weirdly direct message to come from a fae. I would have expected something along the lines of "Perhaps you should cast your eyes on the exiled winged warriors" or "The lost seraphim grow restless, and their plotting grows as well."

"An odd message from a fae," Pele said, noticing my reaction. "It's possible whoever wrote it wasn't fae and simply wrote in that language to throw me off their identity, but I don't know why they would have chosen to write it in a dialect no one uses anymore."

"Where are the children now?" Magos asked.

"One of my safe houses in town. Asmodeus and a couple others of my people are taking turns watching over them."

"So you sent Sigrun to investigate," I said, leaning forward slightly as I thought through the implications of this news. "To find out if they're working with Balor and where they're getting these humans from. Because they're definitely not from this realm."

"She is uniquely suited for this." Pele shrugged. "Both she and her companions can freely move about the realm while invisible. And they're more than capable of taking care of themselves should the need to fight arise."

"Most valkyries would refuse to play spy," Badb noted from her perch in the kitchen.

She and Kalen had arrived an hour earlier and had made themselves at home, apparently having decided they had the right to simply walk in and out of my apartment whenever they pleased.

I was *super* thrilled about that.

"Sigrun isn't like most valkyries," I said.

Badb looked at me, and when I remained silent, she scrunched her nose but let the subject drop. Sigrun's secrets were hers to share or not. She had known my secrets for a long time and never shared them with anyone. I would never share hers. Plus, I would happily seize any opportunity to annoy Badb.

"All right, so we'll have to wait for Sigrun to return to learn where these kids came from. In the meantime, it would probably make sense to take the girl to where the other kids are staying. At least she'll have someone to talk to, and you can continue to watch over them while we're gone."

"I agree about the girl joining the others," Pele said. "However, I will not be available to watch over them."

Here we go.

"And why won't you be available?" I asked sweetly, causing both vampires to tense.

Pele crossed one long leg over the other and leaned back in the chair. "Because I'll be with all of you in the dragon realm."

Godsdamn it all.

Kalen laughed, clearly amused, and I shot him a look before returning my attention to Pele.

"Why?" I asked at the same time Eddie said, "No."

Pele ignored me and looked at Eddie. "I always knew what you were, dragon." Orange flames flowed down her arms, standing out against her deep red skin. "Fire magic isn't common among daemons. Did you know that?" She looked lovingly at her flames before focusing on Eddie again. "Only a few bloodlines possess the ability. Don't you wonder where we got it from? Does it not feel *familiar* to you?"

Eddie sat there, unmoving as his eyes studied the flames before slowly stretching a hand out. The flames dancing across Pele's skin obediently leapt to his palm. Recognition flashed across his face.

"You stole dragon fire," he rumbled in a deep voice, his eyes bright with anger. I tensed, ready to get between them as his fingers curled around the flames as if they were claws.

Pele bared her teeth. "*We* did. Through blood and sacrifice, we took what we needed." With a flick of her fingers, the flames left Eddie's hand and returned to hers. "Dragons are not the lords of fire any longer, nor shall they be for as long as me and mine live."

Eddie's nostrils flared, and I got the distinct impression he was considering shifting to his dragon form and devouring Pele whole.

"How about we remember we're all on the same side?" I

said lightly. "And if anyone burns down this apartment, it's going to be me. It's mine, and I have that right."

Pele slid a glance at me. "It's technically mine. This entire building is mine. I just let you lot live here."

"Semantics." I smiled tightly. "Can you put the flames away and quit antagonizing the dragon?"

After a few beats of silence, Pele relaxed further into her chair and let the flames fade away. I let out a breath but stayed balanced on the seat of the couch in case I needed to move quickly. From the corner of my eye, I could see Magos and Mikhail doing the same. Unfortunately, none of us were fireproof, so I wasn't exactly sure what we'd do if Pele and Eddie decided to throw down.

"How?" Eddie asked flatly, keeping his eyes on the table between him and Pele while his body practically vibrated with tension.

"It was no easy thing for my ancestors to escape their home realm. Once upon a time, the fae were regular visitors to the realm, the sidhe in particular. It was long before we were skilled in magic. The original daemons mostly had telekinetic powers and sometimes an affinity for earth magic." Her eyes flicked to mine. "And of course, the rare telepath."

I couldn't stop my involuntary shiver. It drew the attention of Mikhail, who quirked a questioning eyebrow at me.

"I had an unfortunate encounter with a daemon who was a strong telepath. It was . . . unpleasant." I grimaced. "But it's not relevant."

"We possessed a lot of raw magic," Pele continued. "But we didn't know what to do with it and had no one to teach us.

"The sidhe ignored us in favor of the dragons. It was *their* realm, after all. We were nothing but their amusement and prey. Eventually the sidhe and dragons had a falling out, not surprising considering the arrogance of both species. But the sidhe left a lot of their toys behind. Most were hoarded by the dragons, but not all."

"I've seen some of them," Eddie interrupted. "Most are nothing more than trinkets."

"True. The fae didn't leave anything behind that was truly powerful," Pele acknowledged. "But those minor relics and artifacts were priceless to us because they gave us a path to freedom.

"No one would teach us, so we taught ourselves. We unraveled their spells to understand how they worked. We fixed what was broken, and then we tweaked them to better serve us. Anything to survive."

Something akin to respect flashed across Eddie's face. The daemons might be close to the top of the food chain now, but they had come from nothing. It was one of the many reasons I liked them more than the fae. That and they made practical weapons with all sorts of fun surprises.

"The magic we were able to teach ourselves was useful, and it gave us a fighting chance against the dragons hunting us," she paused before giving Eddie a close-lipped smile. "And then we found something that changed everything. An old fae gateway that had been carved into the rocky side of a mountain. It called to our earth magic and led us to hatching a plan that would change the trajectory of our lives. No more mourning the loss of our children. No more surviving instead of living. The decision was made to leave the realm."

"I always wondered how the daemons made it out," Eddie said. "Before I was exiled, things got bad." He swallowed and flexed his fingers into a fist a few times. "Cerri was convinced her father was going to kill me and was trying to find a way to hide me, or get me out and just hope that the fae would take pity on me." He laughed humorously. "We never found any gateways, but I did find myself outside of the realm."

"You're lucky you weren't killed right away," I said.

The daemons ruthlessly hunted down any dragons that made it out of the dragon realm. Eddie might be yet another complication in my life, but I was glad he had survived and found his way to me.

"Yeah," Eddie said slowly, his eyes lifting from the table until they rested on Pele. "Lucky."

My eyes flicked back and forth between Eddie and Pele. She said earlier that she always knew Eddie was a dragon. I'd assumed that she recognized him as such when he walked through the doors of The Inferno. But I was starting to wonder if Pele had known about Eddie long before then.

"Evacuating an entire people is difficult," Magos said. "We only managed to get out a fraction of our people when our realm was invaded by devourers."

Magos's expression remained calm, but Mikhail's eyes darkened. He'd been a child when he'd fled with his mother, Magos's sister, to the human realm. I wondered who he would have been if he had never come to the human realm. Never become a vampire who served as an assassin for centuries. How would I feel if he had never walked into my life?

It felt like the beating of my heart slowed at the thought of Mikhail not being here. Those intense twilight eyes of his latched on to me, and suddenly my heart that had been struggling to beat raced forward.

Desperate to think about anything else, I turned my attention to Pele. "How did the daemons coordinate getting everyone out?"

Pele looked at me for a long moment, and I knew she was seeing more than I wanted her to. Her eyes briefly flicked to Mikhail before answering my question.

"Lots of slow, methodical planning. It took over a decade to coordinate because there was no way to avoid having a large number of daemons in an open area for at least a few days while we got everyone through the gateway. We needed a way to defend ourselves against the dragons. It was my grandmother who came up with the idea to steal fire from them."

Pele snapped her fingers, and flame erupted briefly from her hand.

"The process was painful and took years to learn, but my grandmother and a few dozen other daemons volunteered. While some planned the escape, my grandmother and the others practiced. By the time everyone was ready to put the plan in motion, the fire daemons were ready to hold the line."

"Hold the line," Elisa repeated. "They didn't think they would survive, did they?"

"Most didn't," Pele said, her words heavy. "My grandmother died that day. So did most of the original fire daemons. It was almost ten years between the time they first got their fire magic and the day the daemons left that realm. Many of them had children, and those children were blessed with fire magic. My mother was one of them."

Eddie remained silent. The tension that had been hardening his features faded, now replaced by sorrow. The dragons had suffered tremendously at the hands of the daemons, but the daemons had suffered just as much under the dragon's reign.

"None of that explains why you want to go back now," I pointed out.

"Maybe I feel that the dragons have paid their dues and I don't want them to suffer anymore." When everyone in the room just continued to stare flatly at her, she rolled her eyes. "There's a strong possibility that the dragons are allied with Balor. Some of them, anyway."

"That's exactly what the Unseelie Queen told me the other night." I narrowed my eyes. "She also suspected the seraphim were allied with Balor. Which one of you is playing the other?"

"We're both playing each other. I know she planted that rumor." A dreamy expression came over her face. "It's kind of hot, to be honest. I mean, I still strongly dislike the fae. But I think I could hate-fuck Elvinia."

That finally managed to snap Eddie out of his discomfort towards Pele, and he barked out a laugh. I snuck a peek at Magos, and he looked absolutely scandalized, which made me chuckle.

"Maybe after you're done fucking her, you could ask her to rethink this whole business about declaring me her knight?" I suggested.

"What the fuck did you just say?" Pele snapped, the dreamy expression immediately gone from her face.

"What, with all our snooping, you didn't know about that?"

"She really made you the Unseelie Knight?" she asked, her tone very serious.

"Yeah," I said softly. "It's one of the many things I would have told you about if you'd just talked to me this week."

"I'm sorry." She gave me an apologetic look. "I really was busy this week arranging a lot of things. I wasn't *just* avoiding you."

I sighed, still annoyed at Pele for hiding from me all week, but it's not like it would have changed anything if she had talked to me sooner. "I'm already going to be looking for evidence of the dragons being allied with Balor while I'm there. You don't need to come."

"That's not the only reason I want to go." She inhaled a deep breath and let it out. "I did mean what I said before about not wanting them to suffer anymore. They've been trapped in that realm with devourers for over a thousand years. Enough is enough. I want to offer the dragons a peace treaty."

Eddie and I both stared at Pele. She was out of her mind.

"And I want to kill any dragons that have allied themselves with Balor." She shot me a sly smile. "Obviously."

"The dragons would never go for a peace treaty," Eddie argued. "And the daemons would never support one."

"I'm sorry, do you think you know what the daemons will do better than me?" She arched a perfectly sculpted eyebrow. "That's odd seeing how I haven't seen *you* in any Assembly meetings lately. And I don't recall *you* being at the last several where *I* worked on the wording and managed to get every single one of the Assembly elders to agree and sign in blood."

Damn. She really had been busy. I was still annoyed at her for not letting me know what she was up to. But I had to begrudgingly respect what she'd managed to accomplish. Luckily, I was perfectly capable of being proud of my friend while also wanting to smack the shit out of her.

Eddie shook his head. "The dragons won't go for it."

"I beg to differ." Pele sniffed.

"You don't know them like I do," he growled.

"You're not the first dragon I've met."

"What?" Eddie blinked.

"I've met others that have been exiled, found them before any other daemons did." She casually shrugged a shoulder. "There are many among the dragons who *want* to parley with the daemons. But the older dragons still clinging to power have refused to do so. I believe it was one of those dragons who was responsible for your exile. So, I will go to them and meet with those dragons who are interested in negotiating."

"Why haven't you already?" I narrowed my eyes at her. "When I told you the truth about Eddie being a dragon, I asked if you could take us to the dragon realm. You said you couldn't, and I didn't push you on it because I was mostly just happy you weren't going to murder my friend. But that's not why, is it?"

"It's no easy thing to contain an entire realm," Pele said casually as she studied her nails. "I'm dying to know how the fae queens accomplished it, but it's not like they'll ever tell me."

"How did the daemons do it?" I pushed.

"The strongest of magic often requires sacrifice." Her face

tightened briefly with pain before she smoothed it away. "We'd already made many sacrifices in our effort to get free. What was one more?"

I sucked in a breath, already knowing what she was going to say.

"We exiled ourselves. Completely cut off any claims we have to that realm. You couldn't have used me to find the dragon realm any more than you could have used Eddie."

Magos looked at the pair of fangs sitting in their box on the coffee table. "How is it that these aren't tainted by the same spell? Why are they still attached to the dragon realm?"

"I don't know," Pele said, shaking her head. "Every dragon I've met has been exiled, just like Eddie. The rumor I sent my cousin to investigate wasn't the first one I'd heard; honestly, I thought it would be a dead end just like all the others. Perhaps we'll learn the answer when we get to the dragon realm. There are many answers I seek and many things I want to accomplish."

I really didn't like the sound of that, but before I could push her about what she meant, Eddie cut in. "Where are they now? The other dragons?"

"Stashed away in some of my more remote safe houses," Pele answered vaguely.

"Why didn't you bring me to one of those?" Eddie asked.

"It took me a while to track you down. I've learned how to detect breaches in the spell placed around the dragon realm, but your dragon nature was bound. You were in Ireland when I tracked you down, and oddly enough you were already planning on coming to Emerald Bay at that point. I was curious about why you would be coming here of all places, so I cleared the path for you and sat back to see what came about."

"Did you know he was looking for me?" I asked curiously. Because I was the reason Eddie had come here.

"No." She shook her head and gave Eddie an impressed look. "You hid your true reason for being here quite well."

"Yeah, well, seeing how I was a dragon in a realm where my kind are hunted down and killed, and I was looking for someone who had magic that shouldn't be possible"—he smirked at me—"and definitely would have gotten them killed. It seemed kind of important to keep motives quiet."

"Touché."

"Pele," I said slowly, "earlier you said that there were several answers you were seeking. What *exactly* are you plotting?"

"Come now, you know me," she drawled. "Why plan for one thing when you can plan for three?"

I held up one finger. "Determine if the dragons have allied themselves with Balor."

She nodded. "And what each side is getting out of it, and what Balor has requested of them. Just knowing they're allied isn't enough."

On that we were in agreement. Even if I hadn't been given that *order* by the Unseelie Queen, I knew it was something that I needed to figure out. Finn was my responsibility, and Balor wanted his son back, which meant I needed to thwart his plans as much as possible. Protecting Finn would become a lot harder if I had seraphim, dragons, and gods knew what else coming for me.

There would probably be retaliation from the seraphim at some point, but they hadn't known I was there. They'd be coming for Sigrun, Kalen, and Badb because they'd done the most damage and were the easiest to identify.

Fuck knew what Sigrun was going to get up to while she was in the seraphim realm. I knew my friend could take care of herself, but it still worried me that the only backup she had was Gunnar and Viggo.

I held up a second finger, and Pele smirked at me. "Negotiate a peace treaty with the dragons and I'm assuming undo the magic that locked them into that realm or get them out of it."

"Probably the latter." She tilted her head to the side as she thought about it. "That realm is fucked thanks to all the devourers in it."

"What's the third thing?" Eddie asked sharply.

"It's really more of a backup plan to the peace treaty option," Pele clarified. "The older dragons hold the most power and are the least likely to want a peace treaty. They are also the ones most likely allied with Balor."

Eddie nodded. "Cerri's father, Thorod, is the one who commands the older generation and unofficially leads all dragons."

"Pit the dragons who aren't allied with Balor against the dragons who are and help them win," Mikhail said thoughtfully. "You'll accomplish everything you want. Thorod and the older dragons won't be there to block the peace treaty, and Balor will lose his allies."

"Pele, tell me you're not seriously planning on staging a coup," I groaned.

"Only if I have to." Pele smiled. "But you have to admit, it'd be kind of fun."

Chapter Seven

"Why did you come with me again?" I asked for the third time as I shoved open the heavy wood door to The Inferno.

"I've never seen anyone ask a loki for a favor before," Mikhail replied. "Seems like it will be entertaining."

"The loki *owes* me a favor," I corrected. "But before we get to that, I want to make sure someone arrived safely."

Mikhail followed me as we wound our way through the crowded bar. Large groups of young daemons were gathered at the back playing pool. More than a few openly stared at Mikhail with a mixture of interest and wariness. The latter was likely because vampires were generally not welcome in daemon establishments and definitely not in Pele's place until recently. That exception had only extended to the vampires living with me, and while Pele had announced it, she hadn't explained why.

The interest was because the daemons were a bunch of horny bastards and Mikhail was dressed in black, form-fitting attire. His long dark hair was braided back away from his face in multiple complex braids. The only reason the daemons weren't propositioning him here and now was because of the silent snarl I'd shot them when one took a step in our direction.

Thanks to Pele dropping that bomb on us earlier, I was very much in the mood for violence.

Our plan had been to go to the dragon realm, find Cerri, and get out. I was going to do a little bit of snooping while we looked for her to see if I could find any evidence that the dragons were indeed working with Balor. But Pele wanted to *talk* to the dragons, which changed our plans drastically.

I promised Eddie that as soon as we found Cerri, I would get them both out of there and the rest of us would remain if that's what they wanted. He'd grumbled something under his breath and walked away from me, so I wasn't exactly sure where he stood that plan.

We made our way up to the third floor, and I walked down a long hallway, stopping in front of the last door on the left. I'd barely finished knocking before the door flung open and a young, slender woman crushed me in a hug.

I stood there frozen, unsure of what to do. Mikhail snickered, and my assailant pulled back, a dark blush spreading across her tawny beige skin.

"Sorry! I know you're not really the hugging type, but I was so surprised to get your message! It's wonderful to see you again!"

I took a step back, putting some space between us, and bumped into Mikhail. Rather than moving forward, I elbowed him sharply. He grunted and stepped back.

"It's good to see you again, Aki." I smiled warmly as I looked her over. It had been a while, and Aki's awkward teenage frame had filled out a little more, but she mostly looked the same. She'd cut her curly brown hair short, which worked well with her delicate features. "How is your grandmother?"

"Oh, she's doing great!" Aki leaned forward and whispered

conspiratorially, "She's with Bahir at his beach house in Croatia. She said she was just going for a weekend trip, but it's been over a month. Methinks they might be more than friends."

I couldn't help but laugh. She hadn't changed at all. I'd met Aki, her grandmother Sekira, and some other Kalari a few years ago. The Kalari had fled to the human realm after their realm had been lost to devourers. They had settled in rather well, but their magic was tied to the waters of their realm, and they eventually lost their empathic abilities. I had taken Aki and a small group back to their home realm to find the springs that could reactivate their magic.

Aki was one of the first Kalari to get her magic back. Even before she had done so, Aki was kind and caring. With her empathic magic on top of that, I was hoping she could help Finn. And perhaps the kids from the seraphim realm.

"I'm glad they've found happiness with each other," I said truthfully. "Did Pele fill you in? A few things have changed since I sent you that message."

Aki's honey-brown eyes darkened. "Yes, I met the kids from the seraphim realm earlier today, including the little girl you rescued. We're working on getting them translation marks. We already have what we need, but I want to work with them a little before we go stabbing them behind the ear."

"It's not stabbing so much as burning."

"Right, that's so much better." Aki rolled her eyes. "I'm excited to meet Finn. Just let me grab my stuff and then I'll be ready to go."

"Take your time and meet us downstairs," I said. "There's one more thing I have to take care of before we head back."

"She seems nice," Mikhail said as we headed down the stairs.

"And?"

"Nothing. Just pointing out that she seems nice."

I whirled on the step and looked up at Mikhail. We were

almost the same height, so the stairs gave him a couple of inches on me. "You had a tone."

"Did I?" His eyes widened.

I started sliding one of the daggers free from the sheath on my forearm, and he grinned.

"Most of your friends are just as violent as you. I've even watched our dear delicate Kaysea slice open someone's throat. I'm pretty sure Aki would feel bad if a bee stung her because it meant it would die."

My lips twitched, and I spun around before Mikhail could see. "That is an accurate assessment of Aki."

"Not going to argue against the other part?"

"Doesn't seem worth it."

When we reached the bottom floor, I scanned the bar again. Pele had seen my quarry earlier, but that didn't mean they were still here. Weaving through the crowd, I paused when I got to the middle of the floor. It was a packed house tonight, and most of the tables were occupied. My gaze settled on a group of three young elves. Two had their back to me, but the young elf sitting across from them stood out in this crowd. With her silvery white hair and delicate features, she was a beacon of light in this dark and raucous setting. I made a beeline for her and didn't pause when I made it to their table. She blinked up at me with pale blue eyes, uncertainty wavering in her expression.

I jerked her up by the front of her tunic and slammed her against the table, back first with one hand wrapped around her throat. Mikhail blocked her friends from interfering, but all they did was grab their mugs to keep their beer from crashing to the ground.

"Rude, Nemain," the elf gasped.

I slammed a dagger into the table, drawing a faint line of blood down the elf's cheek. In a blink, the delicate feminine features were gone, replaced with a strong masculine face and body to match. I took a step back and tucked my dagger back up my sleeve.

"Let's have a chat, Sten." I pulled a chair away from the table and flipped it around so I could straddle it as I sat down. "You owe me for that last job I did for you."

The loki took a seat, a completely innocent look on their face. "I don't know what you're talking about. Perhaps you have me mistaken with a different loki?" They gestured toward the other two loki still seated at the table, who had shifted to match Sten's face and walnut-brown skin. It wasn't Sten's true face. I didn't even know if Sten had a true face, but it was the face they usually wore when interacting with me.

"Leave," I told them.

When they made no move, Mikhail jerked them up by the backs of their tunics and tossed them away from the table. They grumbled their complaints, but Sten just laughed and waved them off.

I growled, "You knew damn well the necklace and artifacts you sent me after belonged to the fae."

"I technically never said they didn't." Sten held up one finger. "I said the ship sank a long time ago and it was unclear who had originally owned them. Which was true. I didn't know which fae family specifically had owned that ship."

"But you knew it was fae!"

"They had over a decade to retrieve what they lost." Sten shrugged. "What's that human expression? Ah, yes! Finders, keepers!"

"That's not the part I'm upset about."

"It's not?" They frowned in confusion. "Then why are you being so pissy?"

"Because someone told them it was me who retrieved those items." The back of the chair creaked as I leaned harder into it. "And it sure as hell wasn't Pele."

The confused expression slid off their face as Sten shot me

a toothy grin. "I couldn't help it! That sidhe had such a stick up her ass. I knew if I sent her your way, you'd cut her down to size. And it was a glorious brawl, if I remember correctly. You took her and her goons out in a few hits."

Of course, they'd been there to witness their mischief. Damned lokis.

"Lucky for you, the debt I'm calling in will allow you to cause more trouble." This was the only way I'd get them to go along with this.

The lokis liked me. I was one of the few beings who was willing to do the occasional odd gig for them. Most of those in the magical community avoided having anything to do with lokis because they loved to cause trouble. They either outright lied or misdirected in almost every conversation, and they absolutely loved to create drama, particularly drama amongst other groups that didn't involve them so they could sit back and watch it unfold.

Pele absolutely hated dealing with them and occasionally would ban them from The Inferno. But I found some perverse joy in taking jobs for them. It was fun trying to figure out what they were up to. It was even more fun to turn the tables on the lokis once I figured it out, which absolutely delighted them. Sten would do me this favor because they liked me, and it would be a good source of entertainment.

"I'm going out of town for a while, but I don't want anybody to know I'm gone. There's still some bad blood between me and the warlocks. I'm pretty sure they have the vampires and some other folks watching me." Not a lie, just not the whole truth.

If it turned out the dragons were directly working with Lir and in communication with him, this ruse wouldn't work, but on the chance they weren't or communication was delayed, it was worth the hassle. Plus, Sten owed me.

"I need you to wear my face around town, make sure

you're seen here and at my apartment. Assuming you think you can convince people you're me for a few weeks."

"Oooh! A challenge!" A subtle change came over them. They didn't shift into a different form, but while they'd previously been lounging in the chair, they sat a little straighter now. Something about their posture promised violence, and their smile held an edge that hadn't been there before. Sten slowly blinked, and emerald-green eyes identical to mine looked at me. "I accept."

I grinned; I had no doubts that Sten would be down for this. "We're leaving tonight. I'll have Pele temporarily update the ward around my place so you can enter. Some friends are staying at my place while I'm gone. I'll let them know to expect your comings and goings. Don't touch my stuff." I pointed a warning finger at them.

"I wouldn't dream of it," Sten replied, not only matching my voice but my cadence. Another loki might struggle to truly impersonate me, but Sten had known me long enough to pull it off. If Lir had spies in town to keep an eye on me, Sten would fool them.

I saw Aki making her way to us, pulling a small suitcase behind her. Pushing off the back of the chair, I rose. "See you around, Sten."

"That was a little disturbing," Mikhail muttered. "Think it'll work?"

"It won't hurt, and I'll take any advantage I can get." I lunged forward as Aki tripped over a pool cue that'd been left on the floor. Setting her upright, I gave her a rueful smile. "I see you're just as observant of your surroundings as you were when we first met."

"I broke my arm last year when I failed to see a step while carrying in groceries," she admitted.

"I'm not the least bit surprised." I looked at Mikhail and jerked my head towards the bar. "Go grab a bottle of whiskey for my brother, something nice so Dante doesn't complain."

He arched an eyebrow at me. "You want me, a vampire that Pele barely tolerates in her bar, to steal whiskey from her? Getting kind of creative in ways to kill me, aren't you?"

"Don't be a scaredy cat. You can clear it with Asmodeus; they're probably still holed up in Pele's office."

Mikhail gave me a flat stare before letting out a long-suffering sigh and making his way to the bar.

"Have I mentioned how happy I am that you reached out?" Aki said. "Based on what I know so far, you definitely need my help."

"Gee, thanks," I said dryly. "I don't think we've been doing *that* bad."

The patient expression I'd so often seen on her grandmother's face settled over Aki's features. "You have one kid who has basically suffered some level of emotional abuse from his parents his entire life *and* is aware there is a prophecy around him stating he will doom us all, and you're giving him cookies to deal."

"They're good cookies!"

"Then you have a young vampire girl," Aki continued, "who has some type of strong psychic magic that none of you understand and that she used to scare the crap out of a centuries-old being . . . and you're just ignoring that whole thing?"

"Right."

"And then we have whatever is going on between you and Mikhail—"

"There's nothing going on," I cut her off. "He's an asshole vampire, and I hate him."

"Mmhmm." She looked over my shoulder towards the bar. "So you don't care at all about that hot daemon with the really nice boobs flirting with him right now?"

"No, of course I—Wait? What?" I whipped around and saw Mikhail walking back to us, whiskey bottle in hand.

"What's going on?" He glanced back and forth between me and a giggling Aki.

"Nothing," I ground out, shooting Aki a dirty look that only made her laugh harder. "Just remembering why I hate being around empaths."

As soon as we got back to the apartment, I introduced Aki to everyone and left her in the first-floor apartment chatting with Magos and the vamp brats while I headed upstairs.

Kaysea had promised to check in regularly, and I knew that between her, Elisa, and Bryn, the kids would be well looked after while the rest of us were gone. But I wanted some additional protection here just in case, especially since Pele wouldn't be around to provide backup. So I'd called in a favor to my brother and his mate, Dante.

Dante might not have Pele's reputation, but he was easily one of the most powerful necromancers in existence. Given he was actually Hades, that wasn't all that surprising. But almost everyone believed Hades was long since dead, and Dante wanted to keep it that way, so he never flaunted his magic and thus flew under the radar. He would be less than pleased about me asking them to come here, which was why I hadn't asked him. I asked my brother, who happily agreed. And wherever Cian went, Dante would follow.

"Hey, sis," Cian said as he hopped through the gateway and enveloped me in a hug. Dante came through a moment later and did *not* give me a hug. As expected.

We were getting along better these days, which made my brother happy, but we still didn't like each other. But tolerating each other begrudgingly was better than outright hating each other. Cian had appreciated the effort on my part and had extended the same courtesy to the vampires I'd befriended despite his, in my opinion, irrational hatred of vampires. He did genuinely like Elisa and the other vamp kids, because my brother was a big softy.

"Everyone is downstairs," I said. "Eddie and Pele are on their way over. We'll leave shortly after they get here."

"Pele is going with you?" Dante asked, sharing an indecipherable look with Cian.

"Yep," I said tiredly. "She sort of invited herself. It's a long story. Elisa can give you all the details. Mikhail and Magos are coming as well. Everyone else is staying here."

"Jinx?" Cian asked.

"He's staying," I said firmly.

My brother frowned at my tone but didn't push. Jinx and I had been inseparable almost my entire life. But if something happened to me on this trip, and I didn't come back . . . I wanted Jinx to be there for Finn. He hadn't liked it when I asked him to do this, but he eventually agreed.

Plus, he was basically bite-size for a dragon.

"My friend, Aki, is also staying in the second-floor apartment. She's an empath, and I'm hoping she can help Finn. He's been through a lot for a kid, and none of us really know what to do to help him. Other than feed him cookies. We go through a lot of cookies."

Cian laughed. "Given that he's living in a building full of killers, cookies and an empath are probably a good idea."

I punched him in the shoulder. "There's also a loki who will be dropping by occasionally wearing my face. Sten. Try not to stab them or anything."

"You're the one who stabs people." Cian grinned, while Dante's mouth formed a hard line at the mention of a loki. "I'm the nice one."

"Whatever. Let's head downstairs."

For the second time in recent memory, I slipped out of the way of a flying projectile after entering a room. Cian might not be much of a fighter, but he was still a feline shapeshifter with excellent reflexes, so he dodged as well. But apparently, old Greek gods don't have the best reflexes, because the plastic dinosaur toy smacked Dante right in the face.

Everyone in the room froze, and I stifled a laugh as Dante turned his dark eyes on me.

"Just consider this practice for when you and Cian have kids," I said brightly. Cian smiled widely, and Dante looked slightly panicked. Heh.

"Sorry about that." Elisa rushed over. "Isabeau has been a little obsessed with dragons lately and has decided throwing dinosaurs through the air basically makes them dragons."

"No worries." Cian hugged her in greeting.

Isabeau came bouncing over, her brown curls flying with every step. She swooped the dinosaur off the ground and looked up at Dante. It would have made a striking photograph. The former god of the underworld with all his dark, harsh beauty staring down at the defiant angelic little girl.

Of course, this little girl was a vampire. And we were all starting to suspect she was also the devil.

"You should have caught it." She brushed imaginary dirt off the dinosaur's bright red scales. "It was literally flying straight towards you. Even a human could have caught that." She squinted at him. "You're not a human, are you?"

Dante's glare was straight from the icy depths of hell. "No."

Isabeau tilted her head quizzically. "Then what are you?"

"Annoyed." Cian coughed, and Dante glanced at him and sighed. "I'm a necromancer. Like Cian."

The young vampire perked up. "Could you bring the dinosaurs back to life?"

"No," Dante said flatly.

"You're kind of useless then, aren't you?" Isabeau scrunched up her cute little nose before she flounced back into the living room. Elisa winced while Cian and I lost it and doubled over in laughter.

Aki got up from where she'd been sitting in the living room and joined us. "I'm guessing you're Nemain's brother?" She held out her hand to Cian.

"I am." He shook her hand and gave her a warm smile. Technically, he was my cousin, but we'd been raised as brother and sister and that's still how we viewed ourselves. "This is my mate, Dante. Don't worry, he's not as grumpy as he looks."

Dante shook Aki's hand while also bumping my brother's shoulder. Cian just smirked at him.

Aki not so subtly gave my brother a once over. I wasn't surprised. Everyone did the first time they saw him. Cian was striking. His ebony black skin had faint silver rosettes that shone as they caught the light. His matching silver hair was pulled away from his face and ran down his back in a long braid. He was a couple of inches shorter than me with a slighter build. Cian also had a softness I didn't have, something that made you gravitate towards him whereas most people ran from me.

"I know," I sighed. "He's obnoxiously gorgeous."

Aki tried to hold back her laugh but ended up making a snorting sound instead. Her hand flew up to her face. "That's not what I was thinking." She glanced at Cian again. "Not wrong, though."

Cian beamed at me, and I crossed my arms and looked away from him.

"That's not why I was staring," Aki went on. "I was wondering if your feline form is the same. I remember when Nemain shifted, her fur was the same color and pattern as her skin."

"Our feline forms come first and determine what our

human forms look like," Cian explained. "We learned to shift into this form"—he gestured at himself—"from the fae. The black panthers originated from the dense, heavily shadowed rainforests that ran across the center of our original realm. They had a slimmer build because they hunted smaller prey, but their bite was bone-crushing. The golden panthers roamed the open grasslands that made up the bulk of our realm. They were built heavier to take down more aggressive, larger prey. Nemain's bite isn't as strong as mine, but her teeth curve back slightly so she can hold onto prey better than I can. But I'm obviously prettier."

I swatted at him, and he easily dodged my halfhearted attempt. "Supposedly there were silver panthers as well that lived in the far northern reaches of the realm where it was cold and snowy year round," I said. "They traveled beyond that area often, but they rarely settled down outside snowy areas. Their coats were thicker, and they were uncomfortable in warmer climates. They were assumed to have been lost when our realm fell to devourers because there had been no gateways close to them that they could flee through. Few of our kind made it out."

Sadness briefly flickered across Aki's face. Most of the Kalari had died when their realm had also fallen to the devourers. The fae had abandoned them, and it was only because of a few gateways held open by daemons that some of their population had escaped.

"Did you meet everyone?" I asked, changing the subject.

"Yes." Aki smiled. "They're all lovely."

"Except Isabeau," Misha said from the kitchen. "She's a damn terror."

"She's just not shy about stating her opinions," Aki hedged. "Besides, I saw you hand her that dinosaur model and whisper something in her ear seconds before Nemain and the others walked in."

Misha's indigo blue eyes lit up, and he grinned. "I might have heard them coming down the stairs and made a suggestion or two."

He's an instigator. Damon's voice popped into my head. Cian, Dante, and Aki glanced around, unsure of where the voice was coming from. *Oh. Sorry. It's uhh . . . me.* A hand shot up from the couch and waved.

"I know you already met everyone, Aki, but I'm guessing they didn't tell you about their magic yet." Aki shook her head. "Elisa can shift into a wolf and is stronger than most vamps. Damon is not only telepathic, but he can branch the minds of non-telepaths together so everyone can hear each other. And Misha—"

The dark-haired vampire appeared abruptly in front of us and froze as Dante tightened his grip around the boy's throat.

"I've warned you about doing that around folks who aren't prepared, Misha," I said dryly.

Misha flinched as Dante squeezed one more time and then released him.

"Right," he grunted and then disappeared, reappearing by the couch where he dropped on top of Damon. The other vampire cursed and tried to shove Misha off him, resulting in both of them thudding to the floor.

Aki smiled at them, and then her gaze went to Isabeau, who was lecturing Finn about something dinosaur related. The quiet fae boy was sitting there, dutifully listening to everything she said.

"I'll do everything I can to help them," she said quietly.

"I know you will."

We watched as Mikhail and Magos said their goodbyes. Magos ruffled Finn's hair gently, and Mikhail not so subtly snuck him another cookie. I heroically did not acknowledge Aki's pointed look in my direction. It was good she was here because there were only so many cookies we could offer this kid.

Please be careful, Luna said. *We'll look after everyone while you're gone. Don't worry about us. Concentrate on what you have to do and come back to us.*

If you have to, throw the vampires in front of any incoming dragons and get out of there, Jinx grumbled.

Magos gave no reaction to having heard Jinx, but Mikhail narrowed his eyes at the black grimalkin. "If you need a break from a certain grumpy cat, you could always feed him to the plant upstairs, Luna."

Luna's musical laughter sounded through my mind, and the silver-colored grimalkin rubbed against Jinx, who just glowered at Mikhail.

"I'm going to say goodbye to Finn. I'll meet you both upstairs." When I knelt on the floor next to Finn, Isabeau paused her dinosaur lecture and glanced between me and him.

A rare, solemn expression filled her face. I didn't think Isabeau's outgoing and loud personality was fake, but I did suspect she often used it to hide her sharp mind and perceptiveness. As if reading my thoughts, which the brat probably was, Isabeau shot me a wicked grin and then leapt up and tackled Misha and Damon.

The teenage vampires immediately collapsed in defeat, and Isabeau giggled. As much as Misha and Damon complained about her, they took their roles as big brothers seriously. None of the vampire kids were related by blood that we knew of, but they were siblings in all the ways that mattered.

Finn watched the three of them interacting as if trying to figure out how it worked. How being playful worked. Sadness hit me like a punch to the chest, but I quickly hid it when he returned his gaze to me. We were all used to his oddly colored eyes now. The autumn gold shone brightly within the ring of spring green.

"You're leaving now," Finn stated.

"Yes—" I started to answer when Isabeau let out an ear-piercing shriek. I flinched and rubbed my ears. My sensitive feline hearing was not meant for this kind of noise. A second later, the sound in the living room all but vanished, and I felt magic settle between us and everyone else. I started at the suddenness of it, and the magic instantly vanished.

"Sorry," Finn whispered.

I gave him an encouraging smile. "There's nothing to be sorry for. I appreciated the quietness. My head could use a break from the chaos of the vamp brats."

Finn gave me a tentative smile, and the magic settled back, dampening the noise once more. As a fae child, Finn should have barely any magic yet and almost no control over what he had. Fae children came into their power with age, and they usually couldn't wield it the way he could until they were well into their fifties or sixties. Finn often tried to use his magic to make us happy, as if he felt that if he didn't, we would turn him away or lose interest in him.

It made me want to find his parents and rip them to shreds for making him feel like he had to earn our love. Given his father was quite possibly the most powerful fae in existence, it would be a hard thing to accomplish, but I was willing to try.

"We'll be back soon. Cian and Dante are going to stay in my apartment on the third floor. Don't let Dante's gruffness throw you off. I think the two of you will get along well. Probably more so than him and Isabeau." Finn's eyes sparked with a twinkle of amusement. "Aki is going to stay with you and Bryn on the second floor."

The light in his eyes dimmed as he looked away from me to his hands draped across his lap. "What if you don't come back?"

"I will," I assured him.

He bit his lip before slowly raising his eyes to meet mine

again. "I know about the prophecy. If you don't come back, I'll hurt people."

"How?" I asked and let out a bone-weary sigh. "Isabeau."

Finn nodded. *Godsdamn it.* Isabeau had been rummaging in our minds again.

"First, I want you to know we were going to tell you about the prophecy. I know what it's like when people hold back information about your heritage, and I didn't want to do that to you. But we wanted you to have some time to get adjusted to living here before telling you about that. Okay?"

I waited to continue until Finn gave me a small nod.

"Second, prophecies change. They are fickle, and more than one being has gone mad trying to decipher all of their meanings. I know the prophecy said you're doomed to this dark fate unless I can save you from it. But I'd rather you save yourself. I'll do everything I can to help you with that, and so will everyone in this room." I gestured to the vampire brats and those gathered in the kitchen. "If I don't come back, and I *will* come back, you are not alone. You will never be alone. We've got your back, kid."

Finn stared at me, blinking a few times before getting up and hugging me. Before I could react, he let the magic around us drop and moved to one of the big armchairs where he could observe the wrestling match still going on. Luna joined him, curling up in his lap, and Jinx jumped up onto the back of the chair. His tail was flicking in annoyance at the noise the vamp kids were making.

I smiled and headed to the door, waving goodbye to Aki and Cian. Dante grabbed my arm before I left and pressed a small dagger into my palm. His cold magic radiated off it, and I wanted to drop it. Instead, I arched an eyebrow at him.

"It's imbued with my magic. I used Cian's blood to spell the sheath. Only you or someone of your blood can remove it, and as long as it's in the sheath, no one will notice its magic." He handed me the sheath, and when I slid the dagger in, the cold magic vanished. "It's a one-shot deal. Use it wisely."

My eyes widened in shock as I stared at him and then at the dagger. Dante had just given me a dagger loaded with his death magic that could kill a dragon in one strike. They were immune to most magic, but death magic had its own rules. There was no cheating death.

"Thank you," I said, still not believing he had given me such a weapon.

Dante shrugged. "I'm finally starting to tolerate you. Try not to get eaten by a dragon."

Chapter Eight

THE FIVE OF us surveyed the vast landscape stretched before us. It was always a little dicey when I used a person, or part of a person in this case, to open a gateway. Sometimes the person could concentrate on a particular location within their realm, and I could open a gateway fairly close to that. But for this gateway, it'd been a bit of a crapshoot since all we had were the fangs of a deceased dragon.

Luckily the gateway hadn't opened us in the middle of a dragon city where we probably would have been killed before getting a chance to explain ourselves. Instead, the gateway had opened us here . . . in what appeared to be the absolute middle of nowhere.

The land was flat and mostly barren, with small scrubby bushes and cacti scattering the landscape here and there. Every once in a while, a plateau would erupt out of the earth, its sides eroded, full of spiraling colors and patterns. Small cracks and fissures weaved through the hard ground. I could see how this realm would greatly benefit any flying creature, because there was nowhere to hide on the ground. I wasn't loving how exposed we were, but it's not like there was anything that could be done about it.

Also, we'd been there for five minutes, and I was dripping in sweat from the unrelenting sun. Pele and Eddie looked no worse for wear. The fire in their blood probably loved this heat. I only liked the sun and heat if I could nap. Mikhail and Magos were stoically dealing with the heat, but they were clearly not thrilled about this, either.

It didn't help that my skin was also tingly from the blood oath between Eddie and me being fulfilled. At least on my end. He had sworn to keep the knowledge of my magic a secret, and I had promised to bring him to a realm of his choosing.

"Thank you," Eddie said, coming to stand by my side. He likely felt the magic of the blood oath rising between us. "You've helped me far beyond what I ever imagined."

I shrugged, feeling awkward about the sincerity in his voice. "You've helped me out more than once. All that blood oath required on your part was to keep my secret, but you've done more than that. You're my friend, Eddie, and I'm happy to help you in any way I can."

"Best friend?" He gave me a sly look.

"Sure. Let's go with that." I wiped the sweat from my brow with the back of my hand. "Do you know where we are? And which way we should head? It all kind of looks the same to me."

Rather than reclaim the entire realm, the dragons had created three safe havens from the devourers: Anspolis, Isonver, and Ralis. The rest of the realm had been abandoned. Our destination was Anspolis.

"I think we lucked out." He pointed at a large plateau with some type of green mineral glittering in the sun where the walls had been drastically eroded. "That green mineral is only found in the southern region below Anspolis. We're probably only a two- or three-day flight away."

"All right," I said with resignation. "Let's get this over with."

Eddie grinned and erupted into flames. We all leapt back as the flames grew and he shifted to his dragon form, towering over us. His sleek reptilian body was covered in black scales with a rainbow iridescence that was breathtaking in sunlight. Not that I'd ever tell him that. If his ego got any bigger, I'd have to kill him myself.

When human, Eddie was average-looking. His only remarkable feature was his burnt, amber-colored eyes. In this form, his eyes practically glowed against his black scales. Black horns stretched out and back from his head, towards the spikes that ran down his neck and spine.

I grimaced. The last time I had ridden on Eddie's back, I'd had to cling to those spikes. I wasn't looking forward to the experience again, but we didn't have any other options. It would take too long to walk, and we would stand out on the ground. Flying was a risk too, but at least Eddie could disappear into the clouds or fly away if we were spotted. We couldn't outrun a dragon on the ground.

You should be excited and honored that I'm willing to let you ride me, Nemain. Eddie's voice rumbled through my mind.

I have no interest in riding you! I snapped back.

Just the vampire then, eh?

Eddie laughed as I glared at him, and I snuck a glance at Mikhail, who was carefully not looking at me. Argh. Eddie must have let him hear our conversation. The damn dragon was perfectly capable of keeping it just between us.

"Let's get on with it," Pele said.

Rather than kneel and let us climb on, Eddie's tail whipped out and wrapped around me, lifting me up to one of the spikes midway down his back. I tucked myself in between two spikes and tried to adjust so I would feel confident about not falling off. A few seconds later, he placed Mikhail behind me. Even with the spike between us, I was acutely aware of his presence. Magos was next, and Pele behind him. Eddie gave us a minute to adjust, and then he leapt straight up into the sky, his leathery wings beating hard.

Magos and Pele both swore behind me, but when I glanced over my shoulder, Mikhail was smiling with unbridled joy. He really was insane.

We flew all day without encountering any dragons or devourers. We had one close call with some fast-moving and rather aggressive birds, but otherwise it was uneventful. By the time the fading light raced us to reach the ground, I could admit to myself that at least the flying was kind of enjoyable. Continuing our journey at night wasn't an option, though. None of us were comfortable continuing in the dark, given Eddie's poor night vision.

"Do you think we're still far enough away that a fire is safe?" I tugged my cloak tighter around myself. As soon as the sun started setting, the temperature drastically dropped, and I was reminded of why I hated deserts so much. The layers of sweat that had been pouring out of me all day were now frozen to my skin.

We should be fine, Eddie replied. *We're still a little over a day away, and patrols never extended out this far before my exile. There was no need to reclaim territory, and it wasn't worth the risk.*

"The devourers were left free to roam this close to the city?" Magos asked, taking a seat next to me.

Mikhail sat on my other side, and I resisted leaning against him for body heat. Pele must have seen the temptation on my face, because she snorted and waved her hand. The small bramble of branches in front of us caught on fire, and I raised my hands to it, soaking in the heat.

Pele sat on the other side of the fire, and Eddie maneuvered so his body and tail wrapped around us, his head resting next to Pele.

Over two-thirds of the dragon population was wiped out during the initial onslaught of the devourers. We simply don't have the numbers to do much more than protect the immediate areas around the city.

I chewed on a piece of dried meat. "What type of devourer is found in this region?"

We call them trakdi. Eddie's tail twitched back and forth, reminding me of Jinx when he was upset. *They're large, almost half my size, with a lupine-like body but the head and jaws of a crocodile. Short, thick quills cover their entire body and protect them from our fire. Fortunately, they can't fly, but they can climb very well. We lost two sanctuaries before we figured out how to safeguard the remaining three against them.*

"Do they hunt at night?" Mikhail asked, accepting a piece of meat I handed him.

They'll hunt at any given opportunity.

Mikhail shifted as he scanned the darkness beyond our fire.

"The infamous vampire assassin of the Council. Scared of camping by the firelight," I teased.

Mikhail's attention snapped to me. "If one of them visits us in the night, I'm not saving you from its jaws, shifter."

I sniffed. "Like I'd ever need you to save me."

Magos and Pele looked at each other and grimaced. Apparently, all it took to bond them together in friendship was their mutual annoyance at the nonstop bickering Mikhail and I were prone to.

"I stretched my magic out as soon as we landed, so I'll know if any devourer comes within half a mile of us."

"Been practicing with Kalen?" Pele gave me an impressed look.

"Yes, I can feel other devourers *without* letting a significant amount of my magic loose." I said proudly and let a tiny bit more of my magic out to gently wrap around her. "Can you feel me using my magic right now?"

She pursed her lips in concentration before slowly shaking her head. "I don't feel anything."

My lips tilted up in a pleased smile. I still had so much to learn about my magic, and after seeing Badb and Kalen fight against the seraphim, I knew I hadn't even begun to scratch the surface of my capabilities. But damn, it felt nice to be making steady progress at least.

"It's a little trickier to feel for devourer hybrids like myself and Balor and his sidhe crew. I have to use more magic, which increases the chances of someone detecting it. Plus, Kalen says that most of the sidhe devourers can use their fae magic to mask their devourer magic, so it's unreliable." I shrugged. "But it's still useful in situations like this. Wouldn't want Mikhail to miss out on his beauty sleep."

"Your jealousy is delicious." A slow, sinful smile spread across Mikhail's face, and I quickly looked into the fire.

What about when you sleep? Eddie asked.

"My magic will wake me. But I probably won't sleep much tonight." I moved back from the fire a little and stretched out. Magos moved over slightly to make more room. Using my pack with my spare clothes, food, and weapons as a pillow, I stared up at the night sky. "It's been a while since I've gotten to lie beneath a new night sky. I want to remember this."

WE'RE APPROACHING THE TOWER.

That was all the warning we got before Eddie's right wing dipped and he dove through the clouds. I gripped the smooth spike in front of me. Someday, I would pay him back for this.

A large stone building rose beneath us, its light sandy tan exterior almost blending in with the landscape. I could see how most dragons would miss it if they were flying high above it. The daemons had mostly lived underground while they were in this realm, but occasionally they needed something built on the surface, so they'd done their best to make it not stand out.

Eddie circled a few times before landing. All of us slid off his back before he stopped moving. As soon as we were a safe distance away, flames erupted over his scales, and he shifted back to his human form. Dragon shifting wasn't like how I shifted to my feline shape. Eddie's clothes remained when he shifted back, similar to how Elisa could shift to her wolf form and back. Personally, I thought that type of shifting was cheating, but whatever.

"We're less than half a day from Anspolis," Eddie said as he adjusted his shirt. "I'll need to figure out a way to contact Cerri without drawing the attention of others. I might have trusted some before my exile, but I have no idea where their allegiances lie now. We can stay here while I figure it out."

He shoved open a rickety wooden door with far more force than necessary and trudged up the stairs.

Mikhail raised his eyebrows at me, but I shrugged and headed into the tower. I wasn't going to be the one to tell Eddie to calm down. He'd been separated from the love of his life for years and was so close to being reunited with her. In his shoes, I'd probably be a little tense, too.

I eyed the old stairs that wound up the inside of the tower. Pieces of them had fallen away, and we had to leap over the gaps. On the plus side, without a quiet way to get up the stairs, we wouldn't have to worry about anyone sneaking up on us from this way. Midway up, an archway revealed a spacious room, and I spotted Eddie standing in front of one of the many tables scattered around the space.

"It's funny," I said as I scanned the room. "This tower is thousands of years old, yet this is still how most daemon workshops look."

"It's a functional layout," Pele said as she quickly started going through various items. "No reason to fix what isn't broken."

Mikhail paused by a table where several books were laid open and glittering gems were stacked in piles. "There's no dust." He ran a finger across the table. "Someone is still using this place."

"Someone is," a voice called out from the book stacks that lined the far side of the room.

Magos, Mikhail, and I pulled our swords free as we spread out across the room. Pele ignored us and walked over to the table, picking up the book Mikhail had casually tossed back on the stack. The owner of the voice appeared in front of the stacks, and I instantly recognized her. Given how many times I had stared at the woman with bright emerald-green eyes and fiery red hair depicted in the painting behind Eddie's desk, it was no surprise.

It was surprising that she was *here*.

"Cerridwyn." Eddie breathed the name like it was the meaning to life.

"I knew you would find your way back to me." A victorious smile spread across her beautiful face, and then she was running towards him.

They crashed into each other, and Eddie swept her up into his arms. She laughed as he spun her, her long red hair swirling around them like living flames.

"I'm so sorry it took me so long. Finding a way back proved more difficult than I imagined. Every time I thought I had it figured out, something else went wrong," Eddie rambled as he set Cerri down.

She pushed a finger to his lips, cutting off his words. Her eyes glistened with tears as a few broke free and streamed down her face. "You're here now, and that's all that matters."

Cerri kissed him deeply, and we all looked away, unsure of

what to do. Except Pele, who was still rifling through the books as if two dragons with an epic love hadn't just been reunited.

"You're okay?" With quivering fingers, he traced her jawline. "Please tell me you're okay."

Gently she grasped his hands, holding them between their bodies. "I'm fine, I promise. You're the one who was exiled. I knew you would survive because I couldn't bear to think otherwise. But I missed you every single day." She roughly wiped her face with the back of her hand.

"I was so worried your father would marry you off once I was gone." He looked down at her hands and ran his fingers along her unadorned ones. Relief flickered through his eyes. "He hasn't bargained away your freedom yet."

"Not for lack of trying," she said wryly, causing Eddie to stiffen. She tilted his chin up, forcing him to look into her eyes. "Did you really think I wouldn't be able to run circles around the old bastard? I demanded a challenge to the right of my hand."

"What challenge?"

Cerri's eyes held a gleam when she answered, "The Nerak."

"Those are extinct. Everyone knows that." Eddie's eyes shone with wonder. "How in the hell did you convince them to go for that?"

"I found a trove of old daemon amulets and gadgets. The magic in them was simple, and I managed to fix one of them up enough to craft a decent illusion spell," she said with smug satisfaction. "I made sure to set it somewhere it would be seen by several prominent families. The first sighting caused quite a stir. Since then, I've set a few other sightings here and there to keep up the excitement."

"You're bloody amazing." He laughed and hugged her fiercely once more.

"I know," she said, her words muffled slightly because her head was still buried against Eddie's shoulder.

My friend looked like he wanted to take Cerri and go, and I didn't blame him at all. We'd assumed we'd have to go looking for Cerri, not find her without setting foot in the remaining dragon cities. I slowly spun around in a circle as I scanned the room from ceiling to floor.

"What are you doing?" Magos asked quietly.

"Cerri finding us here was a stroke of good luck," I whispered back. "I'm never this lucky. The floor is probably going to collapse out from under us or something."

Magos shook his head, lips twitching in amusement. "Maybe it's because Jinx isn't here and he's actually the source of all your bad luck."

"Fair point."

Eddie reluctantly let Cerri go when she pulled away but held onto her hand like he couldn't handle not touching a part of her. She gripped his hand back while she scrutinized each of us, her eyes lingering longest on Pele. If she was angered or frightened at a daemon being in her presence, she didn't show it. I thought that was a testament to both how much she trusted Eddie and how clever she was to portray confidence in a room full of a strangers.

"Who are your friends, Eddie?"

She pronounced his name with an accent, so it sounded more like "Ey-Dee," but it was clearly the same name.

"Wait." I choked back a laugh. "Your name really is Eddie? A dragon named Eddie?"

"Yes." Eddie frowned at me. "Did you think it was a fake name?"

"Of course I thought it was a fake name! It's a ridiculous name for a dragon!"

"There's nothing wrong with my name!" Eddie roared back.

Magos discreetly hid his smile behind his hand, but Mikhail was openly laughing.

"She's right," Pele said, looking up from her leafing through the pages of a book. "It's a ridiculous name."

"Dragons should have more intimidating names. Not Eddie." Laughter poured out of me, and Eddie glared, which only made me laugh harder. "If we run into a dragon named Greg, I'm going to laugh directly in their face. Or punch them in the face. Probably both." Tears streamed down my cheeks as I gulped for air. Even Magos was starting to lose it at this point.

"We don't actually have to worry about introductions, Cerri," Eddie ground out. "Because I'm about to eat all of them."

Cerri looked at me with an amused expression. "His full name is Eydellan, if that helps at all."

"That's slightly better." I wiped the tears from my face and grinned at her. "I'm Nemain. The handsome vampire is Magos." I gestured to Magos, who was once again wearing a calm, pleasant expression. "The ugly vampire that we mostly let tag along out of pity is his nephew, Mikhail."

Mikhail tilted his head as he looked at me, amusement dancing in his twilight eyes. "You're just jealous that you're not the most attractive person in this group."

Before I could get my retort out, Cerri moved to the opposite side of the table from Pele. "And you?" Her voice was even, but tension ran through her shoulders.

Slowly, Pele set the book down on the table and lifted her eyes to meet Cerri's. In that moment, I saw a striking similarity between the two of them, even though they looked nothing alike. Pele was all fire with her deep red skin and short vibrant orange hair. Cerri's fiery red hair was a stark contrast to her creamy white skin. She had a softness that Pele never had. But the intelligence and boldness in Cerri's emerald-green eyes was a match to what I always saw in Pele's turquoise irises.

"I am Pele Das'ki."

Cerri's eyes widened slightly. "So the Das'ki bloodline still survives."

"You know?" Eddie asked, moving to stand by Cerri's side once more. "About the daemons stealing our fire?"

I winced, hoping that Cerri would take that revelation better than Eddie had.

"Yes," she said with a shrug, eyes remaining on Pele. "The daemons didn't leave much behind in terms of writings, but I did find some notes left by Reja Das'ki. It was a good idea, and she executed it beautifully."

"You're not upset by it?" Eddie asked, eyebrows furrowed tightly. "They stole our fire and had to experiment on dragons to do it!"

"It was the actions and decisions by dragons that forced Reja and the other daemons to take such actions. They didn't do it out of greed but for survival, to protect those they loved." Cerri glanced at Eddie. "I know something about taking drastic measures to protect those you love."

Pele's chin dipped slightly in acknowledgment. "That binding you put on Eddie was a gamble. Until recently, he had no access to his dragon magic. It allowed him to blend in easier, but it also left him powerless."

"I had no choice," Cerri said quietly. "There wasn't time for anything else, and we all know what happens when a dragon is found by daemons."

"Not all daemons," Pele responded. "I knew what Eddie was right away, just as I did with the other dragons that came before and after him. There are still some daemons who will happily hunt down any dragons cast into our realm, but the hatred has largely faded. We all know the stories, but all the daemons who originally fled the dragon realm have died off. We are their descendants, and it's hard to keep the hatred alive when we are so far removed from it."

"What does that mean for our people now?"

"It doesn't mean anything," Eddie cut in. "We can leave. Now."

"Eddie . . ." Cerri started.

"I came here for you. To take you away from here, some-place safe." He looked at me desperately. "Please, can we just leave now?"

Navigating the dragon realm without Cerri and Eddie would be challenging. But a promise was a promise.

"I can send the two of you home—to my home," I quickly corrected myself. "But the rests of us can't leave yet."

I was still not happy about Pele's plan to either get a peace treaty or stage a coup. Or both. But it's not like there was anything I could do to stop her, so all I could do was try to keep my friend alive while she worked on her insane plans. And do some investigating to figure out if Balor had sunk his claws into the dragons and why.

"We'll need to ask Cerri some questions first," Pele added. "Just to get some current information about the lay of the land."

"Who is Balor?" Cerri asked, her eyes narrowing on Pele. "What do you really want, daemon?"

"Many, many things," Pele said wickedly. "But to start, I know you and many of your generation would like to negotiate with the daemons to end the lockdown of this realm and allow the dragons to freely move throughout all the realms. Or, if that is not possible, to relocate to a different realm. I'm here to mediate that agreement." Pele flashed her teeth. "Assuming certain requirements are met, of course."

Cerri narrowed her eyes. "And you're authorized to speak on behalf of all daemons?"

"I am. My father, Remil, is the current leader of the Assembly. He's been training me to take his place for decades, and recently the Assembly voted unanimously in my favor. My father and I will be co-leaders for the next few years until he formally retires."

I jerked my gaze away from Cerri and stared at Pele. It was no secret she would be replacing her father one day, but I didn't know it would be so soon. A lot of change had been happening recently amongst the leadership across the realms. Kaysea's father had recently passed the crown of the Tír fo Thuinn to a new queen. Kaysea was happily no longer directly involved with the ruling of the sea fae realm, but she remained the most powerful seer in generations, so she wasn't completely uninvolved. Her brother, Connor, was still helping the new queen transition into her role, whatever that meant.

The fae queens still ruled the rest of the fae realms, but eventually Finn would take over as king. I was having a hard time picturing the shy and reserved young fae boy ruling over the most powerful of realms, but that was at least fifty years away from coming to fruition. And now Pele would be stepping into the role of leading the Daemon Assembly.

Daemons had more of a democratic way of handling things than the fae, so being the leader of the Assembly didn't mean Pele ruled over all the daemons. But the position did come with considerable amounts of political power . . .

I mulled this news over in my head, trying to think about all the political ramifications of so much power shifting over the next few decades. This wasn't my area of expertise, though. I'd shunned politics my entire life, and I just didn't think this way.

My eyes cut to the side where Mikhail was leaning against a table. I'd have to figure out how to pick his brain later without admitting I was way out of my league.

"My father is going to be the largest obstacle in this," Cerri said. "He is the de facto leader and has the support of most of the older generations."

"But there are dragons open to negotiating with the daemons," Pele pushed.

"Yes." Cerri nodded slowly. "But we need to make sure my father doesn't kill you all before the others know you're here."

"Not dying would be great," I said dryly. Mikhail snorted.

"This is insane!" Eddie threw his hands in the air and faced Cerri. "Your father will never let this happen! It's not like dragons haven't challenged his authority." He pointed at his chest. "I was lucky he only had me exiled instead of drawn and quartered. Or staked out in the deserts for the trakdi to feast upon!"

"You think I don't know that!" Cerri raised her voice. "I've watched our friends get brutally killed just as you have! I am well aware of what is at stake! But I will not leave everyone behind just so you and I can live happily ever after! And I know you, Eddie. You wouldn't be happy if we took the coward's way out either!"

The two dragons glared at each other, and I suddenly missed Jinx. He would have made some jibe about smoke coming out of their nostrils or lamented how love made everyone so dramatic.

I let out a long, measured breath. "Look, none of us want to die. How about we discuss this like rational beings and decide if we can't come up with a plan that doesn't equal immediate death, then we'll go back to the human realm. We can always come back later."

Eddie stared at me with a puzzled expression. "Who are you and what have you done with my irrational stabbity friend?"

"I will stab you in your sleep."

"Your father's rule isn't absolute, correct?" Pele said, ignoring my exchange with Eddie. "The dragons have a leadership council of sorts that decides things?"

Cerri nodded. "It's made up of roughly a hundred dragons

broken up into several factions. My father leads one of those factions. It's not the largest, but it consists of the oldest and most powerful dragons."

Pele smiled. "I just need an opportunity to speak to them."

"This week is going to be full of tournaments and celebrations," Cerri said slowly, clearly thinking through our options. "Prior to the opening celebration, those that make up our leadership will be meeting. Every faction will be in attendance, including those who have been pushing to meet with the daemons. We need to get all of you into that meeting. Once it's publicly known that you're here, my father and those loyal to him won't be able to just kill you off."

"Can you get us into that meeting?" I asked.

"No, she can't," Eddie cut in. "Because we're leaving."

Cerri ignored him. "Yes, but I'll need some help." She frowned. "You should all stay here tonight. I'll come get you tomorrow when it's time."

"How did you get here, anyway?" Eddie asked, still glowering at her. "This is a long flight from Anspolis, and your father would never let you go anywhere this far from the city alone."

"I finally fixed those mirrors," Cerri said smugly.

Pele perked up. "Fae mirrors?"

"Yes," Cerri replied, and pointed at a large mirror that rested against the wall. It resembled the mirror in our living room back home that we used for communication. But this one was made of one large piece of glass with a wooden frame of twisting vines.

Pele walked over to the mirror and ran her fingers across the wood, clearly fascinated by its design. "These were what led the fae to design the first gateways between realms. There are so few of them left in existence."

"Some stairs in the back behind the book stacks lead to another room upstairs. I have food stashed up there and blankets as well," Cerri said. "I should head back. I have to make an appearance at a dinner in a few hours."

Eddie reached out and clasped her hand. "What's going on this week? Tournaments mean there is a prize." He searched her face. "What's the prize, Cerri?"

"I am." Eddie's jaw hardened, and Cerri gently traced it with her fingers. "My charade with the Nerak bought me some time, but there was no way to stall the inevitable. My father uses the promise of my hand in marriage as a political prize and the Nerak challenge wasn't going anywhere, so he devised these tournaments instead. I'm promised to be married to the winner."

"Good, we can use this," Pele said.

I gave Pele a pointed look. She might be brilliant at politics, but sometimes she really sucked at reading the room.

"You *will not* use Cerri as a pawn in your scheming." Eddie's eyes glowed, and I let out a sigh, not looking forward to breaking up another fight between them.

Cerri gently turned Eddie's face back to her. "She's right. We can use this to our advantage this week. There are dragons coming in from other cities just for this tournament, and many of them aren't fans of my father's."

"No." Eddie shook his head firmly. "We should get you out of here now. I can't lose you again."

"You never will," Cerri said. "We'll figure this out, my love."

Eddie did not look the least bit convinced by this, and I didn't really blame him. If someone I loved as much as he clearly loved Cerri was putting themselves in danger like this, I would open a gateway and shove them through it. Their anger at me for not respecting their decision would be worth it if they were alive.

"Let's check out the room upstairs. I'm hungry," I told the others to give Cerri and Eddie some time alone. Whatever they decided, I would respect, even if it would make our time here harder.

Pele reluctantly walked away from the mirror, and we headed upstairs. Mikhail and Magos fell into step beside me.

"You're always hungry," Mikhail said. "What if I'm hungry?" He glanced at my neck, and a shiver ran through me. The one and only time Mikhail drank from me, we'd ended up making out against a tree.

"Maybe you can convince Eddie or Pele to feed you, but I wouldn't count on it," I hissed and stomped up the stairs after Pele.

Chapter Nine

THE FOLLOWING day we waited for Cerri to return for us. Being so close to Cerri only to be apart from her again had apparently destroyed any patience Eddie had left. He'd started pacing early that morning, and I'd finally banished him to the book stacks before I had to take more drastic measures. He was currently yanking out various books and reading passages, muttering to himself and shoving them back on the shelf. Magos and Mikhail had posted up on the top of the tower to watch for any signs of dragons and devourers. That left Pele and me in the workshop section of the main floor.

"Cerri has certainly been busy." I picked up a silver amulet that looked like it was meant to be part of a necklace. Some type of sparkly lavender mineral had been used to create a pattern in the silver. I squinted at it. "I think this one was made by a sea fae. It looks like an anemone inspired the design." I tossed it down and picked up a piece of a broken dagger. "She's collected all sorts of relics left behind from the fae."

"Some of these are of daemon make," Pele replied from where she was perched at the window with a book. "Many of these books were left by the fae but clearly ended up in daemon hands. Notes are scribbled in the margins, written in an old daemon dialect."

"Have you found anything written by your grandmother?"

"Yes." Pele paused, her fingers hovering over the pages. "This one, actually. It's mostly a philosophical book written by the fae, but it talks about transference. It's what inspired her plan to transfer the magic from a dragon to the daemons."

"Did you always know?" I peered. "About where your fire magic came from?"

"Yes." In a rare moment of vulnerability, sorrow etched itself across her face. "My mother told me. Not just about where our magic came from, but about her mother. Everything she could remember, no matter how trivial, she told me."

"My parents did the same." The corners of my mouth twitched upward. "Cian and I used to love hearing stories about what the shifter home realm was like. The troublesome things our kin got up to."

"A realm full of felines," Pele said dryly. "I can only imagine."

I walked over to the table closest to Pele and leaned back against it, crossing my arms. "Why didn't you tell me that you were taking over for your father as leader of the Assembly?"

"It not like that's new information." Her gaze returned to the book in her lap. "You knew I would be replacing my father."

"Someday," I replied, not hiding my annoyance. "I knew that *someday* you'd be taking over for your father. You didn't tell me that you were taking over *now*."

"I'm not completely taking over. We'll co-rule for at least a few years." She flipped another page. "Are you annoyed because I didn't tell you? Or because you won't be able to relay this information to the fae queens until we get back from this realm? Worried about messing up in your duties as the new Unseelie Knight?"

I stalked over to the window and snatched the book out of her hands. With rather shocking speed, Pele stood up, directly in front of me. Orange flames ran down her arms.

"I'm worried because the oldest friend I have is stepping into a role that will put new targets on her back." My voice rose with every word. "I'm upset because my best friend is stepping into this role at a time when our enemies are growing, and we don't know who our allies are. I'm *pissed off* because my friend, who I have loved and trusted for centuries, thinks some fucking new title would *ever* stand in the way of my loyalty to her!"

Blue fire erupted from my hands, and I twisted, throwing the book onto the table before my flames reduced it to ashes and frost.

Pele moved until she was standing in front of me once again, studying the blue flames as they danced along my hands and arms. Wicked orange and red flames still danced across her skin as she slowly reached out and grasped my hands. My devourer magic licked at her flames, but she didn't pull back. Blue and orange intertwined, both of us holding our magic in check to keep from hurting the other.

"I'm sorry," she said softly. "My father and I only started discussing this in the last few months. He's tired. While he has excelled at leading the Assembly, it's not something he ever truly wanted. He did it for my mother. They only had a few centuries together, which, when you live for thousands of years, is nothing. When she passed from this world, he threw himself into his job to keep her legacy and dream alive. She was his everything, Nemain."

Her usually bright turquoise eyes dimmed.

"I remember what my father was like when she was alive. He does his best to hide it around me, but I know." She gave me a sad, close-lipped smile. "I've always known. It's like half of his soul is missing. He distracted himself by running the

Assembly, but he can't do it anymore. His heart just isn't in it, and the threat of the devourers led by Balor is too imminent. It's time for me to step in, and for my father to hopefully find something in this world that will bring him peace and purpose. Instead of clinging to my mother's legacy."

I gripped her hands tighter. "I understand, Pele. I really do. I just wish you had told me. You've always been there for me, and gods know I'm a hard person to be friends with."

She snorted, and we finally pulled our hands apart, the flames snuffing out.

I reached over to the table and handed her the book. "Is this the reason you haven't pursued Asmodeus? There's no way you don't know they've carried a torch for you this past century."

"Asmodeus and I are friends." Pele's nostrils flared. "Besides, they work for me."

"They work *with* you," I corrected.

"This isn't up for discussion!" she snapped and went back to her perch on the window.

"I don't understand why you won't explore this!" I threw my hands up in the air. "I know you like them! I've seen the way you watch them when you think no one is looking. Asmodeus is not interested in you as an attempt to climb the political ladder, if that's what you're worried about."

"I know that!" she hissed. "I've watched my father become a shell of his former self because he lost my mother. Love is a double-edged sword. You, of all people, should know that! You fell apart after Myrna died! Kaysea and I had to watch you break yourself for decades! I just can't afford that level of risk right now."

"You're right. Losing Myrna broke me for a while," I rasped as the familiar pain of loss tore through me. "More than a while. All these years later and it still feels like I'm being stabbed in the heart when I hear her name. But I don't regret what we had. You shouldn't deny what you feel for Asmodeus. They've waited a long time, but they won't wait forever."

"You're one to talk." Pele threw the book down, eyes ablaze with fury. "You and that damn vampire have been dancing around each other for months! We all see it! Why not take your own advice and go for it, Nemain?"

"Pele," I warned as I quickly looked over my shoulder to make sure Mikhail hadn't come down.

"Is it because he's the opposite of Andrei?" Pele shoved me, and I took a step back. "That werewolf was a way for you to pretend you are less than you are. A way for you to leave behind the political bullshit you've found yourself ensnared in and just pretend to be a shifter with no special gifts or responsibilities." She shoved me again, and I snarled in her face, but she didn't let up. "But Mikhail comes with baggage and a long list of enemies. He's powerful, clever, and wicked. What are *you* afraid of, Nemain?"

This time when she pushed me, I shoved her back. We both stepped forward until we stood there, glaring at each other, nostrils flaring.

The mirror set against the wall rippled, and we instantly whirled to face it. A man came through instead of Cerri, and I pulled my swords free. Pele moved away from me, giving us both space, a curved dagger with a matte black blade in her hands.

"Wait!" Cerri said as she lunged out of the mirror, moving between us. "He's with me. We need help to pull this off," she said quickly.

Eddie strode up to us, and I instantly knew two things based on the way he was looking at the newcomer. He knew who this dragon was, and he really didn't like him.

"Taliesin." Eddie sank a lot of anger into that word as he moved beside Cerri.

"Told you he'd react like this." The newcomer smirked and

crossed his arms, which did a wonderful job of showing off his carved biceps and rich dark brown skin. He was a handsome bastard.

"Everyone, this is Taliesin."

"Since you're all friends of Cerri's, you may call me Tal." He shot us all a charming grin which did a lovely job of showcasing his dimples.

"He grew up with me and Eddie," Cerri explained, while Eddie muttered under his breath. "He's part of the dragon leadership and will introduce Pele to everyone and make sure you all aren't immediately killed. He's been helping me the last couple years and is on our side. It's difficult for me to move around inside the city, especially in the citadel. I'm always watched outside my rooms. But Tal can move around freely, and nobody questions it when I'm with him."

"And why is that?" Eddie's tone held a dangerous edge.

"Because I'm courting Cerri, of course," Tal replied with a charming grin. "I'm practically a prince among our people. Only makes sense for me to marry the beautiful princess."

A growl rumbled out of Eddie, and he took a step forward, only for Cerri to slam an arm against his chest and shove him back.

"Enough," she snarled.

My eyebrows rose. I didn't think she was the snarling type. I looked at Pele, who had the same surprised expression on her face. We grinned at each other, our argument from earlier temporarily forgotten.

"Need I remind both of you what I did the last time you pulled this alpha bullshit?" Cerri glanced back and forth between the two male dragons.

"I'd like a reminder!" I held my hand up. Pele's hand shot up a second after mine.

Tal smiled widely at both of us. "She knocked both of us out and tied an enchanted fae rope around our hands so we were bound together. Then she refused to undo the knot until we were nice to each other for twenty-four hours and promised to stop fighting over her because, in her words, 'she could make up her own damn mind about what she wanted, and our nonsense just made us both look like unworthy sniveling idiots.'"

I snickered and glanced at Pele. "Can a dragon even be a princess? I thought princesses were supposed to be saved *from* dragons?"

"Why are you asking me this? Daemons don't have monarchies." Pele narrowed her eyes at me. "What do you know about princesses needing saving, anyway?"

"We all have to take turns reading to Isabeau every night. She always makes me read princess nonsense. Or pirate stuff."

"Those kids are rotting your brain."

I shrugged and faced the dragons staring at me and Pele with a mix of amusement and bewilderment.

"It makes so much sense that you're friends with Eddie." Cerri sighed. "Anyway, the fae rope incident was thirty years ago. We are all adults in our eighties now. I didn't have the patience for their bullshit when I was a teenager, and I definitely don't have it now."

"You're only in your eighties?" I gaped at them. "I had just assumed you were like . . . my age?"

"I know." He chuckled. "I thought about correcting you when I first realized you thought I was centuries old, but then I figured the look on your face when you found out the truth would be all kinds of amusing. Glad to confirm I was right."

"How old are you, if you don't mind me asking?" Tal was still wearing that amiable smile as he looked me up and down and then did the same to Pele.

"I'm three hundred and ninety-eight," I said.

"Eight hundred and thirty-one," Pele said with a shrug.

"Both of you are stunning," he replied.

"Oh, shut up," Eddie snapped and then looked at me. "Isn't your birthday coming up?"

The smile slid off my face. "It's in a few days, actually."

"You didn't say anything." Eddie frowned at me.

"We've had kind of a lot going on, in case you hadn't noticed. Besides, I have one every year." I suddenly became acutely aware of everyone's heartbeat and thought about all the bloody hearts that Sebastian had left me each year for my birthday. I wouldn't be getting one this year, but that didn't erase everything he had done. "What's it matter if we skip celebrating one?"

"Yeah, but—"

"I'm going to get Mikhail and Magos so we can get moving." I shoved off the table I'd been leaning against and quickly moved to the stairwell. As I started my ascent, I heard Pele's voice.

"Drop it, Eddie," Pele said quietly.

The voices softened too much for me to hear, and I didn't want to, anyway. I just hoped Eddie would listen and not mention my damn birthday again.

My nose wrinkled as I held back a sneeze. We'd used the mirrors to travel to Cerri's room in the citadel. From there, Tal had scouted ahead to make sure the way was clear as Cerri led us through hallway after hallway to where the dragon leadership met. I was happy we hadn't had to figure out a way to sneak into the citadel. Anspolis was well-guarded.

The downside of this approach was that none of us had any idea of the layout of the citadel or the city in general. Which meant that if we had to flee for our lives later, we'd be running blind down hallways and streets.

Dust continued to assault my nostrils, and I tried breathing through my mouth instead. We'd been waiting in what was basically a storage closet for ten minutes, and given the layers of dust on the empty shelves, it hadn't been used or cleaned in quite some time. Tal had joined the dragon leadership in a large room directly across from us. He would give Cerri a signal when it was time, and then she'd come and get us. I wasn't a huge fan of this plan because of how much it relied on Tal not betraying us. But Eddie trusted Cerri, and she trusted Tal.

If Pele was concerned about walking into a room full of dragons and declaring she was there to negotiate on behalf of the Daemon Assembly, she didn't show it.

On most days, Pele wore well-tailored pantsuits that exuded confidence and authority. That hadn't been practical for this particular adventure. Instead, she wore slim black pants and a button-up long-sleeve shirt with a high collar. It was the daemon answer to needing to appear fancy but still remain functional. It was also identical to what Magos was currently wearing, and I desperately wanted to tease her about it. But given how much I'd pissed her off yesterday and what she was about to do, I'd bitten my tongue.

Everything hinged on Pele being able to convince the dragons to at least hear out her proposal about establishing a peace between the dragons and daemons. We all agreed that we should try for the peace treaty option first and the coup second. That would give us some time to do some searching around the citadel and see what evidence we could find of Balor's presence here. If the peace treaty ultimately failed, Pele would hopefully at least have made some strong connections with the younger dragons and could then put the coup plan into play.

While I agreed with this approach, there was little I could do to help other than keep Pele alive. It made me feel useless, and I didn't like it.

Light footsteps sounded in the hallway outside our hiding spot, and moments later, Cerri appeared. "It's time," was all she said before striding over to the enormous double doors that seemed to be waiting ominously for us. Without missing a beat, she shoved against the doors, and they swung inward, revealing a large, circular room with tiered seating.

Pele strode in behind her, head held high. Magos and I stood on either side of Pele while Mikhail and Eddie guarded our backs.

Silence fell across the chamber as a hundred dragons in human form stared at us. I scanned the room, noting possible exits if we had to make a quick escape.

All three sides of the room were open to the outside. Large archways were cut out of the stone walls, revealing the bright blue sky beyond. To our left and right I could make out stone ledges beyond the room, but I suspected that's all there was. Given only two of us could fly, and all of our potential enemies could definitely fly, fleeing outside didn't seem like a great option. We'd be better off going back the way we'd come; the hallway was too narrow for the dragons to shift to their true forms.

"Ah, my friends have arrived," Tal said brightly from where he was seated on one of the lower tiers.

"What is the meaning of this?" asked a large man with green eyes. White strands wound through his red hair, and his features were harsh and a bit blunt, but there was no mistaking the resemblance. This was Cerri's father. The de facto leader of the dragons and the one responsible for banishing Eddie. Sure enough, he tore his gaze from Pele and skipped over us before landing on Eddie. "You."

"Me." Eddie bared his teeth.

Cerri's father took a step forward, but Tal moved between our group and him. "They're here at my invitation and are therefore our guests. The rules of hospitality apply."

Shouts and growls of outrage filled the chamber, but more than a few dragons leaned forward and whispered in each other's ears while they studied Pele curiously.

Looks like we'd been right about some of the dragons being interested in negotiating with the daemons. I scanned the room once more. Not many, though. Easily half of the dragons looked like they wanted to tear us to pieces. Others seemed to be waiting on how this would play out.

"Those rules only apply to dragons," Thorod snapped, his voice rumbling through the chamber. "And *exiled* dragons lose all claim to them."

"The fae were welcome in our halls once," Tal countered smoothly. "Any dragon is within their right to extend hospitality to a guest."

"He's right, Thorod." One of the few female dragons in the room rose from where she had been sitting halfway up the room. "Taliesin is a dragon in good standing and a leader amongst our community. After all, he's good enough to be courting your daughter, is he not?"

Thorod stared at the female dragon, aggression pouring off him in waves. But after a few moments, he pulled it back in and gave her a close-lipped smile. "Of course, Dindrane. Forgive me for speaking out of turn. My daughter is all I have left of our family, and my protectiveness gets ahead of me sometimes," he said.

Cerri's expression remained one of stone, unmoved by her father's words. But Eddie's eyes glowed brighter.

"If all of you are so eager to hear the lies and tainted gifts the daemons come bearing, so be it." Thorod waved his hand dismissively and returned to his seat. "Nothing will come of this."

Tal made a mocking half bow towards Thorod. "Thank you for allowing us to hear what the daemons have to offer so we can all work together to make sure the future of dragons is strong and eternal." The hostile look Thorod had given Eddie earlier was nothing compared to what he was giving Tal now. When no one else spoke up, Tal turned towards Pele. "My lady." He gestured for her to take the floor.

Pele moved to the center of the room, all eyes once again on her. I cut off the absurd giggle that rose up my throat. After being the center of focus everywhere I had entered for the past few months, it was surreal to have absolutely no one paying any attention to me.

Eddie stood by Cerri, who had taken a seat exactly opposite her father. Mikhail, Magos, and I spread out a little more to defend Pele on all sides. Everything was up to her now.

"I had an aunt, whose name was Kalsa."

Dread coiled in my stomach. Bringing up a dead relative that likely had been murdered by dragons didn't seem like a good way to start, but I trusted Pele to know what she was doing.

"She was thirteen years old when she died," Pele continued evenly. "The daemons stayed underground as much as possible, but it was hard to convince their children to live in the dark. Kalsa went out early one morning to pick wildflowers for her mother's upcoming birthday. A dragon spotted her and decided to have a bit of fun. He picked her up and flew high into the sky and then dropped her."

The only sound I could hear was the rapid beating of my heart. The terror that girl must have felt as she fell through the sky, knowing her death was imminent and she could do nothing about it. Most of the dragons appeared unmoved by Pele's words. But some shifted uncomfortably or looked down, unable to meet the steady gaze of the daemon before them.

"It was the death of her first daughter that set my grandmother on the path that would ultimately free us. That grief and rage is what drove Reja Das'ki to commit unspeakable acts."

Pele held her hands up. Brilliant orange flames sprang forth, causing every dragon in the room to lean forward hungrily. Tal wiped his face in resignation, and out of the corner of my eye, I could see Eddie getting ready to grab Cerri and run out of the room. But I trusted Pele to know what she was doing.

"I could continue listing the names of the daemon children who were brutally slaughtered by dragons. I could recount the horror stories about what life was like for daemons living with the dragons' claws on their necks. I could tell you about all the horrible things we've done in retaliation. The blood *we* have shed. The lives we've cruelly ended.

"But I'm not going to." Pele lowered her hands, the flames winking out of existence. "Because I. Do. Not. Care."

Tal blinked in surprise.

"Every daemon in existence today was born in the human realm. Every dragon left was born after the daemons fled this realm. Our ancestors are dead. It's time for their hatred to die as well."

"A nice sentiment," called out a voice from the upper tier of seats. A tall man rose and leisurely walked down the steps. "But while the daemons have been free to forget about our history with every new generation born, we have been trapped in this realm. Devourers stalk the land outside our sanctuaries. And we get to watch *our* children be hunted down."

I scrutinized the threat as he made his way to the floor. He seemed more like a politician than a warrior with his slim build and impeccable clothing. The dark blue fabric of his tunic complemented his warm brown skin well; the sides of his head were shaved, and his dark hair was pulled back in a neat bun.

Something about him reminded me of Sebastian. I wasn't sure if it was the classically handsome face or the smug arrogance that dripped off him. My magic stirred, but I kept it in check; this was Pele's fight.

"That is why I am here, Vizor. To end the exile and free the dragons once more."

If the dragon was surprised by Pele knowing his name, he didn't show it. Which, point to him, because I was surprised as hell. That surprise was quickly overridden by another. Vizor continued his languid pace, and now I could see the color of his eyes. They were the same burnt amber orange of Eddie's. *Who the hell was this guy?*

The dragon with all-too-familiar eyes stopped and faced Pele. "So you'll free us from this realm, only to hunt us down in another?" He gave her a small pitying smile. "Or are we supposed to ignore the fact that all dragons that have left this realm have been killed by your kind? Brutally based on the bodies you often throw back."

"Leave this realm? You make it sound like they had a choice in the matter." Pele smiled sharply back at him. "While it's true some dragons have found ways to leave this realm of their own accord, I do believe the vast majority have been exiled. My dear friend Eddie was forcibly removed from his realm and separated from his love. Was that not the decision of dragons?"

"Why yes, my *dear* friend, Pele," Eddie said. "It was Thorod himself who evicted me."

Vizor eyed Eddie coldly. "And yet you're here. In the company of a daemon. Perhaps your love for the lovely Cerridwyn isn't that pure, if you had to serve a daemon to survive. Not all of us have the skills, or the stomach, to keep a daemon satisfied."

"So you're still single then?" Eddie drawled.

I snickered, and Vizor glowered at me. His eyes widened slightly, and I stiffened as I pulled my magic deep within me. We'd all agreed it would be best to keep what I was a secret for now. The dragons had enough reasons not to trust us without adding in my devourer magic. Plus, if we had to fight our way out, it was better they not know what I was truly capable of. Vizor continued to study me, and I gave him a lazy grin in return, hoping he hadn't gotten a glimpse of my magic.

"How long has it been since a dragon's body was thrown back into this realm after being exiled?" Pele asked, drawing Vizor's attention back to her.

He didn't respond at first, but awkward silence never bothered Pele, so she continued to wait. Finally, he admitted, "It's been a while."

Pele held her hand out, and I untied the small sack on my belt and threw it to her. She pulled out a necklace and tossed it to Vizor, then proceeded to walk up the stairs, handing out small trinkets to dragons. Based on how she was scanning the audience, I realized she was looking for specific dragons. Several dragons let out relieved sighs; others openly wept and clutched the items to their chest.

"I've done everything I could to ensure no exiled dragon was harmed in the last fifty years." Pele returned to the floor directly in front of Vizor. "I have signed documentation from the ruling Daemon Assembly stating I have authority to negotiate on their behalf. I am not naive. This will be challenging because of our shared history. But I believe we can find a path forward. The question is"—Pele turned away from Vizor, effectively dismissing him as a threat—"are all of you willing to work with me? Or is your hatred more important than your future?"

Chapter Ten

"Well, that was fun." I flopped down onto a pile of blankets, leaving the few chairs to the others.

Cerri had taken us directly to the suite we would be sharing after Pele finished her opening salvo. My relief at getting out of the room full of dragons had been short-lived as Cerri led us through a maze of grey-stoned hallways, deeper into the citadel. There would be no swift escape from this room, so we'd be reliant on me opening a gateway to get us out of here fast. Which was all well and good unless our group got divided later.

Magos and Mikhail had been silent on the walk, but I knew them both well enough to read the tension in their movements. They didn't like the feeling of being trapped either.

"I found the look on Vizor's face priceless," Eddie said. "Makes it almost worth going along with this insane plan instead of getting the hell out when we had the chance."

"Is he always like that?" I asked.

"Yes," Cerri and Eddie said at once.

"He sat by your father at the end, but that's not where he was sitting when we walked in," Pele noted.

"Vizor is"—Cerri pursed her lips—"his own creature. I've never been able to figure out his motives, so I've done my best to stay out of his way. It was a surprise to everyone when he announced he was participating in the tournament."

Eddie stiffened from where he was leaning against the wall.

"The tournament starts tomorrow?" I asked.

"Yes," Cerri said. "Your timing couldn't have been better. Aside from my own personal reasons for being happy you're here,"—she gave Eddie an adoring look—"I think the tournament will help with negotiations because of the amount of young dragons that have come to the city for it, as well as provide distractions for us to investigate my father."

"We'll have to attend the tournament, though," Eddie said. "Cerri will be expected to be there, and it will stand out if we don't attend with her."

"True," Cerri conceded. "But there will be celebrations held after the tournament and that will present some opportunities to go sneaking about."

"Hmm." I eyed Eddie suspiciously. Aside from his initial outburst about the tournament, he'd been very casual about the whole thing. "Is the tournament held close by? I'd like to walk the citadel and surrounding area to get a lay of the land. Wherever the tournament is being held, too. I have no idea where we are right now, and I find that a little unsettling." The vampires nodded in agreement.

Cerri smiled broadly. "I can see how that would be disconcerting. The tournament is held nearby, but it's only accessible by flight . . . or a long climb."

"Great." I wrinkled my nose.

"There is a feast tonight in celebration of the tournament. Most of the dragon leadership will be there, along with their family and friends. Word is already spreading of your presence, but you will be the guests of honor tonight, so by tomorrow morning every dragon in the city will know of you. I think it's best to wait to explore until then or later tonight when everyone is sleeping; otherwise, they might be alarmed at seeing a daemon and outsiders wandering around their homes."

"Fair enough." I understood where Cerri was coming from, but I was already feeling a little stir crazy, and we had hours to go until dinner.

The vampires and I turned our heads to the door as the sound of faint footsteps echoed down the hallway. A moment later, the large door creaked opened and a young woman with auburn hair and lightly tanned skin cautiously entered the room carrying a stack of towels. She halted immediately when she saw us, her eyes flicking to Cerri.

"Thank you, Lynette," Cerri said, her hands moving in deliberate gestures as she spoke. "I can take it from here."

The auburn-haired dragon nodded once, her hands moving quickly in response. Cerri smiled warmly at her, hands flying through different movements. Whatever she told the young dragon caused her to smile slightly. It was there and gone in an instant before she left the room, avoiding making eye contact with any of us.

"She's deaf?" I guessed after the doors closed once more.

"Yes," Cerri confirmed. "It's fairly common amongst our kind. About one-fifth of our children are born deaf. All dragons learn how to sign, along with our spoken language."

"Why not use telepathy to communicate?" Mikhail asked.

Cerri looked towards Eddie, who smirked. "I think your time around Eddie has left you with a false impression of our abilities. We're all telepathic in our dragon forms, but few of us are also telepathic when we're wearing our human skins. Even in our true forms, our telepathic abilities are not particularly strong. Eddie is . . ." She scrunched up her nose.

"Amazing," Eddie offered. "Remarkable? Extraordinary?"

"Exhausting," Pele muttered.

"Unique," Cerri said, glancing sideways at Pele. "But exhausting is also accurate."

"Jealousy is unbecoming on all of you." Eddie grinned. "I'm the last of my bloodline that we know of. I'm not the strongest of dragons, nor is my fire the hottest, but my telepathy is stronger than any other dragon in existence."

"That we know of," Cerri corrected. "It's possible there might be others hiding their abilities."

"Why?" I frowned. "From what I saw in that chamber all afternoon, dragons love to flaunt their powers."

"Because her father is largely responsible for those of my lineage going extinct," Eddie replied. "It's one of the many reasons he doesn't like me."

"Probably not the main reason, though," Mikhail said lightly, his eyes cutting to Cerri.

"My father doesn't like anyone who stands between him and power," Cerri said as she walked over to the back wall.

Her fingers skimmed across the thin seams running between the stonework until they dipped in slightly. She halted her hand and pushed against the wall. A soft click sounded, and a large section of the wall slid back and to the side, displaying a passage behind it.

"An escape route if you need it. I don't think my father will publicly call for your executions, but that doesn't mean he won't try to get rid of you quietly. I'd suggest sleeping in rotation while you're here so someone is always on guard. I can't guarantee no one else knows about these hidden passageways, so there is a risk they could be used by your enemies. But I didn't want to put you in one of the rooms that didn't have a second exit."

"It's worth the risk," Magos agreed, peering inside the passageway. "Where does it lead?"

"Going left will take you on a more direct exit to the outside; going right will loop around most of the citadel before eventually leading to a large outdoor garden that sits in the center of our city." Cerri slid the wall shut and showed each of us how to open and close it, then brushed her hands off. "I'll leave you to get settled while I check on a few things. I'll return in a bit with food." She scrutinized each of us and asked, somewhat hesitantly, "Forgive me for asking, but . . . what exactly are each of you? We have limited food options, but I'll do what I can if you have any dietary needs."

I barked a laugh. "You don't know what we are? And you're only asking now?"

"Well, we had more pressing matters to discuss yesterday!" She threw her hands in the air. "Besides, I wasn't exactly sure how this day would go. There was a very real chance you would be dead by the end of it, in which case it wouldn't really matter what you were."

Well . . . couldn't fault her for the pragmatism.

"You're going to fit in with this group just fine." Magos chuckled. "Mikhail and I are vampires."

Cerri just stared at him blankly.

"Right," I said with a grin. "This realm has been cut off from all the others for over a thousand years, and vampires haven't been around that long. So no one here has heard of vampires or werewolves."

"Lucky them," Pele said dryly.

Ignoring my prickly friend, I continued, "Did sorcerers ever visit this realm?"

"Yes," Cerri replied, sinking a lot of distaste into that one word.

"Yeah, they're no one's favorite," I chuckled. "Sometime in the seventeenth century, they also visited the human realm. Details are a little murky, but two of them had some sort of competition going about who could make the better monster. Long story short, they made devourer human hybrids that we call vampires and werewolves."

"Devourer?" Cerri's emerald-green eyes widened in alarm as she looked at Mikhail and Magos.

I found myself moving between her and them automatically.

"Part devourer." I held my hand out in a calming motion. "And technically, so am I. My mother is a feline shapeshifter, but my father is both sidhe and devourer."

"How is this possible?" She shook her head slowly. "The only devourers I've encountered are beasts, intelligent and powerful, but still beasts."

"It's a long story and part of the reason we're here," I said. "It's a story best told over food . . . and drinks. We'll eat whatever food you have to share."

Magos and Mikhail had gone out and gotten themselves a nice blood meal before we came to this realm. They'd be fine for at least a few weeks unless they were wounded, in which case one of us would be opening up a vein for them.

Cerri stared at us, wariness still clear in her features. Eddie slipped closer to her and whispered something in her ear, too quiet for me to hear. She relaxed slightly and nodded once at me. "Of course. I'll gather some food and be right back. There are three bedrooms, so feel free to choose whichever you like."

Eddie followed her to the suite doors while Pele and I investigated the rooms and discovered a problem.

"Three bedrooms, but only one bedroom has two beds," Pele said. "The others have a single bed."

"A single *large* bed," Eddie corrected. "I'm claiming one of those. I'm fairly certain I can convince Cerri to sneak out from her bedroom at night and protect me from you heathens."

I rolled my eyes at him and turned to Pele. "Why don't Magos and Mikhail take the room with two beds? You and I can share the other room." I grinned at her, a parade of wicked thoughts running through my mind.

"No. Magos and I will share the room with two beds. You and Mikhail can share a bed."

The parade died.

"What?" I asked in a high-pitched voice.

Pele looked at me coolly, arching a single eyebrow. "What's the matter, Nemain? Afraid of something?"

My pulse immediately sped up, and I cursed myself as both vampires swung their heads to look at me. Magos looked concerned. Mikhail looked . . . hungry.

Fuck. My. Life. I should have known Pele wouldn't just let my dig about Asmodeus go. This was payback.

"Fine," I bit out, snatching my bag from where I'd set it on the floor. "I'm going to get cleaned up."

I stalked towards the door on my right, acutely aware of Mikhail following me.

"All the rooms have showers," Eddie called out. "No hot water, though, as dragons tend to run hot. You'll have to figure out another way to warm up."

I slammed the door against his laughter. If things kept going this way, my friends wouldn't have to worry about the dragons murdering them in their sleep. I'd do it my damn self.

I TOSSED my travel bag down and stalked across the large room, halting in front of the massive four-poster bed. Fresh linens that smelled faintly of Lynette covered the mattress. No other furniture was present. Based on the deep grooves in the stone floor, it had likely been dragged out. Probably pillaged to be used in the homes of dragons instead of sitting here in this abandoned section of the citadel. I was surprised such a nice bed had been left behind, but maybe dismantling it to move it had been deemed too much work.

I ran my fingers across the silky dark blue fabric and tried not to think about what Mikhail would look like in it later. I let the fabric drop from my fingers as I violently shoved that thought away.

"You seem rather worked up at the thought of us sharing a bed," Mikhail drawled from where he was leaning against one of the bedposts, a towel tucked under his arm. "Temptation going to be too much for you?"

"Don't flatter yourself," I said flatly. "I just would have preferred Pele is all."

Mikhail moved towards me with liquid grace, tossing the towel onto the bed. Without meaning to, I took a step back, and then another, until I felt the cool stone wall. He braced his hands against the wall on either side of me, boxing me in, and a thrill went up my spine. Those dark twilight eyes were wholly focused on me, causing my heart to beat wildly within my chest.

Mikhail glanced down, no doubt hearing my traitorous heart, before looking at me with a sinful smile that set my skin on fire. "What were you thinking the night we came back from the fae ball?"

"I was thinking about how royally fucked I was at being declared the Unseelie Knight." I was getting really good at bending the truth. I'd be fitting in at the fae courts in no time.

"That's not what sent you running away from me, and you know it."

"What do you want from me, Mikhail?" My voice trembled despite trying to keep my words even.

Uncertainty flickered across his face, and he opened his mouth, only to close it a second later before settling on an answer. "Honesty."

"Fine." Fire replaced the tremble in my voice as I raised my chin and met his stare. "You want to know what I was thinking that night? I was thinking about dragging you to my bed. I was thinking about losing myself with you for a few hours and forgetting about all the other bullshit."

"So why didn't you?" His eyes darkened, but he didn't move an inch.

"You know why." I shoved him away from me and moved so that the wall was no longer at my back. "Whatever this is between us is a complication we can't afford! I didn't mean for everything to happen the way it has with the vamp kids and Finn, but I'm now responsible for more lives than just my own. I can't allow myself to be distracted or have yet another person in my life that I need to take care of!"

"I don't need you or anyone to take care of me." Mikhail smiled wide enough to show his fangs. "I had survived centuries on my own before you were even born. I'm not the damn werewolf pup who needed your coddling and protection."

"Leave Andrei out of this!" I hissed.

"Then stop using him and Myrna as a shield!" Mikhail snarled back.

"Go fuck yourself!" I drew back as if he'd struck me. "You're just being an arrogant asshole who is pissed off that I'm not fawning all over you!"

"You won't give us a chance because I'm nothing like them." He prowled towards me, not the least bit concerned with the anger that was pouring off me in waves. "I'm not good or kind. You can't be with me and forget about all the complications in your life because I'm just as wrapped up in all this as you are. I don't need your protection because I'm not weak and I'm every bit as violent as you."

I held my ground as he took a step closer so that our chests were almost touching.

"You believe you need to find someone to balance out all your bullshit instead of being with someone who sees every inch of your darkness and *likes* it."

I flexed my fingers at my sides, claws digging into my flesh as my blood boiled. He was wrong. Every relationship I'd ever been in had ended badly. Myrna was dead. Sebastian had betrayed me, caused me decades of pain, and was now dead. Losing Andrei had hurt, but at least he'd walked away.

My heart continued to beat wildly even as I inhaled his scent like it was the answer to everything I wanted in life. I needed to put some distance between us and cool down before I tried to tear his head off with my bare hands. Or throw him on the bed and demand that he fuck me until I couldn't think of anything else but how he felt inside me.

Mikhail leaned in, and it took every ounce of my will power not to place my hands on his chest or inhale his scent.

"Tell me, shifter," he purred into my ear, causing me to clench my thighs together, "what are you thinking right now, to make you smell so delicious?"

Fuck.

"I'm not doing this." The words came out too breathy. Space. Distance. That's what I needed. Cold shower. Even better.

Before I made it two steps to the shower, Mikhail grabbed my arm and pulled me back towards him. My fist slammed into his jaw, and he released me, stumbling back a step.

Using the back of his hand, he wiped the blood away from his mouth and grinned at me. "Nice. Got anything else?"

A growl of frustration tore out of me. "I'm done with this conversation, and I'm done with you!"

Mikhail tilted his head, loose dark strands of hair shifting with the movement. "Fine, I'll drop it. For now."

"How about you drop it forever?" I snapped. "Because it's not happening."

"Sure." He grinned, and I narrowed my eyes at him, not believing the sudden shift in his mood or his easy agreement. "I get first dibs on the shower."

He shrugged out of his shirt and unbuttoned the top of his pants. I stared at his well-sculpted chest and the fine trail of hair exposed where his pants opened slightly. Never in my life had I wished so much for a few more buttons to be undone. Realizing I'd been unabashedly staring for several seconds, I jerked my gaze upward.

A sinful smirk played across his lips as he walked across the room, carved muscles wrapped in warm brown skin on full display as he disappeared into the washroom.

Minutes passed by as I stood there, waiting for what, I didn't know. Finally, I snapped out of it and snatched my bag off the floor. Flinging the door open, I stalked over to Eddie's room. I'd use his damn shower.

Chapter Eleven

"Huh," I said from where we stood at the entrance to the dining hall. Cerri had briefed us on what to expect tonight but had clearly downplayed some aspects a little. "Extremely drunk dragons were not what I was expecting."

Cerri winced. "Some of the dragons coming in for the tournament only arrived yesterday. The night before the tournament tends to be more casual and friendly because it's a rare moment for some of us to be together like this. You all being here probably drove a lot of them to drink even more, either in celebration at the possibility of a new future . . . or rage that you're here and not dead yet."

"Conversations this evening will prove interesting then." Pele smiled.

"Food first," I demanded. "Then you can walk around and make nice with the dragons while we make sure no one stabs you in the back."

"We're dragons," Cerri said defensively. "We stab people in the front."

"Of course. How rude of me." I shook my head and

followed after Cerri as she wound her way through the long tables.

The space was massive, with the same stone walls as the rest of the citadel. The back-half of the room opened up to the sky beyond, and I felt it beckoning to me. The view had to be amazing. My lips tilted up into a grin as I wondered if any dragons ever got drunk enough that they stepped off the ledge, forgetting they were in their wingless dragon form.

Thorod was seated at a table across the hall, the same dragons who sat with him in the morning with him now. But aside from that group, there seemed to be a lot more mingling among the rest of the dragons. I recognized some of the young dragons who were part of the leadership, but most of those present were new faces.

Thankfully, there were no signs of Vizor anywhere. I wasn't in the mood to deal with him and his constant verbal jabs. Not that I ever would be. But if I lost my temper and stabbed him, there were an awful lot of witnesses here.

We weaved through the tables, getting a few stares as we went, but no one stopped us or said anything.

Cerri picked a table that was mostly empty, and we all sat down except for Eddie, who ventured over to several large barrels stacked against a wall. He poured several mugs and plopped them down onto the hardwood table, causing some of the ale to slosh out. I eyed the mugs and the drunk dragons around us before looking suspiciously at Eddie.

"I've seen you drink two bottles of whiskey and barely get buzzed. What the fuck is in that?" I pointed a clawed finger at the frothy mugs.

"Don't be such a baby," he said, picking up one of the mugs and taking a deep drink. He let out a contented sigh. "Gods, I missed this."

Cerri smiled and picked up a mug. "It's honey ale. You'll

probably be fine. Most of those present are on their third or fourth mug, so just pace yourself."

Shrugging I picked up the ale and took a tiny sip. Like the name suggested, it was light and sweet. It wasn't what I would normally go for, but it wasn't bad. I continued to sip as I looked over the platters of food that consisted mostly of roasted meats and vegetables. "I'm surprised you have enough food to throw events like this."

"Each city has a designated agriculture area outside its walls that we guard. It's really only the livestock we have to worry about protecting. The devourers don't care about the grains and vegetables we grow. It took a long time for us to get this stable again," Cerri said. "We used to have hundreds of cities throughout the realm. When the devourers were let in, all but ten cities were wiped out within a decade. Over the centuries, those ten dwindled down to three. Anspolis, Isonver, and Ralis."

"Are Isonver and Ralis close to here?" I speared a piece of seared meat and took a bite. *Mmm . . . juicy.*

"Ralis is west, about a three-day flight," Eddie said, carefully placing food onto Cerri's plate. He poked around until he found a nice cut of steak and added that to the assortment before filling his own plate. "Isonver is south and a little further, takes about a week to get there. It's the largest of the cities and the most well defended."

"And yet Anspolis is where the dragon leadership lives?" Pele asked.

"Anspolis is home to our best warriors. It's where the tournaments have always been hosted. It's also central to both the other cities so it naturally became the location for leadership. As to why everyone's families live in Isonver . . ." Cerri's mouth tightened. "That's my father's doing. It took him a while, but he managed to get most of the families of those involved with leadership living in Isonver, mostly by having his supporters build up the city's defenses. Little by little, the city became an impenetrable fortress. Multiple devourer attacks were easily rebuffed, and the city's reputation grew."

"There were four cities back then," Eddie said bitterly. "Elfur was a coastal city that had been secure for decades. But one night, over two dozen trakdi broke through the city gates and slaughtered everything in their path. The only reason so many survived was because an alarm was sounded midway through the attack, waking everyone from their slumber. Even then, a third of the city died, and the damage to the city's defenses was immense."

He took another long drink from his mug, his burning amber eyes seeming haunted. "It didn't make any sense. The trakdi had never attacked like that before, in that large of a group. Everyone on guard duty that night was silently killed, but instead of stopping there and feasting, the trakdi kept going further into the city."

"These trakdi," I said carefully. "They're like most of the devourer species? I mean, they're not like the sidhe devourers?"

"The trakdi are vicious and cunning, but they're just animals," Cerri said quietly. She'd grasped Eddie's hand in hers and held it tightly. "They've never acted that way before."

I looked back and forth between their tightly wound hands and the empty look in Eddie's eyes. "Your mother," I said softly. "That's how she died."

Eddie nodded. "We used to sleep on the roof at night because the inside of the house was often hot and stuffy, and I complained about it. My mother woke in time to see the trakdi climb over the roof. She grabbed me and flung me behind her, screaming at me to shift. When we're young, shifting can be hard, especially when we're panicked. I tried, but the magic kept slipping away. She shifted and fought the trakdi, but my mother was no warrior, and she was on the small side for a dragon. It tore through her and tried to grab me, but she managed to rally the last of her strength and reached me first. She flew us outside the city before faltering and landing hard. By the time I pulled myself out from underneath her wing, she was gone. Her throat had been mostly torn out."

We sat in silence, drinking our honey ale. All of us were familiar with loss and knew there was nothing to be said.

"My father used the attack as a reason to relocate the families to Isonver," Cerri said. "Even some of the families from Ralis relocated there."

"He controls the defenses of the city," Pele said evenly. Her sharp turquoise eyes stared towards the table where Thorod sat. "Attacks in the city wouldn't be good; that would undermine everything he had carefully orchestrated, but I'm guessing there are occasional deaths *outside* the city walls." She looked back at Cerri. "They're explained away as unfortunate incidents of the victim making a mistake or disobeying safety regulations?"

Cerri nodded. "Isonver is the safest place to be. But when those who are part of leadership get in my father's way, they risk their family and friends taking an unfortunate walk outside the walls of Isonver."

"The families are political hostages," Magos said, his voice hard. "And if that doesn't work, he figures out how to exile their loved ones from this realm."

"Brutal." Mikhail took a swig of ale. "But effective."

"We didn't understand how he did it," Cerri said. "How he orchestrated that attack on Elfur. But if he truly is working with who you think, then that would explain it."

"It would," I said grimly. "If anyone knew how to control devourers, it would be Balor."

"That attack was over fifty years ago," Cerri murmured. "That means he's been working with the fae king for far longer than you all thought."

"Good. Fifty years is a long time to keep a secret." Pele

smiled sharply. "If we can find proof of his alliance with Balor and of his orchestration of the slaughter at Elfur, any dragons who are on the fence will come to our side."

"It will also force his hand," Mikhail pointed out. "We don't know what other fun surprises he might have in store for us, beyond his ability to control the devourers of this realm."

"We'll continue to gather information. Carefully." Pele glanced at the drunk dragons and gave Cerri a speculative look. "You said there are dinners like this for the next three nights?"

I smirked as two very drunk, very angry dragons took a swing at each other and both missed by a mile. One crashed into a table, and the other punched a different dragon in the back of the head, causing them to spill their ale. A brawl broke out, and dragons from across the room moved to either join in or drunkenly cheer the participants on.

"If the next three nights are like this, it will definitely provide us with a good opportunity to do some snooping." I looked over the fighting mass of dragons. "Unfortunately, Thorod doesn't seem like the type to get drunk and party all night."

"He's not," Cerri agreed. "But it's also unlikely he'll leave the dining hall early. I'm not sure if the next three nights will be quite this rowdy. The tournament bouts don't have to be to the death, but they can be. Since my father is the one throwing the tournament, he gets to decide whether the loser lives or dies."

I watched Eddie's face carefully, but he gave no signs of being upset by the tournament. "It doesn't upset you at all?" Cerri's bright green eyes met mine, and she arched an eyebrow. "Your father bartering off your hand in marriage like this?"

"Trying," she said lightly. "He's trying to give me away in marriage. I've foiled all his previous attempts."

"Did you have a plan this time around?"

She took a deep gulp of ale. "Not exactly."

I snorted, but before I could tease her more about it and see if I could get Eddie to reveal whatever he was really thinking, Thorod slammed his mug down repeatedly on his table. Within seconds, the too-loud drunken conversations and jeering from those watching the brawlers died as all eyes fell on Thorod.

He took his time ambling to the center of the room. A cruel smile spread across his face as he gestured towards his daughter.

"Join me, Cerridwyn."

With a rigid back, Cerri rose and stood beside her father. She looked so small next to his massive frame, but the fire that burned in her eyes was anything but weak. I slid a glance to Eddie. He'd swung his legs over the bench so he was facing Thorod and casually leaned his back against the table. A dragon in repose.

What are you up to? I pushed the thought towards him.

Me? His lips quirked upward ever so slightly. *I'm here, supporting you all in this foolish plan to save the dragons from themselves.*

That's not all you're doing.

Well, I have to do something to keep myself entertained while the rest of you are plotting or snooping.

Eddie . . .

Before I could question him further, my attention was drawn back to Thorod and Cerri. Seven dragons were kneeling in front of them in the center of the room. I recognized Vizor and Tal but only vaguely knew who the others were. These must be the dragons participating in the tournament.

"I thought there were eight," I said.

Eddie looked at me innocently, and I tensed.

He didn't.

Of all the stupid things to do, he couldn't possibly have

done what I feared he did. "If Cerri doesn't kill you, I will," I ground out.

Before I could stop him, Eddie rose and walked with languid steps to where the others were kneeling.

"Well, this can't be good," Mikhail murmured.

Pele and Magos didn't say anything, but neither of them looked all that surprised by this turn of events. Cerri, however, looked alarmed as she watched her lover approach.

Thorod scanned the room, clearly looking for someone before his gaze stopped on Eddie. Instead of being angry, he looked amused. *Shit.* I should have tackled Eddie when I had the chance. Now all I could do was watch as my friend made a play that would likely get him killed.

"Looks like you're one dragon short," Eddie drawled from where he had stopped just shy of the others. "Lucky for you, I'm here to announce my intent to enter and compete for the right to marry Cerridwyn."

"You will do no such thing!" Cerri snapped. Fear shone in her eyes, and she looked like she wanted to grab Eddie and run. "You can't compete," she tried. "You were exiled from this realm."

"I was officially declared a guest this morning," Eddie said calmly. "I checked the records. We allowed the fae to compete in various tournaments when they passed through our realms."

"That explains where he was all afternoon," Mikhail said.

I tapped my claws against the table. Eddie had disappeared for a bit that afternoon before Cerri came back with lunch. I'd assumed he'd snuck out to have nice little tryst with his lover whom he hadn't seen in years. But apparently, he'd been plotting, and probably murdering whoever the missing dragon was.

"You cannot do this, Eddie," Cerri pleaded. She took a step forward, but her father's arm shot out and stopped her from going any further. "Please—"

"Nonsense," Vizor cut her off, looking over his shoulder

from where he was still kneeling. "Let the boy compete. It'll be fun." He gave Eddie a razor-sharp smile.

Cerri paled, looking quickly between her father, Vizor, and Eddie, clearly trying to come up with some way out of this. But given the satisfied look on Thorod's face, there was no going back.

Eddie met that predatory smile with one of his own. "I've always wanted to wipe that smug grin off your face, Vizor. Might as well take the entire head off."

"Enough," Thorod said, his voice booming across the hall. "Eydellan will take the spot of Gorlois. Rise." The seven dragons stood, and Eddie fell in line with them. "In three days, one of you shall be declared worthy enough to marry my daughter. Some of you will be dead long before then."

"We all know which one that will be," a dark-haired dragon with harsh features said with a laugh.

He was the largest of the contenders by far. He wasn't as tall as Thorod, but he was broader and practically muscle layered on muscle. His shoulders and neck were so thick it was hard to tell where one ended and the other began.

Cerri's father clasped the dragon on the shoulder. "Morholt, you never were one to mince words. I have no bearing on the outcome of this tournament, but know that I would be proud to call you son." The dragon beamed and gave Cerri a lecherous look that she pointedly ignored.

"Why didn't Eddie kill that one?" I muttered.

"Would have been harder to hide the body," Mikhail whispered back. "I don't even think that dragon has a neck."

I snickered. He wasn't wrong. I briefly wondered what the dragon would look like in his true form. Eddie was big but had a sleek and fast build. Something told me Morholt's dragon form would be a tank.

"Let us enjoy the remainder of this night!" Thorod raised a pint of ale into the air. "For some of us, it may be our last!"

Echoing cheers went up around the room as others joined in, but our group remained silent. Eddie and Cerri made their way to us, the latter's face tight with barely contained rage.

Pele looped her arm through Cerri's once she reached us. "How about we head back to the rooms? I'm feeling rather tired."

"Of course." Cerri nodded tightly. "Tomorrow will be a long day."

I tossed my arms over Eddie's shoulders, pulling him in close. "Yes, it will be." He flinched as my claws dug into his flesh. *You are so dead, dragon.*

I'll be fine, he assured me. Cerri looked back at us from where Pele was practically dragging her out of the room. Her green eyes promised murder. Eddie swallowed. *As long as I survive my love's wrath tonight . . . I'll be fine.*

Chapter Twelve

"I'm going to kill you!" Cerri launched herself at Eddie as soon as the doors to our room shut. Eddie nimbly slid out of the way, but Cerri kept coming. He ducked one of her blows but wasn't fast enough to dodge the next she viciously sank into his stomach.

He doubled over and sank to his knees, vomiting some of the ale he'd been drinking all night.

"Gross." I took a step back and gave Cerri an appraising look. For a small thing, she packed one hell of a punch.

"My love—" Eddie started.

"Don't you 'my love' me!" Cerri screamed and kicked him in the ribs.

Eddie groaned as he curled up in the fetal position. "I think you broke some ribs." He clutched his hands to his stomach. "And possibly punctured an organ."

"I'll do more than that, you piece—"

Magos grabbed Cerri as she pulled her foot back to kick Eddie again. She shrieked in rage as he wrapped his arms around her and easily held her off the ground. We waited a few minutes for her to settle down, none of us bothering to help Eddie off the floor.

"You can put me down now," Cerri said with an eerie calmness that would have been more believable if her expression wasn't still promising murder.

Slowly, Magos set her down and backed a few steps away but remained close enough to intervene if she went for Eddie again.

"Care to explain yourself, Eddie?" I asked. "There was no reason for you to join the tournament. I know it sucks to watch Cerri get auctioned off like a prize cow." I cut a look at Cerri. "No offense. But it's not like we would have actually allowed it to happen. Three days. We were gonna be out of here in three days!"

Eddie pushed himself up to a seated position and wiped his mouth. "Do you really think your father wouldn't have attempted to kill me in the next three days?" He looked at Cerri, whose mouth tightened into a hard line. "I can't concentrate on protecting you and keeping the damn daemon alive if I also have to worry about your father trying to rip my head off or send one of his cronies to slit my throat in my sleep. The only thing that would make your father happier than my brutal death would be my very *public* brutal death."

"Right," Cerri bit out. "So your brilliant plan to stay alive is entering a tournament where each bout is potentially to the death and several of your opponents have been wanting to tear you apart for years? That is your plan?"

"Do you have so little faith in me?"

The rage in Cerri's eyes slipped as fear shone through. "I won't watch you die."

Eddie closed the distance between them and wrapped his arms around her. "You won't, I promise," he murmured into her hair. He pulled back and looked her in the eyes. "We will survive this. You and me. Always."

"Always," she whispered back.

"I still think you're an idiot for doing this," I said. Eddie and Cerri looked at me. I shrugged. "Just wanted to make that clear. Anyone else think Eddie is an idiot?"

Only Pele raised her hand.

"Really?" I arched an eyebrow at Magos. "I get Mikhail, he's also an idiot. But I thought you would have more sense than this."

Magos's copper eyes lit with amusement. "Eddie's assessment of Thorod was right. I've seen the way that man has been watching him since we arrived. Eddie is now the safest one in our group, outside the arena. Thorod will not miss out on an opportunity to kill him in such a public manner, which means he only has to worry about straightforward attacks instead of ones to the back."

"Whatever." I cocked my head towards the door. "Someone's coming."

"It's probably Lynette," Cerri said. "She was serving tonight, and I asked her to fill me in on anything she picked up."

"She's your spy?" Pele asked.

"I suppose you could call her that. The other dragons are often careless around her because she can't hear, but it's amazing what you can pick up based on body language alone, and Lynette is excellent at it. Her father is one of my father's fiercest allies, and Lynette plays the timid, doting daughter well."

"Definitely better than you," Eddie said with a grin.

The door swung open, and Lynette slipped inside. She halted once again at seeing all of us, eyes skimming over us warily.

Mikhail stepped forward. *Hello*, his fingers signed with practiced ease. He'd asked Cerri for some basic words and phrases over lunch, and both he and Magos had spent some time practicing.

Hello, Lynette signed back with a shy smile.

The rest of us fumbled through some greetings, Lynette's smile growing as she gently corrected some of our signing. We moved over to the seating area. Eddie tugged Cerri down onto the chaise lounge with him while Pele and Lynette perched on some of the other chairs. I eyed the hidden door along the back wall.

Mikhail followed my gaze. "What are you thinking, shifter?"

"I'm thinking the night is still young, and I have no interest in sitting in this room while those four plot and gossip. They can give us the highlights when we get back."

"It would be nice to get a lay of the land," Magos agreed. "Most of the dragons in the city will be sleeping, so if we move about quietly, no one will see us."

"Will you be all right, Pele?" I asked.

"I'll be fine." She waved towards the hidden passageway. "Just be careful and don't cause any trouble."

"I would never."

Pele let out a long-suffering sigh, and I snickered as I ran my fingers along the back wall where Cerri had earlier. A soft click sounded, and the door slid back. I scrunched up my nose as the musty air hit my nostrils.

"Left or right?" Mikhail asked.

"Right. We'll wind through the citadel and then come out by the garden." I took a step inside and peered down the tunnel. "One of you will need to lead. As soon as this door closes, it's going to be pitch-black, and I'll be as blind as Eddie."

"I'm not that blind at night," the dragon grumbled.

"You really are," I called back over my shoulder.

"I'll go first," Magos said, stepping past me into the passageway.

"Want me to hold your hand?" Mikhail grinned at me.

I flipped him off and started after Magos, leaving Mikhail to close the door behind us.

As we silently made our way in the dark, I wondered if I should have stayed behind to plot and plan with the others. Was that what was expected of me as the Unseelie Knight? I'd had the title for less than a week, and I had no idea what exactly my duties were. The more I thought about my new position among the fae, the more my frustration grew. By the time we made it to the end of the passageway, I was ready to claw my way out of it and find something to fight just to blow off some steam.

I could vaguely make out Magos's broad form in front of me. A soft creak sounded, and a narrow door popped inward. Faint moonlight and fresh air flowed in, and I took a deep breath.

Magos looked at me, worried eyes scanning my face. "Are you all right?"

"Peachy," I grumbled. "Let's go find something to kill."

I squeezed past him and out of the tunnel, quickly scanning the area. As Cerri had said, this side of the passageway ended in a garden. I took a deep breath of the cool, crisp night air. It felt good to be outside after being inside the stone walls of the citadel all day.

"So, this is what passes for a garden around here?" Mikhail sidled up next to me, making no comment about my obvious pissy mood.

"Given the dry, hot climate, it makes sense," Magos said. "I kind of like it. It's simple but resilient."

"That's a nice way of putting it," I said.

This garden was a far cry from the bright and wild ones of the fae realms. The few trees had oddly disjointed branches with thin, prickly leaves. Sparse bushes grew randomly here and there, and large, weathered trunks of trees that had either failed to survive the harsh climate or had been cut down were lying on their sides to provide places to sit. Perhaps the garden looked better in the daylight hours. At night, the branches from the trees looked like skeletal hands reaching towards the dark sky.

I turned around and studied the citadel. Cerri promised to take us on a walk through the city during the day, but I'd been curious about how the citadel looked from the outside. The city sat on top of two mesas; we were on the lower one. The citadel was built into the taller mesa. With its stone walls and spiraling towers, it looked impenetrable.

"I think it would look better with a moat," I declared.

"Not every castle needs a moat," Mikhail replied.

"No, Nemain's right," Magos said. "It needs a moat. And a drawbridge with a portcullis at the entrance."

A few lights flickered on the top levels of the citadel, where I assumed most of the dragon leadership lived, but otherwise it was mostly dark. Some flashes of movement told me where the guards were posted, high on the citadel towers.

I turned away from the scene and walked around aimlessly. Mikhail started to follow after me, but Magos stopped him. They spoke too softly for me to hear, but I imagined Magos was telling Mikhail to give me some space. I appreciated the gesture as I breathed in the crisp night air, trying to let my frustrations over my new title fade, at least for a little while.

Buildings made of sandy brown stone lined the other three sides of the garden. Most of them were dark, but I spotted a few dimly lit torches. From what we'd learned from Cerri over dinner, there was an unofficial curfew after sunset. Dragons were advised to stay indoors at night unless they had a valid reason to be wandering around.

The threat of devourer attacks was real to the surviving

dragons of this city, and I suspected Thorod and others wielded that fear as a political weapon.

My footsteps were silent as I wandered the garden, getting close to the center where a large tree stood. No leaves adorned its branches. The tree had clearly died long ago, but they'd left it standing for some reason.

The feeling of being watched made the hair on the back of my neck stand up, and I halted. A form peeled away from behind the tree, moonlight spilling across their features as they stood in front of me.

Vizor.

"I find it hard to believe Cerri didn't advise you against wandering around after dark. All sorts of dangers lurk in the night." His tone was light, but there was no mistaking the threat.

"Do they?" I tilted my head towards the moonlight, knowing my eyes would reflect the light in an unsettling sheen. "Tell me more about these monsters."

"The arrogance of you and your friends is astounding. You're in a city full of beings who could burn you alive with barely a thought or shift and swallow you whole." He studied me as if I were an interesting bug he'd trapped under a glass. "And yet you stand here, acting as if you present any sort of threat to me. You are alone in my city. Perhaps you should take more care."

"*Your* city?" I chuckled. "I don't think Thorod would like you referring to it as such. And what makes you think I'm alone?"

Vizor flinched a second before Magos's knife dug into his neck. He went still beneath the blade, and for the first time, I saw a hint of emotion on his face. Not fear. Surprise. Vizor wasn't used to someone being able to sneak up on him.

"I expected you to bring the daemon for protection so you

could hide behind her fire," he said calmly as blood trickled down his neck.

"Fire against a dragon?" I scoffed. "Tell me, Vizor, exactly what made you think any of us were fools?"

Magos withdrew the blade and moved to my side. He tucked the dagger away and clasped his hands behind his back in what I had dubbed his polite, non-threatening pose. I also knew he could summon his sword in less than a second and cut through any attack. The pose was a trap. One I really hoped Vizor would fall for, but based on the way he was eyeing Magos with a new sense of caution, I didn't think I'd be so lucky.

Mikhail was nowhere to be seen, which was good. Vizor was likely moving up the threat level of the vampires, but he still had no idea what they were truly capable of.

"Why are you here?" Vizor asked, not bothering to wipe away the blood dripping down his neck.

"Enjoying a midnight stroll." I gave him a lazy grin.

"Not here in the garden," Vizor snapped. "Here in this realm. Why now?"

"Pele explained everything this morning," I said in a bored tone. "Were you too busy planning out your next barbed question to pay attention to what was being discussed?"

"I know there is more going on than what we've been told. The daemons haven't simply had a change of heart. There's a reason you're here *now*, and I will find out what that reason is."

"Where exactly do your allegiances lie?" I cocked my head to the side. "Most of your generation seemed to be inclined to believe Pele and want out of this realm. You're not part of their faction, but you're not one of Thorod's sycophants, either. Despite all your questions this afternoon, it's still not really clear whose side you're on and what you want."

"I'm on my own side," Vizor said flatly. "No one else matters."

"Shocking." I shrugged. "We're going to continue our walk. Lovely chatting with you."

We turned our backs on him and walked away, trusting Mikhail to keep an eye on the dragon in case he tried anything. I didn't think he would, though. Vizor was too smart to attack us when we were expecting it. He'd strike from the shadows when his victory was more guaranteed.

"Thoughts?" I asked, keeping my voice low. Magos didn't openly scheme like the rest of my friends, but he was incredibly observant, and I liked to compare my own internal notes against his.

"Whatever game he's playing, it's his own," he said. "He didn't expect us to actually answer his questions, but perhaps he thought we might accidentally let something slip without Pele here."

"He could still be working with Thorod while also furthering his own agenda. He seems more in line with Thorod and his ilk than the other younger dragons," I said.

Magos hummed in agreement, and we continued our meandering pace, each lost in our own thoughts. Vizor was definitely a problem, and his unknown allegiances bothered me. I'm sure they bothered Pele even more.

We made a large loop around the garden. Mikhail remained unseen, but I sensed him drifting closer to us. The magic Mikhail and Magos used to turn into mist was familiar enough to me now that I could almost always feel it when they were near.

Slowly, I let some of my devourer magic out to explore the area. Remembering everything Kalen had taught me, I released the invisible threads to wind around. The tendrils couldn't be used for defense or any sort of attack, but they would allow me to get a broad sense of what type of magic was in the area. Specifically, if any devourers were nearby. If Thorod or Vizor were working with Balor, it stood to reason some of the sidhe devourers had come to this realm, perhaps even to this very city.

We made a few laps in companionable silence while I looked for traces of any other magic. The tall, ghostly tree at the center of the garden came into view, and I angled towards it so I could get a better look.

"It feels strange to be somewhere where night isn't bustling with activity," I said. "I don't think I've ever been somewhere this quiet at night. I suppose I'll have to adjust if I start spending more time in the fae realms."

"Think of all the extra sneaking around you can do while everyone is sleeping."

"Excellent point," I said with a laugh. "I wonder if—"

A cold, hungry feeling ran up one of my threads.

"What is it?" Magos asked, eyes scanning the houses, looking for whatever threat I sensed.

"I think we're about to meet one of the devourers Eddie told us about. The trakdi." I listened closely for any hints of alarm in the city but heard nothing. "Either it managed to sneak past the guards posted at the perimeter of the mesa, or someone let it through on purpose."

"It would be a convenient way to take us out and keep their hands clean."

"I'll draw its attention to give you and Mikhail an opening."

With a curt nod, Magos vanished into mist. I moved farther into the garden so it couldn't corner me against the stone walls of the houses and to give me more time to study our new friend. It crept forward, unnervingly quiet despite its size.

Eddie's description had been accurate enough, but seeing the trakdi in person was something else. It had the build and grace of a lupine creature and was around ten feet at the shoulder. Its long head hung low in front of it, oversized teeth fully on display in its narrow jaw. The dark quills covering its body were flat and almost looked like scales from this angle. I'd encountered a lot of devourer species in my travels across different realms. This was definitely one of the largest ones I'd ever seen. But it moved quietly and carefully, even keeping its long tail off the ground so it didn't drag.

My magic had given us an early warning to its presence, but we were still too far away from the citadel or our secret entrance to make a run for it. My devourer magic was useless against other devourers, and I was too slow at opening gateways to make use of that tactic. This would be a fight of fangs and claws against swords and daggers.

I was thankful Pele had remained inside the citadel walls. She wasn't bad with her daggers, but she spent her time dealing with politics. Her fire was usually enough of a weapon to keep any physical threats at bay. But her fire was useless in this realm, making her the weakest of our group in a fight. I had to hope that we were the only ones under attack and that whoever was behind this hadn't sent someone else after the others.

Mist swirled slightly behind the trakdi as Mikhail and Magos snapped into existence. They moved to flank the devourer, and it let out a low, rumbling growl.

Even with three-to-one odds, I wasn't loving this. This thing was massive, and it would take us forever to cut through those quills. We needed to find a weak spot, and for that I needed to distract it so the vampires could study it more. Pain was an excellent distraction.

Sprinting towards the devourer, I lunged at the last possible second to avoid its crocodilian jaws closing on me and sliced across its nose. Even its face was covered by short quills, but my strike managed to draw blood. A deep growl tore out of it as it focused on me and gave chase. Its long tail whipped around it, forcing Mikhail back. Magos struck at the beast's left flank, swinging his sword at an angle that split through the raised quills and cut deep into flesh. Instead of whirling to face the new threat, the trakdi's eyes remained locked on me. Apparently, I'd really pissed it off with that strike to its nose.

I barely managed to leap back and avoid the snap of its jaws but wasn't fast enough to dodge its claws. Its front paw slammed into me, sending me flying backwards even as the claws tore through my clothes and flesh.

My back slammed into the trunk of the dead tree, and I dove to the side on pure instinct as the tail collided into the trunk a second later. Bits of bark flew off the tree, and I whirled, putting the trunk between me and the devourer. Pain flooded my senses as my shifter healing kicked in, closing the wounds left by the claws and healing what had to be several cracked ribs.

I'd lost both of my swords when the tail struck me, and breathing hurt. The beast snarled as Mikhail and Magos harried it, giving me time to recover.

The fact that no guards had shown up confirmed my suspicions that the devourer had purposely been let through the perimeter. No one would be coming to help us. That was fine. We could deal with one damn devourer ourselves. I pushed myself up from where I'd been crouching, wincing as my body reminded me it was still very much healing, and peeked around the trunk.

My swords lay on the ground, and the devourer stood between me and them. Magos was bleeding from a head wound, and Mikhail was favoring his right leg. I needed my damn swords.

Taking a few steadying breaths, I concentrated on opening a gateway between here and my swords. My magic rushed up, and I gritted my teeth, pushing it back and trying again. Once again, too much of my magic poured out. *Shit.* I didn't understand how Badb did this so effortlessly. She could open gateways in a fight repeatedly, and I couldn't even do it one damn time to get my swords.

"Uncle!" Mikhail barked out a warning.

The trakdi's back leg kicked out and hit Magos right in the stomach, sending him crashing to the ground. A second later, its tail pinned him to the ground. Mikhail leapt, landing at the base of the creature's neck where the quills weren't long enough to pierce him, and shoved his blade towards the trakdi's spine.

The devourer reared up, and Mikhail's strike went deep but missed severing the spine. He lost his grip on the sword and hit the ground, rolling a second before the trakdi's body would have slammed into him. Mikhail continued rolling to get clear and jumped to his feet, now weaponless, and faced the trakdi.

This time when it lunged for him, he turned to mist and reappeared seconds later where I'd dropped my swords. Somehow, the trakdi had anticipated this and swung its tail, forcing Mikhail to leave the weapons behind.

I moved in front of the tree and let my devourer magic out. Blue flames formed in front of me, and I wielded them into a shield of crystal blue flame. *Here's hoping this works.* With a flick of my wrist, one of the daggers in my bracers slid free, and I hurled it at the trakdi. The blade sunk home, piercing the beast's eye, and it bellowed in pain and lunged at me.

I braced myself against the tree and sank more of my magic into the shield. The trakdi crashed against me, and my magic immediately started to fade. Kalen had warned me about this. We couldn't wield our devourer magic against other devourers. Even using it in defense like this was challenging because our magic revolted at being so close, like two sides of a magnet being forced together.

The trakdi reared back, opening its jaws wide and snapping them closed around me. The tree groaned from the pressure, and my shield slipped a little more.

I had nowhere to go. Rows of teeth closed in around me, gaining ground inch by inch. Claws tore at the front of my shield, and it gave a little more. I screamed when one tore into my thigh. It was taking all of my concentration to keep what was left of the shield in place. I had to hope Mikhail and Magos made the most of this distraction before the devourer shredded me to pieces.

The beast bellowed in rage and shifted its bite around the tree, the long, jagged teeth inches away from my face. Its rancid breath made me want to vomit, but I continued pouring my magic into the shield.

"Now would be a great time for you to do something!" I screamed.

"We're trying!" Mikhail yelled back, something like fear and desperation in his voice.

The jaws ripped free of the tree. My shield fell apart at the same instant, and one tooth snagged my shoulder as the trakdi flung itself wildly around, letting out an earth-shattering bellow.

I crashed to my knees, and the devourer stumbled a few more steps before collapsing to its side. Magos's sword was buried in its one remaining eye. Mist swirled around the sword, and it vanished, only to reappear in Magos's hand. He strode over to the trakdi and thrust the sword into the beast's head once more. It lay still and didn't move. Ideally, we would also cut off its head or tear out its heart, but it seemed to be truly dead. The dragons could deal with it from there.

I hissed through my teeth as I shoved myself up. Blood poured from my shoulder and thigh, plus a number of other places. Mikhail stared at the trakdi and then at the sword Magos still held before whirling away and retrieving the sword he'd dropped and mine. When he came over to me and handed me the twin swords, I took them from him, one at a time, and slid them into the sheaths on my back. My right arm needed more time before it could handle any movement.

"Did you try?" I asked quietly.

Mikhail's jaw flexed as he stared at the damage the beast's jaws had done to the tree. Grooves lined both sides, cutting deep into the trunk. I'd been seconds away from finding out what those jaws would have done to my body.

He knew what I was asking. Mikhail had a mist sword, like Magos. It meant he was never weaponless. Even if someone took it from him or if he lost it in a fight, like he had lost his regular sword in this one, he could summon it again.

But Mikhail no longer believed he was worthy of the sword and hadn't summoned it in centuries. He believed he couldn't anymore.

I believed he wouldn't.

"It won't come to me," Mikhail replied. When I opened my mouth to argue, he cut me off. "Leave it, Nemain."

"Fine," I said, my expression making it clear we were not done with this conversation. I nodded towards the citadel entrance where dragons were finally coming out to investigate. *How nice of them to wait until the devourer was dead.* "Let's deal with the aftermath of this and get back to our rooms. I need a few hours of rest before whatever fun stuff tomorrow brings."

"I still can't believe they're going with the 'oops, our guard fell asleep while on watch and the trakdi just *happened* to sneak in at that moment' excuse." My mouth twisted in annoyance. "Thorod and his goons could have at least been more creative about it."

"There's no reason for them to come up with anything more elaborate," Pele said from where she was leaning against the wall back in our suite. "It's not like we can do anything about it. Luckily you all came out unscathed, and Thorod won't be able to pull that move again. While others on the dragon leadership might be skeptical, they can't prove one way or another what happened. But a trakdi sneaking by all the guards *again* would be too suspicious."

"True." I sighed. "He'll have to use other means of attack if he wants to take us out of the picture, and they'll likely be a lot more devious."

"The city population is really upset about a devourer making it past the guards," Cerri said. "Patrols have been increased, which means any type of similar attack is unlikely. My father will likely try to target you while you're alone and simply make you disappear. Explaining your deaths at this point would be too messy."

Magos eyed the wall that hid the secret passage. I walked over to one of the tables and grabbed one end, and he grabbed the other. We walked it over to the wall and placed it in front of the hidden doorway, then proceeded to move a few chairs and other objects in front of it as well.

"It won't block anyone from accessing the door." I carefully put a few empty ceramic jugs onto the chairs and tables, placing them so that they would fall with the slightest movement. "But it'll give us a heads up if anyone tries. We should still sleep in shifts, though, and have someone on guard at all time."

Everyone nodded in agreement. A yawn escaped my lips before I could hide it.

"I'll take first watch." Pele waved everyone off. "There are some documents I want to review anyway."

"You sure?" I asked. "I can stay up with you if you want."

"No offense, Nemain, but you're not capable of sitting still, and you'd just annoy me."

"Rude," I muttered before glancing at Eddie, who was getting to his feet with the help of Cerri. "You good?"

"Never better." He wiped off some of the lingering smears of blood from his wrist. "Who wouldn't enjoy being snacked on by those two gorgeous bastards."

Magos's lips pressed into a flat line. "I wish you wouldn't have phrased it like that, but thank you for allowing us to drink from you."

"That still sounds so wrong." Cerri shook her head and steered Eddie towards the bedroom he was using. Magos looked at Mikhail and I for a long moment before disappearing into his room.

"I'm going to rinse off and climb into bed," Mikhail said casually before sauntering off into the room we were sharing. I stared after him as horror dawned on me. With everything that had happened over the last few hours, I'd forgotten about the whole one bed thing.

Shit. Fuck. Shit fuck.

"Maybe I should stay with yo—"

"No," Pele cut me off. "Go to bed, Nemain."

I bit my lip and thought over my options. If I got in bed with Mikhail, it was over. Even my stubbornness had a limit, and being in bed with that vampire was well past that limit. He wouldn't even have to do anything. He could just lie on his side and keep his hands to himself, and I'd still be tearing my clothes off within five minutes.

But I couldn't just stay out here all night either. He'd come looking for me, and even if he didn't, Pele would definitely kick me out. She was rapidly skimming through documents that Cerri had dropped off, and she would have zero patience for my bullshit right now.

The sound of falling water came from our bedroom, and all my thoughts immediately went to Mikhail being naked beneath running water right now. An ache started between my thighs, and I became acutely aware of how much dirt and dried blood was still on me. I could use a shower right about now, as well.

No. Bad Nemain.

Before I could give into temptation, I tore off my weapons and clothes, shucking them to the floor. Pele's eyes lifted from the page she was reading, and she watched me strip without comment.

I shot her a look that dared her to comment, and she just gave me a lazy grin in return. Worst best friend ever. Kaysea would have been so much more supportive about this. Maybe. Probably. Like fifty percent more supportive.

Dropping to all fours, I cracked my neck as the shift swept through me. Once it was done, I shook my golden brown fur and huffed in Pele's direction before carefully picking up the sheathed death dagger in my jaws and trotting into the bedroom.

I nudged the door shut and leapt into the bed. Once I tucked the knife under the pillow, I sprawled across the mattress, taking up as much space as my five-hundred-pound form would allow.

A few minutes later, the water shut off, and a still damp Mikhail emerged wearing a loose-fitting pair of pants that hung dangerously low on his hips.

"Really?" He laughed.

I just made a chuffing sound at him even though I was perfectly capable of communicating telepathically in this form. My jaws opened wide as another yawn escaped me.

Mikhail rolled his eyes and walked over to the bed, clearly trying to figure out where he could fit. I lazily flipped my tail back and forth. I closed my eyes. He could sleep on the floor for all I cared.

Strong hands shoved me over, and I snapped my teeth inches from Mikhail's face. He booped me on the nose and I blinked.

He. Booped. Me. On. The. Nose.

While I laid there in stunned silence, he took advantage and claimed more of the bed. Soon, he was lying on his back, one of his sides tucked up against me, while he rested his head on the pillow like he didn't have a care in the world.

"Night, shifter."

I stared at him, outrage still running through me. Then one of his hands ran along my coat once. Twice. Actually, that felt kind of nice. I lowered my head and let him continue stroking me. I could always eat him in the morning.

Chapter Thirteen

"This is the most delicious thing I've ever had in my mouth." I popped another piece of spicy, seasoned meat between my lips.

Mikhail stumbled while Eddie and Pele let out low laughs. I smirked while I licked all my fingers clean, one by one, well aware of Mikhail watching the moment carefully. I considered it payback for all the teasing he'd been giving me all morning.

He'd been stretched out beside me when I woke up with a stupid grin on his face. It'd taken me a moment to realize why. At some point in the night, I'd shifted back and had apparently stolen all the blankets... and cuddled up next to him and started purring. I hardly *ever* purred while wearing my human skin, but just like when I was in feline form, I couldn't control it. It just sort of happened.

I'd jumped out of that bed like it was on fire and had immediately headed for the washroom. Mikhail had found the entire thing very amusing.

The morning session of the dragon leadership had ended shortly before lunch, and we still had a few hours until the first tournament bouts began, so Cerri offered to give us a tour around the city. Our first stop had been at the market because I'd smelled the delicious spices and followed my nose until I found them. The vendors at the market had been wary of us, but that didn't stop them from taking Cerri's money as she bought us all lunch.

I glanced at Eddie, who was chowing down on his third stick of meat. "You sure you're up for fighting today? You should have let Cerri give the vampires blood last night."

"Look, I'm very confident in my looks"—some juice from the meat dribbled down his chin—"but no one is secure enough in their relationship to let those two gorgeous hunks of man flesh drink from their lover." Magos looked embarrassed, but Mikhail just grinned without a trace of humility. "Besides," Eddie continued, "I had a good, long nap, and now I'm full of food. I'm more than ready for the first bout."

"You still should have let me feed them," Cerri said tightly. If Eddie was worried about the day, he was hiding it well, but Cerri had been growing more tense by the hour.

Eddie wiped his mouth with the back of his hand and gripped Cerri by the waist, lifting her up in a spin. "My love, you have no idea how intoxicating a vampire's bite can be. I was barely able to restrain myself, and you know I only have eyes for you." Eddie put Cerri down and spun her away from him as she laughed. His eyes fell on me, and a mischievous smile spread across his lips. "Nemain knows all too well what it's like. Why don't you tell Cerri all about that time you let Mikhail feed off you? You naughty shifter."

Pele snickered as she moved beside Cerri. I felt Mikhail's heated gaze on me but refused to look at him. The memory of Mikhail biting me and us making out against a tree had graced my dreams more than once, and if I looked at him, I feared he would somehow know that.

"Are you trying to die before the tournament? Because I

can make that happen." I slipped a dagger free from the hidden sheath in my bracers."

"Always with the threats." Eddie rolled his eyes. "We both know you'd never—OWWW!"

My dagger sank into his shoulder. "I'm sorry, you were saying?"

"Rude, Nemain." Eddie ripped the dagger out of his shoulder. His dragon healing was fast, and I'd deliberately aimed for a spot where I wouldn't hit anything vital. "That was totally uncalled for."

"It was a little called for." Cerri held up her hand, spacing her index finger and thumb an inch apart. Eddie placed his hand over his heart and gave her a hurt expression. She rolled her eyes at him. "Need I remind you that you *volunteered* to be in a tournament against a bunch of dragons who very much want to kill you?"

Eddie scoffed. "Only half of them want to kill me. The other half are indifferent to my existence."

"Speaking of being indifferent to your existence. . ." I held my hand out, and Eddie shot me a dirty look but returned my dagger. "The tournament starts in less than two hours. Shouldn't you go and get ready?"

"That's probably what Lynnette is here for." Eddie waved brightly at the auburn-haired young woman. In the sunlight, her hair had bright golden streaks.

She gestured towards the blood that had soaked through his shirt, and he rapidly and dramatically signed something back to her. It was too fast for me to begin to follow, but I got the gist of it when Lynette grinned and made a few quick gestures and held her palms up in the air.

"Wow," Eddie replied, giving her the same hurt expression he'd given Cerri earlier. "I didn't expect you to betray me so harshly, Lynette." I paid attention to his hands as he spoke, trying to match up the gestures with the words. It had been a while since I'd learned a new skill that wasn't fighting or magic related, and I found it rather fun.

Lynette looped her arm through Eddie's, not the least bit swayed by his pouty expression, and waved goodbye to all of us. The amusement she'd been feeling moments before slipped from Cerri's face as she watched them walk away.

"He'll be fine," I told her, trying to convey as much confidence as possible.

Eddie wasn't a pushover by any means, but I'd only seen him fight against fae where he had a distinct advantage. Their magic didn't work against him, and once he got the ability to shift back to his true form, he could literally eat them in one gulp. The odds were more than in his favor in those fights. But against another dragon . . . I had no idea how my friend would fare.

I added, "Let's head back the way we came and take a different path back to the citadel."

"You just want more food." Mikhail narrowed his eyes at me.

"She always wants more food," Pele said before I could deny anything.

Cerri looked at me.

"Okay, fine. I want more food," I said.

That managed to get a smile out of her. "Okay, but let's make one stop on the way back." She pulled the knapsack she'd been carrying over her shoulder around and took out a carefully wrapped bundle. When she unfolded it, I recognized the two fangs.

"You know who they belong to?" I asked as she tucked them away again.

"Yes, but I'm not exactly sure how they came to be in a different realm."

"Well, let's find out then."

Cerri nodded and led us down a couple more streets, stopping in front of home with several large sacks of grain outside it. "Ban is a brewer. You can thank him for the honey ale."

She knocked on the door, and a few seconds later it swung open, revealing a dragon who looked a little older than Cerri and Eddie. His leather apron was well-worn, and I could smell the traces of herbs and alcohol on it.

"Cerri?" He wiped his hands on a towel while he looked us over. "I wasn't expecting you . . . or your friends."

"May we come in?" Cerri asked.

After a moment of hesitation, Ban nodded and waved us in. I glanced around the room as we entered. Simple furnishings, including a plate on a table with what looked like lunch. Based on everything I saw, it seemed Ban lived alone.

"What brings you by?" The dragon busied himself by pulling out multiple mugs and sifting through various jugs stashed on a nearby table before selecting one and pouring its contents into the glasses. "Help yourselves. This is my latest batch."

I picked up a mug and took a sip, letting out a pleased sound as the flavors exploded across my tongue.

Ban's eyes lit up as he smiled. He had a kind face, with warm brown eyes. "Never thought I'd see someone who wasn't a dragon try my brew. I'm glad you enjoy it."

"It's delicious," I said truthfully.

The others nodded their agreement as they drank their own. Ban kept glancing at Pele out of the corner of his eye, but he didn't look upset by her being there, more curious than anything.

Cerri set her bag on the table and carefully extracted the contents. Ban's jovial expression slipped from his face as she moved the fabric away. With trembling fingers, he reached out and touched the fangs. He squeezed his eyes shut, tears leaking out of the corners. "Bors," he whispered.

"What happened, Ban?" Cerri asked gently. "How did he get out of this realm? He wasn't exiled."

"No." He inhaled a deep breath and opened his eyes, letting his fingers rest next to the fangs but not touching them. "Our parents died when we were young. Our aunt raised us. Her and her wife. This was long before the fall of Elfur, when a few small villages were still trying to survive outside the cities." He stared at the fangs for a long moment and poured himself some honey ale, taking a deep drink. "My aunt was Olwen."

Cerri stared at him in stunned silence. The rest of us looked at each other, not getting the significance of the name. Lynette tapped Cerri on the shoulder and pointed at me. "You remember the older female dragon that spoke up during that first meeting?" she asked.

Pele nodded. "Dindrane."

"Olwen and Dindrane were married once. But they've been estranged for some time now." Cerri's eyebrows furrowed. "Olwen was one of my father's most outspoken critics within our leadership. He exiled her two years ago on the grounds that she was plotting a sabotage of some supply lines to undermine his authority. He provided several documents as proof."

"The documents were bullshit," Ban said tightly. "Most of them were completely made up, and others he twisted the meaning of."

"Dindrane didn't stop him," Cerri said. "Why didn't she speak in Olwen's defense?"

A hollow laugh rang from Ban's lips. "What would that have accomplished, Cerri? You know your father better than anyone. He probably would have banished Dindrane as well. They were never estranged, still loved each other as fiercely as they did centuries ago. But Olwen was worried about Thorod using that love as a weapon. So when it became clear we would have to live in one of the cities, we all agreed to hide our relationships. My brother and I moved to a city first. No one knew who we were, so it was easy enough to hide our family history. Dindrane and Olwen staged a rather public breakup shortly after moving to Anspolis. We still found ways to see each other, but always in secret and not all that often."

"I'm so sorry," Cerri said, her eyes stricken. "My father has caused so much pain."

He reached out and squeezed her hand. "It's not your fault. None of us ever blamed you."

"Does Bors being outside the dragon realm have to do with Olwen's exile?" I asked.

"Dindrane wanted to go after her. She'd figured out how Thorod was able to punch through the spell around our realm to exile dragons. She wasn't sure if she could guarantee the exact realm, but as long as it was outside the dragon realm, she said she would find her way to whatever realm Olwen was in," Ban said. "But even in her youth, she was never a fighter. We begged her to let us go instead. I don't remember our parents at all. I was a babe when they died, and Bors wasn't much older. Dindrane and Olwen are our mothers. We owe them everything."

His voice cracked, and he looked away. We all sipped our drinks and gave him time to collect himself.

"Dindrane could only send one of us through, so we flipped for it. Bors won the coin toss." Ban swallowed. "And now he's dead."

I stared at the fangs on the table. For a second, I imagined them being smaller and feline but had to shove that thought away as my magic rumbled beneath my skin.

I'd barely survived losing my parents. While I had Badb and Kalen now, it wasn't the same. I didn't know what I would do if I lost Cian, especially in the way that Ban had lost his brother. Bors had simply had the rotten luck of landing in the seraphim realm instead of a realm where Pele might have found him first. A sad end to a sad story.

"Does Olwen have dark blond hair and icy blue eyes? Wears a plain silver ring on a chain around her neck?" Pele asked suddenly.

"Yes." Ban blinked.

"She's alive."

"What?" Cerri asked as Ban stared at Pele in shock.

"She's one of the dragons I found and have stashed in a safe house."

"Should have led with that, Pele," I murmured, shaking my head. I would never understand how Pele was so good at reading people and knowing what made them tick, but still so incredibly bad at handling emotional situations.

"Are you sure?" Ban ran his fingers through his hair. "I have to tell Dindrane. We're not supposed to meet for another couple weeks, but she has to know!"

"Easy, my friend." Cerri placed a hand on his forearm. "You've done well in keeping your family a secret from my father all this time. Don't give it away now. I'll find Dindrane and tell her, I promise."

"Okay." He gripped her hand. "Okay."

"We should be on our way," I said, downing the last of the honey ale. "If anyone asks why we stopped by, just tell them we wanted a drink."

We headed for the door, but Ban intercepted us, stepping in front of Pele and gripping her in a tight hug. "Thank you for saving my mother." She shifted uncomfortably, arms dangling at her sides. Ban released her and took a step back. "Sorry."

"It's fine." I looped an arm around Pele's shoulders. "She's not the hugging type. But she's happy she could at least help your mother."

"I can speak for myself," Pele muttered. I waited, and she sighed. "But what she said is accurate."

We took our leave of Ban and made our way back to the

market. I slowed my pace to walk beside Pele while Mikhail and Magos chatted with Cerri. "You okay?"

"Why wouldn't I be?"

I sighed. "You know you don't have to be a hardass around me all the time, right?"

"We just all but guaranteed the support of Dindrane, who is well-respected among the dragon leadership. I don't know why you think I would be anything other than ecstatic."

"Of course." I rolled my eyes. She could deny it all she wanted, but I knew Pele was happy to give at least some good news to Ban and probably felt guilty for not being able to save his brother. She carried more on her shoulders than she should, but she was loath to let anyone know that. Maybe Asmodeus would have better luck than me. "So what do you think?"

"You'll need to be more specific," she replied. "I think a lot of things. About a lot of things."

I bumped my shoulder against hers. "Don't be dense. You've heard stories about this realm your entire life. Between your family and your magic, you, more than most daemons, have a legacy tied to this realm."

"It feels wrong." Pele's black and turquoise eyes gazed over the buildings. "Everything about this realm feels wrong."

"You don't feel any kinship towards it?" I asked. "This was your home realm once."

"This was never my home. Meenri is my home. It's the realm my parents found each other and fell in love in. It's where I was born. This"—Pele waved a hand around—"is nothing like our home now. This realm is dying. It just doesn't know it."

We continued for a few minutes in silence. I studied the homes as we walked by. Their construction was simple but functional. The red clay blended in with the surroundings, but small prickly green plants were placed underneath windows.

Their bright gold flowers stood out like miniature suns. All of the houses had a patio on top, similar to the seraphim. I supposed it made sense that most flying species liked to be close to the sky.

"I understand what you mean about this realm not being home," I said. Pele glanced at me, an eyebrow raised in question. "I feel the same about the shifter realm. Even if there was a way to get rid of all the devourers and secure the realm, it would always feel strange to me to be there."

"I'm glad I've seen this realm, though," Pele said. "It feels like finally closing a door."

We turned a corner, and another empty street lay before us. Aside from the marketplace, the city had been mostly empty. I suspected most of the dragons had headed to where the tournament was being held. I seized the opportunity to ask Pele more questions; this was the first time I'd been alone with her all day.

"What's your take so far on the negotiations and our speculations about Thorod and his ilk?"

"There's no doubt in my mind that Thorod is working with Balor. I'm curious about how they came into contact to begin with and what Balor is offering. He's managed to create alliances with the warlocks and vampires, and now likely the dragons and seraphim. Impressive for someone who's locked away in his own realm."

"His people aren't, though," I pointed out. "At least, not all of them."

"True. I wish we knew more about Lir."

"Don't we all?" I muttered.

Lir was Balor's second-in-command and had come very close to tracking down Finn before we found him first. When I first encountered Lir, he'd been surprised by my magic and hinted that he knew something about my lineage. I'd asked

Kalen about him, but he didn't know why Lir would have any connection to our family.

"And the negotiations?" I asked. "I kind of tuned out this morning when y'all started talking about trade contracts."

"I suppose I should be glad you didn't fall asleep and start snoring."

"That only happened once!" I said. "And in my defense, I'd come to see you and instead you told me that you just had to make one quick stop by the Assembly. I was sitting outside that room for two hours! And it's not like you could hear me through the doors anyway."

"We totally could." Pele grinned. "Does Mikhail know you snore?"

I gave her a flat stare, and she chuckled. I did *not* snore that loudly.

"To answer your question, negotiations are going as well as can be expected. At least a third of the leadership would sign a treaty right now. There are many more who are interested, but they fear Thorod, so they're trying to appear neutral."

"He's definitely done an excellent job at making every existing dragon scared shitless of him," I agreed.

"I need to convince them that I can secure their safety, and their loved ones' safety, to sway them to our side. Thorod is the immediate threat to this, but there are other players too." Her mouth flattened into a hard line. "Vizor, for one. He bothers me a great deal."

"Because he gave that cunning tongue of yours a challenge?" I smirked.

Vizor was an annoying asshole, and I'd stab him in a heartbeat, but it was *slightly* amusing to see someone give Pele a run for her money. Still seemed likely that I'd be burying more of my places into him before this trip was over though.

"Last I checked"—she gave me a sly glance—"you appreciated my cunning tongue."

I scowled at her. "That was before you pulled the stunt you did with the bed situation.."

She shrugged. "You had it coming. Besides, it's time for you and the vampire to figure yourselves out so the rest of us don't have to stew in your emotional bullshit."

"Now is definitely not the time for us to figure our shit out!" I hissed at her. "In case you haven't noticed, we're in a realm full of beings that want to kill us and are quite possibly plotting with our enemy!"

Pele made a shushing sound. "Only half the dragons want us dead, if that. The rest want to bargain."

"That's not as comforting as you think it is."

"Please." She snorted. "We both know you're enjoying the hell out of this. Besides, when are you not dancing with death, Nemain? There will never be a good time for you to sort out your feelings for Mikhail. Might as well do it now before you potentially end up barbecued."

"I hate you."

"You love me."

"Doesn't mean I won't stab you."

Pele leaned in close. "Doesn't mean I won't *like* it."

I couldn't stop the grin that tugged at my lips as I swatted her away. "You're impossible."

"You love it." She glanced ahead towards the others and laid a hand on my arm, pulling me to a stop. "I know I've been absent lately. There were a lot of things going on that I needed to keep track of and put in motion."

"You mean when you were moving us around like chess pieces for months and then avoiding me when it was clear we knew you were up to something?"

"Yes, that." Her lips twitched in amusement. "Although to be fair, the Unseelie Queen was doing this same to me that I was doing to all of you."

"It really annoys you that she's two steps ahead of you,

doesn't it?" A low husky laugh tumbled out of me. I'd never known anyone who could outmaneuver Pele.

"Yes." She flattened her mouth into the closest expression to a pout I'd ever seen on her face, and it pulled a few more laughs out of me. "I suspected something about the dragons based on the information I'd gotten from the ones I'd been able to save after they were exiled. But I admit . . . I had no idea about the seraphim."

My laughter finally died off, and I tilted my head slightly. "Do you think she's responsible for sending that group of kids your way with the note? Maybe she knows why there are humans in the seraphim realm."

"I thought about that," she said slowly. "But I don't think the note was from her. It might be a good idea for you to ask her directly about the kids when we get back, though."

"I'll make it a formal request from a knight to their queen." I tried to keep my tone light, but it still came out with an edge to it.

"We need to concentrate on getting this treaty in place and staying alive, but when we get back, I'm here if you need to talk about the bullshit the Unseelie Queen pulled." She rested a hand on my shoulder.

"A few years ago, I was just a shifter with freaky magic and a vendetta against a warlock." I gave her a halfhearted smile "I don't even understand how I got here."

Pele shook her head. "You were never just a shifter, Nemain."

"No, I suppose not," I said with a huff. "But at least I'd been able to pretend I was at times."

"But aside from those years with Myrna"—a sharp pain struck deep within my chest even though Pele's tone was gentle —"have you ever been truly happy? You don't have to hide what you are anymore. I've known you for a long time, my friend, and you act like a weight has finally lifted off your shoulders."

"It is freeing," I admitted. "Not having to hide such a large part of myself. But being locked into service for fifty years to the Unseelie Queen isn't exactly the freedom I was hoping for."

"I understand why you're upset over the way she trapped you. But I think you'll find that being the Unseelie Knight suits you well, and we both know you'll do whatever you can to help Finn. Your fate is intertwined with his, which means your future is in the fae courts."

"Ugh." I dropped my forehead to her shoulder, and she patted me on the back of my head. "It's not fair that Kaysea managed to step out of fae politics and I ended up neck-deep in fae shit."

Pele snorted. "First, Kaysea was a princess for centuries and was deep in fae shit during all that time. Second, do you really think just because her father stepped down and the crown passed to someone else that Kaysea isn't still involved in fae politics? Ashling would never let someone as useful as Kaysea fade away. She asked her to be an advisor months ago, and Kaysea accepted after only a week."

"Really?" I lifted my head in surprise. "She never mentioned anything to me."

"Because like you, Kaysea wants a break from fae bullshit sometimes, and you were that break."

"Not anymore," I said wryly.

Pele shrugged. "We've all managed to balance our work responsibilities with our friendships for centuries. We'll figure this out."

"Thank you," I said quietly. "I'm glad we found each other all those years ago. You and Kaysea mean everything to me, and if you ever want to talk about what it means for you to take over your father's role, I'm here for you. Always."

Pele leaned her head against mine. "I'm glad we met too, shifter. Even if you do snore loud enough to shake the walls sometimes."

"Do not." I pulled back and slung my arm around her shoulder. "Now, let's go get more food and then watch some dragons beat on each other. Maybe we can find some of that honey ale, too."

"Food, drink, and violence." Pele shot me a wicked grin. "What more could a daemon ask for?"

Chapter Fourteen

"I'M PRETTY SURE this realm is hell," I complained for what was probably the tenth time in the past hour.

It had been warm during our walk around the city, but between the shade provided by the buildings and the slight breeze, it'd been bearable. The arena for the tournament had been constructed on the land below the city. It sat out in the open, which meant it was almost impossible for any trakdi to sneak up on us, but it also meant hardly any shade from the unrelenting sun. And unlike the top of the mesa, no breeze offered respite down here.

All of us were dripping sweat. Except Pele, whose skin simply soaked in the rays of the sun as if it would add to her fire. In the bright daylight, her vertical slit pupils were practically nonexistent, making her eyes look like a sea of endless turquoise.

"At least we have a shady spot," Magos said. Even sweating, he still managed to look more composed than the rest of us, who were basically sweat monsters at this point. We sat uphill of the large arena where the tournament fights would take place.

A large tree stretched over us, one of the few we'd seen that had leaves wide enough to actually provide some shade instead of the typical thin needle-like leaves we'd seen on most of the fauna in this realm. I suspected this tree and any others like it weren't native to these lands but had been left behind by the fae. Like the large tree that grew in the forests outside Emerald Bay.

"I'm pretty sure, given the chance, you'd shave your head right now." I grinned, eyeing his thick hair pulled back into a bun of sorts.

When I'd first met Magos all those centuries ago, his hair had been in long braids that almost reached his waist. But when he'd reappeared in my life a few years ago, his hair had been shorn down to his scalp. Only recently had he let it grow out again. I assumed he'd be braiding it again at some point. It was a small thing, but it made me happy that my friend was embracing a part of himself that he had lost for so long.

Magos gave me a small smile and summoned some mist around us before letting it go. I sighed in contentment as the cool, moist air ran over my skin. It wasn't as good as air conditioning, but it was better than nothing.

I wondered if this was similar to the climate of my home realm before it had been abandoned to the devourers. I could ask Badb about it. After all, she had been born in that realm, but I had avoided asking her any questions about that place or our family. Kalen had been trying to push Badb and me together in his own subtle but persistent way, but Badb and I seemed destined to always clash.

I couldn't help but compare her to Macha. Badb seemed to be struggling just as much about how to define our relationship.

"May we join you?" Cerri asked, distracting me from my thoughts.

"Of course," Pele answered for us from where she was sitting just outside the shade of the tree.

Mikhail moved over until his arm was brushing mine, and I just barely stopped myself from leaning into him. Him always being around me and finding ways to casually touch me was starting to feel normal. That more than anything had me freaking out.

Cerri sat on the ground between me and Pele, her face and shoulders rigid as she stared at the arena. It hadn't yet been announced who Eddie would be fighting against. All we knew was that there were four rounds today, two fighters each round squaring off in their dragon forms. The winners would move on to the next event. The losers would lose their right to compete for Cerri's hand in marriage, assuming they weren't dead.

Magos rose and pulled a small blanket from the bag he'd packed that morning, stretching it out next to where he'd been sitting. He greeted Lynette and gestured towards the blanket. The hesitant smile she'd been wearing blossomed into a radiant beam as she took a seat on the blanket. Magos moved his fingers hesitantly through some gestures and paused.

Lynette grinned, tapped his hand softly once, and repeated the gestures slowly, making minor corrections.

I knew Magos was just being kind because that's who he was, but if he ever pursued anyone romantically, they wouldn't stand a chance. I smirked at the thought as I looked at our remaining guest, who was lingering in front of us, unsure of where to sit.

"Come on, Lucan. Take a seat." Cerri waved the pale-skinned, dark-haired dragon over. Between his coloring and his lean build, he reminded me of Misha. "Lucan is the younger brother of Uther, who is competing in the tournament," she said matter-of-factly, as if she wasn't talking about one of the many suitors about to fight for the right to marry her, despite her being in love with someone else.

I thought daemons were weird, but dragons were taking it to a whole new level.

"Lucan and I are the same age, born not even a week apart. He's like my brother." She ruffled his hair, and he batted her hand away.

"She's been lording over the fact that she is a week older than me our entire lives," he said with a lopsided grin.

Pele turned her face away from the sun and looked at Lucan. "Does your brother consider Cerri a friend as well? If so, competing in the tournament is an odd way of showing it."

He paled a little at her directness and shuffled nervously. I hid my smile. Pele was perfectly capable of crafting indirect questions to get the answers she wanted, but she was also quite skilled at knowing when to be direct to throw people off their game.

Lucan continued to wilt under Pele's piercing stare, but Cerri rescued him. "Lucan and Uther's parents are some of my father's strongest allies." Her fingers were signing to include Lynette in the conversation. "They've been suggesting marriage between Uther and me for years. He didn't have a choice in entering this tournament any more than Tal did."

"Choosing to sit with us sends a message," Mikhail pointed out.

Lucan cleared his throat and sheepishly looked at Lynette. "I'm . . . uhhh . . ." The tips of his ears turned bright red. "I'm supposed to be courting Lynette."

I put my hand over my mouth to cover my laugh. Mikhail looked at Lynette and then back at Lucan. "Right," he said slowly. "And how's that going for you?"

"Probably better than your attempt to court Nemain," Pele snickered.

Magos barked in laughter and quickly looked away from his nephew's glare.

"It's a shame Asmodeus couldn't join us on this trip." Mikhail narrowed his eyes at Pele. "That outfit they wore last week that showed off their midriff would work well in this heat. It was an odd choice to wear around a tavern, though. Any idea why they would choose such a sinfully tempting outfit to wear to work?"

Flames flickered across Pele's fingers, causing several dragons to focus on us.

"You said you're *supposed* to be courting Lynette," Magos said evenly, drawing attention away from the impending fight. "Not that you *are* courting Lynette."

Cerri pursed her lips while Lucan hesitantly signed something to Lynette. She signed back, and he shook his head, causing her to sign back to him with more forceful gestures. I had no idea what they were saying, but it was clear they were arguing over something.

Lucan sighed and said, "Fine, but I think this is a bad idea. We don't know them."

Lynette looked at all of us, showing no shyness now, just heavy determination. Her gaze fell on me last, and she made a simple gesture.

"Can I trust you?" Lucan translated.

Yes, I signed back. "Cerri trusts you, so we will not do anything to harm you," I said, trusting Lucan to translate for me. "Unless you betray her or us. Then all bets are off."

A savage smile spread across her pretty heart-shaped face, and I was starting to suspect there was another side to Lynette that we didn't know yet.

"I would expect nothing less," Lucan continued to translate as Lynette rapidly signed. "My father and Thorod grew up together. He's Thorod's right-hand at this point. Seven years ago he started talking about potential suitors for me. My mother was opposed to the idea of me getting married so young."

Lynette's hands faltered.

"Our mothers became friends over the years," Cerri said. "Neither of them married for love. Both had been given away by their parents for political advantage. My mother never openly opposed my father, but Lynette's did in small ways. But she flat out refused to allow Lynette to get married."

"They were both killed in a trakdi attack a little over five years ago," Lucan said quietly.

We should just start a dead parents support group at this point, I thought darkly.

Lynette raised her chin, determination showing in her eyes. "I refused to get married after her death," Cerri took a turn at translating. "My father had me locked in one of the citadel towers for defying him. When he found out my friends were sneaking in to give me company and extra food, he had me moved to the dungeon. He withheld food and water for days at a time until finally I relented."

"Your father is a prick," I told her. "Say the word and we'll kill him for you." The vampires smiled broadly as Cerri translated for me, and Lynette returned their smiles.

Thank you, she signed before continuing.

I thought I recognized the phrase as one she had taught us earlier. "It's being handled?" I guessed.

Lynette nodded. We waited for something else beyond those cryptic words, but Lynette folded her hands in her lap and gave us a sweet smile. I looked at Cerri, and she raised her hands with a shrug.

"Lynette has been betrothed five times in the last five years. Each suitor has died before the wedding. The first one could have been a trakdi attack, but the other four definitely weren't." Cerri shot her friend a curious look. "She won't tell us who is doing it. But I know it's not her, and it's not Tal, Lucan, or Uther."

"And Eddie was gone when the most recent one happened," Lucan offered. "So it's not him either."

"Her father is furious," Cerri said. "At first it only raised interest in Lynette. Some dragons are all about a challenge." She rolled her eyes. "But after the last one was left disemboweled with his balls cut off . . . interest waned a bit."

"But you're fine so far," Pele said as she scrutinized Lucan. "So whoever is behind the killings knows you're not actually interested in Lynette or a threat in any way."

Lynette waited for Cerri to finish signing before responding. "Lucan is my friend," Cerri said for her. "We might have to actually go through with a marriage at some point, but we can make it work. It's not ideal, but it might be the best we can manage."

"If the treaty is signed, you'll be free to leave the dragon realm," Pele said. "You can both be free of your parents."

Yes, Lynette signed, with a tentative, hopeful expression.

Our conversation turned to more benign topics as the space around us filled with more dragons. A few had shifted to their human forms when they landed, but most didn't. It was more than a little unnerving to be surrounded by hundreds of dragons, a good number of which probably wanted us dead.

Refusing to be intimidated, I leaned back on my hands and let my gaze roam over those gathered.

An enormous red dragon landed on the opposite side of the arena. Based on how Cerri stiffened, I assumed that was her father. Other dragons landed next to him, but he towered over all of them. Instead of a single row of spikes down his spine, he had twin rows that were slightly shorter than the spikes of the other dragons. His horns also faced forward instead of pointing back.

"Why does your father look different?" I murmured to Cerri.

"It's our bloodline," she replied, not taking her eyes off her father. "Like Eddie, our bloodline is special. Whereas his gives him strong telepathy, ours makes us larger and physically stronger than other dragons."

"You look like that, too?" Mikhail leaned forward so he could look around me at Cerri. She nodded. "Is it rude to ask what color your scales are?"

Cerri looked away from her father and gave Mikhail an amused smile. "I don't think anyone has ever asked me that before, so I don't know if it qualifies as rude or not, but I'm not offended. My scales are blue. I took after my mother."

A low rumble drew our attention. Thorod pushed himself off the ground and leapt into the arena. The earth shook as he landed and let out a roar that had my ears ringing. All the chattering died as gazes fell on him.

Today begins the first of the challenges to determine who has the right to claim my daughter. Eight challengers will enter the arena today. Only four will move on to the next round. Thorod's voice rumbled through my head, but it didn't sound nearly as strong as Eddie's.

I glanced at Cerri and saw she bore a pleasant but blank expression. To those sitting around the arena, she looked like an obedient daughter. Perhaps not happy about her fate, but accepting. But sitting next to her, I could see what they couldn't. Cerri's hands dug into the hard ground as if she had claws, and the look in her eyes was that of a focused predator. I hoped Eddie knew what he was doing by joining this tournament because if anything happened to him, I didn't think we'd be able to stop Cerri from trying to tear her father apart.

Thorod announced the pairs facing off against each other. The tournament would begin with Tal against Lucan's brother, Uther, followed by Eddie squaring off against Morholt.

Thorod beat his wings once and launched himself into the air, returning to his spot on the other side of the arena.

BEGIN!

The command echoed through my mind, and two dragons descended from the sky, landing at opposite ends of the arena. Both dragons were the same size, one with crimson-red scales and the other with a deep green color that reminded me of the evergreen forests found in the human realm.

"Who is who?" I asked.

Lucan swallowed. "Tal is red, and my brother is green."

Cerri moved forward until she was sitting next to Lucan and gripped his hand in hers. I followed Lucan's gaze and found he wasn't staring at Uther, but rather his gaze was locked on Tal.

The two dragons sized each other up as they moved across the arena, and I watched them carefully. Like the trakdi from last night, there was an astonishing amount of grace and fluidity to their movements despite their size. Both dragons had their wings tucked in tight to keep them out of the way. Damaging the wings would hinder their opponent's movability, but it would be far from a death blow. The throat and underbelly were what I would go for. The spikes running down their backs protected their spines and the backs of their necks.

Mikhail leaned forward with me, and I knew he was looking for weak spots, just as I was.

Uther struck at Tal, aiming for his right front leg. Tal nimbly dodged the attack and slammed his tail against Uther but didn't pull it back fast enough. Uther used his tail to pin Tal's and bit down on his rear leg. Bone crushed and Tal roared, his claws raking Uther's sides. They broke apart, with Tal limping heavily and blood pouring down Uther's side. It was then I felt the magic rising from the dragons surrounding the arena.

"Cerri, what's going on?" I asked urgently. "All the dragons are using magic."

"It's part of the tournament," she said, not taking her eyes off the fighting dragons. "They're suppressing the healing of the contenders." Lucan's grip on Cerri's hand tightened until his knuckles were white. His gaze never wavered from Tal.

The dragons clashed again in a sea of red and green scales. Uther pinned Tal to the ground with a roar and latched onto his throat. Tal's claws tore at the green dragon's sides, but he had no leverage from that angle and wasn't doing nearly enough damage.

"No!" Lucan cried and leapt to his feet.

Cerri jumped up and grabbed him as the dragons nearest us tore their gazes away from the arena and focused on the young dragon.

Mikhail and I stepped up to either side of them. I looked back at the arena and saw that Uther still had Tal pinned by the throat. He should have ripped out his throat by that point, but he was hesitating. Only because I was looking for it, I saw the moment he widened his stance and loosened his jaws, giving Tal an opening.

Tal didn't hesitate and thrust his front claws into Uther's underbelly, shoving the red dragon off him and onto his side. Uther didn't move from where he lay, with Tal's claws still buried in his chest. Based on what Eddie had told me about dragon anatomy, I was pretty sure Tal was in a position to rip out the other dragon's heart.

I yield, Uther said, pain etching his voice.

Tal raised his head and looked at Thorod, who swung his gaze to the green dragon sitting next to him. *It seems your son failed to live up to your family's reputation. Should I remove him from the line for you?*

The green dragon gazed down at his son in clear disgust before responding. *I would ask that you spare him, my lord, if only so*

I can make him regret not living up to the family name and make sure his brother understands what it means to choose mercy over strength. The green dragon raised his head and glared coldly at his younger son, who was still clutching Cerri's hand.

Very well, Thorod replied in a bored tone. *Clear the arena for the next match.*

With some obvious effort, both Tal and Uther took to the sky and headed back to the citadel, likely to get patched up. I wasn't sure if their healing ability would kick back in as soon as they cleared the arena or if it took time to come back.

Lucan watched Tal and his brother fly away with obvious concern on his face, but to my surprise, he settled back down next to Cerri and found her hand once again. This time it was her knuckles that turned white as a familiar black dragon landed in the arena.

Eddie's burnt amber eyes locked onto Cerri's, but he didn't say anything as a blue-scaled dragon slammed down into the arena. I wasn't surprised to see that, just like his human form, Morholt's dragon form was broad and bulky. He was roughly the same height as Eddie but clearly outweighed him; grappling with him would be a mistake. Eddie needed to move fast and hit hard if he wanted to survive this. Given Morholt's hostility towards us, there would be no mercy in this fight.

Thorod looked across the arena at Cerri and gave her a crocodilian smile. *Kill the exile.*

Dragons roared in approval as Morholt pounded across the arena towards Eddie, who remained standing in the center. We leapt to our feet. Cerri and Lucan still gripped each other's hand, and it took every ounce of my willpower not to draw my swords and cut my way to the arena.

"He's got this," Mikhail said calmly.

Morholt continued barreling towards Eddie, clearly planning on using his superior size to overpower him.

"What is he doing?" I said. "He can't hold his ground against that tank. He needs to stay mobile."

"Just wait." Mikhail's hand brushed against mine. I grabbed it without thinking, my fingers wrapping tightly around his.

When Morholt had nearly closed the distance between them, Eddie moved unbelievably fast. He slid to the side and thrust his tail towards Morholt as if it were a spear.

Blood sprayed across the sand, and it took me a moment to realize what had happened. Dragon tails ended in a hard point where the scales concentrated together. It wasn't particularly sharp, so I had always dismissed it as a weapon. But as blood poured out of the empty socket on Morholt's face where his eye had once been, I realized how wrong of an assumption that was.

Morholt bellowed a challenge and tried to lock Eddie in a grapple, but with his now-limited vision, his strike was far off. A couple minutes later, Eddie tore out the other eye and proceeded to slowly take the brute of a dragon apart piece by piece before finally ripping out his heart.

Morholt hadn't landed a single hit.

Silence reigned across the arena as all the dragons stared at Eddie, unable to believe what they had just witnessed. Eddie simply faced Thorod and slowly raised the blood-soaked heart to his mouth and swallowed it whole.

"Fuck yes!" I screamed and pumped my fist in the air.

That was all it took for the dragons to let out screams and roars of approval. Thorod stared at Eddie, momentarily shocked, and smoke poured from his nostrils. The dragons seated around him did not cheer. Eddie gave him the same crocodilian smile Thorod had given Cerri earlier.

"I don't know if I want to kiss him or kill him," Cerri growled half-heartedly. "If his strike had missed, Morholt would have torn him apart."

"How'd you know?" I narrowed my eyes at Mikhail.

"Eddie asked me for advice with tactics," he said smugly. "I told him he would have one chance and one chance only to take advantage of how everyone was underestimating him. It was his idea to do the tail thing. Apparently, they used to play a game as kids where they would throw objects at each other and spear them with their tails."

"I remember that game," Cerri murmured. "Eddie always was the best at it."

Thorod waved a clawed hand towards Eddie. *Clear the arena.*

Eddie leapt into the air and flew over to us. He shifted in a flash of flames and plopped down next to Cerri with a satisfied look on his face.

"Oh, get over yourself." I curled my lip up at his perfectly intact clothes.

He grinned. "What bothers you more? That I was right when I told you I had this in the bag, or that I get to keep my clothes when I shift?"

"Personally, I prefer Nemain's method of shifting," Mikhail said.

"I agree with the vampire," Pele said.

"Well, it's not surprising the two of you like a naked Nemain," Eddie said. Lucan gave Eddie a puzzled look and I inwardly groaned. The last thing Eddie needed was encouragement. "You see, Lucan, it's like this. In the human realm there's this thing called 'friends with benefits.' Basically, you're friends, but you also fuck occasionally. That's what Pele and Nemain have going on. Personally, it sounds complicated to me, but they've been doing it for centuries, and it works for them." He waggled his eyebrows suggestively.

Lucan's eyes widened, and he quickly glanced between me and Mikhail. "And them?" He waved his hand back and forth between us.

"Oh, I'm sure you've already picked up on the delicious

tension brewing between them," Eddie announced cheerfully. "It's not a question of will they fuck. It's *when* will they fuck?"

"Do you still want to pummel him?" I asked Cerri. "Because I'll hold him down."

Mikhail lazily wrapped an arm around my shoulders. "You already stabbed him once today. Go easy on him."

I knocked his arm off. "You're sweaty and gross. Don't touch me."

The dragons finished dragging Morholt's corpse from the arena, and our attention focused there once more. With Tal and Eddie's fights out of the way, I was more curious about how the next two fights would go than stressed. A dark form flew through the clouds, and I blinked as a black dragon landed in the arena.

A slight tremor rippled through its wings before it pulled them in tight. The sun was blocked by the thick and heavy clouds, but I could still pick up a slight shimmer in the scales. I noticed a few other black dragons, but none of them shared his iridescent scales like this one. The dragon that landed in the arena could have been Eddie's twin.

"Vizor?" I guessed.

"Yup," Eddie confirmed. "And before you say it, we're not related."

"You sure?" I frowned. "You have the same eye color, and the same iridescent black scales in dragon form."

"Our eyes and scales aren't common, but they're not that rare," he said dismissively. "Trust me. If he shared my bloodline, Thorod would have had him killed by now. No one trusts that dragon."

"Hmm." I continued to study Vizor's dragon form, not entirely convinced, but Eddie would know better than me.

A dragon with bloodred scales landed across from Vizor. He had a lean build, even leaner than Eddie and Vizor, and I could tell he would be wicked fast. I remembered his name was Pellam but knew nothing about him beyond that.

Given how quickly Vizor killed him, I supposed it didn't matter. With ruthless efficiency, Vizor dodged most of the red dragon's attacks and pounced on his back. If you'd asked me before today if it was possible to rip out a dragon's spine, I would have said no, but Vizor proved that theory wrong. Even Magos looked impressed.

"That dragon worries me more and more every day," I said evenly as Vizor left the arena without a word, heading back to the citadel. He had won the bout, but not without taking a few hits.

Lynette had been pale during the fight, and I wondered if Vizor had done something to frighten her in the past. He was a cold-hearted bastard. While more dragons set to cleaning up the arena for the final match, I noticed Lucan and Uther's father jerk his head towards the citadel. Three dragons rose and took off.

Well, that can't be good. I looked at Cerri and saw she had noticed as well. "Lucan, I think you should go check on your brother. I can't leave before the final bout is over."

Lynette watched the dragons fly away before she turned her attention back to the arena.

"I'll go with you." I rose and brushed off my pants.

"*We'll* go with you," Magos corrected as both he and Mikhail moved to stand beside me.

"Pele, are you staying or going?" I asked.

"I'll stay. Elyan is in the last bout, and I'm curious about him."

"All right, let's go."

Lucan moved away and shifted to his dragon form, and we quickly climbed onto his back. I squeezed my eyes shut as he leapt into the sky, which did nothing to prevent my stomach from doing a flip. Hopefully he was a fast flyer, because I doubted the dragons ahead of us had good intentions.

Chapter Fifteen

LUCAN FLEW towards one of the spiraling towers at the back of the citadel and landed on a narrow ledge that jutted out from the tower. We slid off his back and headed towards the door, a flash of heat behind us signaling Lucan's shift to his human form.

Angry shouts came from inside; the three dragons had definitely beat us there. Instead of barging in, I opened the door slowly, and we quietly made our way into the tower. A tidy circular room greeted us, with several empty beds against a wall. Another area had some basic medical supplies stacked on shelves. More angry shouts came from above us, and I spied a narrow staircase that almost perfectly blended into the grey stone walls.

When Lucan shot towards the stairwell, I grabbed him and held my finger to my lips. He tried to pull out of my grasp but stilled when Magos stepped towards him. Once I was sure he wouldn't dart away, I released my grip. I didn't know what we'd be walking into, and I had no idea how Lucan was in a fight. We had surprise on our side, and I didn't want to lose it. I raised my finger to my lips one more time, signaling him to stay quiet, and this time he gave me a tight nod.

But when I pointed to the base of the stairs and mouthed *wait*, his lips flattened into a hard line. He did as he was told, though. Magos spied a walking stick leaning against the wall and picked it up, running his hands along the smooth pale wood. It looked like it'd been carved from a tree similar to the one in the center of the garden.

I glanced at Mikhail. "Get Tal and Uther out," I said, my voice barely a whisper, but with his vampire hearing, he understood just fine.

I slid my daggers free, and we crept up the stairs. The room above us was almost an exact replica of the floor below. Tal and Uther were across the room, both looking more than a little worse for wear. Blood was still seeping from a wound on Uther's chest, and Tal was standing so almost all his weight was on his right foot. Small splotches of blood were soaking into bandages that wrapped around his stomach and upper arm.

Whatever magic the dragons used to suppress healing in that arena clearly took some time to wear off.

In a rare spot of luck, the three dragons we'd followed had their backs to us. Both Tal and Uther were completely focused on them and hadn't noticed us yet. I scanned the room quickly for Vizor but didn't see him anywhere, which wasn't all that surprising. Unless something was in it for him, he didn't seem like the type to help out others. It was a little interesting that he hadn't stayed to help the three newcomers, though. More evidence that whatever he was up to, it really was his own game.

"Get out of the way, Tal," the tallest of the three dragons ordered. "You'll likely meet your end in the arena soon enough."

Tal remained standing in front of Uther, looking like a

slight breeze would knock him over. But his jaw remained set in determination, with nothing but steely resolve in his eyes.

"Have it your way then." The dragon who'd issued the order jerked his head at the other two. "Don't break him so bad that he can't put in a decent showing in the bout tomorrow."

The two dragons took a step towards Tal, but Uther moved around him, placing an arm on the other dragon's forearm. "That's not necessary." He looked at Tal. "I know why you're doing this, I've always known. His happiness is all that matters to me. Take care of him."

My eyebrows rose in surprise.

"Uther—" Tal started.

"Enough of this bullshit," the lead thug snapped. "Grab him and let's get out of here. The last bout is likely over, and everyone will be returning soon."

"I don't think so," I said, moving to the center of the room. Magos stepped up with me, but Mikhail remained in the stairwell, just below the floor out of sight. The three dragons spun to face us, and I twirled my blades around a few times. "You should leave now."

The tall dragon who'd been giving the orders narrowed his eyes at me. His light blond hair was pulled back, making his narrow features look even sharper. Crystal-blue eyes looked me over, dismissing me as a threat, and moved to Magos. I couldn't entirely fault him for that. With his tall and broad build, Magos looked like the bigger threat. Plus, the dragons had largely credited him for taking down the trakdi.

Normally I'd be annoyed, but we needed to get this resolved quickly. If he wanted to take a swing at Magos, more power to him.

"You gonna do something or just stand there and eye-fuck my friend?"

"Vortimer, shut that bitch up," he snarled. "Erec, with me."

One dragon peeled off from the others and started towards me while the other two went after Magos. He swung a meaty fist at me, and I easily ducked beneath it. My daggers sliced into his side, sending blood arcing outward. He snarled and made a grab for me. I spun around him and slammed a dagger hilt into the back of his head; he dropped like a stone. I stared at his unconscious body in mild disappointment. That barely counted as a fight.

Mikhail slid past me and helped Uther down the stairs, with Tal following after them. A grunt sounded from behind me, and I stepped back as a body flew across the room and slammed into the wall. I walked over and prodded the dragon with a toe. Still alive, but based on the angle of his arm, it was broken in a couple of places, and his breathing sounded a little labored. I shrugged; he'd live. Turning around, I watched the remaining dragon square off against Magos.

The dragon held a sword that reminded me a little of a claymore with its length and broad blade. The thing had to be close to four feet long, and it looked slow as hell. I knew from experience that one did not want to be slow around Magos.

The dragon swung the blade upward, going for a diagonal cut across the abdomen. Magos leaned back, and the blade passed an inch from his chest. He thrust the point of the walking stick into the dragon's solar plexus. He gasped and stumbled back, and Magos spun, gaining speed and momentum before smacking the hard wood into the side of the dragon's face.

I winced at the loud cracking sound as the dragon's jaw broke, my body remembering Magos pulling that same move on me a month ago while sparring. The sword slipped from the dragon's fingers, but he remained standing, no doubt seeing stars at the moment. Damn. I'd been out cold for ten minutes after taking that hit.

The dragon shook his head a few times and let out a roar.

He dove towards Magos, apparently deciding brute force was the better option. Magos slid to the side gracefully as if he were dancing and slammed the staff onto the dragon's back. With all his momentum carrying him forward, the force from the blow sent the dragon sprawling. With a groan, he rolled over onto his back and lay there panting.

Magos pointed the tip of the staff at his throat as I sauntered over. I waited until the dragon blinked a few times and focused on me. "You done? I think you're done. Magos, do you think he's done?"

"Yes, I do believe he is."

I leaned down and wiped the blood from my daggers onto the dragon's shirt. "Looks like we're finished here. I trust you'll clean up this mess?" I gestured around us.

"Pay . . . firrr . . . esh," he pushed out, the words mangled by his still-healing jaw.

"Pay for this?" I shoved the daggers back in the hidden sheathes in my bracers. "Unlikely. I mean, what are you going to do? Complain about how your attempt to kidnap an injured dragon was thwarted by us? I don't really think you want everyone to know you got your ass handed to you so easily. Maybe your boss can take a moment to think about how to not be a total douchebag to his sons. Consider this a gift from us to him."

THE FOUR OF us made our way back to our suite without encountering any other dragons. After Mikhail safely delivered Uther to Lucan, the two brothers took off. I wasn't sure what their plan was, but hopefully Uther could hide out somewhere away from the wrath of his father until the treaty was signed. Tal was subdued on our walk back. I wasn't sure if it was because of his injuries or if he had something else on his mind.

Cerri was pacing back and forth when we entered the room. As soon as she saw us, she threw her arms around Tal. "I'm so glad you're okay!" Tal winced but carefully returned her hug. Cerri pulled back and looked over his injuries. "Go sit down and rest while your magic comes back. I'll get you some honey ale."

She hurried out of the room, and Eddie frowned after her before swinging his accusatory gaze to Tal. "She's never doted on me like that before."

"You've been gone a few years," Tal said smugly as he made his way to the lounge chair, still favoring one leg heavily. "Plus, I'm prettier than you."

"I've already rescued you once today, Tal," I said, plopping down on one of the empty chairs. "I'm not doing it again."

"If you're going to brawl, take it outside," Pele said. She was sitting on the floor with a bunch of books and scrolls spread out in front of her. "I'm busy and don't need your alpha male bullshit distracting me."

"Sorry, I couldn't resist." Tal closed his eyes and smiled. "Eddie's always been a bit insecure when it comes to Cerri. Understandable really, considering how far out of his league she is and how everyone has always commented that Cerri and I would make a lovely couple."

Eddie scowled and had just started to take a step towards Tal when the door flung open. Lucan stormed in, not sparing a glance at any of us as he reached Tal and kissed him deeply. Eddie looked at them in confusion and then at Cerri, who was standing in the doorway with a ceramic jug, smirking. Tal and Lucan broke their kiss but stayed in their embrace, foreheads touching.

"Uther?" Tal finally asked.

Lucan swallowed. "Resting in one of the empty towers. As soon as he's healed enough to fly, he'll head to Ralis. He just needs to stay out of our father's grasp for a few weeks until the old bastard's temper cools down."

"I'm sorry," Eddie cut in. "What the hell is this?"

Cerri laughed as she poured the honey ale into several mugs.

Eddie whirled towards her. "You tricky little vixen! You knew!"

"Of course I knew." She passed him a glass and took a sip from her own. "To be fair, I've suspected for a long time, but Tal didn't tell me until after you were exiled."

Eddie shook his head in disbelief as he stared at Tal. "But you were always such a flirtatious bastard. If you weren't going after Cerri, you were pursuing some other female."

"Some of us are better at hiding our secret relationships than others," Tal said. "Your relationship with Cerri was obvious to anyone who remotely knew either of you. Frankly, I'm surprised it took Thorod so long to figure it out."

"We had to keep it a secret," Lucan said quietly. "Tal's parents don't care what he does, but you know how my parents are. They've always planned on arranging politically advantageous marriages for me and Uther."

"Ones that would result in lots of little dragonlings to merge the bloodlines," Tal added.

"Huh." Eddie narrowed his eyes at Tal. "Why didn't you tell me when I got back? Or at least refrain from flirting with Cerri directly in front of me?"

Tal shrugged. "I mean, I have to do something for entertainment around here."

I laughed, and Eddie glared at me. "What?" I lifted my hands. "It's kind of funny."

"Why didn't the two of you just marry while Eddie was in exile?" Mikhail asked Cerri. "You would know it was a marriage of convenience, and it would have solved the problem of your father trying to marry you off."

"Because my father wouldn't have approved," Cerri said. "Tal comes from an old, respected bloodline. But neither of his parents are actively involved in politics or have shown any interest one way or another in my father's scheming."

"So you were hoping Tal would win the tournament and then your father would have to allow the marriage," Mikhail said. "Not a bad plan given your limited options."

"It was a last resort," Cerri said tiredly. "I was hoping to come up with something else before the tournament ended."

"You're still annoying." Eddie walked over towards Tal, causing Lucan to tense slightly. Tal just waited, eyeing Eddie warily. After a few seconds, Eddie clapped him on the shoulder. "I'm glad Cerri had someone like you to help her while I was gone. Someone she could trust."

"You can trust both of us," Tal said, tugging Lucan against his side.

"Might as well fill the both of them in on everything," Pele said distractedly as she unrolled another scroll. "It might be useful to have more ears on the ground while we look for evidence of Balor being involved in dragon affairs and what he wants from them."

"This have anything to do with you lurking outside the city last night?" Tal asked.

"Yes." I nodded and took the honey ale Cerri offered me. "We came to this realm to get Cerri out, but we stayed to see if our enemies are working with Thorod."

Tal and Lucan sat down, and I gave them the rundown of Balor and how he created the devourers. I left out Finn, not because I didn't trust them, but because he wasn't relevant at the moment, and I didn't feel like getting into the prophecy surrounding him and me.

Tal looked at Cerri in speculation. "If Thorod met with these sidhe devourers, he likely did it in that tower of his."

"Agreed." Cerri frowned. "Even I haven't managed to get

in there. There's some type of ward around it. I'd always thought he'd found old artifact of the fae or daemons and was using that to protect the tower, but maybe he's gotten more recent help."

"You can't pass through it?" I asked in surprise. "I've seen Eddie get past fae wards before."

"I could, but it would take a few minutes, and my father has guards posted everywhere. They would catch me before I could break through."

"It's either you or the vampires, then," Eddie said. "Assuming you don't have performance issues getting your gateway magic to work."

I glared at him. "I just can't do it under pressure, but I should be able to pull that off. Magos and Mikhail won't know what to look for, and neither can read fae writing."

"It'll have to be tonight during the celebration," Cerri said. "Everyone will be there. We'll just come up with some sort of explanation for you being absent."

"We'll figure something out." I looked at the simple blue gown Cerri wore and then at my black fighting leathers. "Tell me, Cerri. What exactly does one wear to a dragon party?"

Chapter Sixteen

"Quit pulling at it," Pele said under her breath as we walked around the large ballroom. We'd each borrowed a dress from Cerri, but Pele's fit better. She had a leaner build than the dragon, but the azure dress still complemented her. My options had been severely limited because I outweighed Cerri by a solid forty pounds and had broader shoulders and fuller hips. The only dress she'd had that fit me was made of a soft pink stretchy material, and even then, my boobs were practically falling out of it.

Mikhail and Eddie had laughed so hard they'd cried when I'd walked out of the room after Cerri and Lynette had squeezed me into the dress.

Pele just stared at me, and I knew she was committing every inch of the dress to memory so she could recount it to Kaysea later. Magos managed to hold his laughter in, but there was no mistaking the amusement dancing in his eyes. I was eternally grateful this hadn't happened around the vampire kids in the human realm because they would have taken a thousand pictures with their phones.

To add insult to injury, I had to leave my swords behind. I didn't care how ridiculous they looked with the dress, but apparently it sent a bad message showing up with a bunch of weapons. So no swords for me or Mikhail. I kept my throwing daggers hidden in my silver bracers, and Dante's death dagger was still strapped to my thigh. The leather harness chafed my skin, but I refused to leave the dagger behind.

Cerri still had some of Eddie's old clothes tucked away and had shared those with Mikhail and Magos. Both of them looked perfectly normal in the dark blue tunics, even if that wasn't their usual style of clothing. Only I had to wear the damn pink dress from hell.

"Let's just put our plan into action so I can get out of here," I growled, keeping my voice low.

Pele slid me a glance. "You know what to do."

Fixing a pleasant smile on my face, I slid across the fire-lit ballroom to where Mikhail was speaking with Vizor, of all people. More than a few lustful looks fell on me as I sidled up next to Mikhail, but Vizor's expression remained cold and calculating.

"Dare I ask what you two are chatting about?"

"I was asking what he thought about the fights today," Mikhail said. His lips twitched like he was holding in a laugh. Stupid dress.

"The ones in the arena or the one in the citadel tower that he managed to be absent for?" There was nothing friendly in the smile I gave Vizor.

"Uther chose poorly, and now he'll pay for it. I don't see how that concerns me," Vizor said.

"I haven't been here long, but it seems to me that allies are important in this realm." Sharp amber eyes looked at me, taking my measure. "You're not liked by anyone. No one trusts you. You have no allies. Seems like *you* might have made a poor choice."

Vizor sipped his wine. "One doesn't have to be well-liked to have allies. And one can trust the motivations of an individual without fully trusting said individual." He raised his glass to us and took his leave, joining some other dragons across the room.

"We should just kill him now," I said, only half-jokingly. "Then we won't have to worry about his allegiances and schemes later."

Mikhail let out a low, husky laugh that did all sorts of things to my insides. "I do love it when you talk about killing our enemies," he whispered in my ear. Shivers ran up my spine as the annoyance I'd been feeling at Vizor vanished. "Care to take a spin around the room with me?"

All I could do was nod and let him lead me onto the dance floor. I was suddenly regretting agreeing to this plan earlier even if it did seem like the easiest option. We danced for several songs, growing more and more bold in our movements as our hands roamed over each other.

This was nothing like the elaborate dance we'd done at the fae ball. That dance had been practically tame compared to what we were doing now. Mikhail's fingers set a blazing path down my back before he squeezed my backside possessively, eliciting a low throaty moan out of me. I spun away but he tugged me against him so that my back was against his chest, and something very hard was pressed against my ass.

My acting skills were never great, but I didn't need them at this point because I was on fire everywhere he touched me. I arched into his embrace, and he kissed my neck before twirling me away with the beat of the music. Stares and whispers fell around us as dragons watched us spin around and around.

Finally, Mikhail whispered in my ear, "Ready for the next part?"

I let out a husky laugh in answer and let him pull me off the dance floor. We ducked into a room we'd scouted earlier that was just off the ballroom in plain view of everyone.

Closing the door behind us, I flipped the lock, but before I could do anything else, Mikhail had me pinned against the wall. I sucked in a breath as his lips found my neck, his fingers digging into my hips. Fangs grazed my skin as he trailed upwards, covering my mouth with his. Any thoughts of the plan and what we needed to be doing fled from my mind as I buried my fingers in his hair. Mikhail growled and pulled me closer to him, cupping my ass. I wrapped my legs around his waist as he continued to devour me.

Pulling my dress down, he sucked on a nipple, ripping a moan out of me. Way too many clothes were between us for what I had in mind. Mikhail seemed to be thinking the same, as he leaned back enough to pull the tunic over his head. As he pulled the fabric up, a loud knock sounded, and we both froze.

"Work first, play later," Pele's voice said quietly.

Eddie laughed loudly to cover up her message, and I heard them move away from the door. How they'd known what we were up to, I had no idea.

Mikhail let out a deep sigh and set me down. I pulled my dress back into place, suddenly grateful for Pele's interference. I'd let myself get wrapped up in the dance and allowed this to go too far. There was a long list of reasons why it was a bad idea for me to get involved with Mikhail, but my mind was struggling to remember them at the moment. Which was the problem. This wasn't some passing crush or a quick tryst. My desire for Mikhail went so beyond what I'd felt for almost anyone in my entire life, and that terrified me.

I needed distance between us, and I needed it *now*. But when I tried to move around him, Mikhail stopped me. Fingers lightly ran across my jawline, tilting my face towards him.

Determined twilight eyes held my gaze. "We're going to the tower, completing our mission, but this isn't over, Nemain. You want me every bit as much as I want you."

The heat I'd been feeling was drenched by the cold fear that seized my heart. Mikhail wasn't going to back down. Not this time. "I got carried away," I said, somehow managing an even voice. "It didn't mean anything. I would have gotten turned on by anyone who danced with me like that."

"Really?" Mikhail said. "More than a few dragons were lusting after you out there. Maybe you can pick one of them when we get back."

"Maybe I will!" I hissed loudly and squeezed my eyes shut. Damn him for pushing me on this. I took a couple of deep breaths and opened my eyes once more. "We can fight about this later. Or preferably never. But we need to get going. There's only so long the dragons will fall for our ruse."

"Waiting on you, shifter." The way he was looking at me, I felt like he knew exactly what I was feeling. Like he knew me better than anyone else.

I turned away from his intense stare and focused on letting out the smallest amount of magic. Earlier in the day, we'd taken a walk around the ballroom to scout out this room, but we'd also gone by the tower. The guards were too alert for us to get close, but I'd been able to see enough through some of the open windows. With the destination in mind, I concentrated on opening a gateway. Seconds ticked by before I felt a shift. I let a little more magic out, easing the gateway open until I felt it settle into existence.

"Let's go," I said and stepped through the portal. Mikhail followed after me, and we looked around the circular room. "We'll search together floor by floor."

He nodded and began searching the neat stacks of paper on a nearby table. I tackled the shelving that lined the walls. It was a risk to leave the gateway open, but I didn't want to chance us having to beat a hasty retreat and relying on my ability to open another one quickly. If Eddie noticed Thorod or any of his cronies leaving the party, he'd send me a warning telepathically. It would be faint from this distance, but I'd been able to hear him earlier when we tested it.

Going through the various books and papers was tedious. Our translation marks worked well enough when dragons spoke but didn't work nearly as well on written language. I was a little surprised the daemons had even bothered to include the dragon language at all when they crafted the magic behind the marks, but it probably would have bothered them to leave any known language out. As it was, they'd had to add the dragon language from memory, and it was a little shakier than most of the other languages.

"This one is in fae writing," Mikhail said, going through some letters he'd pulled from a desk on the second floor. I put back the journal I'd been leafing through and took the letter from him.

"I don't recognize any of these names. I don't think these are locations in the human realm." I frowned as I studied the list. Outlined on the paper were names followed by geographical information and human population numbers. "Wait." I pointed at one midway down the list. "That's the seraphim realm."

Mikhail peered at the paper. "We know there are humans in the seraphim realm when there shouldn't be. Is it possible other realms have humans?"

"Maybe," I murmured. "I've been to a lot of realms, though, well over a hundred at this point, and I've never encountered humans in any of them. But something about the humans being in the seraphim realm bothers me . . . make a copy of it, and we'll see what Pele thinks. I'm going to check the room upstairs and then we should head back."

Mikhail pulled out some folded sheets from his pants and flattened them against the paper so they could copy the writing over. Pele had packed a bunch in her pack for just this occasion. I left him to it and jogged up the stairs to the top floor. More shelves lined the walls, with a few wooden crates stacked in front of them. Apparently, this room was used for storage.

A breeze filtered in from the open window, bringing in the cool night air and a familiar scent. I stalked over to the boxes in front of the window and found the source. The box was full of plain off-white fabric that had been tightly wrapped around lavender, sage, and other herbs. I let a little of my devourer magic wrap around the fist-sized balls and felt it snuff out immediately.

"Fuck," I said. After a quick look around the rest of the room, I headed back downstairs. "They're definitely working with Balor, and he's given them several boxes of goodies, courtesy of the warlocks."

I swallowed as memories of what Sebastian had done to me floated to the surface.

"I found some of those damn herb sacks Sebastian used to smother my magic and some other trinkets."

"Balor is making sure the dragons have a way to neutralize the magic of others," Mikhail said. "There's no reason to do that unless he's planning on using the dragons to fight outside of this realm."

I nodded. "What do you want to bet that the seraphim have their own supply of warlock herbs and spells to neutralize magic?"

"Hopefully something in these documents can shed light on where and when they will be attacking," Mikhail tucked the papers into his pocket. "And maybe how Balor planned on getting them out of this realm."

"Let's get out of here," I said. "We can decide tonight with the others if we want to leave this realm tonight or risk staying here another two days."

I closed the gateway as soon as we stepped back inside the storage room and stepped towards the door, but Mikhail blocked me. "You don't look like you've spent the last ten minutes being ravished," he said in a low, thick tone.

"Maybe I'll pretend to leave here disappointed after being so underwhelmed by your mediocre pawing." I arched an eyebrow at him in challenge.

"As if I would ever leave you wanting."

My heart beat wildly in my chest, and by Mikhail's widening grin, he could hear it. Fuck it. We reached for each other at the same time, lips crashing together. He backed me up until my butt bumped into a table, and he lifted me up on it.

One rational thought managed to push itself forward, reminding me this was a bad idea, but I quashed it. Maybe I could just get this out my system and then walk away. Mikhail's mouth tore from mine as he kissed my neck, fangs scraping against my skin. I tilted my head back, giving him better access.

Just one time, I told myself. *Totally walk away after this.*

My thoughts scattered when he sucked hard on my nipple while his hand gripped my other breast. A groan slipped from my lips, and I felt his lips curve into a smile against my skin. His hands trailed down and lifted the fabric from my dress, and he pushed me back on the table. I stretched out, trembling as his fingers slowly traced up my inner thigh.

"Is there something you want from me?"

I bit my tongue as his hand drifted closer to where I wanted it and fell away. I snarled, and he laughed.

"Tell me you want me, Nemain." He leaned over me, one hand still tracing lazy circles on my thigh, the other braced by my head. "Say it," he challenged.

Blood dripped from my lip where I was biting it hard to keep the words back. Like hell would I admit anything to him.

His eyes darkened as he stared at my mouth. I smiled wickedly, and the control he'd been holding onto snapped.

He sucked on my lip at the same time his fingers dove inside me. We both let out sounds somewhere between moans and growls. Mikhail's tongue slipped into my mouth, and I could still taste my coppery blood on it. He kissed me fiercely and pulled back, placing one hand on my chest, pinning me in place, before leaning down and burying his head between my thighs.

"Fuck," I ground out and threw my head back against the table.

Mikhail licked and sucked, and I thrust the sleeve of my dress over my mouth and screamed into it. His hand slid from my chest, and he gripped my thighs, pulling me closer as he devoured me. I bucked against him as my mind unraveled over and over. My body shuddered one more time, and I slumped against the table, feeling wonderfully sated.

Mikhail leaned over me, letting one hand slide up my ribs. He kissed me softly, and I went taut again at the taste of myself on his lips. He pulled back, running his tongue over his fangs, and smirked at me before reaching for a towel on a nearby shelf. He tossed me one as he cleaned himself up.

After a few moments, I was capable of thinking rationally again and something like panic rose in me.

Resisting Mikhail had been difficult before, but now it would be damn near impossible. Based on the knowing grin on his face, Mikhail was very much aware of my thoughts. I schooled my expression into a neutral one as I fixed the dress that had been bunched around my waist.

"Well, if anyone was listening near the door, I think our performance did the job." I yanked the door open before Mikhail could tease me, or worse, start a repeat performance. More than a few dragons watched us walk across the ballroom; my attempt to keep quiet clearly hadn't worked.

"Please tell me you were successful in more than getting off," Pele said under her breath when we joined her off to the side near a balcony.

"Don't start," I warned her. "And yes, to answer your question." I looked around the ballroom, trying to locate the others.

Thorod and his allies were sitting at a table, drinking wine. About half of the other tables were occupied, while the rest of the dragons were meandering around the ballroom or on the dance floor. Eddie and Cerri were dancing and looking at each other like the rest of the world didn't exist. Magos was with Tal and Lynette until they were invited by a group of young dragons to the dance floor; an adventurous red-haired young woman asked Magos to dance, but he politely declined.

"We can discuss it later. I'm going to check in with a few others before the party ends." Pele strode off towards a cluster of young dragons next to the dance floor, leaving me alone with Mikhail.

I was acutely aware of every inch that separated us. Whatever Mikhail was thinking or feeling, he was hiding behind a relaxed pose and amused expression.

I scanned the room, desperately looking for anything to take my mind off the feeling of Mikhail's lips against my skin. My gaze stopped on Magos, and I was surprised by what I saw. He was staring at Eddie and Cerri with a longing I'd never seen on his face before. He seemed to catch himself and covered it up instantly. But it had definitely been there. I knew he wasn't lusting after Cerri specifically. Magos had never shown an interest in anyone before. I knew why and what that type of loss felt like, which was why I never pushed him about it.

"What was she like?" I asked softly. "His wife?"

Mikhail followed my gaze to Magos, understanding dawning in his expression. "Hasina was like the sun rising each day. She was from one of the northern cities, like my father, and when she arrived in our township, she was a force to behold." Mikhail let out a low laugh. "The northern cities had been large, with populations of well over fifty thousand in each city. In the south, we liked our space. So instead of building one large city, we would build towns where a few thousand would live, but all the towns were close to each other. In some ways, I guess they'd be like neighborhoods in the human realm, but with a little more distance between them."

"The feline realm my parents were from was set up in a similar way." I snatched a glass of wine from a passing server and took a sip. *Mmm. Fruity.* "Feline shifters aren't solitary, but we like our space."

"Trading between our regions was a huge priority, and it was complicated to manage. Hasina happened to arrive when the previous steward for our area was looking to retire, and she leapt at the chance." Mikhail watched Pele converse with the young dragons. "She was a lot like Pele, but . . . friendlier."

I smiled into my wine glass as I sipped.

"The trade routes between the south and the north were a common target for others who lived in our realm. Magos was in charge of protecting the traders from our township, so he worked closely with Hasina from the beginning. Everyone could see they liked each other, but Magos was completely oblivious that the woman he was quietly pining after was head over heels in love with him. Until she cornered him at one of our festivals and kissed him in front of everyone." Mikhail smiled at the memory. "It was the first time I'd ever seen my uncle shocked and confused. Once he caught on, he didn't waste any time, though. They were married within six months and together for decades until . . . well, you know what happened." His smile slipped.

I still remembered the pain on Magos's face when he told me what had happened to their people. How their realm had fallen to the devourers and the survivors had fled to the human realm, only to be caught in the war between the vampires and werewolves. Mikhail and Magos had been some of the original vampires created, and when they had spurned the other vampires, it hadn't gone well. Without intending to, they made their people a target, and between vampire and werewolf attacks . . . all their people died. Including Hasina.

"Do you think he'll ever find that kind of love again?" My heart beat wildly in my chest. "After her?"

"You're better suited to answer that question. I've never felt that kind of love before." Mikhail waited a few seconds and asked, "Do you think you can find it again after Myrna?"

The beats of my heart slowed until I was acutely aware of each one. Myrna. The mermaid I had loved so fiercely. Who died because of that love. I swallowed the rest of the wine in one gulp and strode across the room to join Pele, Mikhail's gaze searing me like a brand the entire way.

He didn't follow.

***

"Why are we going to the garden?" I asked again. "I'm really not up for fighting another trakdi. Once was enough, thanks."

Pele continued to ignore my complaints as she ushered me through the halls, Mikhail and Magos behind us. We'd spent the past couple of hours dancing, talking, and eating until the party eventually died down. The younger dragons had all but forgotten their initial wariness of us and had kept us company all night. Thorod made no move to interfere, and eventually he'd left, with most of the older dragons leaving with him.

"It's unlikely there will be another devourer attack after the one last night," Magos said calmly. "Pulling that move twice in a row would be too obvious and wouldn't be worth the political hassle."

Before I could argue, Pele pointed to a bench carved from a

fallen tree. Dutifully, I sat down, and the others joined me. The cool night breeze felt good against my skin.

Physically, I felt fine, but emotionally I was a wreck. All I wanted was to curl up in bed, preferably with another bottle of wine. I tilted my head back and gazed at the stars. Far up in the sky, a fireball streaked across the sky, followed by several others. "What is that?"

"Happy birthday, Nemain," Pele said softly.

I froze as too many emotions competed for supremacy. My birthday had filled me with sadness and dread for decades. It was the day Myrna had died, and in the following years, Sebastian had made sure to remind me of that every year. I hadn't been lying when I'd told Eddie that I just wanted to forget about my birthday and try to pretend it didn't exist. When nobody mentioned my birthday again, I assumed they'd either forgotten or had chosen to heed my wishes. With everything going on today, even I'd been able to shove it to the back of my mind.

But it wasn't sadness I felt as I watched fire dance across the heavens. I had never truly been alone in my life. I'd always had Jinx and my brother. Then Pele and Kaysea. After Myrna, I'd pushed everyone away as best I could, but my friends had never abandoned me. And they never would, I realized.

Now my family and friends had grown to include Mikhail and Magos, plus Finn and the others. Originally, it had terrified me to have so many people in my life that I cared about because I'd only been thinking about what it would cost me if I were to lose them.

But as Cerri, Eddie, and whatever other dragons they'd recruited continued their elaborate display, I realized how much more my found family gave me. They gave me strength and support even when I didn't ask for it or even know it was what I needed. I'd been a fool to only see them as a weakness before.

"Thank you," I managed to say, my voice tight.

"Anytime, child," Magos said gently.

I snorted. "I'm a year shy of being four hundred years old. I don't think I qualify as a child anymore."

Magos shrugged and shot me a mischievous smile that I was used to seeing on Mikhail's face. "I have several centuries on you, and part of me will always think of you as that stubborn child who refused to leave me in the darkness."

"I will always find you in the dark, my friend," I told him, meaning every word. Then I looked at Pele and Mikhail. "I'll find all of you."

"As we will you, Nemain," Pele replied. "Never forget that."

Magos reached behind me and pulled up two familiar-looking ceramic jugs. "We stashed these here earlier," he said, passing one to me and the other to Pele. I took a long drink, enjoying the light, sweet taste of the honey ale. I never would have guessed dragons would like sweet-tasting alcohol, but I was glad they did because this was delicious.

"How do you think the vamp brats are doing?" I asked, passing the ale to Mikhail.

"Almost certainly driving Dante insane," he said. "Cian is probably enjoying himself, though."

"Oh, he definitely is," I agreed. "He comes across as all sweet and nice, but he's a damn instigator."

Pele took a long drink and leaned back on her elbows. "Elisa is working in the tavern all week. I'm sure she's enjoying being out of the chaos of that apartment."

I smirked. "Remember that night she and Bryn were at The Inferno for a date? And those young daemons were making a scene, so Kaysea and Zareen had to explain what daemon puberty is like?"

Pele burst out laughing. "Oh my gods! Asmodeus and I had to excuse ourselves and go hide in my office!"

"What about daemon puberty?" Mikhail asked, grabbing the jug of ale from me.

"Daemons go through puberty later than humans do, usually in their thirties or forties. They're basically young adults at that point."

"Horny young adults," Pele added.

"Horny young adults," I amended. "You've probably noticed from the daemons that hang around The Inferno that they're not exactly shy about sex. They don't see anything shameful in it and think it's just another thing to be enjoyed in life."

"It's an excellent outlook on life," he said coyly.

I snatched the ale back from him. "Well, the daemons have a bit of . . . umm . . . a reputation about the type of parties they throw when going through puberty."

"Orgies for days!" Pele raised the jug high, her quick motion causing some of it to slosh out the top.

Magos carefully took it from her. "No more ale for you," he said, shaking his head. She looked at me, and I took a swig from my jug and passed it to her. Magos sighed.

"So, Zareen is telling Bryn and Elisa all this. And our dear sweet young valkyrie is just blushing harder and harder." I laughed so hard at the memory, tears began streaming down my face. "Meanwhile Elisa is asking for more details. Kaysea chimes in and adds to the story. At which point Bryn cuts in and asks why Kaysea knows so much about all this."

"Oh boy," Mikhail snickered, passing the jug back to me.

"And Kaysea tells her—"

"Nobody fucks like a daemon!" Pele shouted, and we both dissolved into giggles again.

I wiped the tears from my face. "I honestly thought Bryn was going to die right there."

We drank beneath the stars as Pele recounted some of the more ridiculous pranks daemons and lokis had pulled on each other recently. At some point, I'd ended up leaning against Mikhail and sleep tugged at me. I didn't remember drifting off, but I briefly woke as Mikhail placed me in bed back in our shared room.

As I started to stir, he stroked my hair and then slid in behind me and pulled the covers over us. "Sleep, Nemain," he said gently as his arm wrapped around me, and the heat of his body lulled me back into sleep.

Chapter Seventeen

TODAY THE WINNERS *will square off against each other in human form,* Thorod announced. *The winners from today will go on to the third challenge, in which they will fight an opponent of my choosing. If they both survive, then they will fight against each other. The winner will claim my daughter's hand in marriage.*

Dragons roared in approval, but there was a noticeable difference today. Yesterday, the dragons had been more spread out around the arena; now the younger generation of dragons had settled in on our side of the arena. They did not roar and cheer at Thorod's words but instead remained silent or sent glances towards Cerri. Her gaze did not waver from that of her father's as they stared each other down from across the arena.

I wasn't sure if it was nerves or if she wanted to make a statement, but after helping to fly us down to the arena, she had remained in her dragon form. Lucan and Lynette sat with us once again, but they'd shifted back to human.

Thorod didn't miss that the younger dragons had apparently made their decision to throw their support behind us. Instead of looking upset by this, he looked pleased.

"He's plotting something," I murmured.

He always is, Cerri agreed.

Pele had pored over the copies we'd made from what we'd found in Thorod's tower that morning, and I told her about the spells and trinkets of warlock magic I'd found. Aside from the seraphim realm and a couple others, most of the locations were unknown to us. But they each had estimates of human populations which I didn't understand. I'd never encountered humans in any great number outside of the human realm. And these weren't small numbers, either; most listed populations of at least a hundred thousand, and a few were over a million.

Once we were back home, we'd have to investigate these realms to see if we could find them and learn how they came to be. For now, Pele had redirected her focus back to the treaty.

The dragon leadership hadn't met today; everyone agreed they were too tired from the night before. But Pele was planning on meeting individually with a few of its members later, including Dindrane, who was well-respected by several of the dragons still hesitating to say they'd support a treaty.

Nobody outright said it, but everyone was clearly fearful of drawing Thorod's wrath, and I couldn't really fault them for that. We were asking them to trust us not only with their lives, but with the lives of their friends and family.

The first challenge shall be the exile against Taliesin, Thorod said, cutting into my thoughts.

Eddie and Tal entered the arena from opposite sides. Once again, I felt the magic rise from the dragons. There would be no healing for Eddie and Tal for as long as they were in that arena. Neither wore armor. In fact, they wore barely any clothing at all. Both wore loose-fitting pants and carried no weapons.

I studied the arena and noticed some metal objects reflecting the sun in the middle. They must have dumped some weapons for the opponents to fight over.

Based on everything I'd read and my conversations with Cerri, dragons didn't fight as humans that often. Which made sense given the lackluster performance we'd seen from Thorod's thugs yesterday. They trained and practiced for tournaments like this, but in a real fight, they would almost always shift to dragon.

Why fight as a two-hundred-pound human when you could fight as a several-thousand-pound beast with sharp teeth and wicked claws?

Tal had likely practiced his entire life because that was expected of a dragon of his standing. Eddie had sparred occasionally with me and the vampires, but sword fighting definitely wasn't one of his skills. He'd gotten better since I'd known him, but he was still no match for any of us. But then again, few were. I had no doubt I could defeat any of the dragons in a fight of steel. Unfortunately, all they had to do was shift and stomp on me, and that would be the end of that.

"Maybe we should have brought Jinx," I said. "He could have given all of Eddie's opponents bad luck."

It doesn't matter who wins, Cerri said. *As long as they both walk out of that arena alive.*

"Your father will know if they throw the fight," Mikhail said. "They need to make this convincing. Plus, they're both arrogant enough to not want to be the one who throws the fight."

"Tal seemed off this morning when I spoke with him," Lucan said, his features pinched together in concern. "It was after my father pulled him aside and they exchanged a few words."

"Your brother threw the fight yesterday with Tal," Pele said, keeping her voice low. "If your father knows about that, he could be threatening Tal not to throw this fight with Eddie."

"Tal won't kill him," Lucan said firmly. "He knows how

much Eddie means to Cerri, and he would never hurt Cerri like that."

"Not even if your father threatened to kill you if Tal didn't do as he was commanded?" Pele asked.

Lucan paled.

"You know your father better than any of us, Lucan," I said gently. "Would he threaten to kill you? And would Tal believe him?"

Lucan looked down at the hands he'd been wringing in his lap and swallowed. "Uther challenged our father last year about his seemingly unyielding support for Thorod. He'd threatened to ally with the younger dragons and stand up to Thorod and any allied with him. Our father had just shrugged and said he was welcome to do so, but he should know that I would pay the price for such a decision. Uther told him if anything ever happened to me, he'd kill whoever was responsible or die trying."

Lucan paused, a haunted expression filling his eyes.

"It was our mother, our own damn mother, who said they could always make more sons if we were unfit for the responsibilities of our bloodline."

I curled my lip in disgust. My relationship with Badb and Kalen might be complicated, but it was nothing compared to what most of these dragons had with their parents.

Tal would trust us to keep you safe, Lucan, Cerri said.

"After this fight, Lucan, you need to stay with one of us at all times, understand?" I held his gaze until he nodded.

BEGIN! Thorod's voice boomed.

Both Tal and Eddie took off running across the arena and dove for the weapons that had been tossed in the center. Tal snapped up a sword and swiped at Eddie as he reached for his own sword. Eddie pulled his hand back in time to keep from losing it, but Tal's blade grazed the top of his forearm. This was definitely not off to a good start for Eddie, who was backing away from Tal, trying to get him away from the weapons.

Tal didn't hesitate and went after Eddie, who could only dodge the attacks. Cerri tensed as Eddie tripped and Tal slammed his sword into the ground. Eddie barely managed to roll out of the way. Tal wasn't pulling his strikes. If Eddie hadn't moved, he likely would have been dealt a mortal blow.

Maybe Cerri's confidence in Tal was misplaced, and he would choose his lover's life over everything else.

"Come on, Eddie," I urged. "Get around him and get a goddamn weapon."

Tal continued pressing Eddie, who continued dodging his advances. Slowly but surely, Eddie was making his way back to the weapons. Tal thrust forward, lightning quick, and Eddie twisted, letting the blade slide by his stomach, and hammered a kick to Tal's right knee. The dragon grunted and stumbled a step. Eddie didn't hesitate and ran across the arena, grabbing an ax and a sword.

"Drop the damn ax, Eddie," I commanded, as if he could hear me. Wielding two weapons took experience, skill, and speed. It was my preference, but I'd been practicing with my twin blades for centuries. Eddie struggled enough with one sword.

"No," Mikhail said, leaning forward. "I practiced with him before we came here. He knows what he's doing."

My jaw hardened as I watched Tal bear down on Eddie. His usual kind face showed no mercy as he swung his blade. Eddie blocked it with the ax and whipped around with the sword. The blade dug into Tal's shoulder, and he screamed, jerking back.

Eddie went on the offensive. His strikes weren't the best, and he was often off balance, but Tal wasn't a good enough swordsman to take advantage of it. When he managed to counterstrike, Eddie would block with the ax and continue his attacks. Both managed to land a few hits but nothing major enough to end the fight. Almost every inch of their skin was coated in blood, and one of Tal's arms hung at his side. Eddie was limping slightly but still didn't let up.

Tal took a half step to the left and raised his sword to strike at Eddie's side, but I saw it for the feint it was. Panic rose in me as Eddie raised his ax to block the blow, leaving himself open to a different attack. Tal pulled his blade back and plunged it down, straight through Eddie's thigh. Eddie roared in pain and stumbled back. Tal ripped the sword free, flinging blood across the sand.

Cerri screamed, and I saw Thorod bare his teeth, a satisfied look in his eyes as Tal tracked Eddie across the arena. Eddie tried to rise but failed. His life blood was pouring out in the sands. Tal had pierced his femoral artery. He had only minutes to live without his ability to heal. My fingers dug into the earth.

"Get ready," I said under my breath to Mikhail and Magos. They could be down there in an instant to save Eddie. All hell would break loose after that and we'd have to get the hell out of here, but I wasn't about to watch my friend die for this bullshit. They both nodded grimly.

"Wait," Mikhail breathed.

I looked at Eddie, trying to see what Mikhail saw that made him hesitate. Eddie's hand was extended behind him as if looking for something, grim determination on his face.

Tal slowly closed the distance between them, pain etched onto his features, and I knew it wasn't only because of the wounds he'd received in this fight. He had accepted what he had to do to save his lover, and the decision hurt him. When he was a few steps away from being able to make the killing blow, Eddie struck.

Sand flung out as Eddie raised the spear he'd found and threw it at Tal. His aim was true, and Tal's reaction time wasn't fast enough. The spear pierced Tal's body, mere inches from his heart. Tal let out a shocked gasp and fell to his knees, dropping his sword. Eddie crawled over to Tal and gripped the spear, raising the sword to Tal's throat, and looked at Thorod.

Lucan had gone still as a statue.

Cerri's father glowered at Eddie and then at Tal, who was taking in shallow, shuddering breaths. Hatred burned in his eyes, and I knew he was thinking about making Eddie kill Tal, if only because it would hurt his daughter.

Seconds ticked by, and I growled. Both Eddie and Tal would bleed out if they didn't get access to their healing magic. Another dragon with bright red scales rumbled from where he sat near Thorod, who cut a glance at the dragon and turned his gaze back to the arena. *It seems the exile is once again the winner and shall proceed to the next event. Lift the magic so their corpses don't bring shame to the arena.*

Instantly, the magic lifted, and Lucan sprinted to the arena. Cerri leapt into the air to join him.

Not you, daughter, Thorod said coldly. *There is still one more match you must bear witness to.*

Cerri hovered, her mighty wings stirring the air around us with each beat, and lowered to the ground. *Of course, Father.* Even in my mind, her words were stilted. She shifted to human form and sat back down, staring at Lucan, who had shifted to dragon form in the arena.

"I'll go with them," Magos offered.

"Thank you," Cerri said softly. Magos gave her a kind, reassuring smile, and jogged towards the arena.

Lucan stretched a leg out, and Magos nimbly leapt onto his back. Once he was settled, Lucan carefully picked Eddie up with his tail and placed him in front of Magos. Once Eddie was secure, he swiped Tal up with one hand and leapt into the air, flying fast back to the citadel.

On to the next match, Thorod said. Vizor entered the arena on one side, and a dragon with light blond hair and tanned skin entered on the opposite side. Elyan, I remembered.

"That's one of the dragons you were speaking with last night, isn't it, Pele?"

"Yes," she said. "He was courteous and well-spoken and seemed well-versed in dragon history and politics. He's part of a generation in between most of the younger dragons like Cerri and Eddie and the older dragons like Thorod. I'm surprised that he's not part of the dragon leadership and that he entered into this stupid competition. He doesn't seem like the type."

"My father manipulated him into doing so. I don't know the specifics, but I know my father played a hand in this. Elyan is an honorable dragon, unlike Vizor. I hope he survives this bout, but I fear he will not."

Lynette seemed to go still at Cerri's words as she stared at the arena. I gently touched her shoulder, and she jumped slightly, eyes snapping to me.

I signed, *Are you okay?*

Yes. She pointed at Cerri and the arena, and then pressed her hand against her heart, raising it up and down in slow, exaggerated movements. *Stressed.*

I studied her carefully, trying to figure out what I was missing. Maybe she was still shaken from Eddie and Tal's fight. She'd known both of them for a long time. I looked back at the arena to where Vizor was patiently waiting for the fight to begin.

Has he ever bothered you? I stumbled through the gestures, but Lynette seemed to understand me well enough. She vehemently shook her head once.

I'm fine, she signed.

Okay, I told her, still not believing it to be true, but there wasn't much I could do about it now.

She gave me a smile that didn't reach her eyes and returned her attention to the arena.

Thorod raised his tail and slammed it to the ground. *BEGIN!*

Vizor and Elyan reached the center of the arena at the same time and swiped up swords. Elyan went on the offensive first, pushing Vizor back with well-executed blows.

"He's not bad," I murmured.

"He has some skill," Mikhail admitted, sounding reluctant.

"Elyan is two centuries older than us," Cerri said. "He's competed in several tournaments like this and won some of them."

"What did he win at those tournaments?" I asked, then sucked in a breath as Vizor barely managed to block a blow to his neck.

"Not a bride," Cerri said dryly. "Tournaments are held every few years for one reason or another. Usually, my father or one of the other elder dragons coughs up some sort of prize, an old sword with some silly story, a skull of a long-dead beast, but the real prize is bragging rights."

Mikhail leaned forward, eyes focused on Vizor. "Clever, dragon."

I frowned and studied the fighting dragons, trying to pick up on what Mikhail saw that I had missed. Vizor was still on the defensive and bleeding from several wounds on his torso where Elyan had snuck past his guard. He'd been backing up the whole fight, giving ground to Elyan, but he hadn't been taking steps straight back. Instead, he'd made a circle, and they were nearing the center of the arena again.

Oh. Sneaky.

Elyan made a diagonal strike. He'd made the same strike four moves before. He'd fallen into a rhythm and was counting on his superior skill and stamina to eventually break through Vizor's guard. He hadn't noticed where Vizor had been leading them. As Elyan thrust his blade forward, Vizor knocked it to the side, and in an impossibly fast move, he kicked an ax off the ground, sending sand spraying into Elyan's eyes in a move that echoed Eddie's from earlier.

The fair-haired dragon barely parried the brutal strike Vizor had aimed at his gut but couldn't recover fast enough to dodge the ax. He screamed as the ax-head tore into his other side, sliding between the ribs. Without missing a beat, Vizor thrust the sword into his abdomen and ripped it free. Elyan held a hand against his gut, blood seeping through his fingers. His sword slipped from his hand.

"I yield," he pushed out, dropping to one knee, head bent as he took in deep, rattling breaths.

Vizor studied the dragon, a mask of indifference on his face, and looked up at Thorod.

Thorod studied the two of them, satisfaction in his eyes. For whatever reason, he'd wanted Elyan dead, and there was no one to plea on his behalf. Disgust ran through me. Such a waste.

I believe the sands of the arena need more blood, Thorod said. *By all means, help quench that thirst, Vizor.*

Vizor stared at Thorod; no hint of emotion betrayed his thoughts. Moments passed and tension rose in those gathered as they looked back and forth between Thorod and Vizor, confused as to why Vizor hadn't carried out the execution command yet.

"I think enough blood has been spilt for your entertainment." Vizor dropped his sword and ax, the metal clanging against each other as they hit the sand. He strode out of the arena without another glance at Thorod.

"What the fuck?" I stared after him in shock. "What just happened?"

Some of the young dragons swooped in and gathered Elyan before Thorod could order another to do what Vizor had refused to do. I thought Thorod would command them to stop, but he just stared after Vizor, fury burning in his eyes.

"I don't know," Pele said slowly. "Looks like Vizor is a wild-card for everyone."

Chapter Eighteen

No ELABORATE PARTY was planned for that evening. Not even a dinner, really. Food was being served in the large dining hall, but we opted to eat in our suite instead.

Apprehension had lingered in the air since Vizor had walked out of the arena. Everyone seemed to know something was coming, but no one knew what.

Tal and Lucan had been scurrying about, arranging for some of the dragons to come talk to Pele and Cerri. The treaty negotiations weren't anything that I could help with; I would just get in the way. We'd managed to collect some important information from Thorod's tower, and it didn't seem wise to go snooping around tonight given the tense atmosphere. But the idea of spending the rest of the night inside this room made my skin crawl.

I'd just finished sharpening one of my daggers and was starting on the other one when a shadow fell over me. Pele scowled down at me, and I slowly lowered the sword to my lap. "Yes?"

"You're brooding. Which I find annoying in and of itself, but since you do it silently, I can tolerate it." Pele leaned in, setting her hands on each side of the chair and boxing me in. I pushed further back into the chair. "What I *cannot* ignore is the goddamn sound that block makes as you swipe it against your blade."

"I'm bored," I grunted in frustration.

"Go for a walk." She enunciated each word carefully. "Go to the roof. I don't care. Just. Go. Away."

"Not alone though," Eddie said. "Just in case."

"Take the big one." Pele gestured at Magos, who merely gave her a polite smile.

"Fine." I rose from the chair and set aside the sharpening block, sliding my sword back into its sheath. "Care to join me for a walk, Magos?"

"I would be delighted." He rose gracefully to join me.

We left Pele and the others to their political scheming and wandered through the halls of the citadel. Most of the dragons had already retired for the evening, either in their rooms here or in the surrounding houses. The few that passed us merely nodded in greeting and carried on quickly. No one wanted to be out late tonight, it seemed.

Soon, we found a set of stairs and followed them up until we reached a balcony large enough for several dragons in their true forms to lounge about.

Comfortable-looking chairs were gathered in one corner around a fire pit, but I headed towards the thick stone railing that ran around the outer edge of the balcony. I hopped up on it, legs dangling over the edge as I looked out at the city below. Magos leaned against the railing, close enough that he could catch me if I slipped.

I bit back a smile. Magos didn't understand or approve of my fondness for high places. When I was a child and got upset by something, Jinx and I would often climb up onto the roof of our house or find the tallest tree possible and perch at the top. It drove my parents crazy, and they blamed Jinx for encouraging my fondness of high places. I couldn't fly, and a fall from this height would likely break every bone in my body, but it probably wouldn't kill me. I leaned out a little farther, looking down. On second thought . . . it was pretty high.

"I'm not going to fall," I said when Magos moved just a touch closer.

"It would ease my nerves if you wouldn't tempt fate."

I swung one leg over the railing so I was straddling it and grinned at him. "Anything for you, my friend."

Magos shook his head and let out a fatalistic sigh that he seemed to use around me quite often.

"What do you think the brats are up to?" I asked. He'd been quiet last night, content to listen to Pele and me recount ridiculous stories. "Think they've driven Dante insane yet?"

His face broke out into a wide smile. "I think Cian is having fun entertaining Isabeau and probably making sure she doesn't annoy Dante too much, if only so that when Cian starts to bug him about kids, Dante isn't still traumatized from his time with Isabeau." I barked out a laugh, and Magos chuckled. "Elisa is probably hanging on every word Dante says and trying to glean as much information from him as possible. Misha and Damon are likely picking up all sorts of tricks from the loki, who no doubt delights in spreading their brand of mischief and mayhem to the young vampires."

I grunted in agreement. "Gods know what type of things Sten is teaching them."

"Luna and Jinx are probably just letting everything play out and barricading themselves in the second-floor apartment with Finn, while Bryn tries in vain to keep everything in order while we're gone."

"I miss Jinx," I admitted. "He's been one of the few constants in my life. We've been parted before occasionally, but it feels different this time."

"Your lives have changed a lot in the last couple of years," Magos said gently. "And he has Luna now."

"He does," I agreed. "I'm happy for him. For both of them."

"You could have Mikhail."

Full stop. I jerked my gaze away from the rooftops I'd been studying and stared at Magos in disbelief.

He continued looking out into the night, refusing to meet my incredulous stare. It was bad enough that Pele and Eddie were teasing me about this. I did not expect Magos of all people to get involved in my damn love life, especially since he'd always seemed worried about Mikhail and I getting together.

"Are you that eager for me to bang your nephew?"

"I will not be dissuaded from this conversation by crudeness." Magos's tone and expression remained one of calm politeness that said he wouldn't be dropping this. I let out a sigh. Might as well get this over with.

"It's too much." The panic I felt every time I looked into Mikhail's eyes threatened to rise, but I smothered it. "Too complicated."

"Life is complicated. You already know this."

Gods, did I ever. I looked away from my friend and studied the stars, trying to piece together what I was feeling in a way that made sense. "Love makes you weak," I said slowly. "If you give it to the wrong person. Mikhail thinks I reject him because I want to be with someone who balances my often ruthless nature. That I want to be with someone kind and peaceful, and that is why I won't be with him. He's wrong. Everyone forgets that I loved Sebastian, and he loved me."

"He used you," Magos said coldly. The look in his eyes told me that he wished he'd been the one to kill Sebastian. "That wasn't love."

"Life is complicated," I repeated bitterly. "Love even more

so. Sebastian set out to use me. I was powerful, and he knew he could manipulate my grief and anger. Which he did. I was a weapon he wielded for decades against his enemies." A memory of a simple glass sphere played in my mind. A gift and an apology. Something I never would have accepted while he lived but could accept after his death. "But he also loved me."

Magos remained silent.

"It took me a long time to see his manipulation and how I was being used. Love makes you blind to such things. *That* is the weakness I fear."

"You think Mikhail would use you?" He raised an eyebrow at me. "To what end?"

"Not intentionally," I assured him. Magos knew Mikhail had a dark past, but he still loved his nephew. "But he walked away from the Vampire Council. They will come for him, eventually. He would be foolish *not* to use me as a weapon against them."

"Despite what my nephew thinks of himself, he has not fallen so far off the path of our people that he would ever use you in such a manner. Even when he lost his way and joined the Council as their assassin to seek revenge, there were lines he would not cross." Magos's copper eyes bore into me. "Mikhail's greatest flaw isn't that he would use you as a weapon, it's that it wouldn't even cross his mind. He protects those he loves even when they don't need nor want his protection."

My chest tightened, a deep ache pulsing from an old wound that never seemed to heal. I stretched out on the railing, my back against the cool stone, and stared at the night sky.

"What's really bothering you? I know you, Nemain. If you actually thought Mikhail would betray you in such a way, you would have slit his throat while he slept."

I swallowed. He was right. I would have. It would have hurt Magos to lose his nephew like that, which is why I would have hidden the body somewhere he never would have found it. Not a perfect solution, but there rarely was in life. I was content to play the role of being a monster if it kept those I loved safe.

Magos waited for me to answer. The silence between us stretched, feeling like a lifetime, but I knew it had only been a few seconds.

"He's not Myrna," I said, my voice barely above a whisper. "I've loved before. Sebastian. Andrei. But neither compared to what I felt towards Myrna. What if this thing between me and Mikhail, what if it becomes something . . ." The words died in my throat even as the betrayal of what I was suggesting ignited the pain in my chest further.

"Loving him in such a way doesn't discount what you felt towards Myrna," Magos said gently. "If what you and Mikhail have turns into something all-consuming and brings that kind of joy and love into your life, I don't think Myrna would be disappointed in you. Based on everything you've told me about her, I think she would be happy for you. True love is not a competition. You and I are among those who will likely live for a long time; it would be cruel if we couldn't find love again after losing it."

"Will you?" I asked, sitting up so I could look him in the eye. "If you have the opportunity to be with someone again in that way, to give your heart and soul over to them completely, knowing what the cost is of losing that love, would you do it again?"

He looked away from me, turning towards the stars while he thought about my question. His chest rose and fell with a deep breath, and he turned towards me, acceptance brimming in his eyes. "I will, if you will."

Heat pooled behind my eyes, and I jerked my head in a nod and laid back down on the railing.

Magos settled on the ground and leaned his back against the railing, content to enjoy the peace and quiet while we both thought about the truth we'd shared. I still had no idea what I was going to do, but that crushing pain and guilt I'd been feeling started to ease.

Almost an hour had passed when I felt another presence. Magos gracefully rose to his feet and left without a word. I remained frozen where I was still lying on the balcony, heart beating wildly as my magic hummed beneath my skin.

Mist snapped together, and Mikhail stood by the railing. His dark hair fell in loose waves to his shoulders, and his twilight eyes reflected the stars above us.

I forced myself to look away before I lost myself in them.

"Learn anything interesting while you were skulking about?" I asked.

Mikhail braced his hands on the railing, one by my ribs and the other just below my hip. My breath hitched for a few seconds before I focused on breathing. He wasn't even touching me, for crying out loud. Maybe I should just roll off the railing and take my chances on the fall. It couldn't possibly be that bad.

"Nothing new." I risked a quick glance and found his eyes still on the stars. His expression was almost tranquil, but I knew him well enough to see past the mask. Mikhail was every bit as keyed up as I was. "The halls are silent tonight, with tension in the air. The sooner we get out of here, the better."

"The plan is to leave tomorrow after the final bout. Pele is with the last of the dragons she wants to meet so that even if the treaty isn't signed tomorrow, she still has solid contacts here."

"Ah."

Minutes ticked by. Mikhail continued to look up at the stars, making no move to touch me, but I still felt the heat radiating off him. The connection between us was taut as a bowstring, and it was making my magic churn beneath my skin.

Screw this.

In one swift motion, I pulled myself up into a sitting position. As if he anticipated my move, Mikhail raised his arm, letting my legs pass, but didn't move back. The front of my legs brushed against his thighs, and his eyes darkened at the contact, but he made no move to get closer. As it was, we were almost eye level and inches apart.

I sat on that precipice and studied his beautiful face, avoiding those eyes that always seemed to see within my soul.

We'd crossed the line we'd been dancing around last night, but I could still walk away from this. It would be hard; hell, if I was honest with myself, it would be damn near impossible, but I could do it. If I asked him to, Mikhail would leave. He would figure out a way to help us but keep his distance.

The thought of him leaving made me feel cold and hollow. The thought of him staying terrified me. I knew what this was. I recognized this feeling. But I wasn't ready to say it out loud, to admit it. So instead, I said, "This is a bad idea."

"Those are the best kind."

"I'm serious, Mikhail." I lifted my eyes to his and saw the same desperation mirrored in them. "We're both capable of terrible things. Whatever this is between us . . . it will only get stronger if we let it."

"And you're worried about what we would do if the other was taken from us? If we would embrace all the darkness and cruelty in us for the sake of revenge?"

"Yes." No point in lying.

"It's too late for that concern." Mikhail brushed some loose strands of hair behind my ear and ran his fingers down the single long braid that had snaked its way over my shoulder. "If you ask me to leave when we get back, I will do so. But be it a hundred years from now or a thousand, if something ever happened to you, I would spill blood across all the realms and leave them burning until I destroyed everyone who ever raised a hand against you. My uncle wouldn't stop me, nor would your friends."

His fingers ran over the blade on my thigh, and I trembled beneath his touch. "If death came for me, it might be a challenge, but I'm sure I would be victorious."

My breath quickened at his words. "I don't know what's more astounding, your arrogance or your insanity."

"Tell me you wouldn't do the same. Tell me you wouldn't devour the world to get to me." Twilight eyes latched on to me, hiding nothing of himself.

I couldn't bring myself to lie, so I remained silent.

"Decide, Nemain."

I'd already made my decision some time ago. I simply hadn't accepted it yet. I didn't know if it was the right decision, but it was the only one I could make. It was the only one that was real. My fingers wrapped around the back of Mikhail's head, intertwining with his dark hair, and I kissed him.

Mikhail went rigid. My fingers ran through his hair, and I pulled back enough to look at him. A deep purple swirled within his indigo eyes, and I saw the exact moment Mikhail lost control. His mouth crashed back against mine, and the taste of him was intoxicating. I wrapped my legs around his waist, and his hands roamed down to cup my ass, pulling me against him. He licked my jaw, working his way to my throat, and I tilted my head back. He kissed and nipped but didn't break the skin.

I ground against him, and he growled, lifting me off the railing. I laughed as he carried me across the balcony to where the chairs waited for us. He set me on my feet next to one of the longer chaise-style chairs. I missed the heat of him immediately, but he leaned forward, reaching around me, and slowly pulled my swords out of their sheaths. He set them on the ground where they'd be in easy reach. I did the same with his weapons, and we continued pulling weapons off each other, setting them all within reaching distance.

My shirt was next. The cool air brushed against my skin, and Mikhail bent down, sucking one of my nipples into his mouth as his fingers pinched the other. A hiss slipped from my lips as his fang grazed the sensitive skin. He let out a deep-throated chuckle, and I arched my back as his tongue skittered across my skin.

I tugged on his shirt, and he leaned back enough for me to pull it over his head. Mikhail sucked in a breath as I ran my nails over the ridged muscles on his chest and stomach. I cupped the front of his pants, feeling the hard length of him. He let out a growl, and I laughed wickedly as he grabbed the back of my legs and yanked me up, causing me to fall against the chair.

"Two can play that game." He grinned.

I was still laughing when his mouth covered mine, but when his fingers rubbed against the heat pooling between my legs, the laugh turned into a low throaty moan.

"Fuck," he said hoarsely and pulled his hand away. With quick, determined movements, he ripped off my boots and remaining clothes, along with his own. My mouth went dry as I took in the length of him.

"Like what you see?" His eyes were dark as they roamed over my bare skin, drinking in every inch of me.

I leaned back against the chair. "It's all right," I said, sucking in a breath as his fingers ran up the inside of my thighs once more.

"Given how wet you already are, I think you find it more than all right."

My response died on my lips as one of his fingers slipped inside me and pushed in deep. I arched my back, and he slipped in a second finger. Heat spread through me, and I needed more.

Wrapping one leg around his waist, I shoved upward, twisting on top of him.

Mikhail grinned up at me. "So impatient."

"You were taking too long," I snarled. "Fuck. Me."

Mikhail gripped my ass as I leaned down to kiss him. His lips were hot and possessive against mine. My tongue slipped inside his mouth and grazed one of his fangs. The coppery tang spread across my lips as Mikhail licked the drops of blood. He slipped his fingers back inside me, and I thrust forward, riding his hand. His thumb rubbed against my clit, and an orgasm ripped through me. He kept pumping his fingers inside me as I rode it out.

I slowed, trembling over his hand, muscles still twitching. He slid his fingers free, and his cock nudged at my entrance. He looked at me, a question in his eyes, and I responded by sinking onto the full length of him.

"Fuck," he ground out.

His hands gripped my hips, and I sank deeper onto him until he filled every part of me. My body shook as pleasure ripped through me. Gods, this was even better than I thought it would be.

Mikhail rocked his hips up, and I met his thrust with one of my own. I rode him hard, the momentum building faster and faster. Mikhail's fingers dug into my hips as he let out a low growl. When one hand blazed a path up my ribs and squeezed my breast, I arched my back in complete rapture, a heady thrill running through me.

"Gods." Mikhail flipped me over so I was on all fours.

One hand on my hip and the other buried in my hair, he thrust in me. I moaned as pleasure raced through my body. Mikhail kept going, the rhythm building into a frenzy as my body went taut, every thrust bringing me that much closer to the edge.

Finally, the pressure burst, and I cried out as bliss spread through me. Mikhail followed a second later, clutching me tightly against him. My muscles quivered as we sat there, both panting in ecstasy. After a few minutes, Mikhail withdrew and pulled me against him on the chair. I nestled into the heat of his embrace.

Part of me waited for the panic to rise up at what we'd just done, but it never came. Instead, for the first time in ages, I felt completely content.

———

THE FEELING of utter contentment didn't last. The reality that we were naked on a balcony while our enemies roamed beneath us came crashing back. Mikhail seemed to have the same thought.

"We should go back to our room," Mikhail whispered into my ear. "I've got some ideas that would work better with a bed."

"Fine." I rose. "But we're trying my ideas first."

We hastily dressed. Neither of us bothered to put all of our weapons back on. Once I tucked the death dagger back into the sheath on my thigh, I picked up my swords and handed Mikhail his, and we hastily made our way downstairs. I was debating what positions I wanted to try first when the hairs on the back of my neck stood up. I slowed my pace as a dark shadow entered the short hallway from the other end and pulled back his hood.

"Vizor," Mikhail drawled. "Rather late for a dragon to be roaming these halls."

"Shouldn't you be getting your beauty sleep before tomorrow?" I let my fingers slide a little farther up my sword's sheath, closer to the pommel. This hallway was too small for Vizor to shift into his dragon form, but he could still wield fire against us. If he attacked, we'd have to put him down fast or risk getting a little crispy.

Vizor scrutinized us, taking in our misshapen appearance

and the swords in our hands instead of strapped to our backs. His lip curled in distaste. "No trip to the tower tonight, then?"

I willed my face to remain blank even as I wondered how he knew that.

"Nothing to say? Not even going to deny it?" When we continued keeping our mouths shut, Vizor smirked and closed the distance between us, one measured step at a time. "He knows you were in there. Your scents might have faded by the time he got there, but he was taught by the fae he's working with to look for certain signs of gateways being opened."

"Why did you spare Elyan?" I asked, and for a brief second Vizor's cold demeanor wavered at the change in topic before he recovered. "What game are you playing, Vizor?"

"The one where I win."

I took a step away from Mikhail, and he did the same, widening the distance between us and giving Vizor two targets. The corner of his lips tilted up slightly.

He was here for a reason, and I wanted to know why. Telling us about Thorod knowing about our presence in his tower was likely calculated on his part, to make us panic and throw us off our game. But we'd always known it was a risk.

I was more concerned with just how much Thorod knew about my capabilities. It seemed likely Lir was in contact with Thorod; he was in charge of executing Balor's plan. The question was whether Lir told Thorod everything about me. Or did he hold some information back?

"You didn't track us down tonight because you missed our sparkling personalities," I said, tilting my eyes as I inspected him once more. Something was off about him, like he was trying too hard to look unworried.

"Perhaps he's worried about what will happen when we leave this realm?" Mikhail smiled sharply at Vizor, and a flash of uncertainty flickered in the dragon's eyes. "That was quite the move you pulled in the arena earlier."

"That's right." I made a tsking sound. "Going against Thorod's order and sparing Elyan isn't going to endear you to him."

Vizor's eyes flickered between us. His mask slipped a little more, and I saw something in his face I didn't expect. Desperation.

"You're not working with Thorod." I took a step towards him. He stiffened but held his ground. "But that doesn't mean you're on our side."

"I told you before, the only side I'm on is mine."

"No," I said slowly, "I don't think that's true either."

"You know nothing!" he snarled.

"I know you're scared of us leaving," I pushed. "What I don't know is why."

Vizor glared at me, only to take a step back when Mikhail moved closer to him. He shifted back far enough so he could keep us both in his sight. "Are . . ." He stopped. I could practically see the internal war going on in his mind.

I shot Mikhail a baffled look. What the hell had Vizor so freaked out?

"Are you taking anyone with you?" His tone was flat and completely devoid of emotion. This question was important to him. It was the reason he sought us out tonight.

"Who is it that you're concerned about?" Mikhail asked.

I racked my brain trying to think of anyone we'd seen Vizor speak with but came up empty. He had spared Elyan, but I'd never seen them interact outside of the arena. They could be hiding whatever there was between them, or maybe he had someone in one of the other cities he was worried about? Cerri had said all his family was dead, but maybe that wasn't true.

"Tell us who you're so worried about and maybe we can help," I said, ignoring the look Mikhail gave me.

Vizor was an asshole, and I didn't trust him, but he must really care about whoever this person was to be asking us these types of questions. And maybe they were deserving of our help. Even if they weren't, helping them would put Vizor in debt to us, and that would make Pele all kinds of happy.

Vizor stared at me, looking for the answer to something in my face. His expression closed, and he took a step back, shaking his head. "No. You can't even keep your friends safe as it is. I'll handle this myself." He turned to leave.

"Wait!" I called out. "What friends? What are you talking about?" My heart beat rapidly. Had something happened while Mikhail and I were on the roof?

He paused for a moment and looked over his shoulder. "Uther never escaped this city."

Chapter Nineteen

FOR THE THIRD day in a row, we found ourselves seated on the hillside, overlooking the arena. I'd argued we should leave that morning, but Cerri flat out refused because she refused to leave behind Tal and Lucan, neither of whom were willing to leave Uther behind.

Things got interesting when Cerri tried to convince Eddie to leave because she was worried about him. He'd alternated between staring at her like she was insane and laughing maniacally like he was insane.

I tried to get Pele on my side, but she also wanted to stay for the day so that she could finalize plans for how to come back and get the dragons who wanted to sign the treaty out. Once I realized I wasn't going to win this fight, me and the vampires had spent all morning searching the citadel for Uther. We hadn't found a trace of him anywhere, but we also hadn't been able to look in Thorod's tower or the dungeon.

I thought that the dungeon was too obvious a place and that Thorod likely had him locked up in his tower. Magos had argued that Thorod controlled the guards of the city and therefore the dungeon made sense. We still didn't have a plan for what to do about Uther, although secretly I was planning on knocking everyone out and dragging them through a gateway.

Cerri sat in front of me, sandwiched between Lucan and Tal. She'd kept busy all day helping Pele, but she was still beyond pissed off about Eddie refusing to leave. A dark cloud hung over all of us as we waited for the final bouts to begin. We had no idea who Vizor and Eddie would be fighting today, other than not each other. Thorod had only said they would be facing off against an opponent of his choosing and that if they both won their matches, they would fight against each other tomorrow.

My eyes scanned the dragons who had situated themselves around Thorod. I didn't know them all by name, but I recognized most of them now and didn't notice anyone missing. It was possible Thorod had called on dragons from one of the other cities to fight today, but that seemed unlikely. Most of his staunch allies were here, and any dragon entering the tournament now wouldn't have a chance at Cerri's hand, since they hadn't been there from the beginning.

Eddie flew in and landed in the arena. He was up first, so Vizor would have the benefit of knowing what he was up against. Since they had the option of fighting in their dragon or human form, Eddie had chosen to start as a dragon. He could always shift to his human skin if he needed to, but none of us could think of any reason it would make sense to start out that way. Eddie had barely won yesterday, and despite his arrogance, even he admitted his odds were better with scales and claws.

I scanned the dragons who had gathered around the arena. We weren't the only ones wondering what the match would be. They, too, were studying the arena and the surrounding area, trying to figure out what this day would bring.

As my gaze drifted back to the arena, a familiar type of

magic brushed against mine and I froze. "Son of a bitch," I breathed.

"What?" Cerri asked sharply. "Did you see something?"

I concentrated and let out a small sliver of my magic, winding it down to the arena. When it reached the center of the arena, it brushed against that familiar sense and recoiled back to me.

"It's a devourer," I spat. "That's what Eddie and Vizor will be fighting, a godsdamned trakdi."

Mikhail and Magos grimaced. The three of us had barely been able to bring down the trakdi we'd fought against. In his dragon form, Eddie would at least have size on his side, but his flames would be useless, whereas the trakdi could use its devourer magic against Eddie.

"We should have anticipated this," Cerri snarled. "As soon as we discovered he could call them forth, we should have fucking known he would do this. No wonder he was so confident last night."

"What do we do?" Lucan asked.

"We must get him out of there!" Cerri said, trying to keep her voice low. "He can't take on a trakdi by himself!"

"He's fought one before and survived." I rapidly thought through our options for getting Eddie out of this, dismissing them almost as quickly as they came to me. "It was hard for us the other night because we'd never fought one before and the damn things are so big. But they're not as big as a dragon. Eddie is more than double the size of the one we fought, and they can only use their devourer magic against him by physical contact."

"It's been years since he fought one," Cerri argued. "And rarely did he ever fight one alone!"

As if he could sense her worry, Eddie swung his black head towards us, burnt amber eyes completely focused on Cerri. Just as Cerri took a step towards the arena, movement from the other side drew our attention. She halted as dozens of dragons took flight and landed around the arena, guarding the perimeter. The spectator dragons shifted uneasily but remained where they were.

Today's event calls for some protective measures. Some of my friends have volunteered to guard the perimeter and keep everyone safe for these two bouts. Thorod's gaze skimmed over us. *And to prevent any outside interference.*

"Hold for now," I ordered Mikhail and Magos quietly. They could get past the dragons guarding the arena, but getting Eddie out of that arena was another matter.

"And if things go south?" Magos asked in an equally quiet voice.

"Then we'll wing it."

Magos pursed his lips, but Mikhail grinned. He really was insane. And I absolutely adored that about him.

Lucan stood next to Cerri while the rest of us flanked ourselves around them. I hoped Eddie would come out victorious against the devourer. But if he didn't, Mikhail and Magos would go to him, and I'd cause a distraction while Lucan got Cerri the hell out of there. I had no idea how I would accomplish that, and I was kidding myself about Cerri leaving without Eddie, but I was the one who said we would wing it.

As part of the challenge today, the competitors may use whatever means necessary to be victorious, but they cannot leave the arena. A dangerous gleam played in Thorod's emerald-green eyes. *If they leave the arena, they forfeit not only the tournament, but their life.*

The sand at the center of the arena trembled and slipped away, revealing an enormous dark pit. Eddie flexed his black, leathery wings once and tucked them in tight. A low rumble came out of the darkness as the sand continued to pour into its depths. A clawed hand came out of the pit, nearly foot-long talons digging into the ledge, followed by another, then a monstrous head with black eyes and a crocodilian jaw. The trakdi pulled itself up and rose to its full height as the pit closed behind it.

Panicked shouts rose from the dragons seated around the arena, but no one took to the skies. Although those who had been seated further down backed up, creating more distance between them and the arena floor.

"Fuck," I swore as the trakdi seemed to instantly focus on Eddie.

This one was twice as big as the one we'd faced the other night, making it almost the same size as most dragons. Eddie no longer had the advantage of size, and the hope I'd been clinging to vanished. His fire was useless, and if the trakdi sank its jaws or claws into him, its devourer magic would reach out and leech away Eddie's magic as its teeth tore into his flesh.

The dragons guarding our side of the arena angled themselves to keep an eye on both us and the fight. Thorod had the ability to summon the trakdi. He likely had a way to either command it or keep it contained in the arena.

Stationing the dragons around the arena was an excuse; they weren't needed to keep the beast contained, they were only meant to keep us out.

Thorod wanted his daughter to watch her lover get torn to pieces.

All we could do was watch as the trakdi slowly moved across the arena. It looked grotesquely out of place in the bright afternoon sun, a nightmare come to life. Eddie's black scales glistened as he stood his ground but angled his body towards the devourer. The trakdi stopped just short of striking distance and began circling the black dragon. Eddie matched its movements, not allowing the beast to get behind him. Fast as lightning, Eddie spun, his tail aimed at the devourer. But it dodged to the side far faster than it should have been able to given its size, and its massive jaws bit down on Eddie's tail.

Eddie roared, but rather than pull his tail away, he lunged forward, talons aiming for the beast's eyes.

The trakdi released its grip and pulled back, Eddie's talons raking down its long snout and missing the eyes. I flexed my hands at my sides; the dagger strapped to my thigh humming its death magic as if it could sense my need to kill every dragon that stood between me and my friend.

But the dagger could only be used once, and it would be a waste to use it on one of the dragons guarding the arena when half a dozen stood between us and Eddie.

Eddie and the trakdi traded blow after blow. I'd sensed its devourer magic rip into Eddie several times, but so far, he had managed to pull himself free fast enough that the drain on his magic hadn't been too bad. Even still, Eddie was slowing down. The devourer was not. Eddie backed up a step, and metal screeched under his claws. He must be standing on the door that led to the pit where the devourer had been waiting. He stopped in his tracks, and the sound of claws on metal came once more.

"What's he doing?" I said to no one in particular. Even if he got the pit opened again, he couldn't just trap the devourer down there. This fight wasn't over until the devourer was dead, and even if he hurled the devourer down there, I doubted it was deep enough to kill the thing. "Keep moving, Eddie."

Instead of maneuvering around the trakdi, Eddie lunged forward and slammed his tail into the metal door. *Boom! Boom! BOOM!* The door bent inward with each hit until his tail finally broke through. The devourer charged Eddie with a roar. Either the sound of Eddie breaking through the door or his frantic movements had riled it up.

Eddie yanked his tail free, jagged pieces of metal slicing through his scales on the way up. The devourer was too absorbed in its attack to dodge this time as Eddie smashed his tail into its side. The trakdi flew across the arena and crashed into the wall, collapsing before slowly rising and shaking its head. Eddie whirled and grasped the metal door, pulling until half of it fell away, then flipping it so the jagged side was out; his talons punched through the metal, holding it tightly, and in one mighty bound he leapt across the arena. The devourer rose to its feet and faced him and was greeted by Eddie slamming the metal sheet into its neck.

The metal cut into the beast; the quills were thinner on the underside of its neck, and they snapped under the pressure. The devourer was pinned between the wall and Eddie, who was pushing all of his weight onto the metal door that was slowly cutting into flesh.

The trakdi let out a deep growl as it frantically tried to get away. Its jaws snapped open and shut and its tails bashed into Eddie's side, but it couldn't reach him and had no traction. Eddie pushed harder. Inch by inch, the metal slid in further until blood poured onto the arena floor. The trakdi's frantic movements slowed. Eddie pushed himself off the metal door with his front legs and then slammed back down.

The sound of metal hitting stone echoed across the arena, followed by the thud of the devourer's head hitting the ground. I sagged in relief and let out a breath.

Eddie stood over its broken body and roared in triumph. All the dragons that had settled around us roared back and beat their tails against the ground. On the other side of the arena, the dragons remained silent, and several were looking at Eddie with trepidation and fear. Thorod looked at the devourer's remains with amusement. *Looks like the exile isn't completely useless after all. Clear the arena for the next match. We'll see if Vizor is up for the challenge.*

Eddie leapt into the sky and landed behind us, shifting to his human skin in a fiery flash. His wounds had healed, but his skin was pale and clammy, with dark circles under his eyes. The usual bright amber of his eyes had dulled. Healing magic could fix broken bones and tissue damage, but the only thing that helped magic being ripped away was time.

Based on how Eddie looked, the devourer had taken a bigger chunk of his magic than I had realized. Despite the obvious toll the fight had taken on him, he forced himself to stand tall as he strode to us. He gave Cerri a hug and a kiss on the cheek and she moved to the side, with his arm over her shoulder as if she didn't want to let him go. But I could see Eddie's weight shift as he leaned on her slightly.

"Good show," Mikhail said. Magos nodded.

I walked over to Eddie, and he raised a fist in the air. Letting out a sigh, I bumped my fist against his, and he spread his fingers wide as he pulled his hand back, making a whooshing sound.

"The vampire brats are a bad influence on you." I shook my head.

"I like to think we're a bad influence on each other."

Shadows fell over us as ominously dark clouds rolled in. "A storm's coming," Cerri said. "Are you sure you don't want to go back now?"

"No, I'm not missing this," Eddie replied. "If Vizor survives, that means I have to fight the bastard tomorrow. I'd rather him meet his end here and now."

Magos looked up at the storm brewing in the clouds and raised his hand. Mist formed and wound around his fingers. "This is an odd storm."

"We don't get rain all that often," Cerri said. "When it comes, it does not come on gentle winds. Soon, water will pour from the sky and flood the lands. It's why our cities are always built on high ground."

"Can you fly in them?" Mikhail asked.

"Not unless we want to get barbecued," Eddie said with a laugh. "We're immune to fire, not lightning. When the storm kicks into high gear, it's as if a storm god rages above us, and it does not like to share its clouds with dragons."

"The rain likely won't start for another hour or two. This"—Cerri waved her hand towards the sky—"is just the opening salvo."

The dragons finished clearing up the remains of the devourer and returned to the perimeter. Not that they really needed to. We wouldn't be risking our lives for Vizor anytime soon. Lightning flashed in the clouds, followed by thunder. A sleek black dragon descended from the sky and landed clumsily on the arena floor. Odd. Vizor usually moved with more grace than that.

Lynette pulled the shawl she had wrapped around herself tighter. She'd been quiet and withdrawn all morning and now stood slightly behind us. I wondered if she was worried with the tournament drawing to an end. Her father would once again focus on giving her away as a bride. I'd have to assure her after this that we wouldn't let that happen.

It was unlikely Pele would walk away from this with a treaty between the dragons and daemons, but she had turned the small divide between Thorod and the younger generation into a canyon. She would find a way to support the younger dragons. In the meantime, we would help Lynette and any others who were in immediate danger.

Turning my focus back to the arena, I watched as another pit opened and a trakdi clawed its way out. Like the one that had fought Eddie, this one was massive and matched Vizor in size.

The trakdi immediately keyed on Vizor and stalked towards him, drool dripping from the teeth that jutted out from its jaws. The black dragon took a few steps forward, something off in his gait. I squinted. I couldn't see any obvious wounds, but as the dragon moved around the arena, his movements held a sluggish quality. Vizor was a bastard, but he was a graceful bastard. Something was wrong.

I lifted my gaze to Thorod and found him watching Vizor with cool satisfaction. This was punishment, I realized. For Vizor defying him and sparing Elyan yesterday.

"Vizor's going to die," I said with absolute certainty. "Thorod did something to weaken him."

"Vizor must have known my father would never have let his defiance go." Cerri sighed, a hint of finality to it. "He played the game so well all this time. I don't know what he was thinking yesterday."

We watched in silence as the devourer and Vizor fought, the latter barely managing to defend himself. The trakdi sensed the dragon's weakness and was toying with him like a cat torments a mouse. One of Vizor's wings lay at an odd angle where the trakdi had snapped several bones. Blood poured out of a dozen wounds that were no longer healing because the trakdi had stolen huge amounts of magic with every bite.

I couldn't help but feel some respect and pity as Vizor warded off blow after blow. I didn't even know how he was still standing. A growing part of me wanted to help him, despite how much of a prick he was. Based on how Magos and Mikhail were watching Vizor, I suspected they felt the same. But I refused to risk my friends' lives for Vizor's; instead, I prayed for a swift death. It was all I could offer him.

The trakdi surged forward. Vizor tried to swing his tail to bat it aside, but he stumbled. The devourer crashed into his side and pinned the dragon to the ground, its sharp talons ripping into the black scales. A pained sound ripped out of Vizor that sent chills up my spine. It would be over soon.

I turned slightly to check on Lynette but found her gone. "Where is Lynette?"

Both of the vampires snapped their gaze upwards as if they

could sense something moving through the darkening sky. A small golden scaled dragon broke free from the clouds, mist rippling around them as they pinned their wings tight to pick up speed. Snapping their wings open at the last second, they crashed into the trakdi, claws ripping into flesh as the spikes on the back of the devourer pierced the dragon's underside.

The trakdi roared, flinging its head back. The golden dragon didn't hesitate as its claws gripped either side of the crocodilian jaw and pulled. The trakdi frantically flung itself around, trying to dislodge the dragon, but between the dragon's claws and the spike that had impaled their body, the devourer couldn't dislodge them. With one final roar, the dragon ripped the jaws of the trakdi open wide and yanked its head back. Bones cracked as the dragon raised their head above the devourer and shot a steady stream of fire down the devourer's throat.

My mouth hung open as I stared at the barbecued trakdi. That really wasn't how I'd been expecting that fight to go.

With one mighty beat of their wings, the dragon pulled themselves off the devourer, which crashed to the sands, cooked from the inside. Blood poured out the dragon's underside where the spikes had pierced, but they paid no attention to that as they positioned themselves over Vizor's broken body and roared their defiance.

"Well," Mikhail said. "I think we found Lynette."

This is an interesting turn of events, Thorod said. If he was surprised or angry, he hid it well. Which worried me greatly. *Alas, Lady Lynette was not a contender for my daughter's hand in marriage, so she cannot claim it. And I'm inclined to disqualify Vizor based on these events. Which means the exile, Eydellan, is the winner of this tournament and therefore entitled to marry my daughter.*

Both Cerri and Eddie stiffened at his words, at the idea that Cerri was a prize to be given away. *We shall have a feast tonight to celebrate this joyous occasion,* Thorod continued. *All shall be in attendance.*

Once he finished his declaration, Thorod rose up and flew back to the citadel, his allies following after. A few of the dragons that remained looked at Vizor and Lynette, but after a few moments of silent deliberation, they took off back towards the citadel as well. Vizor had done a good job at making himself an enemy to everyone.

Eddie and Cerri looked at each other, some sort of unspoken communication already happening between them. "We're going to figure out what the hell type of veiled threat that just was," Eddie said. "You go help Lynette . . . and Vizor."

Pele looked towards Vizor with obvious distaste. "I'll stay here."

I nodded and took off towards the arena, trusting the vampires to follow after me as I dropped into the arena and sprinted across it to where Lynette was still standing over Vizor's fallen body.

Help him! Lynette's voice crashed into me as I approached them. After conversing with her all week via sign language, it was odd to hear her voice in my head. It suited her, though, soft but with an underlying fierceness.

I slowed my approach and looked over Vizor's form, paying closer attention as my gaze roamed over his scales. Thorod had done something to him. I didn't know much about dragon physiology to know if poison was possible, but I was familiar with warlock magic thanks to hunting Sebastian all those years.

"Don't freak out and bite me," I told Vizor as I closed the distance between us. He raised his head enough to glare at me but didn't flinch as my hands touched his scales.

Slowly, I let my devourer magic seep over him. The magic

within him recoiled, and he snarled at me, but Lynette hushed him. I focused solely on my magic until I felt it, right above his right shoulder, something that was not dragon magic. I climbed onto his front leg, ignoring his warning growl, and pulled one of my swords free. He shifted nervously beneath me but stilled when Lynette nuzzled his head with hers.

I split the scales with my blade and pushed my hand in, trying not to dwell on the squishy insides of a dragon. My fingers closed around something hard, and I pulled it out. A small brown sack sat in the palm of my hands. I couldn't smell anything over the scent of blood and various fluids, but the magic pouring off it felt like warlock magic. I took a few steps back, tossed the bag onto the sand, and flicked my fingers at it. Blue fire engulfed it in an instant, leaving a small circle of ashes behind.

Lynette and Vizor stared at me wide-eyed. Shit. My devourer magic had been itching to be used after watching those two fights, and I hadn't even thought about it. This close, both the dragons would have been able to sense the devourer nature of my magic.

How about we survive the next twenty-four hours and then I'll tell you both everything? I pushed the thought out at both of them.

Lynette nodded, but Vizor continued staring at me. *You're a devourer.*

And you're an asshole, I snapped.

We glared at each other for a few moments until Lynette flexed her claws, biting into Vizor's side. He winced and slowly started to rise. Lynette stood by his side, and I remained where I was, with Magos and Mikhail at my back, refusing to be intimated as Vizor rose to his full height. He lowered his head and angled it slightly, and I met his gaze.

Your terms are acceptable, was all he said before turning and climbing out of the arena.

Thank you, Lynette said, bounding after Vizor.

"I still don't like him," Mikhail said.

"Honestly don't know what Lynette sees in him," Magos agreed.

"Maybe we can talk some sense into her." I looked up at the ever-darkening sky. "For now, let's get the hell out of here."

Chapter Twenty

Hours later, we gathered in the large hall for the final feast. Like before, we sat at a table towards the front of the hall. Unlike the last time, Vizor sat with us, sandwiched between Lynette and Pele. They'd arrived in our suite an hour after we got back, and it was very clear Lynette had all but dragged him there.

Much to Vizor's horror, Lynette told us the entire tale and didn't hold anything back. They'd fallen in love around the same time as Eddie and Cerri, but Lynette's father had already arranged for her to marry another dragon. She'd pleaded with her father to not go through with the marriage; he'd locked her in the dungeon for a week for her disobedience.

A week before the wedding was scheduled, Vizor killed the dragon she was promised to. Elyan saw him do it and helped him cover it up. Elyan didn't ask for anything in return, merely said it was the right thing to do.

Lynette's father always suspected his daughter had somehow arranged the murder of her first betrothed, so he continued promising her hand to dragons known for their cruelty and brutality as punishment, but Vizor kept killing them in spectacularly bloody ways. At first, this only increased interest in marrying Lynette, but by the fifth time, the novelty wore off and few sought her hand, despite the promises her father made if anyone married her.

Elyan never said a word. Never betrayed them.

We all agreed Vizor was still an asshole, but we liked Lynette, so we would tolerate him. He seemed genuinely baffled by this, and his gaze kept darting around the table as if expecting one of us to try to kill him there and then. If our situation wasn't so tense, I would have enjoyed messing with him. But now we were sitting across from our common enemy, waiting for the other shoe to drop, and it wasn't the time for fun and games.

All the dragons that had come to support the idea of a treaty with the daemons were seated around us. Those who opposed the treaty and supported Thorod sat at the outer tables. Which meant we were trapped in the middle.

"We should have left," I said. "I don't like this."

"None of us like this," Pele replied. "But I want to know what his end game is. It seems unlikely he'd make a move now, not with all these dragons here that oppose him. He'll make his move after dinner, which means we can learn more before we leave."

"We still need to get Uther out of the dungeon," Lucan said. "I won't leave my brother behind."

"We'll get him," Tal promised him.

I pushed my plate away and gazed across the room. An obvious tension hung in the air, but that didn't stop the dragons from tearing into the food and wine. We were the only ones whose plates and mugs remained untouched. I didn't think Thorod would poison us, but it was possible. We all agreed not to chance it. Besides, I was far too wound up to eat anything.

My instincts had been dialed up all night, and I was regretting not pushing the others to leave harder. As soon as I could,

I was getting them out. No more arguments. We'd come back later to get everyone else out.

We'd have to do something about Thorod and the remaining dragons working with Balor, but that was something I'd discuss with Kalen, Badb, and the fae queens. Dragons alone were a formidable force, but dragons that were aided by warlock and devourer magic would be deadly. The fae and daemons largely relied on magic to fight and defend themselves; if their magic was neutralized, the dragons would tear them apart.

Thorod rose, and the chatter around the hall died down as everyone looked to him.

His green eyes fell on Cerri and Eddie, and his lips parted in a wide smile, which held nothing friendly. "Thank you all for coming this evening to celebrate the future marriage of Eydellan to Cerridwyn. He has truly proven himself worthy of my beautiful daughter." He raised his mug and slowly everyone did the same, except us.

We all remained rooted to our chairs, our mugs untouched. Thorod's smile only grew, and he sipped from his mug and set it down. "We have more news to celebrate this evening. It seems a majority of the dragon leadership believes we should agree to the proposed peace treaty from the daemons. That we should put the past behind us and form new allies. And I couldn't agree more."

My swords felt heavy on my back, and when I met Mikhail's gaze across the table, I could tell he felt the same. We'd been wrong about Thorod not pulling anything during this meeting, but there was no going back now.

Confused looks passed between the dragons that sat around us, but Thorod's allies stood from their seats and took positions around the hall, forming a ring around all of us. "I, too, believe we should look beyond our past differences and build alliances once again."

A scaled hand reached through one of the large windows, claws digging into the stone as the trakdi pulled itself through the opening and climbed up the wall. More followed, spreading themselves out behind Thorod and the surrounding wall. These were smaller than the ones Eddie and Vizor had fought against, but the numbers made up for their size.

The younger dragons shot to their feet in alarm but had nowhere to go, and the trakdi remained where they were, obeying their master.

"Long ago, we were friendly with the fae who came to our realm. We eventually parted ways due to our many differences, but I have recently learned we have more in common with some of them than we previously believed. Like us, a faction of the fae were unfairly locked away in a realm and shunned by those in power. But they have managed to work around their exile in small ways, and I have been working with them for years to free us from being imprisoned in our own realm." Thorod's eyes locked on Pele. "We will never grovel to those who are beneath us, certainly not daemons. We will soon break free of this realm and will hunt every last one of you down."

"How many, Father?" Cerri's voice rang out across the hall as she rose, shoulders squared back and chin high. "These allies of yours have clearly given you some way to control the trakdi. I suspected you had a way to summon them, but it appears your power over them extends far beyond that. How many dragons have been killed by devourers at your command? How many of our kind did you murder?"

Snarls of outrage tore out of the young dragons, and several looked a hair's breadth away from shifting to their true forms. I leapt to my feet, along with everyone else at our table. There wasn't enough room for every dragon to shift. We'd be crushed in the chaos.

A dark-haired man at the table nearest us doubled over and

vomited black bile all over the stone floor. More dragons bent over, vomiting or collapsing to their knees.

"Poison doesn't work on dragons," Eddie said in confusion as he tried to keep Cerri behind him. Several trakdi leapt down from the walls and crouched in front of Thorod. I took a step back, and the others followed me. We had nowhere to go, but I wanted as much distance between us and the devourers as possible.

Pele swiped a mug off one of the nearby tables and smelled it. The turquoise in her eyes swirled, glowing brighter and shifting to red. "It's not poison. It's fae magic of some kind." She tossed the ceramic mug back on the table, and it shattered, spilling the dark red contents across the worn wood. She backed up and stood next to Magos. "I don't know what it does. I've never felt anything like it before."

Thorod drank deeply from his mug. "It's a shame some of you chose to lower yourselves and bargain with the daemon. If we had more time, I would see every single one of you drawn and quartered, but alas, we have more pressing matters. So instead, you can provide a meal for some very hungry devourers."

He roared and threw a glass sphere onto the ground. It shattered, and light green smoke rose into the air. The dragons that had been groaning in agony moments before froze as if they'd been petrified, and then they simply vanished.

"What the fuck?" Shock ran through me as I stared at the space that had been occupied by hundreds of dragons seconds ago and now lay completely empty. Now it was just us, trapped in a room with Thorod and his allies and a dozen devourers. If we survived this, I was going to tell Pele, "I told you so," for the rest of our damn lives.

"Get us out of here, Nemain," Pele commanded.

"Ya think?" I snapped, my magic already starting to open a gateway.

Pain flared in my thigh a second before Mikhail jerked me back. My head swam as I pulled a dagger from my leg. I held it up and inhaled deeply, letting it fall from my fingers. Reaching for my magic once more, I hissed as agony swept through me. "We have a problem," I said, my words sluggish.

The dragons around the perimeter of the room closed in on us as Thorod laughed. "Lir told me about your abilities to open gateways. I admit I didn't really believe him until you opened one into my tower." He pulled a dagger free from his belt, a twin to the one that lay on the floor at my feet.

"He worked with the warlocks to cook this up just for you. Apparently, the previous method involved using sacks containing the herbs and relied on proximity. These blades are coated with those spelled herbs, and one little scratch works its way into your bloodstream. A lot more potent this way. I was told it would likely be excruciating for you."

My blood was on fire, and every breath hurt. Mikhail gripped my arm. The contact was agony, but I didn't think I could stand without his help. "One. Chance," I pushed the words out. "Run."

Blue flames erupted out of me as I pushed with everything I had left. The dragons that had moved to surround us leapt back. Mikhail swept me into his arms, and we ran for the doors. Blackness clawed at my mind, but I tried to push it back. Roars sounded from behind us from outraged dragons and trakdi, who saw their prey getting away.

I was vaguely aware of us passing through large double doors and the others heaving them shut. As they were about to close, I felt a rush of heat. Eddie and Tal slammed against the doors, heaving them closed, but not before flames shot through and crashed into Magos. He flew back, clothes on fire, and hit the wall. Cerri and Pele ran to him, the flames immediately dying out, but even from where I stood, I could smell burnt flesh.

"This won't hold!" Eddie shouted from where he, Vizor, and Lynette were holding the doors closed as something or someone banged on the other side.

I pushed out of Mikhail's grip and crashed to the floor. He cursed and moved to pick me up again, but I held a hand out to stop him. He knelt beside me, ready to grab me when I passed out. Which I definitely would after this.

Stretching out my hand, I dug deep into myself and pulled out the last of my devourer magic. Gods, it *hurt*. It felt like I was tearing out a piece of my soul. The blue flames flowed around the dragons and covered the doors. Instead of burning through them, the flames solidified into solid ice with patches of ash sprinkled across it. Eddie and the others backed away slowly from the door.

Vizor flicked his fingers towards a torch on the wall and the flames shot towards the door, splashing against the icy barrier before abruptly going out. The ice remained untouched.

He looked at me. "Not just a devourer. You really are a freak of nature."

"You. Still. Asshole." The blackness surged to swallow me whole, and I collapsed.

SOMETHING COOL WAS PRESSED against my face, but the rest of me was still on fire. My fingers brushed against the cool, rough surface. Stone. I was lying on the floor. The sounds of metal clanging against metal and yelling floated to me, and I snapped upright. My head swam at the sudden motion, but I gritted my teeth and pushed myself up to my feet.

Mikhail and Vizor were fighting against half a dozen dragons in human form at one end of the hallway while Eddie, Tal, and Lucan held off more at the other end. Lynette was tending to Magos, who was slumped against the wall, burns covering half his body. With one of my swords in her hand, Cerri stood guard over them. Pele was frantically carving something into a stone wall with a short, curved dagger.

Sweat poured from my forehead as I concentrated on taking a step, then another, and another. Finally, I half-leaned, half-collapsed against the wall next to Pele. Shudders ran through my body, and for a second, I thought I would black out again. I didn't dare reach for my magic. I'd have to let the spell run its course. This couldn't last forever.

"Nice of you to join us," Pele said, not pausing from her rapid scratching of glyphs into the stone. "I'm almost done, then we're going to have to run again."

Words were beyond me, and it didn't matter, anyway. I trusted Pele knew what she was doing, and I couldn't afford to distract her.

A snarl had me twisting my head sharply to the left. Vizor had fallen to one knee, a dragon poised to strike him down. Mikhail appeared in a swirl of mist and beheaded the dragon in one stroke. Their end of the hallway was clear.

"Let's go!" Pele yelled.

Turning, I saw that the section of the wall Pele had been carving into was gone. The tunnel that led to our room loomed in the space behind where the wall had stood. Eddie cut down the last of the dragons at their end of the hallway, and everyone ran to the hole Pele had made.

Cerri bent down and scooped up Magos before diving into the tunnel. I blinked at the sight of the slim-built woman carrying someone who outweighed her by at least a hundred pounds. Apparently, her extra strength in dragon form carried over to her human form. Mikhail reached us and looked me over, a grim look on his face.

"Eddie, take her. I'll cover our exit."

I shoved against Eddie with all the strength I had, which was very little at this point. He grabbed my arm to keep me from falling on my face as I spun to face Mikhail. "No," I breathed.

"I'll be right behind you," Mikhail said with a reassuring smile, and he kissed me deeply. That smile was a lie. I knew it with every fiber of my being.

"Sorry about this, Nemain," Eddie grunted as I weakly fought against him. He threw me over his shoulder and followed after the others.

I screamed but couldn't do anything to stop him. Mikhail followed us, and for a brief moment, I thought we would make it. But then I heard the shouts and footsteps of others running after us. I knew we were heading to the mirror Cerri had tucked away in her room. We could use it to get to the watchtower far from here and smash it from the other side. But it would take a few seconds to activate, and we'd all have to pass through it. Thorod's dragons were closing in on us too fast. We wouldn't have enough time.

We ran down a long stretch of tunnel, and I saw the dragons turn the corner at the other end. Time seemed to slow as Mikhail stopped and whirled to face them.

"Stop!" I screamed hoarsely. I pounded my fist weakly against Eddie's back, but he only gripped my legs tighter and kept running.

Three dragons reached Mikhail, and he ruthlessly cut two of them down but failed to block the third one from stabbing him in the side with a dagger identical to the one Thorod had used. Mikhail thrust his sword through the dragon's chest and collapsed against the wall. Mist briefly swirled around him before vanishing. His magic had been nullified.

For a brief second, our stares connected, and he smiled at me before running in the opposite direction to slow down the other dragons that had just rounded the corner.

I flicked my wrist in a move I had done a thousand times, and the hidden dagger in my gauntlet slid free. Eddie snarled as I stabbed him in the side with the dagger, but he didn't stop running or drop me. That small amount of movement was too much for my overtaxed body and I lost my grip on the dagger.

My vision flickered for the next several minutes, and then we were there, in Cerri's room. She was running her fingers along the frame of the mirror while Eddie and Pele argued over something.

Magos was next to me, still unconscious. I'd only gotten a glimpse of the burns before. Bile rose in my throat now that I could see now how serious they were. Muscle and bone were visible in places. Small parts had healed, but the damage was too extensive for him to finish healing without more magic. His body had shut down in the process, using what little resources it had to keep him alive. I suspected the only reason he still breathed was because he had drank from Eddie days ago; otherwise, he would have gone up like a candle when the dragon's fire hit him.

He would wake, only to learn his nephew had been left behind. Heat burned in my eyes, and I blinked back the tears. Mikhail wasn't lost. I *would* get him back.

The mirror rippled, revealing the familiar workshop and library on the other side. "Let's go," Cerri said urgently.

This time, I didn't resist when Eddie lifted me and walked through the mirror. Tal and Lucan followed with Magos and laid him on top of one of the tables. Lynette held a hand out to Vizor, who frowned at her but handed over a dagger. She made a deep cut on her arm and held it over Magos's mouth, letting the blood drip down.

I didn't realize I'd been holding my breath until a ragged sob tore out of me when Magos finally swallowed. He would be okay.

Pele and Cerri came through the mirror, their arms full of possessions from Cerri's room. "Break the mirror," Pele ordered. "We'll have to hope Nemain regains her strength and can open a gateway before they find us."

Cerri jerked her head in agreement and swiped the sword she'd been wielding earlier off the table. Using every ounce of strength I'd been gathering for the past few minutes, I lunged to my feet and dove through the mirror. I drew my remaining sword, facing my friends on the other side.

"What are you doing, Nemain?" Pele asked. For what might have been the first time, I saw fear on my friend's face.

"I'm sorry, Pele." I shook my head. "But I won't leave him."

"He's gone, Nemain." Pele's tone was gentle but firm. "He sacrificed himself so we could get you out. Don't make that sacrifice meaningless."

"He's still alive. I would know if he wasn't." The pull that has always existed between me and Mikhail was still there. Taut and on the verge of snapping, but still fucking there. I would follow that pull into every hell that existed if I had to.

Pele shook her head. "You're barely clinging to consciousness. This is a stupid plan. Come back and we'll figure something out." She took a step towards the mirror, but halted when I raised the sword.

"The dragons are all about spectacle." I pushed the words out, fighting to remain conscious. "They would have taken him alive so they could execute him later. Or to set a trap for us."

"Obviously!" Pele screamed at me. "And you're walking into that trap!"

"I won't leave him," I repeated.

Pele leapt towards me, her hand outstretched. My sword slammed into the glass and the mirror shattered, taking Pele's image with it. The dragons flooded the room a few minutes later and found me kneeling in front of the broken mirror. I didn't fight them as they put me in shackles and led me away.

Chapter Twenty-One

Cool, damp air filled my lungs as I took a deep breath. Slowly, I opened my eyes, blinking several times as the fog from my mind slowly lifted. I'd either blacked out or they'd knocked me out after putting me in shackles. Dark stone made up the ceiling and floor and the wall behind me. Thick bars boxed me in on all three sides. Dungeon then. Fantastic.

I pulled on my arms that were outstretched above my head. Chains clattered against the stone. My wrists and shoulders ached from the pressure of holding me up. I forced myself to stand straight, but I still could only move my hands a couple of inches. Shorter chains were wrapped around my ankles, further inhibiting my movement.

An old panic flooded my system, and I squeezed my eyes shut. My body didn't feel like it was on fire anymore, but my magic was still out of reach. I focused on taking deep breaths, trying to distract myself from being bound.

"Are you okay?" a strong masculine voice asked.

"Uther?" I guessed.

"Yes," he said after a brief pause.

"Sorry, we were planning on rescuing you." I jiggled my

chains slightly, still keeping my eyes shut as I breathed in and out. "As you can see, it didn't go so well."

"I've been told it's the thought that counts," he said, and I let out a raspy chuckle. "Are you okay?"

"Been better." I gritted my teeth together. "Got stabbed with a spelled dagger. It's blocking me from accessing my magic and causing some other unpleasant side effects. Which might be for the best because I don't handle being bound all that well. Childhood trauma . . ." I paused briefly. "And adult trauma that I'm still working through. So if I did have access to my magic, I'd probably be losing control of it right about now and likely killing you. Which would be bad and make your brother real pissed off at me."

"I'd be kind of pissed about it too, to be honest."

The edge of panic dulled slightly, and I opened my eyes, being careful not to move my arms. I'd have to pretend the shackles weren't there for now and try to concentrate on something else.

Tilting my head to the right, I looked in the cell next to mine and saw Uther chained against the wall in a similar fashion. They'd stripped him down to his pants, a thick metal collar around his neck. Dark purple bruises covered his torso, along with some welts. Whatever they'd been doing to him had slowed down his healing ability. A shadow split from the far wall, and a small trakdi stalked across the dungeon, halting in front of Uther's cell. Its dark eyes were full of hunger as it stared at the chained dragon.

"They let the devourer feed off you?"

"Yes," he said grimly. "My magic is nothing but dregs at this point."

Ignoring the trakdi, I squinted at the cells on the other side of Uther. "Is anyone else here? A vampire?"

"No. You're the first person they've brought down here."

I refused to think about what that could mean. They must

have Mikhail somewhere else. "Guards?" The trakdi definitely posed a problem, but it seemed odd they didn't have other dragons posted.

"Usually there are two of them, but they took off a while ago. Leaving our friend here behind."

"How long have I been here?"

"A few hours at least. I might have fallen asleep for a while, so I'm not sure. My brother." Uther hesitated. "Is he okay?"

"As far as I know, yes." I took a steadying breath and pulled steadily on my chains.

They had zero give and were attached tightly to my wrists. I put my odds of escaping somewhere around highly unlikely. Thorod would have me brought somewhere to trot out on display eventually, or he'd tell Lir about my capture, and he would come for me. I'd need to be prepared to do something then.

I released the pressure as my heart started to thump wildly, and the panic receded slightly. It was still there, but at least I was able to think clearly. "He escaped the city along with my friends, Tal, Lynette, and Vizor."

"Vizor?" Uther asked in surprise.

"Yeah," I grunted. "Don't worry. He's still an asshole."

Uther let out a low laugh but cut it off with a wince. "I've been trying to get out of these chains for days. Unless you have any tricks up your sleeve, I don't think we'll be getting out of here on our own."

"If I had my magic, I could do something about the chains. Does that collar around your neck keep you from shifting?"

"I'm not even sure I have enough magic to shift at the moment even if I wanted to. The collars are specifically designed to imprison us in our human skins. The steel is spelled and will not break or bend when we shift, even when hit with fire. Shifting with one on results in instant decapitation."

"I figured as much." I closed my eyes again. "Don't panic

if I black out again. I'm going to see if I can feel my magic yet. Last time I tried, it was unpleasant."

"I'm not going anywhere."

Instead of diving in and reaching for my magic, I cautiously reached inward, trying to find it. Pain shot through me, and I stopped, but not before I felt a small pull. My shifter magic was still completely out of reach, but my devourer magic was there. Slowly, I reached for it again, being careful not to touch my shifter magic. I felt the barest flicker and smiled.

SWEAT STUNG MY EYES, and I jerked my head, trying to clear them. I'd managed to claw back the smallest amount of my devourer magic. With a little more time, I might be able to use it to break the chains. Uther had fallen silent, sensing that I needed to concentrate on what I was doing. The trakdi had shifted so it was staring at me instead of Uther, and it let out a low hiss every time I pulled more of my magic free.

It swung its head towards a set of stairs that I assumed led out of the dungeon, and the sound of a door swinging open filtered down to us a second later.

Half a dozen guards appeared, two herding the trakdi back away from my cell while two others unlocked the door and entered. I tracked their movements but didn't bother asking any questions. Without a word, they unlatched the chains and thrust my arms behind my back. A hiss of pain escaped me, the muscles across my upper back and shoulders seizing up from the abrupt movement.

"Where are you taking her?" Uther demanded when no guards moved to retrieve him.

"You'll be dealt with later, traitor," one of the guards snapped. "Your father and Thorod have plans for you and your coward of a brother."

Uther roared and pulled against the chains with the little strength he had left. The guards laughed as they pulled me up the stairs, leaving the trakdi to watch over the enraged dragon.

When we reached the garden outside the citadel, I balked at the sight of the blue-scaled dragon that waited for us. I could do nothing as one of the guards shoved me hard, and I stumbled forward and fell hard to my knees. The dragon let out an amused, deep rumble as his tail lashed out and wrapped around me. My insides dropped and my stomach churned as he leapt into the air, whipping me around.

Thunderstorms were still gathering in the sky and the flight was far rougher than any of my previous ones. When we landed in the arena minutes later, the dragon dumped me unceremoniously on the sandy floor. Fire rippled over scales as he shifted to a large human male, dressed head to toe in black-scaled armor.

"Wonderful. The last of our guests has arrived," Thorod said. Most of his dragon allies were in their true forms, perched around the arena walls, but Thorod remained human.

Like the dragon who carried me here, he wore black-scaled armor, but a deep red fabric was attached at the shoulders and flowed over his back. A crown made of twisted dark metal rested on his head. Three large trakdi sat behind him, utterly still like sphinxes. I processed all of this in a split second, vaguely aware I should care about these details.

It was the figure kneeling to the right of Thorod, arms bound in front of him, that held all my attention. A mix of fresh and dried blood seemed to cover every inch of him.

"Mikhail." My voice broke at the sight of him, and I tried to move forward, only to be pulled back and forced on my knees.

Slowly, he raised his head. His eyes flashed with anger and frustration. "You were supposed to run."

"You should have known better." I let out a humorless laugh.

The corner of his lips tilted up. "I really should have."

"How touching," Thorod mocked. "You came to save him. And your friends came to save both of you. And all of you failed."

A shuffle sounded above us, and I looked up in time to see Cerri, Eddie, and, to my astonishment, Vizor shoved into the arena. They landed hard and were immediately jerked up and led over to us. Blood covered their skin and clothing. Eddie's right eye was almost swollen shut, and Vizor had a noticeable limp. They all wore collars identical to the one around Uther's neck. I didn't dare ask about the others. I just had to hope they were still safe in the tower far from here.

Lightning flashed across the sky followed by loud crack of thunder and the scent of ozone filled the air. A few dragons eyed the sky warily.

"A crown?" Cerri sneered. "The dragons have no king."

"We did once," Thorod said coldly. "Before the daemons fled from this realm and tried to destroy us, we were led by kings. We turned our backs on that because of fear, and look where it led us. Centuries of cowering in our cities, watching them fall one by one, while we argued amongst ourselves. No more. I will lead us out of this mess, and we will reclaim our glory once more."

His voice boomed across the arena, and the dragons roared in approval.

"You would make yourself a king?" Eddie let out a cruel laugh. "You're nothing but a servant to the fae now."

Thorod's eyes darkened in rage, and he gripped Eddie by the throat, ripping him away from Cerri. She screamed, but the guards held her back. Eddie clasped his shackled hands around Thorod's wrist as the larger man raised him up in the air.

"You have always been a pathetic excuse of a dragon." Eddie's face darkened as he gasped for air, Thorod's fingers tightening around his throat. "Balor and his ilk are a means to an end. As long as our goals align, we will continue to work with them. But we do not bow down to them and beg for scraps the way the warlocks and those winged bastards do. We are dragons, and we will never serve the fae as long as I live." With one final jerk, Thorod threw Eddie down.

The guards allowed Cerri to pull free, and she crashed to her knees beside Eddie, one hand going to his neck and the other cupping his face. Tears ran down her face as he drew in hoarse breaths.

Thorod looked them over with disgust. "You were always a disappointment, Daughter."

"The feeling is mutual, Father," Cerri spat, pulling Eddie closer to her.

"You look so much like your mother." Thorod's eyes softened for a moment. "I've tolerated you all these years because of it." His expression turned hard as Cerri only raised her chin in defiance. He shook his head, lips curling in disappointment. "No more. None of you are leaving this arena alive."

"You would kill your own daughter?" Cerri asked. There was no hurt in her voice, only contemplation, like this was an answer she needed.

"I no longer recognize our blood," Thorod replied cooly. "You are no daughter of mine." He waved his hand. "Get them in position. The vampire and the shifter can go first. Then the dragons. Cerridwyn last. She will bear witness to her failure."

Buy more time, Vizor's voice said faintly in my head.

I blinked in surprise.

Buy. More. Time.

My eyes flicked to where Cerri was still holding onto Eddie and where one of her hands was behind his neck.

Right next to the collar.

"Lir won't be happy when he learns you killed me," I said quickly. "He's been very insistent on taking me alive."

"As I told Eydellan," Thorod said in a bored tone, "we are working *with* Balor, not *for* him. What his lapdog wants is of no concern to me. Besides, I never told them you were here, and there will be no proof of it."

Guards grabbed Mikhail and me, pulling us to our feet. "I'm the Knight of the Unseelie Queen, and she knows I'm here. Lir has spies within the fae realms. He'll find out sooner or later."

Thorod paused. For all his blustering about dragons not bowing to the fae, he needed Balor. Once the dragons were free of this realm, I had no doubt he would betray the exiled fae king. But he couldn't afford to have them turn on him now. His eyes latched onto the silver bracers on my forearms.

They'd removed my sword and the daggers from the bracers, but they hadn't been able to get the bracers off. The dagger given to me by Dante was still strapped to my thigh as well. They couldn't remove it or the sheath, and given how small it was, they likely hadn't bothered to keep trying. The arrogance of dragons was truly handy sometimes.

"Get those silver bracers off her," Thorod commanded. "We'll find a way to get them out of this realm and leave them somewhere else." He looked at me and smiled. "They'll never find your body here. I'll just tell them you were here and then left."

I doubted the fae queens or Lir would buy that, but given Thorod's astonishing ego, it seemed doubtful I could convince him of that. And he'd likely grow bored if I tried to argue my case. I needed some other way to buy us time.

The dragon who had carried me to the arena smiled and raised a hand in the air. Another dragon on the wall breathed out some flames, and they shot into his outstretched palm, spinning around in a circle. An arm fell around my throat, pulling me to my feet against a hard body. I jerked, trying to get free, but the arm around my throat only tightened.

Two guards released the shackles and pulled my arms to the front, then clasped them together once more. They held onto the short chain, forcing me to keep my arms outstretched.

I swallowed with a grimace. This was going to hurt.

The silver bracers were fae made, a gift from Kaysea. She'd given them to me when I'd first settled in Emerald Bay after escaping Sebastian. In addition to being beautiful, they could absorb magical attacks and had come in handy over the past couple of years. They'd been specifically linked to me, and I was the only one who could remove them. It would take only one thought on my part, and they would unclasp. But Cerri needed more time for whatever she was up to.

I would buy her that time.

The dragon carrying the flames in his palm reached me, his eyes bright with anticipation. Well, at least one of us was going to enjoy this. I clenched my teeth hard enough to make them crack. I thought I'd mentally prepared myself for it, but when he held the flames underneath my arms, I lasted only a few seconds before a scream tore out of me.

Mikhail lunged forward, momentarily breaking free from the grasp of the dragons who held him, but he only made it a few feet before they yanked him back. He snarled as he tried to break free, but they held him fast so all he could do was watch.

The smell of burned flesh filled the air. The dragon temporarily pulled the flames back, and I sagged against the guard holding me, panting and sucking in air hard as the pain threatened to overwhelm me. The silver bracers could only absorb so much magic, and they had quickly been overloaded by the dragon flame. The intricate designs warped slightly but mostly remained intact as the silver burned against my skin. I thought I'd be able to hold out longer against this, but I'd been wrong.

With a savage grin, the dragon held the flames out towards me once more. I fought as hard as I could against my captors and was distantly aware of Mikhail roaring. But nothing stopped those flames from being held under my arms again. Pain like I'd never felt before flooded my body, and I screamed.

Scream after scream tore out of me until I couldn't take it any longer. The bracers slid from my arms, revealing blistered flesh. The guard who'd been holding onto me let go, and I collapsed to the ground, huddling in a ball as tremors shook my body.

One of the dragons that had been holding me swiped the bracers off the ground.

Thorod laughed. "She held out longer than I thought she would."

Several other dragons laughed in agreement. I vomited on the sand and rolled onto my back. My arms had gone blissfully numb. I didn't know if that was a good thing or not.

My healing abilities were knocked offline with the rest of my magic. The small amount of devourer magic I'd been clawing back couldn't heal my arms, and even if it could, I needed to save it for something that could actually help us get out of this. Or at least help some of us get out. I didn't think all of us had a chance of walking away.

Just hold on a little longer, Vizor said, his voice coming through as the barest of whispers. He must be working hard to make sure no other dragons heard him.

With a roar, Eddie leapt from the ground. The collar that had been around his neck lay in Cerri's hands. Flames erupted over him as he shifted to his dragon form and slammed his tail into two of the trakdi crouched behind Thorod.

Vizor took advantage of Eddie's sudden attack and tackled the guard who'd been holding him. The two of them went down, and Cerri lunged to her feet. I tried to get up but couldn't convince my body to move. Another guard joined the two holding Mikhail down as he struggled to rise. Cerri dove towards them but stopped abruptly when Eddie roared in pain.

Two devourers had him pinned to the ground. Cerri ran towards him, even though she could do nothing in that form and with no weapons. I watched helplessly as more guards swarmed Vizor and shoved him to the ground, knees digging into his back. Eddie threw off one of the trakdi and tackled the other. They rolled across the sand until they approached the middle of the arena.

"Nooo!" Cerri screamed.

Eddie rose up, biting down hard onto the neck of the devourer he'd been wrestling with, just as another one crashed into him, and they tumbled into the pit that had been left open from the fight yesterday. Eddie's roar echoed as he disappeared into the darkness, only to be abruptly silenced.

Cerri screamed and tried to dive in after him, but several guards caught her and dragged her back.

"Pity, I was really looking forward to cutting him apart piece by piece myself," Thorod mused.

Cerri didn't acknowledge his words. She just continued staring at the dark hole where Eddie had disappeared, as if she could force him to come back through sheer will alone. Hope glimmered in her eyes. I wanted to feel the same, but Eddie hadn't exactly been at his best, and he had barely won against the devourer yesterday.

"Let's continue as planned. I don't think the shifter is going to last much longer, anyway."

The guards pulled Mikhail up and forced him to his knees a few feet in front of me. Another yanked me up and set me in a kneeling position. Thorod pulled a sword from his side and handed it over to the dragon, who had brought me here. "If you will do the honors, Sarak."

"Of course, my king." Sarak accepted the sword and prowled towards us.

Mikhail raised his head and met my eyes, a storm of emotion brewing in them. I pulled on the little bit of magic I'd continued to claw back, and it rose to the surface, ready to strike. It wouldn't be enough, but it was all I had. "I'm glad I found you, vampire."

"I'm glad I found you too, shifter."

"How touching," Thorod sneered. "Kill the shifter first."

"My pleasure." Sarak reached my side and slowly raised the sword.

I held Mikhail's gaze, refusing to close my eyes or look away. My magic flowed out of me, pausing over my shackles before I urged it on. I only had enough magic to do this once. Ghostly blue flames flickered briefly over the shackles that held Mikhail. So weak that no one noticed, but they were enough to burn through a couple of links. He caught the shackles around his wrists so they didn't fall. The ones around his ankles dropped slightly into the sand.

"*Run,*" I mouthed. At least I would go to my death knowing I bought him a chance. I tried to give him a reassuring smile, to let him know I chose and accepted this. Something broke in Mikhail, and I couldn't stand to see it, so I squeezed my eyes shut.

Some part of me knew the second Sarak started the downward swing, and I braced myself. But the strike never came. Only the sound of metal striking metal. My eyes snapped open, and I looked up, shock running through me. Sarak's strike had been blocked six inches from my neck.

Mikhail stood in front of me, twilight eyes glowing, holding a sword with mist rolling off it.

Chapter Twenty-Two

SARAK GAPED at the sword that had appeared out of nowhere. Before he could process what had happened, Mikhail stabbed the dragon through the chest. I could feel the dragon's magic immediately start to heal the wound, and the smallest amount of my devourer magic stirred in response.

"Somebody kill them!" Thorod commanded. "Keep the other two secure!"

Several dragons immediately started towards us. As one of them passed over the center of the arena, Eddie leapt from the pit and crashed into him. A fierce joy in me surged at the sight of my friend being alive and well enough to be beating the shit out of another dragon.

Chaos broke out as more dragons sprinted towards us and Eddie, while others moved to where Cerri and Vizor were fighting like hell against their guards.

We were still vastly outnumbered. It was only a matter of time before they overwhelmed us again.

"I told you to run," I growled at Mikhail.

He stomped on the back of Sarak's neck when the dragon

tried to rise. "Like you did? You were supposed to leave me behind."

Blue flames flickered down my arms, and Mikhail kicked Sarak towards me. "Eat up. I'll get my own snack." He winked at me as two dragons in human form lunged for him. He dodged their attacks and stabbed one through the heart. The dragon collapsed without a sound, and Mikhail buried his fangs in the neck of the remaining one.

Sarak shoved himself off the sand, one large hand wrapping around my throat. I was still far too weak to fight him off, so I didn't try. "Your vampire lover should have killed me when he had the chance."

A wicked, low laugh spilled from my lips. "That would have been a kindness you didn't deserve," I rasped.

My devourer magic surged, and blue flames twisted around his neck. He released me and fell back, hands going to this throat as if he could pull my flames away. But my fire was nothing like his, and dragon flames held no sway over it. He screamed, and my flames shot down his throat. His magic poured into me, and the small amount of magic I'd been cradling ignited into a bonfire. The last of the spell that had neutralized my power burned away.

I rose to my feet, and the shackles around my wrists crumbled into ashes. With barely a thought, I sent twin streams of flames towards Cerri and Vizor. The collars around their necks fell away in a stream of ashes, and they shifted to their dragon forms.

"Kill the trakdi!" I yelled. "The dragons are mine."

The dragons that had been perched around the arena took to the air, most flying towards me. I could feel their magic rising, intending to burn me away into nothing. Mikhail raced towards me and stopped by my side. Blood coated his mouth and front, and magic pulsed strongly from him.

I stretched my hands out, and crystal-blue flames formed a sphere around us as dozens of dragons unleashed their fire at us. Their orange flames crashed into mine and vanished. Heat spread across my skin, but nothing more. Enraged, they poured more and more of their fire into mine, believing they could breathe through with enough force.

I laughed as my flames absorbed the magic in theirs, a heady feeling coming over me. Magic pooled inside me. The skin on my arms was smooth now, with no hint of blisters, and I felt amazing. This was why Kalen had been so excited about facing off against the seraphim. At the time, I'd thought he was simply crazy and bloodthirsty, but now I understood.

The dragons finally halted their fire-breathing. Their mighty wings beat the air as they stared at me in confusion. Some of them started to recognize the magic that pulsed in my blue flames, and they shot up into the sky. Others weren't so smart.

"My turn." I grinned savagely at the remaining dragons and pointed my hands up. Targeted blue flames flew out and punched into the dragons nearest me. I gasped as their magic crashed into me, and I fell to one knee.

It was so much, too much.

More and more magic poured into me, and it felt like I was coming apart at the seams, but I kept pushing. The flames shot from one dragon to another, creating a web of blue fire. The dragons roared and tried to break free, but my magic held them in place. One by one, they dropped to the arena floor.

My head swam and thinking became difficult. Suddenly, I wasn't sure if I would survive this. Kalen had over a thousand years to build up to holding this amount of power inside him. Panic rose in me as it felt like my mind was ripping apart. I tried to stop the flow of magic, but I had no control over it anymore.

The ground shook as another dragon fell dangerously close

to us, and still more magic poured into me. I shoved hard against my magic, trying to pull it back. It was like trying to stop a tidal wave.

Mikhail's cool magic brushed against me, and his hand slipped into mine. Just like the night of the spring equinox ball, my magic leapt to him and matched what it was doing for me. He stiffened as the power streamed into him. My mind felt a bit clearer as I stepped back from the edge of insanity.

Slowly, I looked around the arena at the havoc I had wrought. The bodies of dragons lay scattered around us, most nothing more than piles of ash, all with a perfect ring of frost around them. At the other end of the arena, Cerri, Eddie, and Vizor battled against the remaining trakdi. All the dragons were either dead or had fled when they realized what I was. Except Thorod. He remained unharmed behind the trakdi in his enormous dragon form.

The last trakdi fell as Mikhail and I reached the others. Vizor pulled back, and I scanned him for injuries. The limp he'd had before was noticeability worse, and two of the spikes along his spine had been snapped off. He shifted back to his human form, and Mikhail gripped him before he collapsed.

"Thank you," Vizor said stiffly, as if uttering those words was foreign to him.

"Thank you for coming," I told him, and meant it.

Vizor shifted uncomfortably. "Lynette asked me to come. It's hard for me to deny her anything."

"I know the feeling," Mikhail replied.

I arched an eyebrow at him. "You tell me no all the time."

"Bold of you to assume I was referring to you."

Cerri and Eddie circled around Thorod, and the three of us watched. Cerri matched her father in size, but Eddie was dwarfed by him. Still, he didn't back down. I scrutinized Thorod, looking for any hints of weakness but finding none. I let a small amount of my devourer magic out, but it stopped inches away from him, as I suspected it would. Whatever Lir had given Thorod to allow him to control the trakdi also protected him from devourer magic.

Too scared to take me on by yourself, daughter? Thorod sneered.

We are a pair. You see that as a weakness. I see it as never fighting alone. Given that you will die today, I think I made the wiser choice in life.

Cerri and Eddie attacked as one. Thorod was a strong fighter and managed to defend against most of their attacks, but not without cost. As they traded blows across the arena, blood smeared across his scales. But his magic was too strong, and the wounds he was being dealt were healing too quickly. I felt the subtle push of magic off him tinged with devourer magic. He was calling more trakdi to him, which meant we were running out of time.

"Tell them more devourers are on the way," I commanded Vizor. "We need to get out of here."

He nodded once in understanding and took on a look of concentration. "Done," he said tiredly. "We still need to get Uther as well."

Eddie dove and bit down hard on Thorod's front leg. The larger red dragon reared up, but instead of pulling away, he bit down hard on Eddie's left wing. A growl tore out of Eddie, but he didn't let go. Thorod bit down harder and pulled back, clearly intending to rip Eddie's wing off. He didn't see Cerri whip her tail around until it was too late.

His eye ruptured as Cerri's tail pierced it, and he roared in pain, releasing Eddie's wing. Eddie didn't hesitate. He might not be as strong as Cerri or Thorod, but he was faster. And he used every ounce of that speed to spin around and claw out Thorod's remaining eye.

Both Cerri and Eddie backed away as Thorod thrashed about, blood pouring down his face. He shifted back to human form, speeding up the healing process. Cerri and Eddie did the same, and I walked up to them, taking a place at Cerri's side.

Thorod kneeled on the ground, a short distance away, both hands over his face. I wanted to finish this quickly and get out of there, but this kill didn't belong to me.

Slowly, Cerri walked towards her father. I knew what it cost Eddie to remain with us, but he knew this wasn't his kill either. Thorod struggled to stand, eventually making it to his feet and letting his hands drop from his face. Both eyes were milky white, but they were there. If he shifted back to dragon form, they'd likely be completely healed. He towered over his daughter as she stopped directly in front of him.

"I'm still your father," he told her. "You won't kill me."

The dagger Cerri had been palming since I slipped it to her earlier slid between her fingers. "I no longer recognize our blood," she said coldly.

Faster than any of us could track, Cerri buried the dagger in her father's heart. He stumbled back a few steps, disbelief etched into his features. The color leeched from his face as the skin withered and turned grey. I could feel the death magic tearing through his body. Thorod took another step back and slipped.

Too late, I realized he was close to the pit Eddie and the devourer had fallen in earlier. His body tumbled into the hole, taking the dagger with it.

"Damn it," Eddie swore. We gathered around the pit and looked down into the darkness. "Should I go and get him?"

A ping of familiar magic reached me. The trakdi were closing in.

"No," I said with a trace of regret as I stared at where the dagger had disappeared. "That dagger was a gift from someone who promised it would deliver a swift death to anyone cut with it. Trust me when I say that person knows what they're talking about when it comes to death. We need to get Uther and collect the others. This city is about to be overrun with devourers." I looked over my shoulder to where I felt the magic. "They'll be here soon, and there are too many for us to fight."

"What about the remaining dragons in the city?" Cerri asked. "Most of those who dwell outside the citadel had nothing to do with my father's scheming."

"You and Eddie can warn them about what's coming. They'll have to fly to one of the other two cities. We'll come back soon, and then they'll have to decide whether they want to leave this realm or remain."

Fat drops of rain started falling and we all gazed up to the ominous clouds where thunder still rolled.

"They'll have to fly low and fast to escape the storm. But they can't remain with the devourers closing in," Cerri said reluctantly. "Meet in the garden?"

I nodded. Cerri and Eddie moved away from us and shifted to dragon form. As they flew back to the city, I concentrated on opening a gateway to the dungeon. Surprisingly, it came easier this time. The air rippled and split, revealing the dimly lit dungeon. The trakdi that had remained to guard Uther let out a hiss and leapt through the gateway. We stepped to the side, and as it whirled to face us, Mikhail thrust a shocked Vizor through the gateway and I stepped through after them. The gateway slammed shut just as the devourer lunged for us.

"Greetings," Uther said. "I trust this rescue attempt is going to be more successful than the last one?"

———

WE WAITED IN THE GARDEN, water dripping from our soaking wet clothes, for Eddie and Cerri to return. Dragons were already taking to the sky, fleeing the onslaught of the incoming wave of devourers. I winced as a dragon with dark green scales barely managed to dodge a lightning strike. Uther kept shooting glances at Vizor as if he couldn't believe the dragon had come to help us. Vizor seemed determined to ignore all of us. Only his occasional look south betrayed his impatience to leave and reunite with Lynette.

"Just how closely are you related to Eddie?" I asked.

Uther startled at my question and gawked at Vizor, who glared at me. He'd probably been hoping I would keep the knowledge of his telepathic abilities to myself. But seeing how he'd been a jerk to us for most of our time here, I wasn't the least bit inclined to do so.

"Distantly," he ground out.

"Cousins?" I pushed, enjoying every moment of his discomfort. Amusement danced in Mikhail's eyes as he watched the exchange.

Vizor let out a long sigh. "Our great-grandfather had an affair. Several, actually. Both Eddie and I are the result of those affairs. No one in our line has ever truly allied with Thorod, and he didn't like the idea of another dragon being able to root around in that brutish mind of his, so he spent the last few centuries trying to hunt down every one of our bloodline. He was mostly successful, but a few of us are out there."

"Hmm," I said.

Vizor turned away from me, looking to the south once more. I wondered what Eddie would think when he learned he had more relatives and that Vizor was one of them.

Delight coursed through me. The look on his face when I told him Vizor was his kin would be priceless.

Shadows passed over us, and I watched as hundreds of dragons took to the sky. Cerri and Eddie must have finished delivering their warning and convinced the remaining dragons to leave. I looked at the items we'd collected from the hall. It should be enough for us to track them down wherever they were. Our first priority was picking up the others, but we all agreed we needed to retrieve the dragons from whatever realm Thorod had sent them to. The dragons who remained in this realm should be safe for a short amount of time now that Thorod was dead.

There were still plenty of Thorod's supporters left as well. We'd have to figure out how to deal with them because they were no doubt regrouping somewhere and someone would rise up to take Thorod's place.

Cerri and Eddie entered the garden, their hands entwined.

"How did it go?" I asked. "Did all of them choose to leave?"

"Not all." Cerri shook her head in frustration. "Some have stubbornly chosen to stay."

Eddie shrugged. "We told them what was coming their way. It's on them at this point. Most will be traveling to Isonver, which is the closest city. There may be supporters of Thorod amongst them. We'll have to figure out how to deal with that when we evacuate everyone."

"I'm sure Pele has taken that into account," I said, then concentrated on opening a gateway into the watchtower.

The portal opened before us, and I walked through, the others following me. Cerri hovered on the other side of the gateway, giving one last look at the citadel she'd called home her entire life, and then joined us in the tower.

The gateway hadn't even closed before Lynette was in Vizor's arms. He held her tightly to him, and a shudder ran through his body. Lucan and Tal greeted Uther while Magos and Pele headed towards us. Something in me loosened at seeing Magos completely healed from his burns.

"You look well, my friend," I said in greeting.

He smiled. "I should hope so after the amount of blood Lynette and Pele poured into me."

I looked at Pele in surprise. She casually shrugged one shoulder. "He makes good coffee."

"What happened?" Magos asked.

"Thorod is dead, and so are most of his allies, but not all,"

I told them and recapped the rest. We'd have time to go over the specifics later. "If you have everything you need from here, we should head to where the other dragons are, and then we can return to the human realm."

Pele pursed her lips. "I can't bring them to The Inferno yet. They won't all fit, and even if they could, it would result in a bloodbath. There's going to be an adjustment period for both the dragons and daemons."

"We'll take them to the forest outside town, near the fae gateway. It's easy enough for me to open a gateway there." I held my hand out to Mikhail, and he passed me the bag full of the items I'd grabbed from the feast hall. "Is everyone ready?"

When they nodded, I stuck my hand into the bag and concentrated on the essences the dragons had left behind on their belongings. It was just enough for me to track them to the realm they'd been thrown into. A gateway snapped open, and we peered through it. I held my magic steady, ready to close the gateway if it was too dangerous to pass through.

Dragons, in both their true and human forms, sat in small groups in a grassy field. Many were wounded, and at least some were lying still, their chests not rising. Seeing no immediate danger, I stepped through the gateway and the others followed me. The dragons looked at us, exhaustion and wariness etched onto their features.

Devourers with feathered wings and sharp beaks lay scattered around the field. I walked over and toed the shredded body of one of them.

"Another new devourer species." I tilted my head as I studied it. "Lovely."

Cerri and the dragons who'd come with us set about getting everyone ready to travel, and soon I opened another gateway. I took a bone from one of the fallen devourers with me so I could return to this realm later; I was curious about what else was there. I walked through the gateway into the familiar forest, breathing in the crisp, piney scent.

While the others ushered the dragons through, Mikhail and Magos trailed after me as I approached the fae tree in the center of the clearing.

The large trunk stretched upwards, towering over the other trees. Within the bark, lines pulsed with light, glowing brighter at my approach. The tree had once served as the fae gateway to this area, but now it was mostly unused. If the fae wanted to come here to meet with someone, they usually used the gateway at The Inferno because that's where most meetings were held. But I had used this gateway several times, and I enjoyed roaming these woods, so this tree and I had a history.

"Hello, friend," I crooned.

A wave of warm magic splashed against me, and I patted the rough bark. The vampires remained a safe distance away. The tree had garnered a bit of a reputation over the years. Some daemon youth that had decided to mess with it a year ago had only recently woken from their comas. But I'd always felt a kinship of sorts towards the tree. It made for an excellent napping spot.

"Are you sure that's safe?" Mikhail asked.

"Of course," I said. "Besides, it's still probably happy about the snack I brought it last month."

"Snack?"

"Emir sent a warlock to spy on us." My lips quirked up in a smile. "The tree is still pissed about the time the warlocks set up their trap in this clearing, so I brought the warlock to it all trussed up as a present." I toed the mossy earth around the roots. "The bones were still here a month ago, but it looks like they've all been absorbed now."

Magos shook his head and let out a long breath.

I looked over my shoulder and saw the last of the dragons pass through the gateway. "Let me check in with Pele and

Cerri to make sure they're all set for now. Then we'll head back to the apartment so we can see how much destruction the vamp brats have caused while we've been gone."

"I'm sure they behaved themselves," Magos said. When Mikhail and I stared at him, he amended his statement. "Probably."

Chapter Twenty-Three

IN WHAT MIGHT HAVE BEEN the greatest shock of my life, Magos had been correct about the kids behaving themselves. The apartments weren't trashed, nothing had caught on fire, and the fae plant was the same ridiculous size it had been when I'd left. Part of me had expected the entire third floor to be lost to the damn thing. I was looking around our apartment when the door opened, and I watched myself walk in through the door.

Mikhail and Magos went still as they eyed the second me stride across the apartment and hop up on the kitchen island, a playful grin on their face.

"The four of us could have all kinds of fun tonight." Light danced in their emerald-green eyes as they looked at me. "I can provide a whole new meaning to fucking yourself, Nemain."

"Really, Sten?" I sighed. "What I want right now is a shower and coffee. I barely have the patience for you on a good day, and certainly not now."

"You're no fun." They pouted from their perch on the island. Magos moved past me and gave me a look that said, *get them out of here, please.* "I did this as a favor for you." Sten gestured at their body.

"You did this because you owed me," I countered. "I'm back now. You can lose my face."

"I kind of like it."

"Lose it," Mikhail growled.

"Fiinnee," Sten drew out. In a blink, they shifted, and now it was Lir who sat in my kitchen.

Even though I knew it wasn't him, I still automatically reached for my swords and grasped nothing but air. My swords, along with my silver bracers, had been lost in the dragon realm. Everything was replaceable, but their loss still annoyed me.

Sten pointed at their face. "This one came looking for you."

"What did he want?"

"Said he wanted to meet and discuss a truce. I found his magic disturbing, so I told him I would think about it." They pulled a glass sphere from their pocket and tossed it to me. "If you want to meet with him, you can use that to summon him. Personally, I think you'd be better off feeding him to Jormundgandr."

Sten shifted to a dark-haired daemon with light red skin and striking feminine features.

They shot me a sinful look as they hopped off the island. "Since none of you will play with me, I'm going to head to The Inferno. Daemons are always up for a little fun." They winked at me and sauntered out the door.

Mikhail gave me a thoughtful look. "Have you ever . . . played with Sten?"

I gave him the same sinful smile Sten had given me. "Obviously. Lokis are all kinds of fun."

Mikhail's eyes sparked with interest, and he gave me a

heated smile in return. Magos cleared his throat. We looked at him as he slid coffee in our direction.

"I'm happy for you both. I truly am." Magos poured himself a cup. "But the same rules as before apply with some new additions. No stabbing each other in this apartment, and no fornicating in the living room or kitchen." With that, Magos grabbed his cup of coffee and left the apartment.

"Wow." I stared blankly at the front door. "Honestly wasn't expecting him to be so upfront about us."

Mikhail laughed and took the coffee cup from my hands, placing it on the counter. He pulled me in close and kissed my neck, working his way up to my jawline.

"How about. . ." He nipped my earlobe, and a small sound escaped my lips. "We go downstairs, make sure the vamp brats all are accounted for, and that they haven't spent the last week traumatizing Finn. Then we come back up here and stay in your bedroom for the next twenty-four hours."

"Every once in a while, you have a good idea, vampire," I said breathlessly.

Mikhail pulled away and placed the coffee back in my hands. "I always have good ideas. You're just too stubborn to recognize them most of the time." He sauntered out of the apartment, and I narrowed my eyes at him, wondering if the rule about no stabbing applied when Magos wasn't in the apartment. Alas, I didn't have any weapons on me.

I followed Mikhail downstairs to a suspiciously quiet apartment. "What are you guys doing?" I asked when I saw everyone crowded in the living room.

All the lights were off, and whatever they were watching on the big screen was dimly lit and was playing ominous music. The movie paused, and Elisa's head popped up over the couch.

"You're back!" She twisted until she was leaning against the back of the couch. "Did everything go okay? Did you find Eddie's dragon lady? Did Pele get them to agree to the treaty?

Are you and Mikhail finally a thing? How many dragons came back with you?"

"Everything's fine. We found Cerri. I'd recommend you don't call her 'dragon lady' to her face. She, Eddie, and Pele are getting the dragons settled now. They're currently in the forest outside of town until we figure out where they can stay temporarily until a long-term solution is found. Nice try on slipping in the Mikhail question, but I'm too old to fall for that trick."

Mikhail slung an arm around my waist. "We are, in fact, a thing, though. Nemain came back to save me and everything. It was all very romantic."

Elisa's fist shot up in the air triumphantly, along with Misha's and Damon's. A few seconds later, Bryn sighed and raised her fist in the air as well. I rolled my eyes and slammed my elbow into Mikhail's ribs. He grunted and removed his arm from around my waist but didn't step away.

"I'll tell you the whole story tomorrow," Mikhail promised.

"Where is Finn?" I stepped further into the living room and saw that Bryn and Elisa were cuddled up on the couch, with Bryn's golden wings sprawled out. Misha and Damon sat on the floor in front of them with a bowl of popcorn. I narrowed my eyes at them. "And Isabeau?"

"Finn and Bo are upstairs with Cian, Dante, and the grumpy grimalkins," Misha said.

"Only one of the grimalkins is grumpy," Damon corrected.

"Fine," Misha said around a handful of popcorn. "One super grumpy grimalkin and one really sweet grimalkin who, for some reason, puts up with the other one."

"You left Isabeau in the same room with Dante?" I raised an eyebrow at Elisa. "I would expect this from the two of them, but not from you."

Misha and Damon looked at me with hurt expressions that

would have been a lot more impactful if they didn't have popcorn butter smeared all over their faces.

"She's passed out," Elisa explained. "We tried to limit how much time we spent outside the apartment while you were gone, but the kids were going stir crazy, which was making Dante go crazy. So he opened a gateway to some death realm that had a big ocean and held it open while Cian took the kids swimming. Tuckered Bo right out. She made it five steps back into the apartment and passed out face first into a bunch of pillows."

"We decided it was the wiser move to just leave her there," Damon said. "We did turn her over so she wouldn't suffocate, though."

"How nice of you," I said dryly.

"Cian fixed Finn some hot chocolate, and he fell asleep shortly after all that. They're still upstairs, but we decided to celebrate by watching some spooky movies."

"All right." I looked at Magos, who was sitting in one of the chairs with a handful of popcorn. "You staying here?"

He nodded. "They told me there are vampires in the movie. I'm morbidly curious. I'll be up in a few hours." He gave me and Mikhail a pointed look. "Don't forget the rules."

"What rules?" Elisa perked up.

Mikhail opened his mouth, and I pointed at him. "Do not answer that." He closed his mouth and smirked at me. "I'm going to check in with my brother and then call it a night. Thanks for not burning down the apartment while we were gone."

The kids waved goodnight, and Mikhail followed me upstairs. We entered the apartment as quietly as we could. Isabeau was a sound sleeper once she was out, but neither of us wanted to risk waking her up and facing her wrath. Both Finn and Isabeau were passed out on a pile of pillows. Luna was asleep, curled up on his feet.

Dante and Cian looked at me from the big dining table behind the couch. I grinned at my brother and stepped towards him when I felt a sudden surge of magic followed by what felt like a two-by-four hitting the back of my legs. My feet flew out from under me, and I fell on my ass.

Jinx leapt onto my chest, using his magic to make his hundred-pound form a lot denser. The air whooshed out of my lungs, and I glared at him.

"What the hell, Jinx?" I snarled.

Where are the silver bracers and your swords? His accusation rumbled through my mind. Trust Jinx to immediately notice what was missing and ask about it.

"Things didn't go exactly as planned. I have no idea where my swords are, but I can now confirm what it feels like to have silver melted off your arms."

Dante's expression hardened, and my brother blanched at my words. Jinx's claws punched through my shirt and bit into my chest.

This is why I can't trust you to go anywhere without me.

"She did it to save me," Mikhail cut in.

Jinx's golden eyes pivoted to Mikhail, and the sudden weight was off my chest as he prowled towards the vampire. *If your idiocy puts her in danger again, I will claw out your heart and leave it to burn in the sun.*

Without another word, Jinx trotted across the living room, only putting his glamour back in place when he reached the pillows so his smaller form could curl up on one. He picked a large pillow between Finn and Isabeau, spun around on it three times, and promptly went to sleep.

My brother looked at me wide-eyed. "I'll explain tomor-row." Mikhail cleared his throat. "Night," I amended. "I'll explain tomorrow. I need a solid day of sleep. I just wanted to let you both know we were back so you can head home."

"Thank the gods," Dante muttered.

I squinted at him. "How does you thanking the gods work exactly?"

Dante glared at me, and I gave him a sweet smile.

"Knock it off," Cian scolded me.

The dark-haired former god rose and extended a hand to my brother, who grasped it and joined him. "The dagger?" Dante asked.

"It did its job, but I lost it," I said apologetically. "It fell into a deep pit within the earth. We might be able to go back and retrieve it. The area is crawling with devourers right now, but they'll move on eventually."

He shook his head. "There's no reason for anyone to look for it. And only someone familiar with my magic would be able to recognize it for what it was now that the magic is spent." Dante opened a gateway to the death realm he and Cian called home. "Swing by tomorrow night and tell us everything." He glanced at the children sleeping on the pillows. "We're off babysitting duty for at least a year. That girl is the devil."

Cian laughed softly as Dante closed the gateway.

"Anyone else you need to check in with?" Mikhail asked.

"No. Pele checked in with Asmodeus and Zareen earlier, and Kaysea was there. Everything else can wait until tomorrow."

"Night," Mikhail purred. "Everything else is waiting until tomorrow night."

"All right, vampire. I'm all yours for the rest of tonight and all day tomorrow. We'll see after that."

Mikhail grabbed my hand and pulled me towards the door. "That's a good start, shifter."

Epilogue

"It's been a long time since I've seen one of your kind."

"Do you mean a human or a warlock?" Emir asked with a charming smile. He had discussed this plan with Balor's second-in-command, Lir, for weeks.

The arrogant fae had felt he should be the one to deliver the message, but Lir had changed his mind. Barely. Lir was used to commanding. He would have strode in there and demanded the goddess and all those who followed her obey him. It would have been a disaster. But Emir came bearing gifts, and he had no problem playing the role of someone with a healthy sense of modesty and a willingness to be subservient.

Because Emir was smarter than all of them, and he would win at the long game. But for now, he had to make sure their short-term goals were successful.

"A human offering themself as a sacrifice." The goddess leaned forward from her golden throne.

Emir was rarely impressed by beauty; he'd been alive for too long to care about such meaningless things anymore, but even he had been momentarily dumbstruck by the goddess. Her perfect olive skin was dusted with gold powder, and while little of it was on display, her modest white tunic still managed to show off her curves. Gold bands wrapped around her biceps, and more strands of gold were wound through her waist-long wavy hair.

She should have looked ridiculous, but instead she looked timeless and powerful. He understood why the humans had worshipped her thousands of years ago.

But Emir had no interest in worshipping a god. He'd rather become one.

"Apologies." He bowed gracefully. "I'm afraid I have not come to offer myself in such a way. Although, if ever I were to do so, it would no doubt be to you."

She gave him an amused smile, but her golden-brown eyes remained cold. "That may not have been your intent, but you are here now in my realm. Tell me why I shouldn't have my hunters rip you apart so your blood may sink into the soil and they may feast upon your flesh."

The seven hounds lounging around her throne raised their heads simultaneously and looked at him. They didn't growl or make any noise whatsoever. Just stared at him with eyes the same golden-brown color of the goddess they served.

Chills ran down his spine, but he kept his expression calm.

"While I might not be offering myself as a sacrifice, I did not come empty-handed." He extended his hand to her with a flourish, and a plain-looking dagger popped into existence on his palm. It was the type of showy magic he personally detested, but it felt fitting under these circumstances. It was well-known that the goddess loved her drama.

She gave him a bored look. "A dagger? That is all you have to offer?"

"The dagger itself is worthless. Its magic has already been used, and now it is nothing more than a hunk of sharpened steel." He flipped the dagger so the blade was in his hand with the hilt extended to her, and slowly but confidently stepped towards the throne.

The dogs did not move or make a sound, but he felt their attention on him with every step. One word from the goddess and they would tear him apart before he could even begin to utter a spell.

It had been a while since he had walked such a fine line, and he found it rather thrilling. He stopped in front of the throne and bent on one knee, holding the dagger out. "The dagger is worthless. But the knowledge of the magic that was embedded in it?" He raised his head and grinned broadly at her. "That is priceless."

Those clever, sharp eyes looked at him and then the dagger. She wrapped her long, slender fingers around it and raised it up. Her eyes glowed as she studied the blade, her magic seeking its knowledge. "It can't be." Her eyes widened, and Emir was pleased he had managed to surprise her. She raised her gaze from the dagger and looked at him with newfound interest. "It seems my hounds will go hungry today."

The dogs lowered their heads once more and closed their eyes. Emir folded his hands in front of him and took a few respectful steps back. "I believe my . . . colleague reached out to you previously, and you were uninterested in his offer."

"I don't waste my time with fae trash," she said dismissively, her eyes once again on the dagger.

"I understand why you would feel that way. Truth be told, I was of the same opinion until he persuaded me otherwise," he said in a hushed, conspiratorial tone. She looked at him once more, this time with amusement in her eyes as well as her smile. "But in this particular case, I think you will realize, as I did, that allying with these particular fae is rather beneficial."

She tossed the dagger into the air, letting it flip a few times before catching it and repeating the process. "But I already have the dagger and the knowledge it holds. It seems to me I don't need you or them anymore."

"True. But your enemy of old is allied with our new enemy. At the very least we can give you more knowledge of everyone involved, and if you are willing, perhaps we can help each other." He chose his next words carefully. "It's my understanding that the last time you and the others went up against this particular enemy, half of you didn't survive. Why not stack the odds in your favor when you go up against him this time?"

Her eyes flashed. "Are you implying I cannot handle him on my own?"

"Of course not," he said confidently, which was a lie. She would almost certainly die. "But he will not be alone, and you don't know what his new friends are capable of. We can help you with that, and more."

After a few tense moments, the goddess Artemis smiled. "Very well, warlock. We'll accept this alliance. In exchange, you will help me capture Hades. Our family reunion is long overdue."

Want to Read More?

The next book in the series, A Shift in Wings is out now! Signed paperbacks with character artwork are available on the Greymalkin Press Shop at www.greymalkinpress.com.

Want to read chapters from Mikhail's POV?

I'm working my way through the books and rewriting some chapters from Mikhail's POV! You can read all the existing ones and get the new ones delivered right to your inbox!

Newsletter subscribers also get the short story of how Nemain and Kaysea met. Hint, it involves a kidnapped kelpie… and Nemain talking a lot of shit.

Visit www.maddoxgreyauthor.com to get your bonus goodies!

Acknowledgments

Thank you so much for reading *A Shift in Ashes*! There were certain scenes in this book that had been living rent free in my head for years (Mikhail's mist sword moment) and I am beyond excited to finally be sending them out into the world!

I know some folks really liked Andrei when they first picked up A Shift in Shadows. And I get it. I adore my sweet werewolf too. But it was always going to be Mikhail for Nemain.

But don't worry, just because they're together now doesn't mean things are going to be boring. If anything them being together just means things will get more unhinged.

Also... I'm not going to leave my golden retriever werewolf hanging. Andrei will be back eventually and he'll get his HEA. I've already promised this to my beta reader and editor, and I'm pretty sure they'll hunt me down if I don't deliver.

If you enjoyed reading this book, it would be incredibly appreciated if you could leave an honest review on Goodreads or whichever platform you prefer. Reviews are super important for authors and we really appreciate it when y'all take the time to leave one! Plus it helps other readers find us :)

Lost Legacies Guide

CHARACTERS:

Bryn - newbie valkyrie; her soul is bonded with Finn's and she is his guardian

Cerridwn - dragon, sweetheart of Eddie; daughter of the dragon who rules their realm

Cian - feline shifter with necromantic magic; twin brother of Nemain; has a strained relationship with her but still loves her fiercely

Damon - teenage vampire on the run from the Vampire Council

Dante - necromancer, incredibly powerful and in a long-term relationship with Nemain's brother Cian

Eddie - a dragon who owns and runs a shop of magical oddities and supplies

Elisa - oldest of the teenage vampire runaways

Emir - leader of the Warlock Circle

Finn - fae child of the exiled fae king Balor; a prophecy about him says he will bring about the end of the realms

Isabeau - child vampire that the teenage vampires take care of and treat as a younger sister

Jinx - a fae cat known as a grimalkin, him and Nemain have been together since she was born; he's grumpy and has the ability to inflict bad luck on others

Kaysea - mermaid princess and bestie of Nemain; Myrna was her twin sister; older brother Connor is very protective of her

Lir - fae devourer hybrid, serves as the right-hand of the exiled fae king, Balor

Luna - another grimalkin (because the only thing better than one cat is two cats); unlike Jinx she is sweet and cuddly

Magos - old vampire warrior, his past is a bit of a mystery but he's loyal to Nemain and their relationship is similar to that of a an uncle/niece despite not being related

Mikhail - former vampire assassin of the Vampire Council; nephew of Magos

Misha - part of the teenage vampire group, looks very similar to Elisa but they don't know for sure if they're actually related, either way they consider each other brother & sister

Nemain - feline shifter and fae hybrid with devourer magic; all around freak of nature; raised by Macha and Nevin who she only learned recently were actually her aunt and uncle; biological parents are Badb and Kalen

Niall - fae devourer hybrid who fought Nemain and lost, but she chose to spare his life

Pele - daemon who runs the local tavern, The Inferno; close friends with Nemain who she has been in an ongoing casual poly relationship with for centuries

Sigrun - valkyrie, exiled from her people after the events of Ragnarok; has a wolf companion named Gunnar and a magical cat named Viggo

REALMS:

  *Note, this is not an extensive list of all the realms because there are many. Only those relevant to the story are mentioned.

Human Realm - the modern world that humans are familiar with; most humans are completely unaware that their realm is one of many or that magical beings walk amongst them
Meenri - the main realm controlled by the daemons after they fled their original home realm

Fae Realms

Mag Ildathach - belongs to the Seelie Court; name means multi-colored plains
Mag Mell - belongs to neither the Seelie or the Unseelie; like all death realms it is difficult to fully comprehend or travel in without necromantic magic; currently where Dante & Cian call home
Tír fo Thuinn - despite being referred to as a realm, this is actually a territory that stretches across all the fae realms, it is the dominion of the sea fae, all the oceans and seas belong to them
Tír na mBeo - only realm shared by the Unseelie & Seelie Queens

Fallen Realms

Kanima - former realm of the feline shifters; this is where Nemain's parents were born; it fell to devourers and the survivors fled to the human realm
Cerulle - former realm of Magos and Mikhail; also fell to devourers; survivors fled to the human realm and were later killed during the vampire and werewolf war

About the Author

After earning a degree in history and political science, Maddox was pulled kicking and screaming from the world of academia and thrust into the tech industry. Because they had bills to pay and nerd muscles to flex.

Whenever possible, they leave reality behind to build fantasy worlds filled with snarky morally grey characters and hot but devious love interests. Maddox currently resides in the northeast, but they'll always consider themselves Californian at heart. They live with their partner and faithful, but often stinky, furry companions.

To get regular email updates about new releases and other announcements, be sure to sign up for the newsletter on maddoxgreyauthor.com

facebook.com/maddoxgrey.author

instagram.com/maddoxgrey.author

tiktok.com/@greymalkinpress